BETHANY CADMAN

DR VANILLA'S SUNFLOWERS

How do you survive when your soul has been stolen?

BETHANY CADMAN

DR VANILLA'S SUNFLOWERS

How do you survive when your soul has been stolen?

MEREO
Cirencester

Mereo Books

1A The Wool Market Dyer Street Cirencester Gloucestershire GL7 2PR
An imprint of Memoirs Publishing www.mereobooks.com

Doctor Vanilla's Sunflowers: 978-1-86151-605-3

First published in Great Britain in 2015
by Mereo Books, an imprint of Memoirs Publishing

The address for Memoirs Publishing Group Limited can be found at
www.memoirspublishing.com

The Memoirs Publishing Group Ltd Reg. No. 7834348

The Memoirs Publishing Group supports both The Forest Stewardship Council®
(FSC®) and the PEFC® leading international forest-certification organisations. Our
books carrying both the FSC label and the PEFC® and are printed on FSC®-certified
paper. FSC® is the only forest-certification scheme supported by the leading
environmental organisations including Greenpeace. Our paper procurement policy
can be found at www.memoirspublishing.com/environment

Typeset in 10/14pt Century Schoolbook
by Wiltshire Associates Publisher Services Ltd. Printed and bound in Great Britain
by Printondemand-Worldwide, Peterborough PE2 6XD

You are a star, you know who you are.

PROLOGUE

The dream begins as it always does, with no air. At first she struggles, screaming bubbles into the darkness as she drags her hands through the water, frantic in her search for an escape. But there is nothing to cling to, nothing that can lead her to an exit or can pull her out. There is only her, surrounded by the fizzy blackness of the sea. Water glugs, settling into the dips of her ears, and her hands glow pale and ghostly, frosted by the moon.

The currents grip her arms and legs and down and down she sinks until her knees touch the grit at the bottom. Her head moves in slow motion as she looks around, trying to make out shapes in the darkness. Mottled shadows quiver and peer out through crevices of rock. Their jagged outlines look like huge mouths that curve over her. There is certainly something wicked here, but it does not reach her – she is numb and, like a soft floating statue, she drifts on.

A curtain of silver fish, with pure white eyes, flicker into view. They flash and spark through tangles of weed emerging from the darkness, and there is a faint tug, a flutter at the back of her heart that tells her to follow them. Whispers of tongue-twisters float gently through the currents. From all sides they come. They are important and so she listens.

Peter Piper picked a peck of pickled peppers. How many pickled peppers did Peter Piper pick?

The voices are hushed and terribly sad and she does not recognise that they are her own. She then remembers she should not be alone, and twists around to look for him swimming this way and that.

"Where are you? Why aren't you here?" The words come out muffled, get trapped in bubbles and then drift away. He is not here, though he said he would come, that they would do it together. He said they would no longer be soulless, hopeless things, that they would find their souls and be able to live. She can't do this without him, she is certain of that.

It is when she realises that she is truly alone and that he will never come that the fear takes hold. It starts at the tips of her toes before smashing through her blood as she senses the thing; something black, fat and huge slowly gliding beside her. She stiffens, rotates and kicks. She scratches at rocks to find a way out, but cannot.

She goes on and on this way, unable to speak or breathe, with the dark shape by her side. It is a bad thing, the shape. Something so awful it is almost unbearable. It presses down on her, gets right into her bones, but she can't swim faster than it, nor can she slow down and drop away. Gently the shape cocoons around her, its wet flesh sucking her in, its stinking, sweating skin trying to suffocate and seal her up.

It is just before she is nearly gone that the light appears. It is a far-away light which glimmers a bright sapphire blue. It always seems to be calling out to her with a desperate, high-pitched song.

She wakes from this dream as usual, tangled in a sticky nest of linen and sweat with such a terrible feeling of misery and hatred towards the world that it feels as though she has been soaked in lemons. Eyes shift to the clock. A curse is muffled and she shoves her face deep into her pillows. With no hope of returning to dreams she clambers out of bed with shallow breath and stiff knees and eyes still clinging to sleep. Sitting by the window on a little wooden chair she begins to make lists – lists of anything – things she needs, or things that must be done, but soon, as always, she grows tired of this and writes lists of words that rhyme, of all the street names she can remember in the town where she used to live, or of all the people she once knew. She sticks them on the wall around the solitary picture that hangs there – a rough shadowy painting of a man holding a flower stretched up above his head in a despairing offering to the stormy skies that swirl around him. It is a focused and diligent task, one which dismisses the noises that filter through the walls of her room – the moans and groans that come in the night – ignoring the footsteps and the shadow that passes by momentarily blocking out the light which glows through the gap where her door meets the floor. When she is satisfied, she turns back towards the window and stares at the glass. On catching glimpses of her face she glares at the faint creases on her forehead which, to her, serve as cruel reminders of age and of death.

CHAPTER 1

DEBORAH

There was nothing left to do

My son is dead and he is gone. These were the eight words that repeated themselves over and over in Deborah's head like an annoying song to which she knew only a single line, being stuck, wedged in her brain until it slowly drove her mad. It was not the first time she'd thought this, of course, but so far she'd always found a way to distract herself, to think of something else. Tonight, however, it didn't seem these thoughts were going to go away.

Deborah was curled like a cat on her sofa, a shabby, uncomfortable two-seater affair with a thin dusting of crumbs over the burgundy cushions and a half-empty bottle of gin stuck firmly down the middle. Her feet were tucked neatly under her, chin resting on her hands, elbows resting on knees. She stared at the television, which flickered and crackled, barely revealing the picture on the screen, as if the people within it were drowning in the middle of a huge, snowy blizzard. This did not matter to Deborah because 'Germ busters!' was on – it was her very favourite show. Glaring at the screen she hoped that, if she concentrated hard enough, she would forget those words that were incessantly being sung in her head. *My son is dead and he is gone.*

Today a woman in a pink suit and perfectly neat hair was swabbing the backs of people's necks, their shoes, the insides of their sleeves and their coats. This woman would then inform the viewer, with unnecessary pleasure, that millions of germs were breeding all over them. The swabbed ones appeared mostly unfazed by this. Some would half-heartedly try to please her, coiling their faces into expressions of shock and dismay. Most would just shrug and then mutter "Oh well" before flashing the woman a feeble grin and then cracking a joke about eating dinner from the toilet seat.

Today Deborah's face was like a fruit basket; plum and peach around the eyes, banana yellow and cherry red on her forehead where week-old scratches had formed scabs. She pulled up her T-shirt and winced at the red mark on her stomach and the dark, blood-speckled bruise that formed around it. She held some ice wrapped in cloth and was cradling it to her chest like a baby, then winced as she raised it to her swollen cheek.

Today had not been a good day – not from the beginning, when the screech of the alarm had forced her, naked and wrinkle-faced out of sleep. There was always that split second, before morning stuck its claws in, when she forgot. *My son is dead and he is gone.*

It had been six years since Deborah's son had been born. They'd named him Jamie after her late grandfather. In a haze of screams and blood he'd squeezed his way out. He was a pink-skinned, bug-eyed scab of a thing. She remembered holding him. He'd had such a serious face! He frowned up at her as if to say "you are not what I bargained for" before letting his displeasure be heard with a huge red scream. Deborah had never been more frightened in all her life. In that moment, just for a split second, she'd toyed with the idea of calmly handing him back and then making a run for it down the hospital corridor, arse exposed, gown flapping in the breeze.

Before she'd got pregnant, it had just been the two of them. They'd rented this huge run-down cottage right by the loch and scraped a life together, surviving off cereal and watery cans of potato soup. Jack, her husband, though unqualified, had charmed his way into getting some building work in the town, while she had pulled pints for the local drunks in the shabby, sour-smelling pub down the road. On a Saturday, as a tradition, they'd walk up to the top of the hill behind their house, armed with a bottle of vodka, singing love ballads at the tops of their voices. Slogged up to the eyeballs, drunk as skunks and high as kites, they'd paraded around like a couple of thugs in love without a care in the world. They'd wedge close together, wrap themselves up in an itchy woollen blanket and stay all night long, looking up at the stars and slurring dreamily about all the greatness and the riches that were right around the corner.

A piss on a stick and everything changed. They got sensible. They had to leave, to get proper jobs, to be adults. So they'd upped sticks and moved, to their own little slice of the city to be a family. And that they were. Deborah had never felt it again, after that day in the hospital; she'd never regretted her son for an instant.

She sighed and raised the ice up to her face again, still staring at the television. She took a huge slug of gin from her glass, swilling it around her cheeks like a mouthwash to get a good sting before gulping it down. The woman on TV was now talking to a man in a white coat in a lab. There was a large window at one end of this lab and behind it a room with beige walls that appeared to have nothing in it. The woman in the pink suit and the man in the white coat were peering into the microscope in front of them and, each in turn, came up with faces of equal and appropriate horror. The man then said something and the woman in pink laughed, a lusty crinkled laugh, before touching his arm.

Deborah sighed again. No, it had not been a good day at all. She'd arrived at work just moments before Jo-Jo, the new PA, had bustled in making her usual spectacular entrance. Jo-Jo was so polished you could almost see your reflection if you looked into her shiny, perfect face. She would walk into the office, heels clip-clopping like a show pony across the floor, hair glossy, and swishing back and forth in time with her hips. She was so bloody perfect and so nice to everyone too – one of those 'couldn't say a bad word about her' types. It was nonsense of course. Deborah had it on good authority that Jo-Jo was a nympho bulimic who had only got the job because she'd seduced Gary from accounts. Besides, Deborah was of the opinion that there was always something one could find to say that was bad about a person if one really truly tried.

Today, mere moments after Jo-Jo's arrival, Deborah had been called in to Mr Dogman's office. It was then that the day really took a turn for the worse. He had sat her down with a look of practised concern and explained to her that he thought it was best for the company's 'image' if she took some time off.

"Miss Green," he sighed, sitting unnecessarily close to her on the edge of his desk as he loosened his tie, as if to say 'we're all friends here, you can tell me things.' "I want you to know how much we value you here. I don't want you to think what I'm saying is a reflection on your ability as a member of the team. However, we do think it would be best for everyone if you took a little break."

He then smacked his lips together and sighed. He had big crusts of sleep in clumps around his eyelashes and there was a blotch of something yellow and greasy on his tie. "Don't worry – we're happy to pay you up until the end of the month and of course keep your position open until you" - he paused and looked at the floor - "feel better."

There had been a dreadful moment, a split second when Deborah had thought she might cry. It wasn't that she wanted to cry. What she wanted to do was say something extraordinarily witty and suitably scathing – a perfect sentence that would encapsulate how little she enjoyed working for his poorly paid, no prospects, sad little company. That he could stick his job and that she couldn't care less if she never set foot in his pathetic office again. The words just wouldn't come though, and she became distinctly aware that there was a large lump in her throat. In the end she said little in protest and instead did what was normal and sensible by quietly packing her things in a box, shaking his hand and smiling and nodding when he said he would be in touch.

It hadn't been a shock, of course. In many ways she was surprised that the self-important idiot had let her stay that long. When her son had died, naturally everyone had been suitably sympathetic. They'd given her time off and when she'd returned everyone had expressed how very sorry they were. It was the months after that the problems started, the days where she couldn't get out of bed, the days where she couldn't even be bothered to pick up the phone to tell them that she couldn't be bothered to get out of bed. Then the rumours started that when she did show up she was drinking at work. It was when the bruises appeared that Deborah realised how uncomfortable they were around her. Everyone would hush when she walked to the vending machine and no one could quite look her in the eye.

She stifled a sob, took another gulp from her drink and glanced to the window. It had begun to rain. It wasn't ordinary rain – the kind that starts in tiptoes while it makes up its mind whether to continue. It stamped from the sky in gusts, right up to the glass, insisting on her attention. She shut her eyes and wished it could wash away the words that spun in her head, around and around like a revolving door – one which was moving too fast to let her out. She wished that the rain would become so strong that it would dissolve the walls of her apartment and that everything would just be washed away until it was only her, on her sofa, surrounded by a vast sea. In fact Deborah wished that it would rain so hard that her skin would give in, and slip from her, and she would be nothing but a mess of veins and insides which would swell like balloons, great giant organs floating in solitude, until, too fat to stay afloat, they would sink to the bottom, and only then the rain would stop.

It was after their son had died that it had begun to brew in Jack. Deborah had seen it curdling in his eyes, all the sadness, all the regret, all the things he didn't know how to put into words. It had started with a shove after an argument as he'd pushed past her to storm out of the house. It had been a reasonable reaction – that's what she'd told herself while she rubbed the bruises on her arms and waited for him to come home. A shove and an apology – that's how it started. Then the shove became a punch and the apology became extinct.

Deborah reached for the remote to turn the TV off. Just as she did, she swore in the flash before it went dead that she could see herself in the empty room leading off from the lab, her hands and face pressed up tightly against the glass.

The living room was large and square, with two sofas forming an L shape in the centre. Both were ratty and dirty and they didn't match. In the corner, the TV sat unsteadily on a pile of books with torn edges and next to this a mantelpiece overhung a fireplace from which a hissing electric fire gave off a dusty, sour-smelling heat. On the shelves above stood an unloved, browning plant in a stone pot, empty photo frames, more books, and a row of tiny studded trinket boxes lined up neatly in silver and blue. A bare bulb hung precariously from a thin stretch of wire in the middle of the ceiling, casting a shadowy glaze over everything as it almost imperceptibly moved back and forth.

Deborah stood up and walked towards the window at the back of the room where she looked out at the skyline of endless cement. It wasn't a bad area of the city they'd moved to, just up from the tube. The flat was ex-council, but it had suited them well enough and they'd been happy here for a time. Even so, she'd always missed the country. It was where she had felt most at home – where she'd first met Jack, with his ice-blue eyes and that slight curl upwards of his top lip whenever he was laughing that made him look so mean, but so attractive at the same time. It wasn't just the sense of freedom they'd had back then, the 'us against the world' attitude that they'd adopted fuelled by booze and youth. She also missed the weaves of the trees, the smells of bonfires and wild flowers and sounds of crickets and birds competing to be heard as the sun, as round and fresh as an orange, dipped low over the weather beaten hills. She missed the rain, the freezing winters, even the mice in the cupboards. Here a constant groan of traffic, a view of grey bricks and a smoke-sliced sky was all that greeted her.

Deborah turned and walked to the bathroom, just off the small hallway through a door on the left. This was her favourite room in the flat, mostly due to the huge free-standing bath that stood in the middle. The porcelain was a bit cracked and the water took ages to heat up but, even so, every time she lay in that bath she felt she was living in the lap of luxury. She leaned down and turned on the taps, rinsing away the rim of scum that had formed around the edges, before pushing the plug in. She listened to the familiar hiss before the water spluttered and coughed its way out. After a while the room filled with a thick steam and she stood back upright, faced towards the mirror, and watched herself fade away.

He's gone. He is really gone. He is never coming back.

Deborah glanced at the clock above the sink. In exactly five minutes it would be precisely seven days since he'd left. She frowned as she tried to remember how it had happened – her on the floor, him leaning over her, leg cocked like a pissing dog. But he hadn't been pissing, he'd been kicking. Every muscle, every tendon, was all coiled up like a spring, until he'd smashed it down over and over again, and she had felt her head knock back against the wall. She had tried to cover her face with her hands, but not before her tongue had split and the warm metallic taste of blood filled up her mouth until she was coughing and choking and spitting it everywhere.

He had been leaning over her, leg still raised for one last

kick, and then, just like that, something in him had snapped like an elastic band. Suddenly he was no longer taut and ready to strike but instead a loose, rubbery thing that slumped to the floor. He'd pawed at the wall, crimson-faced and wailing like a child. Then he got up. He didn't say sorry. He didn't beg for her to forgive him. He just left – his final way of screwing her up.

Deborah took a deep breath and sighed into the empty room, her head throbbing. The memory of that night always exhausted her. For some reason, every time she thought of it she would find it harder and harder to remember the details. Must be blocking it out, she supposed.

As she waited for the bathtub to fill she crossed the hall to her bedroom. The window was wide open, propped up with a huge red-backed book with gold letters down the spine. The mirror which hung above her bed was a smudged circle of glass in a blue plastic frame. Walking to it, she gently pulled down the bits of paper that had been stuffed around its edge – the little scribbled reminders of things she had yet to do. When she had taken them all down she carefully gathered up the bits, walked over to the window and threw them out. The rain had stopped now. The buildings opposite glistened, illuminated by streetlights and framed by the night sky. A bus pulled up at the stop on the street below. A frail old man helped a frailer old lady step down and they shuffled off together arm in arm.

Deborah slammed the window down, pushing the memories out into the night, as if they were solid things, as if this would keep them out. She then stared at her feet, hoping an explanation would somehow creep out of them – a worm of hope that would make her change her mind. Nothing happened. There was nothing left to do.

It was as though she should be thinking something,

doing something more significant – perhaps weeping as she clutched photos depicting scenes from her childhood, or writing heartfelt letters to her nearest and dearest with some sort of explanation or an appeal to them not to blame themselves. But it all seemed rather pointless. What she was about to do was so insignificant, so inconsequential in the grand scheme of things, that she didn't want to flatter herself by thinking that anyone would truly care about it, least of all people that knew her.

With her bath almost full, Deborah carefully smoothed the bedspread down and left her bedroom. Outside she paused and looked at the room opposite for a moment, its door firmly shut. If she turned her head in a certain light she could still make out the greasy outlines of little handprints on the paint.

"Happy birthday," she whispered, and her face pinched, sour with grief as she forced herself away, and moved to the kitchen to check it one last time before switching off the light.

As the room absorbed itself into the night, Deborah turned and stretched for the black-bladed knife that was lying ready on the counter, grinning up at her through the darkness.

My son is dead and he is gone. She walked back towards the bathroom door. As she opened it steam poured out and enclosed her, making her appear momentarily indistinct, as if neither dead nor alive. Then she disappeared into it and slowly, purposefully, shut the door behind her.

CHAPTER 2

DEBORAH

No trip to the dentist

Deborah paused and craned her neck to check the street sign before frowning at the piece of paper in the hope that the information on it would coincide. It did not. Pulling her coat tight around her with one hand she flexed her fingers, careful not to drop the coffee she clutched with the other. She took a sip and winced as it scalded her tongue and the back of her throat.

"Excuse me?" Deborah tapped a man in a fluorescent jacket on the shoulder, took off her sunglasses, and offered him a smile. The man was standing by a lamppost clutching a large brush in one hand and a cigarette in the other. He looked at her curiously and said nothing.

"Sorry to disturb." She smiled again. "Can you tell me how to get here, please?"

She waved the paper in front of his face before dropping it on the floor. A breeze picked it up, hungry for playmates, and tossed it into the air.

"Oh God. Sorry. Hang on."

The man propped up his elbow on his broom and watched with bemusement as Deborah set off down the street chasing her directions which teased her by settling then, just as she cornered them, sashaying off again as though controlled by a cruel puppeteer. Eventually she managed to trap a corner with her foot. Turning back, she saw that the man was now a mere orange spot in the distance. Since there was no one else around to start with afresh and embarrassment free, she hurried back towards him, avoiding the drains where ice had spread in frosty tentacles, hanging down in the gaps between the grates.

"Sorry about that."

She brushed her hair back from her face, once again presenting the piece of paper where she had scribbled the directions down. The man paused and looked at her carefully before taking it between his finger and thumb, observing it with distaste as drain water dripped from its edges. After considering, he spoke.

"Down that way." He stabbed the air behind him with a grubby thumb. "Turn right at the traffic lights, cross over, and right again. Is it the dentists you're after?"

Deborah nodded and glanced at her watch. 4.01pm. She was late. Thanking him she hurried down the road.

Moments later, she found herself staring at the grey-bricked walls that made up the three-storey building. It was one of those clean, monotonous buildings which were scattered all over the city. With square windows in rows of four across the sides it had the look of a schoolmarm, prim and displeased. The private cosmetic dentist's surgery, which made up the first two floors, was advertised by a poster of the smuggest looking family Deborah had ever seen. Their faces were plastered up against the window in matching pastel polo necks with shockingly white teeth that glittered through the glass. *Look how happy we are*, they commanded, *just think how happy you could be too.* Deborah felt a small part of herself consider it. A part of her brain whispered to her that a dazzling white smile would be all that she needed, that it was the key to solving all her problems and leading a wonderful fulfilling life – that it was that simple. If only it were.

She sighed, pulled open the door and walked past. There was a sign on the wall which told her that Doctor Vanilla's office was on the top floor of the building. She peered up at the winding staircase and tried to catch her breath.

Doctor Vanilla had been the one to contact her. Deborah thought back to the day he had called. It had been exactly five weeks after she had attempted to take her own life and she'd been sitting in her dressing gown, a sausagey heap on her kitchen floor, eating cereal from the box. The phone had rung. Since no one else usually called apart from her mother, Deborah ignored it and let the answering machine click on. She remembered her surprise as this strange man's voice had filled the room. His message had been brief and matter of fact, explaining that the hospital had made a referral and that he believed he could be of service as he specialised in cases like hers. He suggested if she would like to meet him for an initial discussion he had an appointment available on Tuesday at four.

Stopping halfway up the stairs, Deborah peered back down and admired the way they spiralled to the ground like a helter-skelter. A brief urge to fling herself off the top and pirouette her way to her death flashed in her head. It would be wonderfully ironic though, dead at the doorstep of the therapist who'd set out to cure her.

At the top of the stairs she smoothed down her hair, a long, static mass of fallow brown. She was not an obviously pretty woman, with features that didn't quite match; pale freckled skin, large dark eyes, a plump nose which inclined slightly to the left and a wide, thin mouth. Even with the bruises now fading she looked rather like a rag doll, somewhat carelessly thrown together, but there was an innocence about her face that made her look a lot younger than her thirty-two years.

She pulled at the bottom of her T-shirt, trying to tug out the creases and wishing she had given more thought to her outfit. She winced as it grazed the red mark on her stomach – that was the only injury that persisted, taking forever to heal as a cruel reminder of what had happened.

Deborah turned to the door. There was a silver panel screwed to the centre and the name 'Dr Ouranos Vanilla' engraved in the middle. She tried the handle. It was locked and there was no doorbell. Pressing her ear against the wood, and still leaning, Deborah raised her fist to knock. The door was then abruptly pulled open and she fell to the floor with a thud.

Lying still for a moment, Deborah weighed up her options. She briefly toyed with the idea of just remaining still. Perhaps if they thought she was really hurt it would somehow be less embarrassing. She screwed her eyes shut, her face full of carpet, and tried to ignore the taste of moth in her mouth.

"Ahem."

A glossy shoe distorted her face in its shine. Rising to her knees, Deborah got to her feet. Flustered and brushing imaginary crumbs from her thighs, she then looked up and smiled in an attempt to show that she was OK, and had the good sense to find humour in the situation.

"Quite an entrance, huh?" The man she addressed looked startled at the sound of her voice. He stepped back and something flashed across his eyes but was gone before Deborah had a chance to work it out. He said nothing but nodded towards the door behind her and took a step forward so he was unnaturally close to her face. "Right, sorry," she muttered and stepped aside, turning to watch as he hurriedly departed down the stairs. "Idiot!" she muttered after him under her breath. There was no need to be like that. It was half his fault anyway.

She took a breath and smoothed down her hair once more. A thousand questions bubbled inside her head. Was he another patient? Why hadn't he said anything? Why was it so hard now to picture his face? She had been told, in the past, that she over-thought everything. It was a common complaint voiced by her mother and several ex-boyfriends. One even used the word 'depressing' to describe watching her pick apart every action, every careless word.

"Sometimes," he'd said to her with that weary tone reserved when talking to infants or senile relatives, "there aren't any hidden meanings or innuendos or anything. Sometimes words are just words and things are just what they seem." Deborah had pointed out that what he had said didn't really mean anything, to which the ex had sighed and smugly replied, "Exactly my point," and then swivelled back around in his chair and turned on the TV, signalling the end of the conversation.

Deborah sighed and looked around the empty room again, extracting a piece of fluff from her hair. The room was much like any other waiting room she'd been in – the clinical smell, the forced hospitality of the magazines and rows of hard-backed chairs. This one was narrow with beige walls and a thin, rather grubby looking, blue carpet. There were two chairs side by side on the left, and a door at the end. A small plastic table stood in the centre on which sat a glass bowl filled with what looked like dead leaves but was, on closer inspection, potpourri. Next to this the untouched magazines were fanned out in a perfect, unbroken ring.

Deborah walked towards the door and pushed it open.

"Hello?"

There was no response. A small wooden arch to her left was padlocked shut and a wide corridor with great high ceilings stretched out ahead of her. Bookshelves lined the walls either side. They were crammed with leather-bound journals, bulging at the seams where leaves of extra paper had been stuffed in. All were covered in a thin haze of dust and held together with yellowing bits of string.

Something creaked ahead of her and a high, rhythm-less whirring sound began. Deborah strained to work out where it was coming from but could not.

"Hello?" she called again.

"Come in, please."

The reply was distant and tinged with echo. The voice low and lispy. Navigating around the bookcases, Deborah turned the corner. The room opened up into a huge space, diamond in shape, with more bookcases around the edges and old wood-panelled walls. Sagging, pale lemon cloths hung in several places. Deborah reached up and touched the edge of one and got a waft of something strangely buttery. The material was embroidered with thousands of tiny brown stitches in a pattern that made no symmetry or sense.

A vast bay window was smothered by velvet curtains in

a faded turtle green which blocked all sunlight from the room. A large mahogany desk stood near to the window. The only thing on its surface was a newspaper which sat at a neat right angle to the edge. To the left of this a Chaise Longue upholstered in cream silk with a delicate wooden trim stood at odds with the rest of the room. The whole place had a strange air about it, like it was out of an old film or something.

The strangest of all was above the desk, where a large painting of sunflowers hung. Deborah couldn't help but stare at the flowers. Their heads, which were all upturned towards the sky, seemed longing, as if they wished to uproot themselves and be free. She knew the feeling. Even the flowers were trying desperately to escape.

Doctor Vanilla stood in the far corner of the room with his back turned. He appeared to be distracted and was humming quietly to himself. Deborah realised that the whirring noise she'd heard earlier had been coming from him.

"Doctor Vanilla? Hi. I'm Deborah Green. I have an appointment."

"Take a seat."

Glancing around, Deborah stepped towards the silk couch. As she did, the feel of the floor beneath her changed; she looked down and found her feet engulfed in a thick meat-red rug. She sat on the couch, balanced uncertainly on the edge. The silk was thin, like tracing paper, and she could feel the feathers beneath prickling the backs of her thighs. Deborah exhaled slowly and dug her nails into the palm of her hands. This was definitely a mistake. What on earth was she supposed to say when Doctor Vanilla turned to face her?

From where she sat he looked perfectly ordinary. He was

younger than she expected – couldn't have been more than forty – average height, hair almost white and pushed back from his forehead, sitting stiffly on his head. He wore an expensive-looking linen suit in peacock blue which struck Deborah as slightly inappropriate for the brisk February weather. The suit jacket was open, revealing a mustard yellow shirt which strained a little around the middle, showing the barest hint of a pot belly. His choice of footwear was also odd; his scuffed green trainers, which looked a little too large, didn't appear to fit in with the rest of his appearance.

"Please do not sit on that."

Doctor Vanilla's voice shook a little as he carefully emphasised each word. He gestured to an uncomfortable-looking metal chair by his desk as he made his way around the back, and sat, hunched down, as if ready to pounce.

"Sorry." Deborah got up.

Approaching the desk made her realise how wrong she'd been about the ordinariness of Doctor Vanilla's appearance. As she got closer she could see that a pale scar was emerging from beneath his skin. The light caught his face as he turned his head towards her and it seemed to swell from his temples in a thick diagonal stripe, pulling down his thin eyelids so they hooked low over his eyes. It spread down further, like spilt milk onto his left cheek, slacking the skin and finishing in a saggy flap which hung off his chin like tissue paper. Deborah looked down at the desk ahead and tried not to stare. She pushed her lips into what she hoped looked like a smile. His eyes were the worst kind of grey, like clouds right before the rain came.

"Deborah."

He said her name like a snake. His tongue, which too long for his mouth, flicked restlessly around his lips before disappearing. He pulled his lips into a firm line and little creases scribbled from the corners out towards the sides of his head.

"I want you to know you may find some of my methods a little unconventional. If you were expecting cardigans and cups of tea then I suggest you think again. I am here to help you and in order to be helped, you must trust me and trust my process without question."

Deborah nodded and hoped that her revulsion wasn't obvious. A thin veil of sweat had appeared on his upper lip and his eyes darted vacantly back and forth as he spoke. His head, held still, was tilted at a crooked angle and she could see a deep pink crease in his neck where his collar had dug into his skin.

Doctor Vanilla began the session by asking general details about her past: her childhood (average), her relationship with her parents (they were divorced) and her current situation (suicidal, obviously). He jotted notes of her answers down in a notebook. He looked unimpressed with her one-word, and often sarcastic, responses and would sometimes pause, breathing heavily, his eyebrows arched and disapproving as he positioned his pen over the book, expecting her to continue. Occasionally he would glance up when she had finished, locking his eyes onto hers in silence, until she had found it too uncomfortable and had to look away.

"Where did you grow up?" Doctor Vanilla asked, eyebrows scrunched, pen poised to write.

"Devon," Deborah replied. "I grew up in the countryside."

"With your family?"

"My parents split when I was nine. I haven't seen my father since," she said, still stubbornly refusing to give him anything but the barest of detail. Deborah had had no contact with her father since the day he walked out on them. Her father, whose sweet good nature she had blocked from her mind, was replaced with the image of the vile, pathetic and cowardly man that her mother often referred to as 'Judas'.

"And your mother?" Doctor Vanilla ignored her childish tone and tapped his nails noisily on the desk.

"My mother and I are close," Deborah lied, while wondering if closeness was judged by frequency of contact. They certainly had that. Her mother had moved, unasked, from their family home very shortly after Deborah had arrived in the city. Apparently she and Jack would have been 'incapable' of looking after a child by themselves – a comment which, though insulting, was probably true. Deborah had only just managed to dissuade her mother from moving in. She now lived a thirty-minute drive away with a new partner and, if she had it her way, she spoke to Deborah on the phone at least once a day, saw her at least once a week, and fretted about her all the time in between.

"And you've been married, haven't you?"

Deborah tensed, hackles up, as he mentioned it. She certainly didn't want to talk about Jack yet. She dug her fingernails into her palms again and shook her head. Doctor Vanilla ignored her and simply repeated the question.

"You've been married, yes, haven't you?"

Deborah bit her lip. There was something about his tone, something resigned like he found it excruciatingly boring that he had to ask again. Strangely, she found this comforting. If he acted like he didn't care, telling him for some reason felt easier. If she was going to get anything out of the extortionate amount of money he was no doubt getting paid for her to sit here, she should at least attempt to answer him.

"I still am, actually. His name is Jack. We met in Scotland. I was visiting a friend. Jack was her plumber. A pipe burst, he came round, and that was it." Deborah smiled, indulging in the memory for a moment, before she went on. "We were married within the year, and then... then..." Deborah shrugged, trailing off as she tried to find the words. "When I got pregnant we moved here. But we're not together any more. He left me a couple of months back. I haven't seen him since."

"And your son?" Deborah pressed her nails in tighter, watching as all the blood disappeared from her knuckles.

"My son is dead." She looked up at Doctor Vanilla defiantly, determined not to cry. He held her gaze and nodded, showing no hint of emotion or sympathy. He didn't tilt his head, or reach out to touch her hand. These were all motions Deborah had come to expect when she told people, 'My son is dead'. Doctor Vanilla did neither of these things. He just looked at her for a moment and then began scribbling furiously into his notepad.

As the session continued, the questions Doctor Vanilla asked felt more and more peculiar. It wasn't that he was asking her anything particularly personal, more that he seemed predominantly interested in the physical details of things, asking her to describe the houses, the places and the people she mentioned in very exact and excruciating detail. Then, when the hour was up he took a new leather-bound journal from his drawer and passed it to her.

"What's this?" Deborah asked. He leant back in his chair and folded his arms neatly in front of him.

"I'd like you to keep a dream journal," he said. "I know this may be an unusual request but I strongly believe that our dreams are extremely significant in allowing us to unlock our subconscious thoughts and desires. I would therefore ask that you write down every dream you have from now on. No detail is insignificant. No matter what they are about you must promise to do this."

"What if I don't remember my dreams?" Deborah asked.

Doctor Vanilla's features suddenly dropped as if his skin was beginning to melt. His lip curled upwards and his milk scar darkened as speckles of blood battled their way to the surface. Something furious flashed, just for a second, in his eyes and then they glazed over again, back to his cool impassive gaze.

"Just trust my process," he said.

As Deborah got up to leave, Doctor Vanilla turned away. He then picked up the newspaper that had been lying on his desk. A page had been turned back at the corner and the story's headline had been circled in red: 'TEENAGE GIRL ALMOST DIES AFTER LEAPING FROM 4th FLOOR COUNCIL BLOCK.' Turning to go she swore that, just as she did so, she saw Doctor Vanilla's lips twist into a smile.

CHAPTER 3

GRACE

On the outside now

She was a ghost. At least she felt like one: a faint shadowy thing flipping carelessly through space. At first she was nothing, like the dark air that surrounded her, but hours turned to days and days to weeks and slowly she began to grow. An outline at first but then she filled out with bones and flesh and skin. She had a container all of her own.

She clutched at her stomach as the pain seared through her body. Having a body was an awful, dreadful thing. But this was her punishment and so she would have to bear it. Would this be her life now? An endless, twisting darkness that would show her just how foolish and careless she had been? Surely this couldn't be it? If this was it, it would all be so, well... pointless.

Then one day she fell, crashing through the darkness down and down and hitting the earth with a thud. Winded and scarcely able to breathe, she tried to keep her eyes open, but the world spun around her. It wasn't long before the darkness came again, and then there was nothing.

It was impossible to tell how long it had been when she finally woke. Minutes, hours, even days could have passed. She blinked and turned, trying to understand where she was. The morning light scorched her eyes as she looked to the sky. The ground was damp and cool. The air smelt of dried out grass and earthy manure, and clouds of pearl and dandelion grey were splodged carelessly across the horizon.

She reached up to touch her face, and then looked at her fingers – pale, thin skin, threads of blue veins. She was cold. Her heart beat faster.

My Heart? MY HEART.

"Christ."

Soggy leaves peeled gently from her back and fell in papier mâché clumps to the ground. She pulled her knees up towards her chest and wrapped her arms around them, trying to mould herself into a single ball of flesh.

"Oh Deborah, what have you done?"

Gathering herself, she used a nearby fence to take her weight and pulled upwards. Acres of fields surrounded her: churned-up pockets of mud, a scattering of wide-eyed sheep, huge willowy trees bent backward by the wind. There was a small lake a few hundred yards to her right; slowly she picked out a path towards it.

At its edge she glared down at her reflection, hands on hips at first, then slowly gliding them all over, wincing when passing over her stomach where a huge blistering red mark formed a perfect ring around her belly button. Her face was sharp and pointed, her ears misshapen, one slightly larger than the other. Her body was made up of soft folds of flesh and near-translucent new-born skin, eyebrows neat and thin, round amber eyes and thick, soft waves of golden hair stretching down the arch of her back.

So this was it. The very worst thing in the world had occurred. She, Deborah's soul, had totally messed up. Deborah was gone, and she was alone. It was a total and utter disaster.

A soul should never leave its body, from the moment it is born until its very last breath. She knew that of course - it was the most important rule after all. Bodies needed their souls to live, and it was the job of a soul to try and keep their designated bodies emotions neatly under control. That's not to say it was up to her to keep Deborah happy all the time, that would have been impossible, and in fact, it was sometimes good to feel bad. No, her purpose was to be with her, to give her hope, to make her feel wonder, to give her faith that, in the end, everything would be all right. Deborah could cry and laugh, feel joy and sadness, jealousy, hysteria, even pain as much as she liked, as long as she never let one take over, as long as they were all kept at levels that were considered reasonable and normal, then she wasn't doing too bad a job.

Governing the emotions was a tricky task, the problem being that it was almost impossible to control any circumstances that took place in the outside world. It was all well and good holding it together from the inside, but she couldn't predict whether someone would be horrible to Deborah that day, or if she ate a bad sandwich and got sick, or if someone ran her over, or if someone close to her died. She could have her shit totally together and then wham bam! An event beyond her control could spiral her into a whirlwind of sadness, anger and bitterness towards the world, and it would be her souls job to try and piece her back together.

So really, it was no surprise that when all the bad things started happening to Deborah it all became too difficult to regulate. She'd been unlucky for sure. And she had tried, she'd really tried. Could she have done any more to hold Deborah together? Perhaps. If she could have she was certainly paying the price for it now. For here she was, ripped apart from Deborah, who was God knows where and almost certainly in a whole lot of trouble. The fact of the matter was this; if she didn't get back to her soon, then Deborah would certainly die.

With that in mind she started to walk: across the field at first, slipping and squelching through the mud, then onto a dual carriageway where shining cars roared and squealed, making the rain splash her skin as they whooshed on past. Finally she came across the first high-rise buildings, shining beetle black against the skyline. She headed for them, towards the people, towards the city.

She tried to remember a time before Deborah, racking her brains as best she could. Perhaps there hadn't been one. Every time she said Deborah's name in her head her stomach ached; it was a strange kind of pain, one not entirely physical. She glanced down at her feet and manoeuvred her way through the cars, swearing at ignorant drivers who skidded too close. Her toes were bruised yellow and black and she could feel the acrid rub as blisters began to form between them. As she walked she tried to untangle the mess in her head, and to think of a plan.

She had to find Deborah. That was the most important thing. She hoped that wouldn't be too difficult. Deborah had barely left the house in recent weeks so if she headed there she was sure she could find her. But then what? How would it work? Bodies couldn't see their souls, of course they couldn't! Would it be different now she was on the outside? Would she just be able to walk up to Deborah and say, 'hey I'm your soul, kind of a big deal actually, do you mind if I just pop back inside you and keep doing my job?'

It's not like she had been given a manual on this sort of situation, a 'Dummies' Guide To Retrieving Your Body'. What if it were just impossible? If it were already too late? Deborah had already tried to kill herself once. Without anyone there to control her emotions it was only a matter of time before she tried it again.

"You bloody idiot!" she coughed and spat onto the tarmac as a fraught sob rose up and the brutal pain of being half of what she should be began to press down on her shoulders. They had gone through everything together – first days at school, first dates, first jobs. She'd watched with regret as Deborah had married Jack, that great oaf of a boy, but laughed and shouted with her every time the vodka took over. Alcohol was the worst for the souls, and Deborah had become rather partial to it of late. Drinking was not something souls had any power over though. If Deborah chose to put it in her body, and as a side effect of that she got her soul pissed as a newt, that was her problem, and there was nothing that could be done about it.

Of course, when Deborah had gotten pregnant it was a great day. There was suddenly this extra little life to take care of. It had been a true honour to be there at the very first stages, before Deborah or Jack even knew it had happened. She had been there as a witness to the first tiny blossoms of a new human being. She knew that after Deborah's son was born he would have his own soul to take care of him, but for a while, however short, it was just the two of them and there was nothing more wonderful for a soul than to be part of that.

After the birth, it felt like everything was going to work out for Jack and Deborah. Jack calmed down, he became responsible. Their son gave them all something to fight for.

When they lost him, the change happened instantly. It was as if something just shut down inside of Deborah the very moment she knew. That somehow her son had been a key component to keeping her functioning and happy, and as soon as he was gone the loss created a raging sickness inside her.

It became impossible to do anything. Fury, fear and anguish was all Deborah ever felt, and it took her over. Was there anything a soul could do in those circumstances? Should she have tried harder, done something more to try and counteract it, to make things better? She had tried so hard, tried to take it all on board, to process all the anger and all the despair and the unfairness of it all, but eventually, and perhaps inevitably, it became too much and there was just no way of controlling it any longer.

Of course that was around the time that Jack had started drinking for real. What it must have been like to be in charge of his emotions God only knew. Someone must have been doing it, for everybody was divided in the same way: a body and a soul working together to weave their way through the highs and lows of life. In a way it was his fault: Jack's soul, whoever he or she was, they had obviously been doing an incredibly bad job of holding it together, and it had made it so much worse for Deborah and her. She had let Deborah down, sure, but Jack? Well, by the end it was clear his soul hadn't managed to keep any control over him at all.

It was the shock that had done it – the sudden realisation that that was it, that Deborah was really trying to end it all. It had knocked her right out of Deborah's body. She remembered the split second of being released, being catapulted out. The next thing she knew she had been on the outside, sort of hovering above her. At first she could see Deborah's body, seemingly lifeless, below her and then that was it. The darkness had come, that endless, monotonous tunnel that captured her in a strange world, seesawing her gently between life and death.

She looked down at the great red mark on her stomach once more. It throbbed and ached, and seemed to pulsate when she touched it again. The wound was where she had been ripped from Deborah. They were the very essence of one another and now, just like that, both of them were alone.

On entering the city she came to a shop, 'Judy's Jackets'. The bitter winter air was chilling her to the bone and so she went in to find something to cover her up. The inside was small and smelt of damp sawdust and stale perfume. Rows and rows of second-hand jackets on rusty hangers created a five foot maze of material around her, so only her head poked out above them. She tiptoed around, feeling strangely conscious of her nudity, before spotting a woollen coat. It was cherry red with wooden toggles and an oversized hood, and it was exactly what she needed. Taking a deep breath she reached out to grab it, not noticing that a woman had appeared beside her. It was only when their skin brushed one another and the searing pain shot through her arm that she realised. It made her squeal and instinctively duck to the floor. The woman grabbed a cropped denim jacket, inspected it for a moment, and then shuffled towards the counter, blissfully unaware that anything had happened. Clutching at the coats, the soul pulled herself back upright as the pain slowly faded. As she reached out for the red coat once more it melted into the air, leaving the hanger swinging like a metal skeleton on the rail. She smiled to herself. Not being seen by the bodies was one thing, but being able to touch things and turn them invisible was definitely a bonus, for now at least.

Heading for the exit, she hoped that they would blame the wind for the door as she pushed it open and closed it behind her.

The coat was warm and itchy, and she shrugged her shoulders and bent down to rub her knees, slowly beginning to get the feeling back into her body. She looked down the street, carefully checking for other people to be aware of, but there were only bin bags billowing in the wind like devilish ghosts as they spewed out rubbish onto the road. So she began to walk, concentrating on the pavement as she picked her way through the shards of glass and slushy puddles that riddled the way ahead.

As she turned the corner she smacked right into him. The shock of the real physical contact, of the resistance as their bodies collided, sent her staggering backwards. She tripped over her feet, landing with a hard bump on the concrete of the pavement below.

"Heeyyy, whoa there! Are you OK?"

He had an accent but she couldn't work out where from – kind of an Irish drawl. Looking up, she observed leather-clad legs, scuffed Doc Martens with smiley faces tippexed all over them and undone purple laces, soggy from puddles, trailing like caterpillars on the ground behind him. A red-knuckled hand extended towards her. She shook her head and scrambled to her feet. His hair was a mess of shaggy ginger curls. He was wearing sunglasses which he pushed back on his forehead, revealing warm chestnut eyes. He squinted, flashed a grin, and shrugged while shoving his rejected hand back into his trouser pocket.

"How... I don't understand... are you?"

She had known there would be others, of course, but she had not thought she would have seen one so soon. Stepping back she took a breath.

"Are you lost, too?"

The man's eyes glazed over and he bit his lip. Turning his head away from hers, he drew a sharp breath. His features stiffened as he struggled with a sadness that crept from the collar of his t-shirt. His eyes moved from hers and focused down the street. He then exhaled hard and pulled his hand from his pocket, extending it towards her once more.

"I'm Peter," he said. "And yes, I'm lost too."

"Oh. Hi. Um, I'm..." She frowned, "I don't really know."

Peter tilted his head to the side and laughed. "You just got here, right?"

She nodded.

"Yeah, you can tell you just got here. I didn't know either when I first arrived. I mean, I still don't really, but it's nice to have a name, don't you think? A sense of identity, you know?"

She shrugged. "Why would I want a sense of identity?"

Peter laughed again. "Yes, you are definitely new. How about you just humour me, yeah?"

"I guess."

He grinned. "Great. Well let's see. We could name you after the shop you just stole that jacket from? I assume this is your first steal, right?"

"Right."

"Hmmm, but I'm not sure it suits you." His eyes suddenly widened as if remembering something of great importance. "Hey, hang on, my guy had a pet goldfish once – Popeye he was called – what about that? You've kind of got big eyes, like a fish."

"Are you making fun of me?"

"Nah." He grinned again, then gripped her arm excitedly. "OK. How about this. My guy, you know, my body, he really liked this girl when he was younger. She was a movie star or something. He had a proper crush on her so he did. She had a pretty name though – Grace. What do you think of that? It's a nice name, right?"

"OK."

"OK!" He smacked his hands together and did a strange jig. "So that's who you are now. It's you and me, Grace, and it looks as though you could do with a little help."

She frowned. "What do you mean?"

He smiled at her, softer now, and pointed to her feet which were almost purple from the cold. "I reckon you could do with some shoes."

They talked only a little as they walked through the streets, carefully avoiding the people. There was so much to say, and yet they were both still reeling with the shock of having found one another that they maintained a friendly silence for the time being, each quietly thinking about what it might mean. Peter knew the 'perfect place' to get shoes. There was a market down the road that sold hundreds of pairs. It was busy and noisy. A risk of being touched, he knew, but no one would notice a thing.

"That's where I got these bad boys from," he told her, his boyish grin making another appearance while gesturing to his feet. Grace smiled, unsure how to comment on his choice of footwear. "You'll need a sturdy pair of shoes for what we have to do."

"We?" Grace asked.

He smiled at her. "We're here," he said and he grabbed her hand before hurrying her in.

The market was in a huge building with a high vaulted ceiling. Just as Peter had said, there were people everywhere yelling, bartering, holding up shoes by their laces and swinging them over their shoulders, or kneeling or squatting on the ground trying on shoes of all shapes and sizes. Berry-faced old men with money belts strapped tight below their bellies sweated and heaved as they operated the stalls. Young girls giggled and leant on each other as they attempted glittering heels; workmen smoked over boots, holding them close to their faces and inspecting every inch. Mothers leaned protectively over their children as they tried on Wellington boots with frogs' eyes on them and let out delighted squeals.

Peter expertly weaved his way through the crowd, avoiding contact with the people and pulling Grace behind him. He stopped by a stall filled with hiking boots, old sports trainers and his beloved Doc Martens.

"Pick a pair," he said. Grace scanned the shoes before settling on a pair of sandy hiking boots. Peter nodded in approval and grabbed them by the heels. He then opened his coat, which had hooks fastened into the lining. Keys, padlocks, chains and numerous strange small items hung from them. He bent the laces over one and fastened it back around his chest. "Let's go!" he called to her, pulling her back through the crowds and never once letting go of her hand.

In the park across the street they lay side by side on their backs. Peter presented her with a pair of thick woollen socks that he had conjured from his seemingly never-ending pockets and Grace, now warm and dry, began to think about her situation and the impossible task that lay ahead. She struggled as a cheerless lump formed in her throat; she never thought it would happen to her. Even when things got really bad, she had never suspected it would come to this.

"What was yours like?" Grace asked him in a shy pause as they looked at the sky.

"What's he like?" Peter turned towards her with a shocked expression on his face.

"Come on – really? You really want to talk about them?"

"I don't know," Grace shrugged. "What – are we not supposed to or something?"

Peter kept silent for a while as if weighing this up, then turned on his side towards her, and propped up his head with his hand.

"It's not that. It's just, well I don't know Grace, I just think it's kind of personal that's all. Don't get me wrong, I want to help you and, you know, maybe you'll even end up helping me. But all the details, all the stories about how we ended up here, about how we failed, I just don't think I want to share it, OK?"

"OK." Grace changed the subject. "How long have you been here for?"

"About four weeks now," he sighed. "I guess it's not that long but let's face it, it's not like we have all the time in the world".

"No." Grace matched his sigh with her own and nodded her head.

"You still have no idea where he is?"

"Not much." Peter reached his hand to the sky and opened and closed his fingers, creating stripes of sunshine and shadow on his face. His arm was long, white and muscular, and covered in tattoos in black and red ink.

"What are they for?" Grace asked. "You didn't come with them, did you?"

Peter snorted and dropped his hand back down to his side.

"No, I didn't come with them. It's just stuff I think I might need to remember, from the dreams, you know?"

"The dreams?"

Peter smiled at her sadly. "I bet you thought you could just walk back into her house and somehow get back inside, huh? No, I'm afraid it's not that easy. The dreams are how we find them again. When they go to sleep, in a way so do we. We kind of get pulled in. They'll only see us in their dreams, you see. They wouldn't believe it when they are awake. But dreams are where anything can happen. They are tough places to be though, there is no logic, no rules."

Grace felt her head grow hot. She had no idea it would be like this. Why did it have to be so hard? She turned her face away and stared fiercely at the ground as Peter went on.

"I use the tattoos to keep a note of clues because that way they are always with me, so I won't forget. It's all such a muddle so you need to keep track. Sometimes it's almost like things happen that have happened before, or I see something and I recognise it but I can't quite remember. But if I check my arm and it's there, then things can start to fit into place. That's how it works, I think. You know that deep down they want to find us too, so they try, they try to help us. Even though they don't know they are doing it, something on a subconscious level knows that we are missing, knows that without us they will die. So in the dreams I swear stuff repeats itself and so if it happens more than once I put it on here."

He pointed to his arm then jumped up and walked a few paces away from her. He pushed his hands into his pockets and kicked at a stone, agitated.

"We can only find them when they're asleep and even then it's only if they dream. We could be standing right next to them when they are awake and they wouldn't even know we were there. But then I guess they might not want us back if they knew, you know, that we're the key to their survival? They tried to kill themselves after all. But when they sleep, that's when their subconscious wakes up, and all it wants to do is keep them alive. So being in their dreams, in their subconscious, it's the best shot we have to find them, to hope they know us and they'll want us back. You must know they won't last long without us..." Peter's voice trembled and he cleared his throat before carrying on. "But of course it's not exactly easy, and we have to try and figure out what it all means. Their dreams - they're so erratic, it's not like they are just there in front of you, smiling and waving. Sometimes they don't even appear as themselves, did you know that? Plus it's risky. You could just end up anywhere."

Peter shook his head and trailed off in exasperated despair.

Grace sat up and patted the ground. He squatted down beside her. She bit her lip and felt an unfamiliar ache; a cold, fat toad was crawling in her stomach.

"Aren't you scared he won't recognise you?"

The toad crawled up her throat, and she swallowed hard. Peter's hand found hers amongst the damp blades of grass.

"If we can find them, they will know who we are." He said it firmly, though his voice still shook a little. "I promise you, Grace, if we find them they will know who we are."

CHAPTER 4

DEBORAH

The first dream

"Take off your shoes."

Deborah turned the corner of Doctor Vanilla's office and found him much the same as last time, with his back to her in the far corner of the room. He was flicking through the pages of one of the journals, and did not look up at her when he spoke.

She glanced down at her feet; flat black boots in worn leather stuck out from underneath her jeans. Last time Doctor Vanilla had made it clear he'd been less than impressed with her appearance, looking her up and down with an unnerving contempt as she'd huffed and puffed her way through the session. It was as though he was judging her somewhat dishevelled exterior to be a reflection of what was happening on the inside. It was a ridiculous notion, in Deborah's opinion, that somehow, if she slipped on a power suit and brushed her hair, her problems would puff away into the sky. However, the previous night, after many gins and a great deal of thought, she had decided to give the therapy a proper chance, and had therefore spent the rest of the night trying to create the perfect 'I'm fine, I'm together, I am fit for society' outfit.

She had teamed her boots and jeans with an ashy blue shirt she had found at the bottom of her linen closet. It had been there since her mother had come round and insisted on ironing all of her 'nice clothes' in the hope this would encourage Deborah to wear them. Her hair was scraped back into a tight bun and a she had put on some blusher and crimson lipstick that had been a birthday gift – another attempt by her mother to smarten her up. Why he was asking her to take her shoes off she had no idea. Perhaps it was an attempt to get her to feel more relaxed, or perhaps he just didn't want her traipsing street dirt onto his expensive-looking rug. Whatever the reason, Deborah felt little need to argue so kicked off her boots with an ungraceful stagger and placed them neatly side by side by the door.

Doctor Vanilla moved towards his desk and gestured silently for her to sit down. He lowered himself into his chair and clasped his hands in front of his chest. He wore a silver ring on the middle finger of his left hand. Three deep-set diagonal lines were scratched across it, as though it had been swiped at by something with claws.

It had been a week since her last visit. After she left his office Deborah had decided to take a walk in the park near her house. She'd had a stomach ache and thought perhaps that some fresh air would help. It was mild at first, but it soon got stronger until it felt as though someone was pummelling furiously at her insides.

She had sat on one of the benches. On the back a bronze plaque had been screwed into the centre of it:

74 years was far too short. But in that time we knew quite an extraordinary man. For Brian, a son, a father a husband, a friend, you were always cherished; you will be forever missed.

Deborah had smiled, one of those tight-lipped quivering smiles, as if her mouth were trying to rein in the pain that could come flooding out at any moment in a great gush of indignity. Beside the plaque someone had scrawled with a black pen, 'Lucy sucked it here.' Deborah couldn't imagine how she would feel if someone had done that on a bench she'd put up as a memory to her son. The very thought of it made her want to find Lucy and whatever it was she sucked and slap them until they realised what awful, insolent monsters they were.

Deborah had stayed on the bench for over an hour facing the stretch of grass ahead. The people came and went in hordes, stamping through the leaves. They'd all looked so angry as though the park was in their way. Coffee and newspaper clutching they'd hurried past her in suits, grasping their brief cases as if they were the most precious things in the world, and talking sternly into mobile phones. They had no time to notice how the trees, with their forked faces, were leaning so delicately through the silver sky, how the grass, peppered in frost, looked sugar-coated and sweet. *I have all the time in the world*, she'd thought, and smiled again as her blood ached with a sorrow she could not explain in words.

Doctor Vanilla coughed, jerking Deborah away from the memory. Some phlegm caught in his throat and a momentary panic flared up in his eyes. He tried to clear it and a fleck of spit appeared on his bottom lip.

Today he was wearing a dark blue silk shirt with a crimson tie. The shirt looked a little too tight around the neck and a little too short around the cuffs. His hair was pulled up and over to the right hand side of his face, leaving his scar on the left fully exposed. It was even more noticeable today, the lines, the skin all illuminated in the light. Deborah felt her stomach turn as she looked at it.

He cleared his throat again.

He'd asked her a question. *I wonder if it was for me to remove more items of clothing*, Deborah joked to herself. She snorted, a large, nervous snort which hung in the air between them, and Doctor Vanilla's eyes narrowed in disgust.

"I repeat," he sighed, leaning back in his chair, "did you bring your journal with you today?" Looking away from her as he spoke, his eyes seemed to be constantly trying to catch up with one another; one looked right and then the other followed, as if they could never quite agree to go the same way. Deborah nodded and rummaged in the rucksack by her feet before pulling the journal out and placing it on his desk.

Doctor Vanilla let out a sigh and his skin flushed pink. He reached across the desk and Deborah couldn't help but notice his hands were trembling. He was like a dog with a bone, juddering with excitement, wagging his tail. His desperation to see what was inside made her nervous and instinctively she pulled the journal back from the desk and clutched it protectively to her chest.

Doctor Vanilla cocked his head to one side and sighed a second time. It seemed that her reaction had been expected.

His mouth pressed into a shrivelled pout like a satsuma left in the sun and he leant forward, pushing his face closer to hers.

"Deborah," his lisp coated his words, making them come out in a strange mix of condescension and threat. "I know it seems uncommon to hand over information that you may feel is private, however you need to understand that we are safe here. Try to think of this little office and me as a bubble, one that you yourself have blown. When you arrive you enter the bubble, and when you leave we stay here, floating and sealed until your next visit. And when you are better you can burst the bubble and all that we've shared will evaporate into the air."

He fluttered his fingers towards the ceiling and leant even further forward until Deborah felt his breath on her forehead. It smelt syrupy and dense as it drifted, sickly-sweet, into her nostrils.

"You do want to get better, don't you, Deborah? You do want me to help you, don't you?"

Deborah clutched the journal a little tighter. There was something about him; she didn't trust him, but it was more than that. There was something unsettling, queer, almost ghostly, about him. She just couldn't put her finger on exactly what it was.

Of course she had no real reason to believe that there was anything hostile or unpleasant in him really. His outward appearance was a little unusual, sure, but that wasn't a fair reason not to give him a proper chance. Besides she was the kind of person who tended to escalate situations in her head. In her mind everyone had the potential to be evil or dangerous in some way. It was ridiculous, of course, and she could recognise that. For her initial position was always to be suspicious, and to think the worst in people, but why not let them prove otherwise? That way she would always be on her guard. That way she would never let anyone treat her badly again.

However, at this moment, the situation was more than a little uncomfortable. Doctor Vanilla was looking at her expectantly and she was unreasonably holding onto her journal like a baby with a rattle. Besides, if nothing else, she knew he was a good therapist – she'd researched him a little after receiving his initial call and he certainly had a solid reputation. She'd scrolled through his website – he had all the qualifications, a member of BCAP, accredited by UKCP. She didn't really know what any of this meant, of course, but it all appeared to be pretty legitimate. Anyway she was too tired to protest. She felt like she hadn't slept all week. Even when she had managed to relax enough to drift off it had only been those weak, static, restless sleeps that only seemed to last for a few minutes at a time.

The question remained hanging in the air between them. Did she want to get better? It would be ridiculous if her answer would be anything other than 'yes', but yet she couldn't quite bring herself to say it. Deborah suddenly flashed back to the bathtub, the memory squeezing into every last inch of her mind. She remembered how surprising it was that the knife had so easily cut through her skin, and her wonder at the blood all thick and shiny and new as it trickled down and mixed with the water. It seemed happy somehow, the blood, as if it had always wanted to escape. And the water was so pretty, turning such a lovely shade of pink.

She didn't remember any pain, but something had stopped her letting it happen. Something in the back of her mind had made her panic and she was suddenly overcome with regret. A voice that didn't seem like hers had popped into her head. "What a silly, silly girl you've been," it said, over and over again.

The next thing she knew was waking up in the hospital, her mother by her side. Her mother had seemed like an outline of herself, all withered and crumpled up and hunched in a chair. Deborah had looked down at the wires, little life-giving worms that dug into her skin, and had felt so angry to be alive that she wanted to punch things, and scream, and rip everything off. Instead she'd pushed her head back against the pillows and dug her nails deep into the palm of her hands. Then the guilt and the shame and the discomfort all arrived, right on cue, when her mother saw she was awake and had begun to cry.

Deborah nodded her head and slid the journal towards Doctor Vanilla across the desk. "Of course, I want to get better," she said.

With her reluctant consent, Doctor Vanilla flicked through the pages. Deborah watched him as he hungrily feasted on each word. As soon as she had let go of the journal, she wished she had not given it to him. There was something peculiar about how desperate he had been to look at it. Surely it was all nonsense anyway. What could her dreams possibly tell him about her state of mind? She felt embarrassed that he was reading about a part of her brain over which she had no control, and felt a low wave of regret absorb its way, feet first, up through her body.

Carefully Deborah watched him as his eyes scanned the pages. Occasionally he would pause and stab his finger violently on a word, his skin quivering repulsively as he did, and then he would flick open his notebook and scribble something down. He was excited. Deborah assumed this meant that something good was happening, that, ridiculously, he thought he had found something that he could build on. He didn't speak one word to her as he did this, completely absorbed in his task; it was as though she was no longer in the room.

Deborah shifted in her seat and glanced around. Her eyes were drawn once again to the painting of sunflowers that had so disturbed her last time she had come. It looked different from before; the ones at the front looked taller, as though they had trampled their way forwards, anxious to be seen. The yellow looked paler, the sallow petals hanging limply like a frame of rotten fangs around their centres, as though they were baring their teeth to give her some sort of warning. It was as though they had been disfigured in some way, and were trying to break away from the captive of the canvas, away from the dark earth that had swallowed their roots and held them prisoner there.

Doctor Vanilla slammed the journal shut, making Deborah jump, and for a moment her heart felt as though it was beating in her mouth. A puff of dust appeared around his face, hazing it out momentarily before it cleared. He was smiling a tight and artificial-looking smile.

"Good, Deborah. Very good. Progress is being made."

"OK..." Deborah replied, confused. "But how do you know? I mean, I am not sure I understand..."

She trailed off. He seemed so pleased that she almost didn't want to spoil it with her questions. He was the professional after all. But she didn't feel any different at all. He could say that she was progressing all he liked, but if she didn't feel any different, then what was the point?

"Doctor Vanilla," she tried again, 'I'm glad and everything, you know, that you think things are going well. But I'm not sure I get it. I mean, aren't we supposed to talk more? You've barely asked me anything today."

Deborah clenched and unclenched her hands and crossed

her legs before continuing. "I mean, I'm not even sure if I've got anything to say, but isn't that what we are supposed to do here?"

Doctor Vanilla leant back in his chair and sighed. He appeared frustrated, as if her questions and her uncertainty were utterly beneath him.

"Miss Green," he addressed her as if he was gently scolding a child. "Do you recall what I told you when you first came here?"

Deborah opened her mouth to answer, but the question was clearly a rhetorical one and she was silenced by his raised hand. "I told you that you may find some of my methods unconventional, did I not?" Again he prevented her from answering and continued. "So please, let me do my job." He then pulled forwards again and smiled, tapping his nose in an oddly mischievous gesture as he handed the journal back to her. "Keep dreaming, Miss Green," he whispered. "Rest, sleep and dream – and trust me." He then rose from his desk and made for the door. "I shall be back shortly," he added before striding purposefully from the room.

Deborah stared ahead. The heat of his office was crushing; she could feel damp patches forming under her arms. Her lungs were shrinking, withering to tiny sinewy sacks with each breath. Deborah walked to the window and shoved fistfuls of velvet curtain to the side as she tried to tug it upwards. Slices of sunshine cut across the room as she struggled and squatted, pushing up from the knees. The window wouldn't budge. Deborah checked for a lock but there was none; it was as though it had been cemented shut, never to be opened again.

Suddenly a whisper floated from behind her, sealed in a pocket of air and dust. "*Help us!*" it murmured softly. Deborah turned with a start and the curtain fell to the ground, once again blocking out all natural light. The hairs on her arms and the back of her neck prickled and she felt a cool shiver run over her body. She stared into the corners of the room, slitting her eyes as if this would somehow help her to see more clearly. No, there was definitely no one else there. But the painting – the sunflowers – they had moved, she could swear it. Their heads were bent in crippled hunches and they pointed down to the desk beneath them. Her eyes followed and fell on the notebook Doctor Vanilla had left on its surface.

Deborah stepped towards it, neck craning, eyes wide. Her heart felt as though it had paused, caught in a tight net in her chest. Reaching his desk, she looked from the pad to the corner which led to the door out of the office. She listened for Doctor Vanilla's returning footsteps, then quickly flicked the notebook open. She took a step back, suddenly afraid of what it would contain, as though the words might leap off the page and into her head with new and dreadful meaning.

The date was at the top. Beneath there were only five words.

Old heroines
Pairs
Loss
Love

Deborah scowled. None of these was related to what she had written in her dream journal, nor what her dreams had been about. She turned over the page. There was nothing more. That was it. Before she had a chance to read any more, Deborah heard the creak of the door and so she slammed the notebook shut, and hurriedly sat back down in her chair.

Doctor Vanilla emerged around the corner. He seemed to be smiling, but the smile didn't look right. It was rigid, as though someone had stitched it onto his face. When he got to the desk he handed the journal back to her.

"Thank you, Miss Green." Then, glancing at his watch, he raised a single eyebrow into a perfect triangular point. "I'll see you next week."

Deborah walked down the corridor to collect her boots from where she had left them by the door. They were no longer there. Perplexed, she turned to go back and almost collided with Doctor Vanilla, who had followed her soundlessly. He was holding her boots in front of him.

"Forget something?"

The way he said it implied that he believed she would have left and trudged barefoot along the pavement, unable to comprehend why her feet were so cold. Deborah had never seen his face so close before and his scar seemed to wriggle beneath his skin. Like bloodless tentacles the lines writhed as he spoke.

"Thanks." She took her boots from him and stepped into the corridor.

A young girl who couldn't have been older than about fifteen or sixteen was sitting in one of the chairs in the hallway, her head nestled in her hands. Doctor Vanilla cleared his throat and the girl looked up. She had the face of a winter moon, distant, round and silvery pale. Her hair was waist length, her legs long and impossibly thin. As she got up her frayed grey satchel swung forlornly from her shoulder. One of her arms was in a full cast, which had been decorated with messages and pictures in green and blue biro. She passed Deborah silently, quickly glancing up at her with strange piercing blue eyes, before looking fixedly back down to the floor as she entered Doctor Vanilla's office.

Outside, Deborah devoured the air, and she felt quite refreshed before the same strange stomach ache started again. It was well past lunchtime and she hadn't eaten yet that day. Perhaps some food would help it settle. She remembered walking past a supermarket two streets down. Rifling through her bag for her phone, Deborah began walking in the direction of the shop. She had no messages and frowned at herself for the disappointment she felt. Who was she expecting a call from? She had no idea.

It had been different before, when she'd been happy. When she'd had a family. They'd had friends then, friends they'd go out with, do things with. They would have each other round for dinner, or go to watch a film together then have a few drinks in the pub. But after it all happened there just didn't seem any point any more and Deborah had shut them all out. They'd tried, of course, to keep calling, to keep 'dropping by', but eventually had given up. Deborah didn't blame them. There is only so much you can do for another person when they refuse to give anything back.

When she reached the supermarket the doors of the shop parted, opening silver jaws to reveal rows upon rows of packets, boxes and cans, all being supervised by the blinding eyes of the fluorescent strip lighting above. Deborah made her way round the aisles, becoming lost, hypnotised by the mass maze of produce. She strolled up and down each section, occasionally pausing and feigning interest at special offers on cans of soup. She knew she was stalling for time, avoiding going home.

Finally, armed with some pills, some bread rolls and a packet of cheap, glossy cheese slices, Deborah arrived at the till. The checkout girl had a name-tag pinned to her navy uniform. It was one of those names that made the owner of it seem as though they could be nothing but irritating:

'Kaithey'. Deborah repeated it over in her head in a singsong voice. Kaithey regarded Deborah with world-weary eyes, her gold earrings glittering under the lights as she swivelled in her chair and began to scan the items through.

"Bags?" she asked. Deborah shook her head.

That was when she saw him, the man she had so briefly encountered at Doctor Vanilla's. He was two queues up from her, standing at the till, biting his lip. He looked up momentarily and his eyes caught Deborah's. His face was unshaven and sparse tufts of hair grew in coarse patches on his skin which had turned a vigorous crimson in the cold air. Thick eyebrows demanded all the attention from his face, united in their quest for domination, and squatted over his eyes, which hesitated in an expression that hovered somewhere between anger and panic. He was tall, his jaw square, jutting out just a little too much so an air of petulance hovered near his chin. He wore a crumpled blue suit that sat awkwardly on his heavy frame, the sleeves and cuffs just a little too short which made him look like an overgrown schoolboy squeezed into a sibling's old uniform. Deborah smiled at him.

He stepped backwards as though an invisible wind had kicked him in the shins. Tugging a tatty canvas wallet from the back pocket of his trousers, he hastily pulled out a handful of notes and threw them down on the counter. Not waiting for change, he picked up his bags and marched to the exit, grazing a sign that said '5 cans for 4' as he passed. It swayed, momentarily paused in time, and then fell to the ground with a resounding and final clatter. The shop assistant looked after him open-mouthed. She had the pocked face of a sponge. It trembled as she blinked rapidly. It looked as though she was about to cry.

Deborah stared after him. She had almost thought about

going up to him, saying hello or at least offering him a conspiratorial wave or a wink, yet he'd looked so horrified to have seen her again, as if her knowledge that he saw a therapist too, made seeing her in a setting that was ordinary and real just too much for him to bear.

At home, she lay face down on her kitchen table with her arms dangling over the sides. All she could think about was being thirteen and at school. She had been sitting alone, unsuccessfully trying to make daisy chains with too-fat thumbs. A group of girls in the year above had approached her. "Billy Ricks likes you," they'd said.

Billy Ricks played football on the proper team, and wore the best kind of shoes. In the five minutes between then and what happened next, Deborah had imagined the following: holding his hand, lying in a field making pictures from the clouds, their first kiss behind the science labs where everyone that got to kiss kissed, and eating fish fingers and peas at his house, where his mum would pass her the ketchup and smile.

None of this was due to happen as she found out when she approached Billy, her stomach a blubber of nerves, and he had informed her that he did not like her, quite the opposite in fact. Instead he pushed her, spat and said, "Don't talk to me". The girls had laughed.

"Don't talk to him, Deb BORE rah!" they'd gleefully shouted, and then turned and ran away, leaving echoes of cruel giggles behind them.

A moan escaped from Deborah's lips and vibrated through the table top. Sitting up, she slid from the down, flicked on the kettle and pulled a cheese slice from the packet, absent-mindedly nibbling it at the corner. Then she pulled her journal from her rucksack, leant against the worktop and began to read what she had written, cringing at the thought that this was what she had let Doctor Vanilla read, too.

I'm falling and falling and drowning, drowning, drowning. There is water all around me and I can't breathe. I am nervous, afraid. I know I shouldn't be here and that something has gone terribly wrong. I can feel my heart pounding. It's beating so fast because it can tell that this is the end. I reach up to touch it. I try and soothe it, but it knows, it knows that it is too late. I try to kick my legs, try to swim upwards, but it's like they are stuck in cement. I look around trying to see something, anything that will help me, but I am in the dark. There is nothing but the dark; the dark has come to take me away.

The kettle frothed at the mouth and clicked off, sighing steam into the air. Ignoring it, Deborah continued to read.

And just when I think that's it, I see him. I see Jack swimming towards me. His face is bruised and battered. There are leaves in his hair and a paleness to his skin that scares me at first. He stretches his hand out towards me, in it there is a ring. His hair flows out behind him, pulling the skin back on his face; I can see the outline of his bones underneath it.

Deborah walked, the journal still in her hand. She kicked out a chair and sat, not taking her eyes from the page.

I take it from him and as soon as I do he smiles. It is the saddest smile I have ever seen. I want to touch him, to tell him I forgive him and that things will be OK, but I can't bring myself to do it, and when I look in his eyes I know he knows I never will. Then it is over. His eyes bulge, they roll back in his head. He starts to drift away from me and suddenly I am free. I want to save him, but I can't, I can't. So I swim up, kicking desperately, swallowing water and gasping for air. When I break the surface of the water with one last push that takes the last of my energy and my head is finally above the top, I drink in the air. It is only after a moment that I notice the thousands and thousands of pale fish floating lifelessly on the surface, and there is nothing else around as far as the eye can see.

Deborah slammed the journal closed. Old heroines, partners, love and loss. What the hell had that got to do with anything?

CHAPTER 5

GRACE

Avoid the crowds

Peter was fading away. He tried to smile reassuringly, but it only went as far as his cheeks; the fear in his eyes had made a wall around his eyelashes which couldn't be broken. Grace reached out her hand to touch him, to pull him back, but he was now merely an outline of himself and soon was no longer visible as he was carried away by the shadows of sleep.

She was alone. Lying back on the mattress, she clamped her hand over her face – it smelt of dust and mould. The stench stung her eyes and clung to the back of her throat. She stared up at the fractured ceiling, the cracks in the plaster forming a web of pity above her. Floorboards creaked from the rooms upstairs and she heard a shout, the slam of a door, and stuttered, hiccupy sobs muffled through the walls as somewhere nearby, a child began to cry.

Anger. That was what overwhelmed her now. Why had she followed the stupid, stupid boy? He had led her here, to this stale, crumbling half-life, and then just drifted away. He had promised he would help her, that they would search together, but now he had gone and she was alone, lying in this squatter's house all by herself. She didn't even really know where they were. She didn't have a plan. She didn't even have the first idea of how to get back to Deborah.

Peter had tried to explain to her what would happen, what it felt like. "Kind of like melting but without any heat," was the best he'd come up with. Then he'd reached for her hand. "It doesn't hurt," he'd added, and given it a little squeeze.

She had thought they could do it together, that it would happen to them at the same time, and somehow they would end up in the same place. He had not promised her any of this, of course, but he had said "we". He had told her "we" – and not just once – but now he was gone. Turning her head to the wall, Grace sighed and fought back the tears as she watched the damp seep in fat patches through the paint.

Why hadn't Deborah fallen asleep yet? Why hadn't she been pulled into a dream? Just sitting here waiting was torture. Peter had said it would happen. He had said it would happen soon.

"Foolish, foolish fool. Liar!"

Grace pounded her fists onto the mattress, awakening fresh wafts of the smell. Sitting up she then took a huge breath and tried to calm down. "Enough," she announced to the empty room and got to her feet.

Outside the air hung low; an apathetic fog blanketed the rooftops, revealing glimpses of thick, grey slate in the breaks where it thinned. Grace tilted her head skywards, enjoying the freshness of the cold on her cheeks. Her stomach made a disagreeable gurgle, and she could feel something wriggle underneath her skin, as though there was someone trying to struggle from within it. Looking down she unbuttoned her coat, pulling up the faded T-shirt Peter had lent her to reveal a creamy white belly button. She gently stroked her stomach, trying not to wince at the large red mark that seemed to have grown bigger and bigger each time she inspected it. She looked to the sky once again. The fog had drifted and the clouds were huddling together in dense clumps of grey.

Walking along the pavement, Grace repeated the instructions Peter had given her the night before.

"Numero uno," he'd said, "Avoid the crowds, any place that has the words 'market' or 'mall' in them – do not go in. If you get hungry, some of the shops on Blachingham Street have stalls of fruit and vegetables outside – get something from there. They're quiet and the keepers are always too busy on the phone or ogling some sort of dirty magazine to notice. It's easy to steal from there," he'd grinned, "especially if they can't see you in the first place!"

Grace reached into her coat pocket and pulled out the scribbled directions, studying them carefully. He had drawn them in such detail that there was no way of getting lost. The names of the shops, the street signs, the traffic lights – he had even drawn a sketch of the drunk who always sat on the bench by the corner of the park. She'd asked him at the time why he couldn't just show her himself. "Just in case," he'd replied.

Grace felt her anger rise up through her throat in a hot swell. If he had known it would happen so soon why hadn't he just warned her outright?

The road he'd drawn was a narrow street with jutting-out roofs topping the houses either side and stretching out towards each other, almost blocking out all light. There were several shops along the street; all had stalls, carelessly heaped with red and green apples, flaking onions, bruised bananas, potatoes, withered-looking herbs and one with a solitary pineapple. Grace made her way to the first one and glanced in. She smiled against her will. It was just as Peter had said. The shopkeeper, leaning nonchalantly over the counter, was flicking through a magazine with ink-stained fingers. Its cover had a photo of a shiny car and a near-naked girl spread at an uncomfortable-looking angle on its bonnet. His phone was jammed to his ear with his shrugged-up shoulder and he was frowning, speaking loudly in a language she did not understand. His face was jagged, angular, like you could fish with it, and his wiry moustache twitched as he spoke.

None of the food on the stalls was what she wanted. It was a strange feeling to crave food for herself. Grace's stomach rumbled again and she hovered, moth-like, by the doorway. There was no one else in the shop. Inside there were shelves of bread, fridges of cheese, butter, croissants, crisps and chocolate. *Deborah likes these things,* Grace thought, and a little sadness nudged at her throat.

She remembered Deborah's face clearly, and thought back to a favourite memory of her laughing in the rain. It was just after their son had been born. Deborah's mother had offered to babysit, so she and Jack headed out for a night out on the town. They'd only made it about ten minutes down the road before the heavens had opened. It had soaked them through, dripping in tadpoles down Deborah's face, making black lines of mascara streak down her cheeks like war paint. Jack had wiped them away with his fingertips, a gesture so tender that had made Deborah shudder – and not because of the cold. The two of them had been drinking of course. Grace remembered the tickle and burn of vodka as they had passed the bottle between them. They'd huddled under a shop doorway before making a run for it, crashing through the puddles with stupid fat grins and hands clutched together as if their lives depended on it.

Grace remembered the tinkle of the bell as they'd pushed open the door of the cafe. "Good day to you," Jack had called to the startled waitress, taking a drippy bow, and making Deborah giggle as they slid into a booth. The wall was lined with pictures of black and white movie stars: beautiful, glamorous people who were now long gone. They ordered steaming mugs of coffee that they had sneakily topped up, and a thick slice of cake. They'd shared a fork. They had been so in love, and neither Deborah nor Grace had realised it was so frail, that it would so soon be taken away from them.

Grace frowned. She wanted that feeling back so badly, and she wanted Deborah to feel it as well. She hated that she missed Jack. He'd been so awful and so selfishly cruel in those last few months before he left, but she didn't believe he'd ever stopped loving Deborah. It broke Grace's heart that he had gone. She knew getting a cake wouldn't make any difference but, just for a moment, perhaps it would help to make the current situation feel less utterly and stupidly hopeless.

"Rule number dos," Peter had been laughing, dancing a stupid jig in circles around her, trying to make her smile. "Don't take risks. Even if it's not busy, it's not worth it. If you have the choice, stay as far away from the people as you can, OK?"

"You take risks," Grace had pointed out. "What about the shoe market? That was jammed and I was fine."

"You were with me," he'd said.

"Why wouldn't I be with you?" she'd asked

To that he had said nothing. Instead he had grinned. "Why aren't you dancing?" he'd asked, and banged her with his hip.

Grace edged her way around the shelves. The scent of old milk and cheap floor cleaner clung to the back of her throat. The shopkeeper had now pulled up a metal stool with a plastic seat and was perched on its edge, still yelling into his phone, occasionally pausing, tilting his head back and roaring a huge gruff laugh before he continued to shout. Grace stood by the fridge and carefully slipped in some wedges of cheese wrapped in cellophane slices, shoving them deep into her pockets, before continuing to the bread aisle and grabbing some rolls which she jammed in on top. There was a voice in her head that told her to leave, but she ignored it and continued to walk down the aisle, further and further away from the exit.

Bingo! There it was. Out of the corner of her eye she spotted it, sitting on a shelf above the fridge: a huge chocolate cake, three layers, cemented together with a thick spread of buttercream. Peter's warning echoed in her mind but then another voice shouted louder. The shopkeeper had turned his back and was idly skimming his fingers across the packets of cigarettes lined up neatly behind him. Grace saw her chance and reached up.

A breeze from the shop entrance tickled her ankles, and with it a chorus of voices. A crowd of teenagers entered the shop, spotted faces glowing out from hoods, they were shouting, laughing, shoving each other about. The shopkeeper slammed his phone onto the counter and glared.

"Oi, oi, oi!" His voice was thick with accent. "Two at a time. Read the sign." He jutted his head towards the door. The kids stopped and looked at him. There was a silence, a pause during which tension crept in and tightened the air between them. Then they laughed. The tallest one punched at one of the shelves, sending packets and cans flying through the air before clattering to the floor.

"What? You gonna make us, Paki man?"

His friends gathered behind him, sneering, jeering and banging shoulders. One of them grabbed a carton of milk. He peeled open the sides and took a huge gulp, holding it in his mouth. His eyes glistened spitefully, acne-scarred cheeks swelling out as he poured it in.

His friends parted and he spat, sowing the counter and the man behind it with seeds of milk and saliva. The shopkeeper yelled in vain and thumped his fist. Grace tried to run, but her feet wouldn't move. It was too late.

The boys went wild, tearing at the shop and trampling anything they could get their hands on. They egged each other on, caught up in an untamed frenzy that grew with each item they broke. Grace squeezed herself into a nook at the back of the shop and covered her head with her hands.

The leader appeared round the corner. He skidded on a can of beans that had washed the floor in a sticky mess of orange lumps. Grace looked up and stretched her arms out in protest as if this might stop him. Time slowed down as he glided towards her, looking momentarily graceful, like an ice skater, until his lanky body slammed into hers.

It was not like the first time, in the coat shop, when the woman's skin had brushed hers before. He was all in her, and every part of her skin stung. She tore at her hair, which fell in clumps to the ground as she uselessly tried to shove him away. A black balloon was inflating in her head. She saw threads of white flash between her temples and a swarm of dots appeared either side, closing in on her until everything went black.

The boy lay laughing and panting in the corner. His hood had fallen from his head, revealing a slicked-back segment of hair which shone like a wet fish under the lights. There was a siren in the distance. The shopkeeper was huddled, shaking, behind the counter, his anger hijacked by shock and fear.

"Cm'on, man, let's go!" A hand reached down and the boy was pulled up by another. Grace stayed, limp and invisible to all, as the spilt liquids formed a puddle around her body.

She could not tell how long she had been lying there before she finally came to. It was a bristly nudge that jolted her from the rich blankness only souls can feel. Opening her eyes she rolled out of the way as the shopkeeper, whose face was puffy and pink-eyed, bent over her, clutching a brush.

Grace quickly struggled to her feet to get away from him, grasping the shelves for balance as sharp pains shot through her body. The skin on her hands which had once been smooth and pale was now covered in huge screaming blisters. She pulled up her sleeves, wincing as the rough cloth of her coat rubbed on her wounds. Reaching up to touch her head, Grace moaned – there was nothing but straggling knots and red raw patches of scalp. She glimpsed at her reflection distorted by the metal of the fridge and a hollow sickness formed a space in her stomach.

How could I have been so stupid?

She closed her eyes for a moment, then stumbled back out into the street.

The walk back took forever; Grace limped and bent and staggered like a drunk in a painful daze. She finally reached the place where she and Peter had been staying and, pushing open the door, she saw him. Crouched by the corner of mattress his hands were knotted into fists in his hair. His eyes were pink, just as the shopkeeper's had been. Peter opened his mouth to say something but nothing came out and he had a funny expression in his eyes. They had glazed over. It was as though he wished to look away but he couldn't. Instead he held her gaze until Grace bent double and fell to her knees.

"You left me." The whisper floated gracefully across the room and fell at Peter's feet. He got up and ran towards her and she felt him, arms strong and tight, as he clamped them around her, and pulled her in.

"You left me, you left me, you left me!" Grace felt the hysteria scale her throat as she struggled away, her scabbed fists beating onto him as sour, gummy tears trickled into her mouth. Peter held on, his hands moving to the back of her head and pressing it into his chest. She could feel it rise and fall as he wrapped himself around her like a blanket. Her breathing slowed. She felt his mouth hot on her ear.

"I am sorry." He then squeezed her tighter. "I love you," he said.

CHAPTER 6

DEBORAH

The man who helped her home

There was a tapping. She could feel it – someone knocking, someone trying with all their might to get her attention as she slept. Then came the whisper that gradually grew louder. "*Find me,*" they cried. "*Find me. I'm here. Find me.*"

Sunlight grazed Deborah's eyelids as she flickered in and out of consciousness. She stirred and rolled over, pulling the sheet from the corner of her mattress. The edges of her lips twitched. They were smeared with a smudge of red that was caked in soft cracks at the corners of her mouth. A breeze from the open window pushed the catch of her bedroom door open, making it swing back and forth, and its tapping replaced the calls of those inside, whose cries were lost to dreams, as Deborah began to stir.

Her leg, heavy from sleep, was first to emerge from the mass of cushions, blankets and clothes that covered her. It flopped its way to the floor and a groan emerged from deep within. Deborah stayed like this for a moment, motionless bar the scrunching of her toes, sniffing at the carpet as if trying to understand their new surroundings. Next was a hand, hesitant at first, nails broken and brown with dirt, skimming the lines of the pillow case. Then, as though electrified, she started into action, fisting at cushions and knocking them to the ground, clutching at blankets with furious tugs, tossing them aside to reveal her body piece by piece: a soft, pale thigh; a torso clad in a navy blue T-shirt; her face twisted away from the light; and a puff of brown hair muddled around a face which was contorted, held rigid by the cobwebs of dreams.

Deborah sat up and stared at the wall ahead. She blinked a couple of times and swallowed hard. Her throat was dry and her eyes stung. She reached up to touch her head.

Yep, it was definitely a hangover, and a bad one at that.

Memories crawled in, sticky and slow. She remembered a bar, music and laughter, large whisky shots served in short, dirty glasses. Someone pushing her, the abrupt night air and a man steadying her towards a taxi rank. Deborah squeezed her eyes shut and thudded back down onto her pillows. Her brain was on fire. The memories were simply flashes like photographs, with nothing to fill what had happened in between.

She lay still for a while until the throbbing in her head lessened and then, little by little, as if on a winch, she eased herself upright again and this time got out of bed. Pulling a dressing gown from the hook at the back of her door she shuffled towards the kitchen. Water would help. She drank three glasses one after the other before flicking on the kettle. As it boiled she wandered into the bathroom, pulled off her T-shirt and carefully began to unwind the bandage around her stomach. The mark looked worse if anything. Wincing, Deborah took a cloth and washed it gently, smoothed a thin layer of antiseptic cream on the area, and wound the bandage back around as tight as she could bear, cursing Jack all the while as she did so. When it was done she returned to the kitchen. Then, with a cup of tea firmly clutched in her hand, she collapsed on her sofa and curled her feet under her in the usual position.

She remembered coming home, the frustration of not being able to understand the words that Doctor Vanilla had written. She had sat in her kitchen for what felt like hours, silence and night both closing in around her. She remembered pouring a drink from a sticky bottle of vodka she had found by clawing at the back of her cupboard, where she'd 'hidden' it from herself behind tins of soup and canned mushy peas. There was that pleasant feeling as it slipped down her throat, the heat in her belly, and the sigh of relief that had escaped her lips. She remembered the clatter and crash as she had thrown the empty bottle with a slurry arm and it had smashed into the corner next to her bin. Brimmed up with liquor, she'd grabbed her keys and headed out into the coldness of the night, which hit the back of her neck and made her eyes water. The cobbles of the street had grinned up at her like huge, flat teeth as she'd weaved her way towards the city. There she was in amongst the business of a Friday night – smells of sorrow, people pushing around her, a crowd of men yelling, leering.

"It's a bit cold without a jacket, love. Do you want warming up?"

She'd found a bar and stumbled in. There was warmth,

darkness and odours of spilt liquor, both sweet and sour, which had crept up from the floorboards. She had slumped, avoiding the eyes of the barman who'd served her shot after shot with growing reluctance.

After this point Deborah became uncertain. Had she gone somewhere else or stayed? And who was the man who had helped her home? She tried to picture his face but through the dark night and blurred vision she came up with nothing. There were no words, no memories, no matter how hard she thought back, and now here she was, in her apartment, all alone.

Deborah buried her head in between her knees and sighed. She wasn't supposed to be drinking; that was definitely breaking one of the 'rules' that had been set for her after she'd been discharged from hospital. It had hardly been her fault though, after the strange session she'd had with Doctor Vanilla, his creepy office, that peculiar painting. Besides she hadn't slept in days. She had needed something to try and knock her out. No one was exactly going to prescribe her sleeping pills in her oh-so-fragile state, so what else was she supposed to do?

As Deborah sat, new memories came forward; they weren't of last night but of her dream. Deborah smiled despite herself at the irony that the dream was coming back to her, crystal clear, as if it wished to take over reality itself. She grabbed her journal, picked up a pen and began to write.

I am in a cube. It's not a cube-shaped room – something smaller, more rubbery I guess. I am trapped inside it, cemented in. I don't know how I know it's a cube because all I can see is my feet, my chest and my hands. My head is wedged still. I struggle to move it but it's locked in, tilted downward so I can feel the fat of my neck with my chin. And suddenly it starts to move – not me, the cube I mean. It shakes and twists and I can feel that I am spinning, trapped and twisting and unable to stop.

Then it drops.

I open my mouth to scream but the cube melts into me. The rubber is like a balloon clawing at the back of my throat and I can't breathe. And I think, "This is it, this is how I am going to die." But I don't die. I just keep on spinning. I keep on dropping down.

And then I notice the button. It can't have been there before because it's a huge red button, right by my hand. It says 'stop'. It looks like a warning 'STOP!' I press it but I'm still falling. I can't see that I am falling because I'm still inside, but I can feel the sensation in my stomach, and the tips of my fingers and toes.

And then I land with a bump. A crack appears above my head, I see a flash of sky. The whole cube then crumbles around me like an egg, revealing bits of the picture piece by piece, and eventually I can see where I am.

I'm in a nest. An immense breezy nest made from sticks and string. I look up and a huge blackbird squawks above me. It seems impatient, as if I should be doing something else, as if it is waiting for me to act. It hovers for a moment and then flies off. I run to the edge to watch it leave.

Then I see the loveliness of the place I am in. There are hills and rivers and streams, of all different colours, like a rainbow has been stitched onto the land. They stretch out for miles all around. Giant yellow flowers tower above me, swooping their heads back and forth. They seem like they are scanning the ground, like spotlights surveying the land, or looking for something, or someone, on it.

Then the bird arrives back with a sharp flap of its wings. I see that it has another cube in its claws. When it gets to the nest it hovers over me and looks confused. The sky changes and giant thunderous clouds roll in. "You shouldn't still be here," the crow says and then drops the cube right on top of me.

So I jump, just in time, right over the edge and then I am falling through this landscape of colours. All the yellow flowers turn on me like spotlights and I see that within their petals are faces, and they are outraged. They are so angry with me. "You shouldn't still be here!" they scream, and they toss me about. And then suddenly the phone rings...

Deborah shook her head. That wasn't right; the phone did not ring. She closed her journal. It was only then that she realised that the phone was indeed ringing, at that very moment, in her flat. She leant across to the table and picked up the receiver.

"Hello?"

"Deborah. Christ almighty! Where on earth have you been? I rang yesterday, seven times and no reply. I left messages; did you not get my messages? I have been worried sick."

The voice was shrill, loud, so high pitched, Deborah thought, that really only dogs should be able to hear it. She held the receiver away from her ear as it continued to megaphone down the wires.

"Bloody worried sick I've been. I couldn't eat, and David had cooked beef Wellington. Beef sodding Wellington, I ask you. We had to give it to the cat in the end; you should've seen the look on her face, smug as anything she was. Smug as flippin' anything. While I, your poor mother, paced around the house all night like a clucking hen, starving to death I was. But I thought, no, no, I am not going to eat. Not a morsel of food will go down this throat until I hear from her. Worried. Bloody. Sick."

"Mum, sorry, I just..."

"Yes, yes, you just forgot, you were just busy. Busy? Hmmm? Too busy to put my mind at rest while I slowly waste away on my own doorstep? You know the rules, Deborah. You KNOW the rules. I really think I am going to have to tell someone about this, my love. I really think I am."

"Mum!" Deborah shouted. She knew the threat; she knew what was meant by 'Someone' and she knew her mother would do it. She also knew what would happen to her if 'Someone' was informed. There was no way that was happening.

"It's no use shouting, dear," her mother continued. "I am hardly deaf. Hungry? Yes. Hurt? Very much so. But not deaf." She paused, a rare occurrence, and Deborah took her chance.

"Mum look, I am sorry. I know you're not deaf. I'm sorry you were worried, but I'm fine. I just..." A memory flashed back, like a charge of lightning through the fog. Oh Christ! The man, the man who had helped her home, she remembered who he was!

"Deborah?" Anxiety fluttered around the word. "Deborah, are you still there? Deborah!"

"Mum, sorry. Yes, sorry. Jesus! I just fell asleep that's all. I went for a big walk, a really, really long walk, after my appointment. I came home, took my pills – you know how they make me drowsy. I told you how they make me drowsy, right?"

She didn't wait for a reply. "Well, that's what happened. I had my appointment, took my pills and crashed out. I only just woke up, just now, to the phone ringing."

The lie slid with practised ease from Deborah's throat and landed gracelessly, an ugly slug, on her living room floor. She thought of her nightstand, picturing the bottle of pills, seal unbroken – a little plastic container for her dishonesty.

"Hmm... yes, you did tell me they made you drowsy, after the last time you didn't return my calls." Deborah's mother emphasised the 't' of 'last' like she was tutting the word.

"I know, and I'm sorry, but I'm OK. Okay?"

"I think I should come over," and then there was a click as her mother hung up.

Deborah pushed her head back into the cushions of her sofa and let the phone dangle from her fingers. Crap. Well it wasn't as bad as it could have been. Her mother's coming round meant she was persuadable; she had bought some time. Deborah did a quick sum in her head. She had about forty-five minutes to extinguish all evidence of the night before and convince her mother that she was a stable, functioning and normal human being.

Looking around her flat, Deborah concluded that it was no worse than usual – luckily she appeared not to have devastated it too much when she had come home last night. There were no empty cans, overflowing ashtrays or greasy wrappers of takeout food. It seemed last night she had been so drunk she had simply collapsed in bed: last night, when a man called Luke had found her sitting, shoes off, on the pavement, staring up at the night sky. A man called Luke whom she had only seen twice before in her life, and both times he had run away from her. A man with whom she had her very worst thing in common.

Deborah walked to the window and opened it, letting a sharp stab of winter air poke its way in. She looked down to the street below. It was one of those bitter February mornings when people were dribbled onto the world. The sky was a matted grey and the few souls who dared to brave the cold merged with the pavement. Heads bent down they scuttled about, as if they were not really there, as if they were exoskeletons of themselves.

Just to be on the safe side Deborah spent the next half an hour hurriedly stuffing clothes into drawers, unwashed plates into cupboards, and cramming litter into the dustbin. When she was finished she glanced at the clock. It had been thirty-six minutes since her mother had rung. "Bollocks", she muttered and began to undress, throwing the clothes into her bedroom as she passed it.

In the bathroom she flicked on the shower switch and waited for the water to heat. Half way in and the phone rang again. Deborah paused, one leg already damp from the drool of the water. It was likely to be her mother again checking she had loo roll or milk or something else horribly patronising, so she ignored it and climbed in.

The water scalded her skin. Deborah liked her showers uncomfortably hot – so hot that when she got out her skin felt all warm and pink and new. She quickly rubbed a stick of soap over her legs, stomach and arms, swearing as it slipped from her hands and into the plug hole. She then dipped her head under the water and rubbed her eyes with the back of her hands, trying to get the makeup off. The buzzer sounded just as she stepped out and quickly Deborah tugged on jeans and a sweater, muttering a brief prayer that somehow they would be clean. Straightening up and combing her fingers through her hair she then picked up the entry phone.

"Hello?"

"About time, dear."

Deborah pressed the buzzer and opened the door, leaning against the frame as she heard wheezing and puffing below. Her mother arrived at the top of the stairs and busied her way past, shaking an oversized umbrella so raindrops sprinkled onto the walls, before handing it with her coat to her daughter. Joan Green was a large woman with a sensible face; thin, perfectly arched eyebrows framed her eyes which were small, dark and shrewd. She wore a checked brown and grey suit with a cream polo neck underneath the jacket which pushed her neck upwards so two frills of fat poked out from the top of it. Her mouth was tight and puckered into a displeased pout.

"What a mess you are!" She took hold of Deborah's cheek with two damp hands and kissed the air either side of her face. "What's wrong with your face... and what on earth are you wearing?"

"What, I..." Deborah glanced turned to face the mirror. "Oh."

Thick black streaks of mascara stretched from her eyes to her chin and the crimson smear of lipstick had now spread across one side of her cheek. She looked like a clown that had been hit by a truck. Worse still she had managed to pull, of all her sweaters, the one it had been her overwhelming pleasure to receive at the annual office secret Santa last Christmas. Seemingly normal from the back – a bottle-green knit – she had failed to notice that on the front a huge pink arse had been knitted. There was a Santa hat resting on its festive plump cheeks and the words 'Merry Christm–arse!' underneath.

Deborah sighed. If there was one thing that makes one look mental, wearing a Christmas arse jumper in the middle of February could be it. She smiled at her mother.

"Just doing a big laundry load, that's all. It's my laundry top. Cup of tea?"

Her mother's eyes narrowed, vole-like, but she let it go.

"Right, yes. Don't worry, I will do it. I brought some milk

just in case – go and sit down." Without waiting for her daughter to protest, she bustled off to the kitchen.

Deborah wandered back through to the living room and threw herself onto the sofa. It was a few moments before she noticed that the light on her answering machine was flashing.

"Mum, did you leave me a message?" Deborah asked, calling through to her mother, leaning her head back round the door. Her mother was already in full swing, rubber-gloved and armed with spray, humming and fussing her way around the kitchen.

Deborah got up and gently closed the living room door behind her, then perched on the arm of the sofa and pressed 'play'. There was a crackle as the message began, and a fuzzy sound in the background. This continued, crackle-fuzz, as Deborah leant forward, her brow crinkled and concentrated, barely breathing to make sure she didn't miss anything.

Suddenly there was a voice. "Deborah?" A man, shouting uncertainly over the fuzz. "Deborah, its Luke. Um, I just wanted to make sure you got home OK last night and um, well, I have your shoes."

There was a pause, then silence: no more voice, no more crackling noise, as if the place where he was speaking from had suddenly ceased to exist. Then it faded back in. "So you probably didn't want to hear that but, well, I just thought... I thought maybe we could talk about it, or at least I could give you your shoes back. You kind of ran off without them in the end. Jesus, this damn rain! Sorry, um OK, bye... oh my number, it's 07352 843137. OK. Sorry. Talk to you later, I hope... shit!"

The line went dead.

Deborah clasped the arm of the sofa and watched her

knuckles turn white. How drunk had she been last night? She did not remember giving Luke her number, and what had he said in the gap that she "probably wouldn't want to hear"? Deborah moaned and pushed her head onto a cushion. Her hangover, which had been bad enough, suddenly intensified, creeping forward with spicy fingers and a wicked grin.

She looked out of her window once again and frowned. The sky was tight with rain, but a minute ago she could have sworn it had been fine.

"Deborah?" Her mother's voice echoed through the hall. "Deborah, do you take sugar? I can't remember. And where do you keep your sponges? What... for goodness sake girl, why are there dirty cups in the plate cupboard? For heaven's sake!"

Footsteps resonated across the floor; they sounded slurred, distant. The living room door pushed open.

"Are you all right?"

Deborah shook her head. Thoughts which had cemented themselves on top of one another slowly began to shift and drip, messing themselves together. She looked up and tried to smile, but her lips were heavy and remained flat.

"God, I'm fine, Mum," she managed. Even to Deborah, her voice sounded unconvincing. "You just didn't, well you didn't exactly give me much warning, did you? And you know what you're like – you're so...well, I just couldn't deal with another lecture – OK?"

There was no reply, just a stare, as Deborah continued, weaker, whinier, feeling herself shrivel back into a spotty teenager before her mother's gaze.

"I was going to do it, you know, you just didn't give me much warning, like I said."

Deborah looked down. She felt two stiff, cold hands being

placed uncomfortably on her shoulders. She resisted the urge to shake them off, scream and run from the room.

"I just worry, my dear. You know how I worry. How can I not after...?"

Deborah could feel the gaze as it shifted down towards her throat and the scar on her neck. She quickly tugged the top of her sweater upwards and turned her head away, pushing herself into the arm of the sofa.

"I know. I get it, Mum. I do. I am so much better now though, honestly." Deborah turned, forcing herself to meet her mother's stare. "Really. Look, I take my pills, I see that therapist, Doctor Vanilla – I told you about him, didn't I?"

As she said his name, Doctor Vanilla's face appeared in her mind's eye: the pale, veiny skin, the scar and those strange, lifeless eyes. Deborah ignored the image, blinking it away.

"Please, Mum, I can deal with this. I'm OK now. It was just, just a stupid... thing."

She looked up, hoping to convince, but her mother had turned her head away and was biting her lip, carefully stroking down the imaginary creases in her skirt.

"Well OK then, dear, I'd best be off."

She stood up hurriedly, avoiding Deborah's gaze. "I have a hair appointment, you see. It was just a flying visit really. You take care – no need to get up, I'll let myself out."

Deborah watched her mother as she walked half way across the living room floor before turning back. She wanted to say 'I love you', Deborah could tell, but no words came, just the pause, then a stiff clearing of the throat and a click of the door as her mother left the room.

Deborah stared after her for a moment and then leant towards her answering machine, pressing play and listening to the message once more. He sounded anxious. She took a deep breath and pressed the numbers on the keypad. She let it ring twice before she lost her nerve and hung up.

She remembered it clearly now. She had been looking up at the sky and feeling so overwhelmed as the world bobbed and swung around her through her drunken eyes. She had blinked and gulped in the air, aware of how drunk she was and yet too drunk to know how to fix it. She had felt that familiar feeling of pointlessness creep through her body that always made her want to cry. The dull pain in her stomach had begun to ache again. She had just wanted to lie down and press her head into the tarmac and stay still until she was all gone. The stars had seemed friendly, hopeful, winking at her through the night, but she had felt nothing but resentment and sadness, and she had wished she could scissor them from the sky.

Suddenly she'd felt his shadow over her and there was Luke. Deborah had found it difficult to place him at first. But as he sat next to her she realised who he was. She'd tried to talk but the words wouldn't come out properly, so he'd picked up her shoes, offered her an arm, and helped her home.

At least that's what she thought had happened, but he had said something about her running off. She couldn't work it out, and why hadn't she put her shoes back on?

Deborah groaned. Oh she was embarrassed all right. But there was something more than that. His voice on the message had sounded so urgent, and the urgency made her afraid.

"Don't be a coward," she muttered to herself and picked up the receiver, dialling again, this time letting it ring.

"Hello?" The voice sounded coarse, sleepy.

"Hi, is that Luke?"

"This is Luke."

"It's Deborah. Um, you have my shoes, I think?" She felt her face tingle and grow hot as there was a silence on the other end of the line. Then suddenly he spoke:

"Hi, yes, I have your shoes. You got my message then?"

"Yes, but it kept breaking up and there was lots of crackling in the background so I didn't get all of it."

"Right, sorry, it was pouring with rain. I could barely hear myself. Sorry, I should have waited. Idiot."

"What?"

"God, no. Sorry, I'm an idiot. I wasn't calling you and... Listen, do you want to meet up at all? I guess you'll want your shoes back?"

"Right," said Deborah. She cursed herself for not thinking before she called him. She'd known he'd wanted to meet her but hadn't decided if she had wanted to meet him. She could've told him just to drop the shoes at Doctor Vanilla's office, but it was too late now.

"I was thinking," he cut into her thoughts, "we could just go for a coffee, tonight maybe?" Then his voice changed. "Look, do you even remember what happened to you last night?"

"Not really."

"Well I think maybe you ought to know. Sorry, I don't mean to sound like this; it's just difficult to talk on the phone. Will you meet me, say tonight at eight where the bridge meets Clapton Hill?"

"OK," said Deborah, "see you there." And then she hung up.

CHAPTER 7

GRACE

An introduction to The Creature

"What?" Grace struggled out of Peter's arms. "You what?"

"I love you," Peter repeated. He stepped back. The distance between them solidified, preventing either from returning to the embrace. Grace slowly nodded her head. She understood why this was happening; she understood it perfectly. Things were different now that they were outside their bodies. All their nerves were exposed; all their feelings were heightened. Peter had been out here longer than her. He was lonely and afraid. The fact that they had found each other was nothing short of a miracle, and they needed each other. For Peter's feelings towards her to be mistaken for love was perfectly understandable. But still, how could he? Grace reached up and winced as she touched her straggling knots of hair again. No matter how easy it was to explain, how could anyone love her when she looked like this?

"You love me?" She looked up at him and laughed. "You love me!" Reaching up, Grace pointed to her burnt skin. "Look at me, Peter. Look at my face –I'm a freak."

Her voice came out strange – harsh and hysterical. She was angry. This wasn't what she wanted. She knew love. She knew what it brought – what it had brought for Deborah anyway. Turning away from him she stumbled backwards. The walls were vibrating around her. It felt as though her head had transformed into a huge maraca and someone was shaking her up and down. She could feel the grains inside, pouring endlessly over one another, wearing away the lining of her skull.

Grace clamped her hand over her mouth to block it. She was afraid of what words might come out of it if she didn't. Staggering towards the furthest corner away from him she crouched down, and gasped for air.

Her stomach was aching. It had been doing so from the moment she'd come to on the floor of the shop, but suddenly it got really bad. Moaning, she bent double and curled into a ball.

Peter stepped forward, his brow furrowed with worry, but Grace held her hand up to stop him. The memories! They were coming, fast and thick, ploughing their way through Grace's mind and forming gritty pictures in her head until she could see it all. Suddenly she could see Jack's face, and Deborah's face. There they both were, waving and smiling. There! There was the outline of a little boy a few metres away, she remembered him too, with his big, beautiful grin, his neat little blazer and tiny, shiny shoes. He was waving and smiling, too, clutching a satchel close to his chest. The sun was behind him. He was glowing like something wonderful and beautiful from another world.

Grace let out a whimper – she didn't want to remember. She didn't want to recall the awfulness of that day. She clawed at her hair, trying to drag the memories out, but they wouldn't stop.

She remembered that sudden split second when all their faces had altered. Deborah and Jack were suddenly frozen still, like two wide-eyed corpses just staring forward, staring straight at their little boy.

The images kept coming, dragging Grace back to when it had happened. They were blurry at first, then the specks would peel away one by one, cruelly revealing the scene until she could see it all crystal clear. The echoes of sounds, the screech of tyres and the low, wretched scream that came from Deborah's lips.

It was right at the time of the scream that it had happened, that Grace had been jerked outside, out of Deborah's body. It had been the scare that had done it, that brutal raw fear that lurched her away from the inside. It had disconnected her from Deborah and left her swinging like a balloon, still only attached by a thin line of light.

Grace had been able to see her; she was looking right at Deborah's face! Her eyes darted frantically from Deborah to Jack, trying to see if they could see her, but nothing registered. Grace looked at their hands, watched them grip tighter to one another, as if the squeeze would somehow stop what was happening in front of them.

Grace couldn't see, but she had still known. She could still feel through the cord that held her to Deborah even though she couldn't turn round to see it for herself. It happened so quickly – the panic, the revulsion, and that desperate moment when only stopping time would prevent it. But time had a noose around everyone's neck that day, and there was nothing that any of them could do about it.

Grace remembered a nauseating thud and then suddenly being dragged back inside, desperately trying to hold Deborah together as her insides collapsed around her. She looked through Deborah's eyes but could only see the top of a precious blonde head, stained with blood, and hear the dreadful scream that Deborah made as she clutched her limp son to her chest.

Grace buried her head in her hands; she could hear the weight of Peter's footsteps coming carefully towards her, the tickle of his shoelaces brushing against the floorboards as they trailed behind him. She snapped her head up. He stopped. His huge green eyes looked bruised, his jaw slightly apart. He stared at her without saying a word.

"Don't!"

It came out feral. Peter closed his mouth and then his eyes. One by one he closed them, first the right then the left, his eyelids tucking them in. Grace watched him as he breathed in and out, his hand slightly raised towards her as if to trying catch the words so he could push them away. They stayed like this, both silent, her crouching, him standing still, both of them breathing. In and out hers came in stuttery hiccups, tugging at the spaces around her. His was slow, deliberate and even. Grace shut her eyes and listened to his breathing, and finally the faces fizzled away.

When she opened her eyes Peter was gone. She looked to the door and saw it had been left slightly ajar. A cool breeze eddied around the room and a rectangle of light cut across the floor, resting at her feet.

Grace uncurled herself from the corner; easing out of it limb by limb. She then walked to the mirror that hung on a rusty nail at the back of the room and looked at her reflection.

What? Grace frowned. *How can it?*

Moving closer, she held her hand up in front of her face and waved it around. The mirror wasn't lying. Her hand was transparent, the light was shining right through it, right through her. Where her body should have blocked it out, she could see the wall behind her, the cracks running down it, the streaks of damp, and the dirty lamp that stood in the corner where Peter had flung his coat when they had first arrived.

It was happening. She was fading.

It was the strangest feeling. Her limbs separated and moved independently in a slow, floating dance around her. Her feet became liquid, dripping through the floorboards. She tried to touch her face, tried to open her mouth to gasp, to say something, anything, but could not.

In the final moments the door swung open and there Peter stood. The sun silhouetted his outline as if a ring of fire had been carefully etched all the way around his body. They watched one another. Peter dropped the bags he was carrying; a lettuce rolled out, so round and ordinary it seemed, as it tumbled towards her.

"Good luck," Peter mouthed, and then she was gone.

***

Wordless whispers glided from the shadows. Grace was travelling forward. At least she thought she was, but it was hard to tell. She looked down and her feet glowed luminously through the darkness. Was she afraid? It was happening so fast she couldn't be sure.

She outstretched her arms, trying to gauge her surroundings. Her fingertips brushed something soft, like wisps of thread which delicately traced over her skin. A light wind trembled through the thin cotton of a lilac dress that she had not been wearing before. Her hair was flowing; her thick golden curls had returned, streaming behind her. Grace reached up to touch it. It felt softer and stronger than before. The pain and the wounds had all healed. She had been restored.

The whispers continued and a dull light cast itself quietly over the tunnel. Straining her eyes, Grace made out outlines of doors shimmering through the darkness. Tiny wooden arches with padlocks lined the sides, each with a Roman numeral above them. The doors were in differing states of wear – some flaked and crumbling, almost disintegrating right before her eyes. The whispers grew louder as Grace passed these, and soon she was able to make out the words 'Mine, mine, mine, mine', murmured over and over again. Once she had passed by the words ceased, and all she could hear were deep and mournful cries full of longing and despair.

Some of the doors had red crosses painted over them. Grace felt sick as she saw liquid dripping over these in sinewy lines onto the floor of the tunnel. No noise came from them; there was no hope for them now.

The newer doors had wood that was freshly glossed. Grace caught wafts of paint smell as she floated past. Their locks were shiny and the voices that called to her from these were more timid and hopeful. 'Mine?' It was with a shy optimism that they questioned. But these, too, descended into the terrible wails once she had moved on.

Faster still she travelled until the wisps of cotton whipped at her arms and her hair tugged out behind her, pulling her face back until it felt tight and heavy, as if its weight alone could rip the skin from her bones. Reaching out, Grace tried to stiffen her arms against the sides of the tunnel, to wedge herself in and make it stop, but she could not. The cries continued, closer, the breath of their anger on her ears as they screamed 'MINE MINE MINE!'. The threads clutched tighter. They twisted her round and tossed her about.

Suddenly it was over. The noise vanished. The lights went out. Within seconds a wooden door lit up in front of her and its silver padlock dropped to floor. Two long-fingered hands glowed through the darkness; they snatched at her ankles and pulled her in.

Grace landed, thumping hard onto the earth. Her eyes were screwed shut as she felt the echo of the screams ring in her ears.

"Open up."

Grace felt a weight press down on her shoulder and slowly opened her eyes.

The Creature that stood above her was a bizarre sight. He crouched on two long hind legs which were as thick as tree trunks and covered in a bushy layer of stiff, grey hair. His torso was that of a leopard, dappled and muscular. His skin rippled as he moved around her. His features resembled a cat: paws and claws, whiskers, a long spotted tail and short pointed ears which twitched restlessly back and forth. His eyes and mouth, however, were distinctly human.

Gasping, Grace sat up and quickly backed away from him. "Who are you? Where am I?"

She glanced around. She was in a desert, or something like it. Miles of sand stretched around her. She could see sand dunes far in the distance which moved as if the sand were constantly pouring down over itself like a waterfall. Apart from the sand, there was nothing bar a few sparse trees dotted around and a large slate rock in the distance. The sky was cloudless and still.

The Creature moved over towards a shady tree, curled

himself around it and began idly licking and inspecting his paws with small, decisive movements. He grinned, revealing a set of perfectly straight, perfectly white, teeth.

"Time," he replied.

"Time for what?" asked Grace.

The Creature tilted his head back and laughed. His laugh was huge and deep and echoed over the sands as he thumped his tail on the ground.

"Time," he repeated. "Your time, Deborah's time, all time."

The Creature's voice was croaky as if there was dust caught in the back of his throat. He got up and slowly padded towards her. The length of his hind legs caused his rear end to stick up in an almost comical fashion. He paced in a circle close around her so she could feel the hairs of his legs tickle against her own.

"You know Deborah?" Grace asked. "Where is she? Can you help me find her? Please!"

"What do you think of me?" the Creature asked, pushing his face up against hers. His eyes were icy blue and brimmed with sorrow.

"Um, I don't know. You seem... you seem nice."

The Creature snorted. "Liar! I can see. I can see you, you know. You are afraid of me. Of course you are! Of my strength, my size, my power. I am very powerful, you know. Very powerful. Look!"

He suddenly bolted and ran across the earth, then galloped in a wide circle around her. His muscles rippled and his fur gleamed in the sun. He then turned and charged, head down low, his eyes fixated on his prize. Grace turned and began to run as fast as she could away from him, then felt a huge shadow loom over her as the Creature leapt far above her head. He landed about ten feet away before he turned around and grinned proudly, thumping his heavy tail on the ground. Grace skidded to a halt.

"Impressive," she muttered, breathing heavily.

The Creature smiled, pleased with himself, and sat down. Grace looked up at him.

"So what am I supposed to do now?"

The Creature shrugged sadly. "I don't know," he said.

Grace sat down and put her head in her hands. "You don't know?" She mumbled it from the crevice in between her knees, then again more loudly. "You don't know! Well what the hell is the point in you then? What the hell was all that with the tunnel and the doors? Isn't this supposed to be my chance, my chance to help, to change all of this? I'm supposed to be able to find her! But there is nothing, just nothing. Except you, with your running, and your showing off, and your trying to scare me. What is the point in you?"

The Creature looked hurt. His whiskers twitched and his lips trembled.

"I'm a checkpoint, aren't I?" He got up and began to pace back and forth, disturbed. "You come here, then you go on and I stay and crumble, bit by bit, until I'm all gone."

"What? What are you talking about?"

Grace wiped her forehead with the back of her hand. She suddenly felt exhausted. She looked up at the sky, a bright slab of powder blue. There were no clouds, no sun, no nothing. It appeared almost fake, like it had been painted on, like she could reach up to touch it and wipe it all away with her hands.

Suddenly Grace spotted something on the horizon. A black bird was flying in the distance over the sand dunes. It was clutching something white in its talons and she felt her heart pull urgently towards it. But why? It was all too much; nothing made any sense. Grace turned back to the Creature.

"WHAT DO YOU MEAN?" she screamed at him again.

He turned to face her and she saw that his eyes were filled with tears.

"You have to go now," he whispered, sadly. "I don't want you to go. I want you to stay here with me. If you stay here then I'll always be strong. I'll always be powerful. Please won't you stay?"

His voice had risen to a feeble whine and he pushed his face towards hers again, his eyes wide, imploring her to consider it. Cautiously, Grace moved towards him, then gently stretched up to touch him. Barely being able to reach above his chest, she settled for patting him softly on the leg.

"Please," she asked, calmer now. "Please tell me what you mean. I don't even understand how I can leave when there isn't any way out. What am I supposed to do? If you tell me, you can come with me. Or if you wait here, when I'm finished I'll come back and get you."

The Creature raised his head and looked her in the eye. "I can't wait for you. I can't wait for anyone," he said, unhappily. "And even if I could you wouldn't wait for me. Nobody waits. Nobody comes back. Nobody cares."

He cocked his head to the side and pushed his lips into a haughty pout. "It's time for you to go now," he repeated and lifted one of his huge paws to gesture behind her.

Grace turned around. From nowhere, three shrubs had sprouted from the sand. The one nearest to her was tall and thin with spiky mint-green leaves. The middle one had a stocky base and long, waxy leaves which curled over, casually skimming the sand below. The furthest one from her was a strange, shapeless thing in shades of pine green and brown. Its twigs pleated round one another and tiny buds sprouted sporadically from its ends.

"Pick one," the Creature said.

Grace stepped forward. As she did so, the shrubs grew towards her, each one seeming to beg for her attention.

"What? What for?" she asked.

The Creature pressed his lips together firmly and nodded to the plants.

Grace stared at them. She didn't understand, yet perhaps if she just chose then at least she would move on, and moving on meant a chance of finding Deborah.

"They all look the so different. How can I choose if I don't know what they mean?"

The Creature sighed. "Perhaps it doesn't matter," he said. "I'm only ever allowed to go this far so I don't know. They are always like this, so perhaps it is not important after all."

Grace frowned. It seemed to her completely illogical that one would be presented with a choice if, in fact, there was no choice to be made. But then perhaps that was the way with all choices. Once you had chosen you could never know what would have happened if you had chosen something different, or whether you would have just ended up in the same situation anyway.

"Fine," she said. Stepping closer, she pointed to the shrub furthest away from her with the mint green leaves, prodding it angrily with her forefinger.

"What now?"

The Creature smiled, his lips curled up in a thin, cruel line and his eyes narrowed into tiny slits of pale blue.

"They always pick that one," he muttered, and then he disappeared.

CHAPTER 8

DEBORAH

The meeting at Rivercross Bridge

It was the coldest night they'd had so far this winter. Deborah had made it thirty seconds down the road before she noticed this and now realised how underdressed for the occasion she was. It was not one of her talents, dressing. She always seemed to get it wrong somehow, wearing too many clothes in the warmer months so she ended up sweating profusely and having to lug the excessive layers about with her all day. In winter, however, she never managed to wear enough, often leaving the flat, as she had done tonight, in pumps and a light jacket before realising that if she didn't want to freeze to death she would have to return to change.

Quickly, she turned around. Back inside her flat she tugged on a fawn knitted jumper, some black ankle boots and her warmest coat, a long black Puffa jacket with a fur-trimmed hood, before setting out again. Outside her door she paused for a moment and contemplated whether she was doing the right thing. She knew nothing of Luke apart from that he went to a therapist – not a great start, though it would be somewhat hypocritical to hold that against him.

Deborah couldn't help but feel nervous though. The fact that she could remember so little of the night before, and the urgency in Luke's voice in the message he'd left her, and again when they'd spoken on the phone, had unsettled her. How did she know he wasn't a serial killer or a schizophrenic? He had been nice to her last night, as far as she knew. He certainly hadn't done anything untoward, as she had made it home safely, but what if he was just biding his time? What if he was actually planning to throw her off the bridge or lure her back to his apartment and keep her there forever in a cage? He hadn't explained why he needed to see her so desperately. How could she know that he wasn't going to do something terrible?

Deborah shook her head and tutted to herself. She was always letting her imagination get the better of her. Her natural inclination was to expect the worst in people, scaring herself that they were out to get her, or were going to harm her in some way. She had always been like that, confiding in very few people and not letting many get close. After losing Jamie, however, it had become almost impossible for her to trust anyone any more. It was not so much a fear of being hurt, more a weariness; she just didn't see the point. Then Jack had left her, too. The person she'd loved most in the world was dead and the person she'd trusted most in the world had been the one who'd hurt her more than anyone.

Who was she kidding, though? There was no way she could not go. Despite the possibilities of murderous intent, she still needed to find out what Luke wanted. There was something about him which had caught her interest; she couldn't quite put her finger on it, but there was no going back now.

Rivercross Bridge was a ten-minute walk from her flat. Deborah kept her head down and moved fast, wrapping her coat tightly around her as she walked.

Just before the bridge was Clapton Hill, a steeply-curved, pot hole-scattered road that led to the main shops in the area above. Its incline was most inconvenient to all who lived there and residents both old and new to the area always commented on how ridiculous it seemed having to trudge up a 'mountain' just to get a carton of milk. Deborah remembered how when they'd moved here, with her just about ready to pop, they'd joked that she'd need a pulley to get her up. She remembered how she'd laughed and sighed, and then her smile would fade as it always did, and she'd wonder if they had made the right choice to leave their pleasant and simple life, to keep the kid, to start over again. Whenever Jack saw that look, he'd turn to her and smile and rub her belly affectionately. It was his way of telling her that everything was going to be OK.

Deborah's eyes scanned the street searching for Luke. There was a young couple stumbling down the hill laughing and holding hands while their shopping bags clinked and strained with liquid fuel for the night ahead. A woman with her hood up and head bent low was pushing a pram with one hand and swearing angrily down the phone with the other.

And there, on the far side of the bridge, she spotted him. He was wearing light blue jeans and a calf-length black coat with the collar tugged up in an attempt to cover his ears. A large yellow scarf was wrapped around his neck and chin. One hand was idly rubbing his stomach, while the other clutched a cigarette which he held to his lips, taking a drag and holding it in for longer than necessary. He had his head tilted back. He exhaled slowly, his eyes closed, then opened them and watched as the smoke gently twisted into the sky. He then dropped the cigarette over the side, leaning over to watch it fall. A carrier bag sat on the pavement wedged beneath his feet.

Deborah walked towards him and cleared her throat. She glanced over the side of the bridge. There was a fifty-foot drop and then the water whirled and rushed away, constantly chasing itself down towards the sea. Suddenly she felt very nervous, to the point of sickness almost. Her head began to spin. She stopped abruptly, jamming her hands into the pockets of her jacket. He looked over.

"Hi," she said. "Sorry, can you come over here? I feel a bit weird – it's the height or something."

He picked up the carrier bag, looking nervous, and walked towards her.

"Your shoes." He nodded to the bag before holding it out in front of her.

Deborah reached forwards to take it. Their hands brushed slightly in the handover. They both pulled away and the bag dropped to the floor. A shoe rolled out onto the road.

"Sorry."

"Sorry."

Their apologies were unanimous and awkward as they both went to pick it up.

"It's fine, I've got it," Deborah said. The words came out harsher then she'd meant them to.

"OK, sorry." He stepped back sounding a little hurt.

She straightened herself back upright and put the shoe back in the bag. "Thanks – I appreciate it." She smiled, pushing her hair back from her face and raising her eyebrows a little at him, as if to say 'is that it?'

He turned towards the river and pulled a pack of cigarettes from his pocket. He offered her one; she shook her head. He took one from the packet using his teeth, fished a lighter from a pocket in the top of his coat and lit up.

"I wasn't sure if you'd come," he said after taking another monstrous drag.

"Well, these are my favourites," she smiled, jostling the bag she now held. She rubbed the side of her arm with her free hand. "Pretty cold out here tonight, huh?"

His head snapped round to face her and he flicked his barely-smoked cigarette over the side, suddenly looking flustered. "God. I'm sorry. I should have thought. I wasn't sure. I mean, I just didn't know if you'd want to, like, go for a drink or anything, or if that would be too... do you want to? There is a place just down from here. I know the owner – it's all right..." He looked at her earnestly.

Deborah nodded. "Lead the way."

She followed behind him as he took a left at the end of the bridge. She couldn't figure him out. He appeared to change from being so distant that he almost seemed cold to a bumbling, overly polite, stuttering English gentleman type in an instant. Maybe he was just nervous, or embarrassed about the way he'd spoken to her on the phone. But there was obviously something she'd done last night that had upset him, something more than the usual drunken antics, something that made him feel he had to see her and talk to her about it again.

She hurried behind him as he strode ahead. He didn't turn around to see if she was following and a couple of minutes later they turned onto a street where a little pub was illuminated on the corner. A sign swung from a metal hook that had been screwed into the side of the building. It was rusty around the edges and had a picture of a duck, fully clad in a suit of armour, wielding a sword. Underneath were the words, 'The Mighty Duck!' scrawled in green italics.

"This is it," he called behind him. He turned to see her looking up at the sign. "Don't ask," he said, rolling his eyes.

Inside the ceilings were low, supported by dark wooden beams. A fire snapped and crackled in the far corner and the whole place was filled with mismatched furniture. No two chairs or tables were the same. Mirrors hung in wooden frames and endless pictures and photos of different types of birds, mostly ducks, were all over the walls. A few random china ornaments of houses and dolls sat on some shelves in the corner, and above the bar two silver swords which crossed over a bronze shield were screwed into the wood. The whole place smelt of malt and pine. He pointed to the table by the fire.

"I'll get us a drink," he said.

A man appeared from a door to the side of the bar. He stopped as soon as he saw them and put his hands on his hips, staring expressionless for a moment until his face crinkled into a huge, beaming smile.

"Luke! Bloody hell, son, I almost thought I'd seen a ghost there! Where've you been, my lad? I haven't seen you in bloody ages. How long has it been? Months? Years? God, it hasn't been years, has it? He pushed the door back open. "Linda! Linda, get your big arse down here. Bloody Luke's here. Ahhh, Bingo, my wee lad – look who's here!"

A huge black Labrador pushed its way out and under the bar. Its fur was clumpy and speckled with crusts of mud and it had a shiny pink collar fastened around its neck. Running over to Luke, it promptly jumped up, sniffing frantically at his crotch, panting and whimpering, its tail shaking quickly from side to side. Luke looked mildly embarrassed and a faint crimson glow appeared on his cheeks. He reached down and pushed the dog's head away before ruffling its ears. "Every time," he murmured. He then nodded towards the man at the bar, his expression changing to one of deep affection.

"It's good to see you, John," he said quietly.

The two men held each other's gaze and Deborah stood behind Luke shifting the weight between her feet, not knowing where to look.

Suddenly there was a clatter upstairs followed, by several large thuds. The door was pushed open again, this time revealing a very large, red-faced woman with piggy eyes, neon orange skin and a huge peroxide blonde perm. She was wearing a T-shirt that was exactly the same shade of pink as the dog's collar. Over this an apron which strained over her gargantuan chest had a picture of a much slimmer, naked woman's body on it, with a couple of slices of cumber modestly placed over the nipples.

"I don't bloody believe it!" she bellowed. "Bloody Luke, John, it's bloody Luke!"

She pulled up the bar hatch and waddled over to him as fast as she was able before enveloping him in her apron-clad bosom.

"All right. Bloody hell Linda, don't suffocate the lad!" Linda pulled back and the pair of them stared at Luke, both of them shining and watery with the pleasure of seeing him again. Then John's face turned serious. "Luke, your mum, lad – you know don't you?" Luke nodded his head. "We're so sorry, son. We tried to get hold of you but no one knew where you were." He paused. "Is everything OK, son?"

Luke nodded his head and put his hand up to stop them. He nodded towards Deborah and changed the subject. "This is my friend. Deborah, this is John and that's Linda." John stared at Luke for another moment before pulling the bar hatch up and walking over to her, smiling warmly and offering her his hand. "Well well!" He smiled, not letting go as she shook it, "what do we have here?" He turned back to Luke. "Is this why we haven't seen you for so long, boy?!" His eyes narrowed before letting out a huge honking laugh. "A fine young woman, a fine-looking woman indeed. What's your name then, missy?"

"Deborah," she replied, struggling to keep up with the scene that was unravelling before her. She had now caught the attention of Linda, who beamed at her before promptly clipping Luke around the back of the head.

"What's the meaning of this, Luke, keeping a new girlfriend all to yourself? What have you been hiding her away for? How long has it been going on?" She took a breath, then her face settled into a sterner look. "You stopped answering my calls. You disappeared. We taught you better than that, did we not?" She suddenly looked as though she might cry. Luke stepped back and roughly tugged his hand through his hair.

"I'm sorry," he said, before nodding at Deborah. "It's not like that with us."

"Oh, please!" Her chin began wobbling furiously so she smacked her lips together and rubbed her throat, trying to regain her composure. "You've never been one who's shy with the ladies, but you always let us know. She must be very special for you to have kept her hidden from us, eh? Or have you two just been so busy you forgot to pick up the phone?" She turned to wink at Deborah, who smiled uncomfortably back at her.

"It's not like that, OK?" Luke said. The irritation in his tone was unmistakable.

Linda's mouth formed an 'O' shape and her skin flushed as she fussily patted down her curls. There was a horrible pause as she seemed to struggle with what to say next. Deborah couldn't bear silences like these; she felt like yelling out or pulling a silly face - anything to end it.

"Well," Linda finally spoke, somewhat subdued. "It's nice to see you again, that's all. What can we get for you two to drink?"

Luke turned to Deborah. "Beer OK with you?" he asked.

Deborah nodded. "Two beers, please," he said and then walked towards the table to find a seat, leaving Linda busily muttering to herself as she waddled back behind the bar to fetch the drinks.

Luke nodded towards John again. "We need to talk for a bit," he said about Deborah. "But then we'll catch up properly, yeah?"

John nodded. "Sounds good to me, son," he said quietly and then turned back towards the bar, whistling softly as he stacked glasses on the shelves.

Luke eased himself into a large armchair by the fire that was upholstered in maroon velvet. Deborah noticed he grimaced slightly as he did so, as if in pain. Bingo padded over and lay at his feet, resting his head on the carrier bag containing Deborah's shoes. Luke clasped his hands together, holding them uncomfortably over his stomach and sighed. He looked like a character from a period drama with his long coat, dark curls and serious face.

"Sorry about that," he said.

"That's OK," Deborah replied. "They seem nice." She desperately wanted to interrogate him, but held back. From what she knew of him so far he didn't seem like a man who enjoyed sharing his feelings. It wasn't out of a politeness that she refrained from prying – she just didn't want to scare him off.

Luke nodded. "They can just be a bit much sometimes, you know?"

"Is that why you've been avoiding them?" It slipped out of her mouth before she had a chance to stop herself, then bit her lip. "Sorry, it's probably none of my business," she quickly retracted.

Luke leant back in his chair and looked at her while scratching his chin. He appeared to be weighing up whether he could trust her or not. Linda arrived plonking two bottles of beer in front of them. Deborah could feel her eyes burning into her but refused to look up until she heard Linda sigh and walk away.

Deborah played with the bottle top of her beer, feeling strangely shy under Luke's gaze.

Finally he spoke. "It's difficult." He paused, as if trying to find the perfect words so that she would be sure to understand it from his point of view. "They sort of brought me up, you see. They knew my parents and then, well, something happened and my parents weren't able to look after me any more. So John and Linda, they took me in. I haven't lived here for a while, of course, but it still feels like home.

I used to come back and visit them quite a lot, Sunday lunches, that sort of thing. I know they might seem a bit loud, a bit crude, but they're really the kindest and most honest people I know."

He sighed, seeming reluctant to say more, and took a slug of his beer, wiping his mouth with the back of his hand, eyeing Deborah uncertainly all the while.

"So yeah, I just haven't come back in a while. Well, really, the truth is something happened and I couldn't come back, and even after that was all over and I could have come to see them, I didn't think I should come back. I didn't think I should get them involved, didn't think it was right. After all they've been so good to me..."

Luke trailed off and leant back in his chair, tugging his hand through his hair again. "Sorry, I don't know why I'm telling you all of this. I don't really know why I brought you here in the first place."

Deborah smiled at him, she felt a pang of sadness for this strange and uncomfortable man.

"Don't worry about it. I guess sometimes it's hard to avoid the things you love, even when you know you should. Trust me, I know something about that myself. Sometimes no matter how clear it is that you need to leave them you can't quite ever seem to let go..."

Deborah paused, noticing how Luke's expression had changed. It was clear she wasn't talking about him and she caught herself before she said too much.

"Maybe you're telling me because sometimes it's easier to talk to strangers about things that are hard to talk about. And maybe you chose me because you know that, if nothing else, I'm hardly in a position to judge you for not being able to cope sometimes, or for needing to talk about things." Deborah bit her lip. Until this point neither of them had mentioned the fact that they both went to the same therapist – a therapist who, from what he'd told Deborah, only handled attempted suicide cases. She hoped he didn't mind her making reference to it.

Luke looked at her for a moment, then shook his head. "Yeah, maybe." He sounded dismissive, then took a deep breath and tried to smile. He seemed to be gearing himself up to say something important.

"But you see that's the thing, Deborah, I do know you, well, sort of anyway. At least, I feel like I do. I think that's why I feel like I can talk to you, because we sort of talk all the time actually. Really that's why I wanted to meet you tonight, and why I brought us here, to test it – and it worked." He stopped to take another sip of his drink.

"I mean, that first time in the supermarket, remember that? I was just too shocked. It was all too weird, you know? Seeing you there, just standing in the aisle." The corners of his mouth turned upwards as he smiled and shook his head as if even he didn't quite believe what he was saying.

"It just caught me off guard, that's all. But then last night, when I found you, you were just sitting there so peacefully and then you looked at me with that look, that spaced-out look, and it was just the same as I've always seen it. You know, where you're looking right at me but you're not. Like you're looking into me, right inside, but also through me and past me all at once."

He paused again and caught his breath. His eyes had a frantic look about them and beads of sweat bubbled on his brow. He was excited, nodding his head enthusiastically at the sound of his own voice, as if he expected her to get it. He then stared, his face stiff with sincerity, desperately trying to make her understand, then frowning when it became obvious that she didn't.

Deborah leant forwards and touched his arm, trying to calm him down. He wasn't making any sense. She suddenly felt very nervous and wished that she hadn't come. Perhaps he was crazy after all. It wasn't what she'd bargained for –

another crazy person in her life. She spoke firmly and slowly to make sure he got it.

"Luke, I don't understand. What are you talking about? This is the second time I've spoken to you in my life, and I don't even really remember the first. What do you mean 'we talk all the time'? I've only just met you."

"No!" Luke cut her off and shook his head emphatically. "I see you all the time, Deborah. Every night, without fail. God, this is going to come out so weird." He sighed and shook his head again. "I dream about you every night, Deborah. From the very first time that I bumped into you in Doctor Vanilla's office. I mean I barely even noticed you at the time, no offence or anything. God, this isn't coming out well at all."

He stopped and looked at her, breathing heavily. Linda then appeared, obviously unaware of the tension between them, and began bustling around the table, leaning between them to clear the beers away.

"Another?" she asked, hands on hips, still clearly a little wounded by Luke's harsh tone earlier. Neither Deborah nor Luke responded. They stayed still, both looking at one another, trying to work each other out. Linda shook her head and wandered off muttering something about the youth of today. Finally Luke spoke again.

"I'm so sorry. I didn't mean it to come out like that."

Deborah glanced down at the table. Her leg was twitching. She pressed her foot hard into the floor to try to stop it. Her mind felt as though it was twisting, whirling around so fast that she couldn't seem to slow it down or hold onto any of the thoughts that were spiralling around within it. Finally she managed to speak.

"I'm sorry. I don't understand. You dream about me? All the time? What do you mean by all the time? What kind of dreams? This is all a bit much, Luke. I get that you might have had a dream about me – it's not that uncommon, I guess, to dream about someone you've seen and stuff – but I don't get it. What do you mean by 'all the time'?"

He leant onto his elbows and looked at her solemnly. "Yes, it's all the time, Deborah. Every time I go to sleep I dream about you. And it's not just ordinary dreams either. It's like you are always there, like you always have been. It doesn't matter what I'm dreaming about. Like the other day, right, I dreamt I was having Christmas with my family, and I'm talking my real family, my mum and my dad and everything. And there you were, just sitting there with us, like there was nothing weird about it. I don't know..." He tried to touch her arm, she pulled away.

"I just had to tell you. There is something about the way you're there. It's like it means something, like it means something more, you know?"

Deborah leant back, pressing herself into her chair to get as far away as possible. She pulled her sleeves over her hands so he couldn't see them shaking. Her face felt unnaturally hot.

It felt as though by him dreaming about her he had pried into her privacy. The fact that she was there, in his dreams, in his subconscious, and she had no control over what she did there, felt perverse somehow and very wrong. It was just all too strange. What right did he have to tell her all this anyway? Why did he have to make it seem so significant, to share whatever was going on in his weird, obsessed, messed up head, to make it seem like it was a problem that they should work out together. She didn't need this, she simply didn't want to know.

"No, I'm sorry," she said, getting up. "This is all a bit weird. I mean, you lure me here, acting like I did something crazy last night, and then you come out with all of this. I don't get it. If you don't know what it means yourself, why are you telling me all of this? It's nothing to do with me really. No. I'm sorry, it's just all too much."

Deborah pulled the bag from under Bingo's head making him help in surprise. John and Linda looked up from the bar where they had been huddled over the crossword section of the newspaper, jostling one another and bickering over the answers.

"I have to go." Deborah got up, hastily grabbing her coat from the back of the chair, and refusing to look Luke in the eye.

It was only as she pulled open the door that the realisation dawned on her. She'd forgotten one very important detail in all of this.

Deborah turned around slowly. "Do you keep a dream journal?" she asked, her stomach suddenly a pit of nerves.

Luke looked down at the table. "I need to talk to you about that, too," he said.

CHAPTER 9

GRACE

Closer to nothing

The sands formed a whirlpool around her. They twisted, slowly at first in eddying circles, but soon a wind picked up and blew them higher, harder, and they beat into her skin. Grace fell to her knees and shielded her face with her hands. The sands ripped at her dress and it billowed out into a great wide circle, like a parachute in the wind, as she was pulled about, knocking her this way and that and dragging her from side to side. The air was roaring in her ears like a huge ravenous beast pummelling angrily at her ear drums.

"Make it stop. Make it stop," she muttered, peering out between the gaps in her fingers. She didn't dare uncover her face in case the grains went into her eyes. She could already feel them stinging her arms and legs scratching at every part where her skin was exposed.

Suddenly everything stopped. The winds dropped and there was no further noise, no further movement. Slowly Grace peeled her hands from her face. The desert had disappeared, replaced by nothing but a glaring white light.

Grace pressed her hands down to where the ground had once been. It felt firm so carefully she got to her feet, leaning on the backs of her heels as though if she stepped forward she might suddenly fall through space. Looking around, she saw nothing but white. Was that possible? To have only white, only a colour? Grace sighed, feeling suddenly exhausted, and tried to focus on what to do next. She gazed into the distance and cocked her head to the side as she spotted something. It was barely visible, like a tiny speck of dust in the sky. She squinted and blinked, trying desperately to make it out. As she did so, it got bigger. It was moving, flying through the nothingness right towards her. Grace squatted on her heels and tilted her head up as it came closer. It was travelling at a phenomenal speed and soon she could clearly make out what it was.

A blackbird with huge wings was gliding towards her. Its feathers were bristled upright and shining brightly. They reflected the white that was all around and shone so much they looked as though they had been dipped in glass. As it drew nearer it dropped until it was hovering just a little way away from her, looking at her quizzically with its currant-black eyes.

From nowhere a tree suddenly sprouted out of the earth by Grace's feet. She shrieked in surprise and stumbled backwards. The bird ignored her and settled itself down in one of the lower branches.

"Hello." It turned to Grace. Its beak, a mustard yellow,

was pulled downwards in a disapproving curve. It hopped down a branch and scratched at it impatiently.

"I said, hello!" it repeated.

"Hi." Grace stepped towards it uncertainly. "Sorry, I... I just wasn't expecting... Sorry, what is this? Do you live here?"

The bird began to peck at its feathers, pulling them out in great clumps and spitting them aside, before clearing its throat to reply.

"Do I live here? Don't be so absurd! You can't live here! God, I do hate travellers - always asking such bloody stupid questions." Its accent was feminine and plummy, slightly upper class, and tinged with the impatience of an exasperated schoolteacher. It swept its wing back, gesturing to their surroundings.

"We're in a dream, of course. I am but a figment of the imagination, so to speak."

"A dream?" Grace smiled. "I'm in a dream? Is it Deborah's? Where is she?"

The blackbird laughed, cocked its head to the side and pulled out another clump of feathers with its beak.

"Too late," it replied in a sing-song voice.

"What do you mean, too late?" Grace moved to the base of the tree and looked up angrily at the bird. It hopped down the branch until its beak was practically touching the tip of Grace's nose.

"I mean, TOO LATE!" it shrieked, flapping its remaining feathers and puffing out its chest. "You already missed the last one completely. You are really not doing very well at all are you, my dear? In this one, well, there is hardly any point bothering at this point. We are just fragments. We're fading away now." It looked away from her and into the distance with a wistful stare, as if it were seeing things she could not.

"This used to be a beautiful place, vivid, full of imaginings, and now I'm the only thing left. There is no one here to imagine new things apart from me. Of course, I can't imagine things myself, for I am not real, and besides, I am just a bird."

The bird dipped its head modestly. Grace couldn't decide if it was being sincere.

"You'd better hurry up next time or you'll never find her," it said. It grabbed another chunk of feathers and angrily spat them to the floor. Grace then noticed that instead of patches underneath there was nothing, just more of the whiteness that was all around them.

"Such problems," it muttered. "There is no organisation, that's the issue. Godforsaken travellers wandering about all over the place. Too late! Wrong place, wrong time, you name it." It looked at her again. "And now I must go," it announced.

"No!" Grace cried. She shook at the tree. It crumbled to dust and immediately disappeared in her hands. She felt extremely hot, and her body heavy, like something was pushing her down, as though she was imploding in on herself.

The bird, now barely there, called out to her again.

"Remember, hurry up next time or you'll never find her." Then with a sickening pop his final feathers melted into the background and, as they did, Grace felt herself, too, fade away.

***

When she came to, Peter was standing over her. She was back in the room they shared, on the mattress. The familiar smells of dust and damp felt strangely comforting. Grace tried to sit up and immediately winced and flopped back down, squeezing her eyes shut as waves of nausea pulsated through her body. Her head felt as though someone had pricked it with a thousand needles, and she was incredibly hot.

"Easy," Peter whispered as he carefully pushed back her hair from her face. "It'll hurt for a minute or so but it doesn't last long. It helps if you stay as still as possible."

Grace looked up at him; his eyes were awash with concern and affection. "I'm sorry," she whispered. Her tongue felt as though it had been wrapped in tissue paper.

Peter handed her a bottle of water and tilted her head forward, his hand gently pressed to the back of her neck while she drank.

"I'm sorry," she repeated. "I'm so sorry about what happened before I was taken away. I shouldn't have yelled at you like that. I was just afraid. I didn't know what to make of it. I didn't believe you, but it wasn't fair and I didn't mean it."

She felt a lump form in her throat and closed her eyes tightly.

"I just couldn't believe you. I saw myself after what happened in that shop. I saw myself, my face, my hair. I was ruined. And I knew I deserved it because I had ignored you, after I had been so stupid and angry with you when you were only trying to protect me. I knew you would get taken away at some point, but I guess I didn't realise how afraid I'd be when you did."

She turned her head away from him and felt a warm tear begin to bubble in the corner of her eye.

"It was just hard, you know," she continued. "When you first realise that you've been separated – from your body I mean – you feel so alone and all you can think about is getting back to them. You don't expect to find someone else, to have someone who understands, who feels it too. I guess I just didn't realise how much I liked having you around and then when you faded away, it felt like I had lost someone again. I'm such an idiot. Jesus!"

She curled herself into a ball trying to hide from him. Tears were pouring down her face now – tears! Crying was a strange feeling indeed. She had seen Deborah do it many times, of course, but it was so ridiculous. Souls didn't cry! She pinched the insides of her wrists, which helped a little.

"How could anyone love me? I mean, look at me," she whispered.

Peter pulled her round to face him and smiled at her. He got up and took the mirror down from the wall.

"Sit up," he commanded. Grace did as she was told and Peter held the mirror in front of her.

"Oh my God, what? How did that...?" Grace reached up and touched her face. She had thought she would only be restored in the dream world, that when she returned her injuries would still be there, that she would still be scarred and burnt. But her reflection told a different story. She looked, if anything, stronger and healthier than before. Her hair shone, her eyes were so bright they seemed to glow, and her skin was flushed with youth and vitality. Grace reached up to touch her face.

"I don't understand," she said. "I thought I would be the same." She turned to him. "Did you know? Did you know that I would be better when I came back?"

Peter shook his head. "Honestly," he replied, "I didn't think it would happen. I knew that when you go into the dreams you return to your original state, like how you are on the inside. But you're not supposed to stay that way; that's not the point. If anything, the longer we're away from them the worse we become. But you! Well, you may be stubborn and you may be a lot of things but, well, you look amazing!"

He blushed at his own outburst and scratched his chin before he carried on. "I don't understand it though, Grace. It's not supposed to be this way. Something is different. Something has definitely changed."

Grace took his hand. "Well, at the moment I'm just glad to be back," she said, "and glad to see you again. We'll figure out what's going on, I'm sure of it."

She hoped she sounded convincing, knowing that questions would come about what had happened to her while she was away, and she couldn't bear to tell him that she hadn't even made it into a proper dream, that she was so far behind. It felt like finding Deborah would never happen and she was terrified that soon she would be taken away for good.

"What have you got to eat? I'm starving."

Peter nodded. "Yeah, it's not surprising. It takes a lot out of you going into the dreams. OK, I'll get something sorted for us, but then I want to hear all about it. Deal?"

Grace nodded weakly and watched as Peter jumped up and began banging around in cupboards and rustling in bags. A small fridge stood next to a sink and under the window there was a stained electric cooker with rusty brown hobs. After a couple of kicks it would usually work. Peter set to making the food with astonishing efficiency. Grace watched him from the mattress and soon the comforting crackle and the sweet, fat smell of sausages slowly filled the room.

When the food was ready Peter pulled up an imaginary chair for Grace. "Madame?" he said, laughing, and then they both sat in the middle of the floor.

"Right," he said between mouthfuls. "What happened? I need to know everything so don't hold back on any details. No matter how insignificant you think they might be, everything counts. If you didn't find her in this one it doesn't matter, but everything you saw might mean something or might come back in the next dream. It's only by being totally observant, totally on guard and clever, that we will find them."

He paused and looked at her. "Well, come on then. Spill the beans."

Grace opened her mouth but nothing came out. He was so happy, so positive that he would be able to help. It was almost unbearable. She pushed her plate to one side and put her head in her hands.

"Whoa, what's the matter? It's OK. What happened?" Peter knelt beside her and she felt the weight and warmth of his hands on her shoulders. She stared at the floor and spoke through her hands.

"I didn't get into the dream. It was so horrible. I mean at first there were these tunnels and doors, and then I got pulled through one of them. Then I met this creature thing, and he played tricks on me, and then I picked a shrub, and then I was in this nothing, and then this crow said I was too late! He said I was too late, and then he disappeared!" She looked up at him. "It's terrible, Peter. I'm bloody terrible at this. I'm not going to find her. It's too hard." Grace realised she was sobbing again, harder this time. "Urgh!" she screamed. "Why can't I keep it together?!"

She glanced over at Peter, expecting him to be shocked at her outburst but instead he was staring at her, eyes wide with confusion. His face had turned greyish in colour and his whole body was shaking.

"Peter!" Grace knelt back upright and held his arms with her hands. "What's going on? Are you OK?"

"Say that again."

"Say what again? Peter, you're really beginning to scare me now."

"Say what you said, about the doors and the creature and the shrub and the crow."

Grace shook her head. "I don't understand. What do you mean, what do you want to know?"

"Grace," Peter took a deep breath, and grabbed her hands tightly. "I'm pretty sure the exact same thing happened to me."

CHAPTER 10

DEBORAH

The Apple tree

Deborah turned back round towards him, letting go of the door, which swung back shut. Linda and John had paused and were both standing open mouthed, staring at her. They were completely stationary apart from Linda's bottom chin, which was wobbling ever so slightly as if caught in a soft breeze. Her plump fingers were still clutched around the edge of the newspaper page that she'd been about to turn. John, too, stood still, his fingers frozen in space as they reached out towards his pint of ale. It was as though someone had reached down from the heavens and pressed 'pause' on this little scene in the world. Even Luke remained motionless; he was half out of his seat, knees bent, knuckles growing white as he gripped the edge of the table. His eyes were locked on hers, imploring her, begging her to stay, to hear him out. Deborah felt sure that she could do anything in this moment, that she could scream or sing or strip off all her clothes and run around naked smashing things up. But she did not do this. Instead she remained silent and still.

Suddenly Bingo appeared from behind the bar, his immense flopping jaws snuffling along the floor. He looked up and seemed amused at the scene that confronted him, cocking his head to the side for a moment before lumbering towards them, jumping over a chair, sending a half-empty wine glass crashing to the floor in the process. He bounded over to Deborah and leapt up at her, his huge dusty paws pressing against her coat and his tail wagging furiously.

"Bingo, NO!" John was the first to react. Breaking his mannequin stance he came hurrying over, red faced, apologetic and fussy. He pulled the dog down by its collar and shoved him roughly away. "So sorry about that, love. He's never usually so bold with strangers." He then turned and called over his shoulder to his wife: "Linda, get a cloth, will you? Bloody hell, there's glass everywhere. Bingo! Stay! Bloody stupid dog."

Deborah shook her head as she brushed down her coat with her hands. "No, look, it's fine, honestly. Don't worry about it. It's really old anyway and I'm sure it will come out in the wash. It's just a bit of mud. Really, it's seen worse. It's fine."

She backed away from his apologies and turned to face Luke. A labyrinth of furniture lay between them. She squeezed herself behind a white wicker table by the wall, which wobbled dangerously as she went past, and then manoeuvred her way towards a set of shabby-looking patio furniture which took pride of place in the centre of the room, shuffling her way round both it and an old pub bench before she got back to him. She looked back at John and Linda, who were now both on their hands and knees, preoccupied with the mess that Bingo had created, and sat back down.

"I'll take it as a yes then," she said. Luke nodded.

"So he makes you write one too."

Luke looked uncomfortable and pushed his hands deep into his pockets. "He makes everyone write one. I mean he must do. You've seen his office, Deborah. There must be thousands of them."

She shrugged, 'Well, maybe, but you don't know what's in them, do you? It could be other stuff. Aren't you supposed to keep stuff like that locked up, for patient confidentiality and all that?"

Now it was Luke's turn to shrug. "I don't know. Never really thought about it, I suppose." He leant forward and looked at her with that earnest expression on his face again. "Look, I know how weird this must be for you. It's weird for me too, you know. But I want to get past this, to move on and, well, Doctor Vanilla, he seems to think that dreams are the way to make us reconnect with ourselves or something. At least that's what he's said to me."

Deborah snorted, disbelieving. Luke sighed. His face shifted a little and he suddenly looked very tired. "I thought it was bullshit at first. I almost didn't go back after the first day when he shoved that stupid book into my hands. I thought 'controlling my dreams is pretty far down my list of priorities, mate'. I thought he was a joke. I felt like a right mug for going to him in the first place. I hadn't looked for him but, well, I was at rock bottom, you know, after what I did. I didn't want any help, but then he called me, and there's something about him. I don't know what it was. The way he spoke to me somehow resonated with me, you know?

So I went along to see. I thought to hell with it, I don't deserve it but I owe it to them at least."

He nodded at Linda and John who had now resumed their positions behind the bar. John had his arm draped around Linda's shoulders. Sensing eyes on her, she looked over at them and smiled, then elbowed John in the ribs and whispered something in his ear.

Luke continued. He was no longer looking at her but staring into the top of his beer bottle as though it were the barrel of a gun. "She'd be so disappointed, so hurt, if she knew..." He trailed off and cleared his throat. "But the thing is, recently, I've just been going for it. I've been writing my dreams down and everything. And I do sort of feel better, like I might actually be getting somewhere. And then suddenly you were in them and it's all sort of become confusing again."

Deborah pulled his empty bottle from his hands and stood up. "I need another drink," she said and weaved her way towards the bar, leaving Luke staring after her. Linda beamed as she approached. "Glad you two are making up over there, ducky. Another couple of beers for the lovebirds, yes?"

Deborah could feel Luke's eyes burning holes in her back. Linda looked so hopeful that there was almost something strange about it. As if it was necessary for her to believe that they were in a relationship. As if she needed there to be a reason why Luke hadn't been back for so long.

Deborah smiled. Unable to bring herself to lie, she simply nodded. "Another two beers would be great, thanks."

Back at the table Deborah took a long gulp, letting the liquid rest in her mouth before swallowing, enjoying the sharp tickle of the bubbles as they burst on her tongue. Linda was now staring at them both; her piggy eyes had narrowed, both suspicious and eager to be a part of the conversation. Deborah watched as she exchanged a sideways glance with John, whose expression said 'mind your own business', before Deborah turned back to face Luke.

"Look," she said, trying to take it all in. "That's great for you and everything. You seem like a good guy, and it's good that things are progressing for you and you feel better and all that. But let me try to get you to see it from my point of view."

She leant back in her chair and took a deep breath. She wasn't even sure if what she was about to say was what she wanted to say, if it was what she really meant. But it was just too much, too intense, too creepy, and she needed time to think.

"You write a dream journal, right? Which you show to your therapist? Your therapist is telling you that these dreams you have are somehow the key to making you feel better. You believe him, and write the journal, and begin to feel better. Fine. But then you have dreams about me. So when you're writing about your dreams, you're actually writing about me, and your therapist sees this. Which would all be fine, I guess, except that your therapist is also my therapist, which makes this whole thing completely messed up."

Deborah felt her throat suddenly contract and she pressed her tongue against the roof of her mouth. Panic was setting in and the walls of the pub appeared to curve and bend around her. She groped the table for something solid to hold onto and continued.

"Does he tell you...' Deborah asked, the panic worsening, "does he tell you what it means when you dream of me? Because he sure as hell hasn't give me any insight into my own dreams! Do you think it actually means something, that

I am here to save you or something? Luke? Please don't tell me you think I can save you. I don't even think I can save myself."

She stood up. Bingo whimpered from a corner somewhere.

"Well that's it. I'm going to call him tomorrow and quit. Maybe this whole 'your dreams will save you' crap is working for you, but it sure as hell isn't working for me! I'm sorry but I can't be a strange pawn in whatever game you two think you are playing. I am out. I am never going back there again."

She marched towards the door and turned to Linda. "I'm sorry," she said to her quietly. As she reached the exit she turned and saw Luke, who was now bent forward and leaning his head in his hands, which were gripped in tight fists around the side of his head. He was rocking slightly back and forth and looked as though he might hit something or cry or both. Linda rushed over to him and glared at Deborah before enveloping him in her huge bosom. Bingo let out another whine. John stood still by the counter. He nodded at her sternly. Deborah nodded back at him then pushed the door and hurried outside.

She reached her flat about fifteen minutes later. She had walked fast but had taken a slightly longer route, overcome with a strange paranoia that she was being followed. The streets in the area were a criss-cross of almost identical-looking roads with a frustrating lack of street names. Her street looked the same as any with a row of two up two down, modest-looking houses either side and a slightly shabby block of flats at the end, one of which was hers. When they had first moved here Deborah had only been able to tell her road by the apple tree which grew in the garden of the first house as you turned in. She had never seen the person that lived there, but the garden was always beautifully well kept. The tree itself, however, was what had caught her attention over the years, as it seemed to change so suddenly in appearance.

Sometimes it looked so withered and old that it seemed a shame to keep it standing amongst the beautifully manicured lawns, and neat, pretty rows of posies and crocuses. Its branches would coil downwards into gnarly fists and its leaves became crisp and brown. On other days, however, it defied both nature and the seasons and would spurt back to life, its branches strong and scattered with a fragile blossom in the subtlest shades of pink and cream. Then the fruit would appear in plump, succulent spheres which hung delicately from the branches. Deborah had always admired its strength, the way it would fight and always come back from the brink of despair.

When she arrived home, she looked back out onto the street from her doorway before heading inside. It was a relatively quiet neighbourhood and there was hardly ever any noise to speak of after dark, yet still she felt uneasy, as if someone was watching her every move. Climbing the stairs of the communal hallway to her front door she entered her flat, hooking her keys to the back of the door like she always did. She then sat, knees together, hands on her lap, crouched on the edge of her sofa in the dim evening light.

The tears came unexpectedly, and once she started she couldn't stop. She clutched her sides trying to hold it in, as though if she let go they might burst open and her living room would be flooded with a great pool of sadness.

She remembered the times when she had never felt alone, when all three of them had been in this room, playing games or watching TV. She and Jack would curl around each other on the sofa, with their beautiful, precious sandy-haired boy sitting on the floor below them, mumbling and burbling to himself as he played with his toys.

She remembered the day it happened. How ordinary that day had been. The sun had been shining. Deborah always found it hard to understand how such a lovely day had been the one that chose to rip them apart. It didn't seem right somehow that it happened in daylight with the birds singing and a warmth in the air. It should have been raining and dark, the skies grey and ominous, and clapping with thunder, something that might have warned them, that might have made them stay inside.

The worst bit was after it happened; the hope that they had clung onto so desperately; the little flashes of faith as they sat side by side in the hospital, day after day, night after night, barely able to speak; the hope that got ripped from her throat when they had taken him to surgery and the doctor came out of that door and told them, with a grim smile and a shake of his head, that Jamie was gone.

Then there was the time that came after, where they'd had to go home without him. The house had been so quiet – that awful deafening quietness that silently suffocated them both. Bit by bit the silence smothered them, until they were gasping for breath. Deborah shook her head, trying not to think about what came next, what happened to her and Jack, and how it all ended.

It hadn't been his fault. She'd always believed that. He'd blamed himself for what happened to Jamie, thought he should have been watching, should have run out into the road and got him. He got so angry, but he didn't know how to manage that anger, so he'd turned it on her, and it had broken them. When Jack had left the silence was worse than ever; it came with a gleeful dance and wrapped itself around her, ready to take her away.

Deborah peeled her face from her hands and looked around the room. So little had changed since that day. It was as if she'd been afraid to move anything in case he came back. She would take him back of, course; she knew it. Even now, after everything, all would be forgiven. The day after he left she had given in and, unable to take the silence, had called her mother. They had sat on the sofa and Deborah had told her the very same thing – that she would take him back in a heartbeat. Her mother had said nothing but her face tightened with worry and pain as she listened to her daughter. She didn't mention the bruises, didn't try to call the police, didn't even say a bad word about Jack, which was unusual for her. She simply held her daughter's hand and sat with her and talked about things so the silence was no longer there.

Deborah shook her head and got up. She moved down the hall. Her whole body felt heavy, as if gravity had decided to push down harder on her and crumple her into the earth. She paused at the kitchen and thought how easy it would be to just try again, to be careful this time, to be better at it, be less of a coward and make sure that it worked.

In her bedroom Deborah lay down on her bed. She'd call Doctor Vanilla the next day and cancel her remaining appointments. There would be someone else, someone not creepy, someone normal who didn't have an obsession with prying into people's dreams, and then she could get better and work things out. Deborah turned on her side and squeezed her eyes tight shut as if trying to press this new resolution deep into her mind, to convince herself things would somehow be OK.

The events of the day had been overwhelming, and soon she was asleep.

That night she dreamt of him.

CHAPTER 11

GRACE

Forgotten memories .

Peter and Grace walked arm in arm along the riverbank. The river was high for this time of day. It swirled and groped at the sides, desperate to spread itself over the edges and be still. Grace looked up. The sun was dipped low over the horizon, sinking through the sky and bleeding into the clouds. Oranges and purples kneaded themselves into the skyline like huge, fresh bruises that floated against a backdrop of crisp, azure blue.

Unsure of what to make of the similar dreams into which they had both been pulled, they had decided to go for a walk to clear their heads. Each had an ice cream clutched in their hands which Peter had cunningly stolen from a lone ice cream van that had been parked on the street outside their flat. Even though only contending against one man, it had been difficult to get them in such a confined space without being noticed. At one point the man's arm had brushed against Peter's side which he now rubbed with his ice cream-free hand, wincing in pain.

Grace frowned at him. "You shouldn't have done it. I told you not to bother," she scolded.

Peter grinned at her and took a huge lick of his cone. "It was so worth it," he replied.

Grace wasn't sure she agreed. It was nice enough but Deborah had never been a huge ice cream fan so it just tasted rather strange to her. They'd hardly ever had it in the house, apart from when Jack sometimes would sneak it in. Having it on a day like today was pretty ridiculous, though. It was freezing and the ice cream certainly wasn't helping. She looked up again. "It's going to be dark soon," she said.

Peter ignored her, too busy devouring his ice cream. "Mmmm?" He turned to her with a shiny outline of white around his lips. Grace couldn't help but smile. She gently pulled his face towards hers and wiped it away with her sleeve. He acted in such a childlike way sometimes.

Peter nodded towards a bench set back from the river; it was surrounded by a scattering of snowdrops that had pushed their way out, despite the rigid soil. They walked towards it. They sat down side by side and Grace leant her head on his shoulder, gazing out at the river. Dusk was falling and the sun had almost fallen into the land.

"What happened to him, Peter?"

Peter sighed and his lip trembled. "I don't think I can tell you," he said.

Grace picked up his hand and squeezed it hard. "You can tell me anything," she said.

Peter shook his head, cleared his throat and turned to her. "OK, I will tell you something right, but please, please just hear me out and try not to get angry, OK?"

"OK."

Peter nodded his head as if to reassure himself that he believed her before he continued.

"The thing is, Grace, I can't really tell you anything about him because, well, the truth is, I don't remember anything. I've wanted to tell you for ages but I just haven't been able to. I guess I've felt ashamed."

Grace sat up and looked at him quizzically. "Go on."

"I just can't remember anything about him," Peter whispered.

"What do you mean?"

He shook his head and cleared his throat again. "I can't remember him, Grace."

Grace abruptly pulled away from him and tried to take it in. What he was saying made no sense at all. He couldn't remember his body? It was impossible, surely. She remembered Deborah – everything about her, from the very first moment she'd been born until the second they had been separated. Some of the bad memories took a while to come forward, but that was just the way it was, a natural reaction to try to soften the blow. But to not remember at all? It just wasn't possible. It couldn't be.

"What do you mean?" she repeated, her head reeling. "You don't remember anything? But what about my name? You called me Grace because you said he liked old movies or something? And that thing about the fish. You must remember some things about him?"

Peter shook his head and stared at the ground. "It's hard to explain. To be honest I only remembered those things when I met you. Before that there was nothing, but when I bumped into you that day, stuff like your name, it just came to me in a flash. I don't know why, but it was the happiest I've felt in ages. I didn't want to tell you at the time because I don't know what you would have thought of me. But all the important things – his name, his family, even what he looks like, it's all just kind of *fuzzy*, you know? Ever since I got here I have been struggling as hard as I can to figure out something, to remember something to cling on to. But all there is is just empty space."

His voice was trembling now and he paused to wipe a tear from his cheek. "I can't even tell you how bad it feels, not to remember him. I feel so lost and scared and I don't know what it means. I get pulled into these awful dreams and I don't even have the first clue of what I am supposed to look for."

He pointed to the tattoos on his arm. "Even these, these stupid scars, I don't even know if it's worth it at all."

Peter's voice was barely audible now. A breeze had picked up and pushed his hair into his eyes which he fiercely brushed away. The sun had disappeared and a dusky light cast itself over them. The shadow of the bench stretched out behind them. The clouds had changed to thickets of grey; only the faintest slashes of sky could be seen as they moved in closer around them.

Grace pulled her arm around Peter and stared at him determinedly. "OK, well it must mean something then, that we are together, and you remembered something when you met me, don't you think, Peter? It must mean something. There must be a reason why we met each other. I mean, what are the chances, right?"

Peter's forehead was crumpled into thick rims and his mouth was trembling at the edges. He looked up at her. His eyes were serious; they looked darker, a winter green like the pine trees that grew like tall, wise gentlemen on the hills across the river. Grace strained to hear him as he mumbled into the collar of his coat.

"I'm afraid that what he did, what we did, what I couldn't control, was so bad that I have somehow blocked it all out."

She shook her head fiercely. "There's no way, Peter. There is just no way. Look at you! How good, and kind, and gentle you are. There must be another reason why. I won't believe that he is some sort of monster, and you shouldn't too, OK?" She put her arms around him and pulled him closer. "I'm here now and it's clear from the dreams that something is pushing us together. We need each other and maybe our bodies need each other, too."

"I guess," Peter replied. He took another deep breath that puffed out cold and white into the night air. "I just hope you're right. It's just, well what if I do find him and he's this awful guy? What if I find out that I was so awful at controlling him that he did these terrible things? What if when I find him I realise that what he did, by trying to end it all, was actually something I wanted, something I put in his mind and when I'm faced with it I don't even want to go back to him?"

Peter's eyes brimmed up with shame and sorrow. Then he gasped suddenly and let out a cry of alarm. Grace jumped to her feet. "Peter! What is it?"

He stared up at her, his whole body trembling. "I just remembered how he did it. How he tried to end it."

Grace took a deep breath and sat back down. *Please,* she thought to herself, *please don't let him turn out to be awful. I need him.* She reached for his hand and held her breath, nodding for him to go on.

"I can't remember exactly, just that it was a cold night. I can't see his face, but he's walking. He has this thin coat on.

It's too cold to be wearing that kind of coat, but he doesn't seem to care. The collar's all done up round his neck. He's heading towards the bridge." Peter closed his eyes slowly, struggling with the memory. "God, I don't know. I think he jumped, Grace. I don't know why but I think he jumped. Oh God, I don't want him to do it!" Peter abruptly opened his eyes and began to sob, huge shaking sobs that ran right through his body.

Grace looked up towards him. Gently she took his face in her hands and with her thumbs brushed away the tears that were falling onto his cheeks. There were so many more things she wanted to ask him and so much that she wanted to say.

"You still can't remember his name?" she asked.

Peter took her hands and smiled at her gratefully. "It's not important any more," he replied.

Grace shook her head. "You're wrong, Peter. It is. Listen, you know now that you didn't want him to do it, OK? That's a good thing, Peter. And we are going to find them – both of them – and everything is going to be all right. I know it."

She said it firmly and held his gaze until Peter nodded his head.

"And I love you, too," she said.

CHAPTER 12

DEBORAH

Little plastic pills

Deborah looked at her watch and then back up at the building, and she was already five minutes late. She had been pacing back and forth outside for almost twenty minutes now.

She hadn't cancelled. She had been so sure she would do after her meeting with Luke, but then she had had the dream, the dream where Luke's face had appeared so clearly beside her, where his shadow had followed hers as she had walked the corridors of her old school, listening to the faceless laughter that echoed through the locker-lined walls. He was there with her the whole time, and he had made her feel less afraid.

Deborah put her hand into her coat pocket and felt for

the paper inside. She had written the dream in her journal as she usually did now, instinctively grabbing for it in its place on her bedside table as soon as she woke up. But later, as she was about to pack it into her rucksack on her way here, she had ripped out the page. It had not been a rash decision; she had done it slowly, carefully, in order to make sure that there would be no way Doctor Vanilla could tell.

Why had she done it? Because something deep inside had told her that showing it to Doctor Vanilla would be a mistake. As she massaged the edges of the paper between her finger and thumb she recalled the dream and the words she had written the night before.

At first I see nothing; it's like I am awake but with my eyes closed. Its noises I hear first, shuffles and whispers of things that are barely there. Then suddenly a light switches on, and then another. They start far away from me but then gallop towards me one by one, illuminating the walls of a huge corridor, yet I am kept in the dark until the final moment possible, and when the light above my head flickers to life it makes a low, sad, groaning sound as if it hurts to shine upon me, to make me seen.

I am in my high school, in the hallway. I feel that same low, sick feeling I always felt when I was here.

I take a step forward and there he is, right beside me. I don't know where he came from because there is only a door at the end. I am backed against a wall. But however it happened he suddenly appeared, and I know I feel glad that he's here.

I take a step forward – so does he, mimicking my movement. He is looking, his eyes firmly set on the double doors at the far end which mark our exit. He glances over at me and frowns, and puts a finger to his lips. I know not to talk. He takes my hand. I slowly look around; I see a spider creeping down the side of the locker nearest to me. He notices it, too, and seems angry and brushes it away with his fingers.

Then the bell rings.

The pupils pour out and fall into regimented lines. They are all facing us and they look really angry, and I realise I am looking back at a thousand faces of myself.

Deborah took a deep breath and looked up. It was a horrible day. The wind was blowing with gusto, whipping her hair across her face. Strings of drizzle were worming their way through the sky, leaving everything damp and dreary. She shivered, tugging the sleeves of her light corduroy jacket over her arms as she shifted the weight of her feet from side to side, full of regret at her choice of footwear – her beloved five-year-old high top trainers with a hole in the sole and grubby white laces. She had stopped caring about trying to impress Doctor Vanilla. At first she had simply wanted him to certify her sane and then leave her alone forever. She thought that perhaps pencil skirts and shiny hair had been the way to do this, but from her last visit she realised that it made no difference to him what she wore. In fact, it often felt as if it would have made no difference to him if she were not there at all. As long as she dropped off her dream journal, returned to collect it and then wrote more for the next session they could probably continue in this way forever.

What is he up to? she thought to herself, torn between the curiosity to find out, a rising concern that there was something sinister or dangerous about him, and an overwhelming desire to simply return home, slither into bed and never get out of it again. Yes, bed was appealing – too appealing to ignore, in fact. Deborah looked up at Doctor Vanilla's office again and sighed. Sod it. She would call him from home and tell him she wasn't well, then she could buy more time to decide whether this therapy thing was a good idea. Nodding her head to confirm this decision, Deborah turned and began to make her way home.

Thirty seconds into the walk, she paused by a set of traffic lights. A young boy darted past, closely followed by another, slightly smaller one. Both were red faced, with waves of messy blonde hair that stopped just over their ears. It was puffed up, bouffant style, making them look like miniature pop stars. They were wearing matching red anoraks with pockets that were bulging furiously, and were giggling excitedly and calling to each other as they ran on pudgy pink and white legs. The second boy, the younger of the two, called something and then stopped abruptly a few feet away from her. As he did so his pocket burst open and three golden green apples rolled out onto the street.

The boy looked at Deborah as one of the apples rolled up towards her. Deborah's heart stiffened and her stomach lurched down to her knees. She could feel her face automatically crumple with a grief that was impossible to contain.

Oh God! He looked just like him, just like Jamie. She wanted to reach out, to touch him, to grab hold of him and never let him go. But she couldn't move and before she knew it the boy had turned, running away from her back down the street.

Deborah knelt down and picked up the apple, digging her fingers into its waxy skin. She stayed kneeling on the ground for a moment, trying to get the feeling back into her legs. It wasn't him – she knew that. She knew he was not coming back, that nothing could be done to change what had happened – that her son was dead. She rubbed at her chest where her heart was stinging.

"Be like the apple tree," she whispered to herself.

A man with grey hair and a perfectly twirled moustache glared at her suspiciously. Deborah smiled at him, pulled herself up, turned and ran back towards Doctor Vanilla's office.

Five minutes later she was inside, red faced, sitting up stiffly on the uncomfortable metal chair in his office, trying desperately to control her wheezing from running up all his stairs. Doctor Vanilla was watching her with a steady gaze. His distaste at her late arrival was summed up with a pointed tap of his watch and an exaggerated sigh. He seemed quite disgruntled by her general appearance and inability to get her breath back, wrinkling his nose at her in distaste and pushing a box of tissues towards her. Deborah shook her head and rummaged in her rucksack for some water.

He looked different. His hair was slightly flatter and looked dull under the gentle glow of the antique lamps which lit his office. Dark circles were forming under his red-rimmed eyes. His scar had changed, too – it had turned ashy in colour. Before, it had seemed almost alive, as though it wriggled across his face when he moved. Now it was like dead matter, like a stream of useless, greying cells washed up underneath his skin. He had put on weight, too. His shirt, this time a deep scarlet with amber buttons, strained at the chest and gut. His hands were swollen and purple, and the silver ring he wore was definitely too tight, cutting off all circulation in his finger.

"How long have we been seeing each other for?" Doctor Vanilla leant back in his chair and raised an eyebrow, looking at her sternly.

Deborah glanced down at the table, struggling to remember. "About six weeks now, I think," she replied.

He smiled a tight-lipped smile. "Is that so? Well then, you must be ready."

"Ready for what?"

Doctor Vanilla leant forwards in his chair and Deborah smelt his strange, sweet, charred perfume once again. Her stomach turned. There was something very unsettling about it; it was like burnt hair and overripe fruit mixed together. The hairs on the back of her neck stood up.

"Do you trust me, Deborah?" He opened his eyes very wide as he said this and reached over the desk, gently laying his hand over hers. It took everything in her not to jump up and pull it away. She didn't know what to say. Of course she didn't trust him! But when someone you don't trust asks you if you do, you are almost forced into a lie because you don't trust them enough to tell them that you don't. It was quite a predicament, but there was really only one answer she could give.

"Yes," she replied, not meeting his gaze.

"Very well."

Doctor Vanilla reached into a drawer underneath his desk, careful not to allow her to see the contents, and rummaged around in it, his head bent, murmuring to himself quietly as he did so. Once he had found what he was looking for he slammed the drawer shut and took a deep intake of breath before turning back towards her again. He cocked his head to one side, appearing oddly unsure of himself, and his fingers twitched and jumped as if small insects were crawling inside his sleeves.

"You see, Deborah, for you to be able to get better, you need to appreciate yourself as a person. You need to be able to believe that you are worth fighting for, that you are worth living for. Do you feel like that right now?"

Deborah looked at him dubiously. This was far from his usual style.

"Um, I guess so. I mean I think I do. I want to try and figure this out, you know, for my mum and stuff..."

She trailed off as Doctor Vanilla shook his head violently from side to side.

"You need to want to get better for you," he said. "Don't you see that that is the key? You'll never find your way back if you don't want to. You need to want to."

He paused, got up from his desk and walked slowly over to the window. "It's not your fault, you know." He said it softly in a curling whisper as he fingered the velvet of the curtains. "What I think is this; the things that have happened to you are things that you have convinced yourself you made happen – that somehow you are responsible. So you have turned all this pain in on yourself and it's eaten away at your own sense of worth. You don't feel like you deserve to be happy, so you won't allow yourself to be happy."

He had turned to face her now and was staring deeply into her eyes.

"Do you ever forget?" he asked.

"What do you mean?" Deborah felt her heart beat faster, because she knew what he meant and she did forget sometimes. Some days she would wake up and she wouldn't immediately smell the pillow on his side of the bed or open the wardrobe and touch the few shirts he had left behind. Other days she would get out of bed and go straight to the kitchen and put on the kettle. She would just walk straight past her son's door, as if it was just a door in her house, as if it wasn't a room that she hadn't set foot in since the day he died. She bit her lip and barely nodded. Doctor Vanilla continued.

"You can't keep forcing yourself not to move on. You have to accept, accept what happened to you, you hear me, Miss Green? What happened to you, not what you did. And then you need to allow yourself to heal."

He nodded to her journal, which she had pulled from her rucksack at the beginning of the session.

"Your dreams tell me this," he explained. "They are full of images of sadness, of self-hatred, of being out of control. You need to take back that control, otherwise she'll never find you."

He had moved closer to her now. His hands were clutched around the back of his chair and she could see they were shaking. As soon as he had said these words Deborah saw him clench his knuckles, which flashed white as he saw her brow wrinkle in confusion and she opened her mouth to speak. He hurriedly corrected himself.

"What I mean by this is that you'll never find you. You need to find yourself, to become reconnected to yourself. Do you see what I mean?"

The question appeared to be rhetorical, as he did not let her answer. He pulled the drawer open again with a flourish and from it took a small yellow tub which rattled as he moved it.

Deborah sighed. "Pills. More pills."

Doctor Vanilla snapped his head up. "Of course not," he replied.

He opened the cap and carefully tilted the bottle, tapping it with his long nail, which Deborah noticed was tinged a soft yellow and ragged at the tip. A small gel capsule, also yellow, and oval in shape, fell onto the table.

"They certainly look like pills," Deborah commented, folding her arms and eyeing him suspiciously.

A dark shadow crossed over Doctor Vanilla's face.

"Put one of these in a shallow cup of some sort, then cover it with warm water. Once dissolved, drink. They are calming, natural. They unlock the mind and they will help you. If you can reconcile with yourself in your subconscious, it is my belief that you can then begin to repair the conscious. Work from the inside out, so to speak."

Deborah snorted, leaning back in her chair. She scooped up the pills and jammed them in her jacket pocket. As she did so she felt the edges of the paper where she had written her dream.

Then she remembered something. She remembered that the dream, that particular dream, hadn't ended like the others. Up until this point all the dreams she had had were strange, haunting and full of uncertainty. It was fair enough that Doctor Vanilla, upon reading her dream journal, might believe that these dreams were somehow reflective of her subconscious. But last night's dream had been different. If Doctor Vanilla was right and her dreams were an indicator of how she was truly feeling, then surely that meant she was obviously getting somewhere by herself, and, if she was getting better by herself she didn't need whatever it was he had given her, didn't need his stupid pills.

Deborah looked at Doctor Vanilla and forced a smile as he sat back down in his seat.

"And now, as usual, may I see your dream journal please?"

His eyes lit up like a gleeful child when he said the words and he flipped open his notebook and clutched a pen, his hand hovering expectantly over the paper.

Deborah pushed her journal towards him. He opened it, immediately flicking through the pages before a thunderous frown settled on his forehead. He rocked back and forth in his chair and his scar momentarily flashed white and stretched monstrously across his face.

"No new dreams, I see." He looked at her. There was fear in his eyes and his skin turned white and wet with sweat at the same time. He carefully placed the pen back down and clasped and unclasped his hands over his notepad.

Deborah shrugged. "I just didn't remember any of them, I guess," she said.

She crossed her legs and leant back further in her chair, adopting what she hoped was a casual pose as she put her hand in her pocket once again to reassure herself that the paper with her dream written on it was still there.

His disappointment was too strange. There was something more going on here, there had to be. Whatever he believed in, he clearly wanted her to get better. But it was the way he encouraged her, the way he talked of 'getting better' and 'finding herself'. There was a desperation about it, an urgency in his voice which made her think there was so much more to it than just pills and money. There must be a clue in the dream, a clue that Doctor Vanilla would not find out first. She cleared her throat and smiled, diverting his attention back to her.

"Sorry, I haven't really been sleeping all that well." She waited for him to reply, but he did not. "I guess that's it then," she continued, keeping the smile plastered to her face.

Doctor Vanilla looked anxious and angry at the same time. His face had reddened so his greying scar was now highlighted against a deep flush of crimson.

"Yes," he replied slowly. "I guess so, for now."

Deborah got up to leave and as she did so her eyes rested on the sunflower painting above her. She stifled a gasp. There was nothing so wrong that someone who had not seen the painting before would notice. However, it had caught

Deborah's attention before so she could see the changes. The flowers nearest the front looked fiercer, angrier. Their petals were curved upwards like Samurai swords with shiny black heads that were dense with menace. The sky had also changed; it was now speckled with tiny flecks of red paint that Deborah could have sworn had not been there before. But the strangest thing was the shape of the painting itself. It looked as though the whole thing was curved outwards, as if it had swollen, just like Doctor Vanilla's belly. It looked as if someone were blowing a huge bubble behind it and it might burst at any moment.

Doctor Vanilla coughed purposefully and Deborah jumped and turned towards him. He was looking at her intently, his expression dormant apart from a slight downwards twist of the left side of his mouth.

"I have another client now, Miss Green," he said.

Deborah nodded and grabbed her rucksack from beneath his desk, fumbling with the zip as it caught on the edge of a scarf which she had hastily stuffed inside.

"Bye," she muttered and quickly made for the door, pausing briefly as she turned the corner to stare at the shelves and shelves of journals either side of her. They were layered ceiling high and packed in tight together. The total must have been well into the thousands. What was it all for? She couldn't even fathom how he had managed to gather so many. If they were, as she suspected, each dedicated to a person's dreams then he must have gone through more patients than it seemed possible for him to have had in several lifetimes. It simply didn't make any sense. Deborah sighed, frustrated, before walking to the end of the hallway and pulling the door open to leave.

Outside sat Luke. He looked up at her from the paper he had been reading then immediately looked away again, carefully folding and placing it neatly back on the table as if to buy himself time. His skin was darker than before, and it looked as though he hadn't shaved for a few days, the stubble now beginning to form a beard which was tufting through, longer on the sides of his face than on his chin which remained, oddly, almost bare.

"Hi," he said.

"Hi," Deborah replied. She could hear Doctor Vanilla rustling papers at his desk round the corner. She stepped forwards, bending down to him so their faces were parallel and only inches apart.

"Look, I need to talk to you, OK?" Deborah whispered. "Just don't tell him anything. If you've had another dream about me, or anything like that, just don't tell him, you understand? There's something..." She trailed off as she heard Doctor Vanilla's footsteps approaching.

"Just don't tell him anything about me, OK?" she repeated firmly, then hurried past him just as Doctor Vanilla approached behind her, hoping with all her might that he hadn't seen them speak.

When she got home, there was a letter on the doormat. She pulled the door shut and stared at it for a long while. Her name and address had been typed and there was no stamp. It made her nervous immediately. Jack. He always used to type his letters.

She knelt down and picked it up, holding it away from her as if this would stop it hurting her. Slowly she walked with it into the living room, and stared at it for a long while before opening the envelope.

Dear Debs,
I don't even know where to begin. I can't even say I am sorry
for what I have done to you because I know that sorry just

isn't enough. What happened to us is the worst thing imaginable. But it happened to us, not me, and I am just realising that now.

I blamed you – for making us late that day, for not holding his hand tighter, for making us move here in the first place. I couldn't see anything more.

I should have been loving you, grieving with you, taking care of what was left of our family but instead I did everything wrong. I never deserved you. I knew that from the moment I met you, but you made me different somehow. I never appreciated that until I let you go and now all the good parts of me are let go, too.

Please know this. You are the love of my life. You are free. Don't forgive me. Be happy. Live on.
Jack.

Deborah heard a moan. She glanced around the room, surprised at the noise, before realising that it had come from her. She wiped away tears that didn't feel like tears but more like a river bursting, streaming all over her face. Why now? And what did it even mean? It was so unlike Jack to do something like that, to be so sentimental. Even when they had been most in love, been most happy, it had always been that rugged, rough, gruff sort of love, not filled with poetry and roses, but real and tough. A love that should have lasted, yet hadn't.

Deborah shook her head. It hadn't lasted and that's what she needed to remember. She wiped her face with the back of her sleeve, took a deep breath and read the letter once more.

Don't forgive me. Be happy. Live on. Perhaps that was all she needed to hear.

CHAPTER 13

GRACE

Dream leak

Grace rolled over and smiled. There he was lying beside her, his chest moving gently up and down as he slept. He muttered something through his lips and they trembled slightly. As his eyelashes twitched she saw a flash of green before he squeezed them tight, moaned softly and then turned his head away. He was sleeping like the bodies did. If he was asleep it meant his body must be awake and therefore he had little chance of being pulled away from her and into a dream.

Grace sat up and pulled her knees to her chest. Reaching over she pushed his hair back from his forehead, careful not to wake him. If only it could always be like this, if only they just needed each other to survive this world instead of their bodies.

She could still feel the emptiness, the void where Deborah should be. She looked down at the mark on Peter's stomach, the one just like hers which reminded her that he felt it too. However, this morning was different. She had thought when they had first separated that the pain, the hollowness that churned inside her would never fade, that she would wake every morning with that same feeling, that lonely hunger, that aching sorrow which pulled at her stomach. But now, with him, perhaps it could start to be better.

Grace rolled off the mattress they had shared, stood up and pulled on some jeans. They were a pair Peter had found lying on the pavement next to a bin and were far too large, so they hung off her hips and dragged along the ground. Grace searched the floor for the string they had used to hold them up. Finding it, she tied a knot tight around her waist, then pulled a sweater over her head and some thick navy socks onto her feet before shuffling over to the door, to go and have a look at the day.

There was a slight breeze still, stiff with winter's chill, and the air was cool and refreshing on her skin. Grace looked up to the sky to see the sun was finding its way through the clouds and creating agitated shadows on the ground below; they stretched out, then collapsed back in on themselves. The whole world was moving, turning all different shades of light and dark.

On the opposite side of the road an old woman, back bent to the floor almost at a right angle, carefully hobbled down the street. She had a bright headscarf wrapped tightly around her head. It was the colour of sunset and silvery wisps of her hair escaped and streamed out from beneath it. She had on a long tawny skirt stopping just at her ankles which looked swollen, puffed up and sore as they bulged in neat fat rims out over the top of her shoes. Grace felt sad as she watched her struggle up the street. "I hope you are not lonely," she whispered, and then turned back inside.

Filling the kettle and setting it to boil on the stove, Grace then fished around in the cupboards to see what food they had left. She found a can of alphabet spaghetti at the back – another of Peter's obsessions. She poured it into a saucepan and turned the heat low, then poured herself some Coco Pops into a mug and leant against the sink, smiling a little as she replayed the events of the night before. After she had said the words 'I love you' to him, everything had seemed like a dream – not like the dream they were pulled into by the bodies, which were dark, frantic and despairing, but one of the wonderful ones, like the ones Deborah sometimes used to have when she was back on the inside.

It was rare for Deborah to have good dreams. Instead they were often draining and fraught with sadness. But sometimes, when she was carried through the layers of consciousness, soft shapes would begin to fade in, and the dream would suddenly be beautifully sunny. Deborah would be flying or lying in the grass or holding her son by the hand. Deborah was so at peace in these dreams. It was the only time Grace felt like she could truly relax, that she didn't need to monitor Deborah's every move to make sure she was OK.

She had felt exactly the same last night when Peter had held her face and kissed her and they had walked hand in hand back to the flat, and without words had lain down on the floor. The sex for souls was perfunctory. They did as their bodies would have done, but they did not feel as bodies did. The pleasure for them came afterwards, when they rested, their limbs entangled in one another. There they lay as two souls melting together and were momentarily as one.

Grace stirred the spaghetti as it bubbled on the stove. She heard a great yawn from behind her and turned to see Peter pull a shabby brown blanket over his head.

"Too light," he mumbled. "Sleep more. Where are you? Why aren't you still in bed with me?"

Grace softly padded over to him, then ripped the blanket from his face. Peter groaned and rolled away from her.

"It's time you got up," Grace said and grinned as he pulled her down gently beside him onto the mattress.

"I don't want to," he said, pressing his lips together firmly.

Grace leant into the warmth of his body, wishing that they could just lie here on this horrible mattress in this filthy place forever. She didn't think anything could make her happier, at least not while she was separate from Deborah. She turned to face him and looked into his eyes. They were full of sleep, slitty but smiling. He gently took a lock of her hair and twisted it round his fingers.

"We have to find them," she said. "Nothing's changed. We still have to find them."

There was a flash in Peter's eyes. It was only for a moment, but it was definitely there. It broke the smile in them and they changed. His lips moved as if to speak, but then he hesitated, and instead he let all his breath out in a huge, raggedy sigh.

"You're absolutely right," he said. "We have to find them, and soon. And we are certainly not going to find them here."

He sat up and turned to her, his face locked back in its smiling position.

"Is that spaghetti I can smell burning?"

"Shit!" Grace jumped up and ran over to the stove. Sure enough the liquid had all evaporated, leaving the spaghetti hissing in a pile of dried up blackened orange mess. Grace turned off the cooker, then turned back to him.

"Cereal?"

He nodded, laughing, and threw a cushion at her head.

Grace poured him a bowl and they sat down together and began trying to go through everything they already knew. She carefully recounted all the details of the dream she had been pulled into so that Peter could see if there were any differences. She started with the tunnel, shuddering at the memory of the screams and the dripping crosses over the doors. They decided the tunnel was something everyone in their position had to go through. The doors were obviously doors to the dream-worlds of their individual bodies and, when you stopped, you were pulled through to the one that was yours. The problem with this was that it seemed as though they had both been pulled through the same door, just at different times. How could that happen? And why? Could it be possible that there was some connection between their bodies that meant that their minds were dreaming the same thing?

"When did it happen to you? Was it your first one, like me, or did it happen after that?" Grace asked.

"It was that one, that one after I had met you, where I left and then when I came back you weren't there." He looked up at her. "I thought something awful had happened to you, you know. You can tell if someone's been pulled away into a dream. There is something different in the air, so I knew you hadn't, and I waited. I waited for you to come back and then you didn't – you'd been gone for so long..."

He trailed off. Grace put her hand on his shoulder.

"I'm really sorry," she said. "It must have been horrible for you."

Peter nodded and smiled so she knew it was all right, before he continued.

"So it was that one. I didn't get a chance to tell you about it because, well, when you came back we had that fight and then you disappeared. Besides, I didn't think much of it at the time. It had been a pretty useless one. I mean there was nothing there to give me a clue with all the colours and those weird faces in the sky."

Grace took her hand from his shoulder sharply.

"What faces? What colours? I didn't see any of that, Peter. I just had that infuriating crow on a tree, telling me everything was gone and I was too late."

"Oh." Peter stared at her wide-eyed for a moment before he sat up straight and crossed his legs.

"Well, that is different. I guess we didn't really talk about it much when you first told me, huh? Let's see. Ah, yes, I remember, I did see this funny white object in a tree. It looked really out of place. Nothing else was white, you see, which is really weird in dreams. Most of the time colours are really faded, but this one, wow, there were so many colours and it was so vivid, and there were these drippy, inky rainbow faces coming through the sky. It didn't seem real. It's not like one I've had before. The ones I go into are much simpler, like black and white films – you know it makes me think maybe my guy watched old films or something like that, when I was on the inside. Maybe that's why his dreams are like that, you know? It's how I can best describe it, anyway. Everything has got this sort of softness, and it's kind of blurry and sad. But this one, this one was so different, and that white thing, all the way up in the tree, it caught my attention, and I got this feeling, like it was all wrong... that's when I decided the dream was a dud and wasn't going to help me. You can tell if you're in a dream where your body is there, too, you get this pull, this tug deep inside. And I didn't get it, so I assumed maybe I was just too late and he'd already gone on. And then moments later I was pulled back out, so I figured I was right – that I'd got there too late and he'd already moved on."

Peter paused to take a mouthful of cereal and chewed slowly before continuing. "That's the problem with them, you see, they dream so fast, they can just skip from one into the next so suddenly. And we're so much slower because we're trying to work stuff out. By the time we've realised they aren't there, we're behind them – in the dreams I mean. Then they might wake up and bang! We're pulled out, just like that." He paused. "Sorry, it's probably all really confusing to you, but you'll get it, too, when you've been pulled into them more."

"A tug on the inside," Grace said vacantly. She was thinking hard, trying to pull the pieces together.

"Exactly," Peter replied, not understanding. "If you're in there, in the right one, you can feel it. They draw you towards them whether they like it or not, kind of like magnets... why?"

Grace turned to him excitedly. "I felt it. I felt it when I was with the Creature. I saw it then, when I saw that bird in the distance and could see the white thing he was carrying. I felt it then, I swear."

Peter shook his head. "But that's impossible," he said. "The Creature isn't part of the dream. We know that. The Creature is the check point. It tells us how we're doing – it's not part of it. You can't be in the dream while you're with him."

"What if it leaked?" Grace asked.

"What do you mean?"

"That white thing was Deborah. I'm sure of it. If you saw it, too, then maybe..." She trailed off and they looked at each other uncertainly.

"Maybe I was in a dream that was meant for you," Peter finished, "and you think that's making the dream leak out into another part, a different layer?"

Grace nodded. "That's what I think," she said.

They looked at each other, both not daring to believe that it could be true. Yet neither of them could deny it either. Peter leant back and lay down on the floor staring at the ceiling with his hands crossed firmly over his chest.

"OK, say that is true," he contemplated. "Why would it be happening? I mean, that's just not how it works, you know. If we're released, the dream-worlds are our chance to try and find our way back, our only chance. Our bodies know this, so they pull us in. It's magnetic, like I told you. You can't break that, Grace, there's no way. Why would I be pulled into dreams that were meant for you? If that's true, then our task is just impossible. We'll never find them."

Peter sighed. He sounded angry and hurt, as if he thought his body was rejecting him, that it didn't care, that their connection wasn't strong enough for them to find their way back to each other.

He turned to her. "It's hard enough as it is, Grace, but if this is what's happening then we really don't have a chance."

Grace looked at him. He had turned away from her again and was staring at the wall opposite, so she squatted down beside him to make sure he was listening.

"I think you're wrong, Peter," she said. "You said yourself that our connections with our bodies are magnetic; they are unbreakable. It's just the way it is. There's got to be a reason." She put her head between her knees and stared at the floor, trying to concentrate. There was silence between them as they both sunk into their own thoughts.

"They must be trying to help us," Grace murmured to herself. She refused to believe anything other than this. It was impossible for them to give up on each other. There was just no way. They were designed to be together. Without each other neither could survive, so it was instinct that they fought to find each other, and they would keep fighting until it was over, one way or another.

She raised her head slowly and touched Peter's arm so that he rolled over to face her. He looked up at her, dewy-eyed and despairing.

"They must be trying to help us," she repeated louder, growing suddenly more excited and determined.

"Peter, maybe that's it! Of course they are trying to help us – of course!" She was on her feet now and paced over to the window. Peter sat up and rubbed his head, looking at her, somewhat confused.

"What if they are trying to pull us together?" Grace continued. "Don't you think it's strange that we met, straight away pretty much, as soon as I arrived? Maybe our bodies did that. Maybe they are directing us so that we are together, and then somehow they are trying to dream together so that maybe we get pulled into the same dream, at the same time. Imagine that happened – that we were able to be in the same dreams together. We'd have a much better chance of finding them then, wouldn't we?"

Peter looked unconvinced. 'I don't know. I mean, how would they even know how to do that? They must be pretty lost themselves you know, without us looking after them. I reckon most of their energy is taken up with just carrying on, you know? Trying to convince themselves that they can keep going as normal, trying to convince themselves they'll get better. That's what they do without us, and it can work for a while, but then if things start to go wrong, even the slightest thing really, without us there to help them, to fix it, it just sticks. They're like ticking time bombs and eventually there'll be so much wrong, so much sorrow and anger and hate just floating around inside them, that they'll try to do it again." He bit his lip. "And without us inside, there is no way they will survive it again."

Grace frowned at him; she could feel herself getting angry. Why did he have to be so practical, to ask so many questions?

"I don't know how they did it, OK?" she snapped. "But they did, I'm sure of it. And we've got to try. What do you want us to do, just stop and give up and die?"

Something flashed across Peter's eyes again, as it had done earlier that morning. He opened his mouth, bursting with a secret he wanted to tell her, but again it was only for the briefest of moments before it had gone. Instead he relented.

"Of course I don't want to give up, and I especially don't want you to give up. You deserve to have her back, Grace. I know that. You deserve to be happy." He took a breath before continuing. "So suppose what you're saying is true. Are we just supposed to sit here and wait, and hope that somehow we're right and we get pulled into a dream together?"

"No," said Grace, and sat back down beside him. "If it does happen we've got to be prepared."

"And how do we do that?"

She smiled. "We've got to learn about each other's bodies. We need to know them like we know our own, so that if we do get pulled in we can recognise the signs for both of them. I think we need a trip to that tattoo place, and I need you to tell me everything you know."

CHAPTER 14

DEBORAH

A song about a boy, and a longing to go home

Deborah was sitting in her flat waiting for the phone to ring. She had been staring at it for over an hour, ever since she had got back from Doctor Vanilla's office. She glared at it, sighing huffily, as if by vocalising her impatience she could make it suddenly ring.

She was anxious. What if Luke had ignored what she'd told him? He had every right to. She hadn't exactly left things on a high note between them when she'd left last time. There he had been, pouring his heart out to her, trying to make her understand, and she had just freaked out and left him. She wondered what had happened after she'd left, what he'd said to Linda and John. She wondered whether he had told them the whole story. He hadn't said at the time, but she was pretty sure they didn't know he was in therapy. Perhaps it was a good thing she had left. Perhaps he had told them everything, told them whatever it was that he had done that he was so ashamed of. "Perhaps," she muttered out loud, failing to convince herself while still trying to concentrate on the phone.

Soon her mind strayed off again and she wondered what Luke had already told Doctor Vanilla; she hadn't given him much of a chance to explain. Maybe he hadn't even said anything to him. He obviously had found it strange when she had started appearing in his dreams. Perhaps he had wanted to talk to her first, to see if she could shed some light, to try to make sense of it all.

Deborah clenched her hand tightly, digging her nails into the arm of the sofa. Why oh why did she have to be so stupid? If only she'd just listened, just let him finish, then she would know so much more!

She leant down and picked up her coat from the floor, feeling in the pocket for the bottle of pills Doctor Vanilla had given her. Carefully she unscrewed the cap and tipped one into her hands. Holding it up to the light between her forefinger and thumb, she inspected it closely. The pill was oval in shape with a tinted yellow plastic coating. If she held it in a certain way she was able to see the liquid contained within it. Cautiously tilting it from side to side, she watched as it oozed back and forth.

She put the pill down and switched on her laptop, dragging it from the floor onto her knees. She turned the bottle of the pills so she could read the label. 'Viatel 12mg' was printed down one side. Typing this into the search engine, she hit 'return' and waited.

Nothing came up. Doctor Vanilla had said they were herbal, but surely there would still be some information about them? Deborah looked at the pills dubiously once more, then got up and went into her bedroom, placing them beside the others on her bedside table before returning to the living room.

She resumed her position on the sofa and continued to stare at the phone. Finally it rang. Deborah jumped up to get it, tripping on the laptop cable and tumbling forward into a full-on sprawl. She slid ungracefully over the floor, chin first, until she came to a stop by the table upon which the phone sat.

"Hello?" Deborah pressed the receiver to her ear and touched her chin, which was stinging. She drew her hand away and her fingers were covered in blood.

There was a sigh which travelled down the receiver and then a huge intake of breath. Deborah knew immediately who it was.

"Hi, Mum," she said, before her mother had a chance to unleash. Deborah pushed herself backwards to lean against the wall and brace herself for what was about to come.

"Deborah." The tone was stern. "I will not tell you again. If you refuse to return my calls, that is it. I am going to voice my concerns to the appropriate bodies and we shall have what I believe is called an intervention, and they'll take you away, my girl. Back to where you were when you first woke up after, you know, or somewhere similar. Now what do you think about that?"

Deborah sighed, clutching her chin. "Mum, I don't think they can commit you for not returning phone calls."

Her mother remained unamused. "I think you'll find, dear, that it is about much more than that. It's about your own safety. We need to make sure you are all right. We need to make sure you are not falling backwards, that any consideration of doing... what you did before is completely out of your head."

"Why can't you say it, Mum?" Deborah closed her eyes and pressed her head back against the wall. A wave of exhaustion washed over her.

"Now, Deborah, don't get clever with me, darling, OK." It was not a question. Her voice had gone up a couple of octaves. It was the warning voice.

"I'm not being clever with you, Mum, but you know, maybe you should think about why you can't. I tried to kill myself, didn't I? Why can't you say it? It's like if you don't, you think it didn't happen."

Deborah coiled the telephone wire in between her fingers and held her breath. She hoped it would work, that she had managed to switch things round so her mother would begin to question herself and would therefore leave her alone.

Silence.

"Look, Mum, I'm sorry. I have to go now, OK? My chin's bleeding all over the floor."

"What? You're bleeding? Oh my god, Deborah, what have you done?"

"Mum, Mum! I just grazed my chin. I'm fine, but I do need to go. We can meet up if you like, yeah? Let's have lunch tomorrow, here – I'll cook and you can see for yourself that everything is fine."

Her mother snorted at the suggestion, but was appeased. "All right, I'll be there at midday, and Deborah?"

"Yes, Mum."

"I'll cook."

Then there was a click and she was gone.

Deborah got up and went into the bathroom. Reaching for some toilet paper she looked in the mirror and pressed it to her chin. A drip of blood dropped onto her toe, then dribbled down her shoe to the floor. She looked at it, a fat splash of red on the tiles. Her head began to buzz and sing and she was taken suddenly back to the day she had done it, and remembered how wonderfully vibrant the blood had looked against the ceramic.

Deborah shook her head, trying to force the memory away. She could see herself in the bath watching the blood slowly eddy out of her and into the water. It seemed so distant now it almost felt like it couldn't be real.

She had only saved herself because the panic had set in. She had instinctively covered her neck with her hand. She remembered how she had coughed and spluttered as she realised she was choking. She'd clasped her hand to her throat, desperately trying to stop it, her mind repeating, "You don't want this" over and over again in different, childish voices. She'd struggled out of the bathtub, dragged a towel off the rail, the horror almost freezing her as it soaked through, and her own blood smeared all over her hands. There had been blood everywhere, so much blood.

She had stumbled out of the room and down the hallway, sobbing, gasping, suffocating as she went, reaching for the phone and only just managing to cough out her address before she was no longer able to speak as the room began to spin and darken around her.

The last thing she heard was the tongue twister. It was one that always haunted her dreams and she heard it being perfectly spoken, booming in her ears. She'd heard it so clearly she would always believe it had not come from her, and swore in that moment she saw a strange dark shape loom over her, before it had gone fuzzy, then grey, and then black.

The tissue had soaked through. It was only this and another drip on the tiles that pulled Deborah back from the memory and she realised she had been standing, staring vacantly at her own reflection, her hand clutching an invisible wound at her neck. She looked harder. She didn't even look like herself these days. She twisted her face this way and that, trying to find a hint of recognition, but the person staring back at her barely seemed real.

Grabbing for some more tissue and dampening it this time, Deborah pressed it onto her chin. She then fumbled in the cabinet above the sink, found a large square plaster and a chunk of cotton wool and carefully stuck them both over the wound.

In her bedroom she carefully looked up and down the rows of books until she found what she had been looking for. The cover was creased and curled at the edges. On the front was a cartoon of a big smiling man, bushy-haired and open-mouthed, sticking a tongue out which was inappropriately long. Across the top it read 'Tongue Twisters – The Classics!' Deborah smiled as she flicked through; it had been a gift on her sixth birthday. She thumbed the pages, then smiled at the inscription scrawled in the front. 'Dearest Deborah, I hope you have fun with these. Have a wonderful day. Love, Grandma.'

Her grandma had been the tongue twister champion. She was unbeatable. She could do them all at any speed; sometimes she'd do them backwards. Deborah remembered the days, sitting on her lap in the conservatory with open doors, the smell of the honeysuckle that twisted up the sides of the house drifting gently towards them. They would sit for hours, Deborah with her hands gripped around a glass of lemonade, listening to the faint buzz of insects, and practising the tongue twisters over and over again. When Deborah got one right her grandmother would act as if it was the most wonderful thing in the world and would applaud and throw her upwards before they settled down to concentrate on the next one.

Deborah closed the book and felt the familiar wave of sadness, for everything that had been lost, start to wash over her once again.

The phone rang and she felt her stomach flip over. It was him. It had to be him. She jumped off her bed, throwing the book down on the bed, and ran through to the living room, pausing to take a deep breath before she answered.

"Hello?" she said. Her voice sounded high pitched, squeaky almost. She rubbed her stomach, trying to flatten the nerves that were hopping about within it.

"Deborah?" He sounded unsure. "Is that Deborah? It's Luke. We really need to talk."

They agreed to meet in a café on Whitehawk Lane, which was just across the park from where Deborah lived. She peered through the curtains before she left, resolute that she would dress in a manner appropriate for the occasion. The sky was a deep, frosty blue with heavy-looking clouds drawing in from either side, as if they were curtains across a stage. She pulled on her boots and coat, adding a thick, purple woollen scarf and matching gloves and a grey knitted bobble hat with snowflakes stitched in a neat pattern around the rim. Grabbing her bag from the living room and keys from behind the door, she left the flat.

Deborah walked quickly to the end of the road, trying to work out what she might say when faced with Luke. As she passed the last house on the street she looked to the apple tree, as had become her tradition when going by. The unusually cold winter had clearly taken its toll. The branches were limp and sodden from frost and mist, the bark was stained with curled patches of brown moss and the whole tree seemed curved to the left, as if it were about to topple over at any minute. Deborah paused and stared at it, finding herself willing it to get better. She looked at the house behind it. It was like any other on the street, painted a dull shade of white on the outside, with a charcoal-coloured slate roof and a large bay window at the bottom left which she assumed was the window of the living room. There was another window to the right and then two smaller ones on the floor above. All the curtains were pressed tightly shut and there was no way of telling if anyone was home.

She was halfway across the park when it began to snow. She didn't see it at first, only felt it as little frosted drops spat onto her cheeks and nose. Then it came down harder, settling almost immediately onto the ground. Deborah tilted her head upwards and watched the snowflakes swirl and dance in the wind. Dusk was setting in and the flakes shimmered against the sky. Deborah stuck out her tongue and smiled. For a moment she forgot herself and could only think of how beautiful it was.

She arrived at the café right on time. '*Mama Che's*'. She had never been before even though it was so close to her house. The walls were painted a warm yellow and the tables and chairs were wooden and few. There was a counter in the far corner: behind it a hatch, and a door to the right, both of which she assumed led to the kitchen. The room was stuffy and the windows had steamed up. Luke wasn't there yet, so Deborah chose a seat at a table in the middle. She shrugged out of her coat and leant back, taking a deep breath as the smell of coffee and spices flowed towards her.

The kitchen door creaked open and Deborah looked up to see an exquisitely beautiful African woman standing behind the counter. She began to quietly arrange the cakes in the display with her long, slender fingers.

She had a woven cloth wrapped tightly round her head with citrus-coloured stripes over it. Huge gold hoops were fastened to her ears, brushing her shoulders as she leant forward to move the scones. She wore a loose grey shirt with yellow buttons and as she came around the counter, Deborah saw she had a short, white apron tied tightly around her waist which partly covered a floor-length skirt in a vibrant lime green which perfectly matched the green in her headscarf. She looked up to see Deborah staring over and offered her a wide smile.

"Good afternoon," she said, lowering long eyelashes demurely. Her voice low, it sounded as though she had been sucking on toffees. She turned and picked up a small notepad which was lying on the side behind her, then came over to the table where Deborah was sitting.

"What can I get for you?" Her voice was almost hypnotic and Deborah found herself blushing a little as she replied.

"Um, I'm waiting for my friend, actually. Maybe just some tea for now?"

The woman nodded graciously and tucked the notepad into the top pocket of her shirt, not bothering to write this down. She then walked back towards the counter, her many gold bracelets creating a faint tinkle as she did so.

Suddenly the door was pushed open, hard. It slammed back against the wall with a loud bang causing, both Deborah and the woman to gasp. Deborah jumped up defensively as she saw a figure stumble though the entrance. It was Luke. He had a huge army green-coloured Puffa jacket on and the same yellow scarf she had seen before wound closely around his face and jaw. A crimson hat was pulled down over his head, covering his eyebrows so the only part of his face visible was his eyes. He wore khaki trousers with large pockets down the sides and on his feet were green trainers which Deborah felt she had seen before. He was covered in snow and soaking wet. He twisted round awkwardly, restricted by his layers, and snow fell in clumps from his sleeves as he did so. Deborah moved to his side and tapped him on the shoulder.

"Luke."

He turned round and mumbled a greeting though his scarf. He then pulled his scarf and hat off before he tried in vain to wipe the snow off his boots on the wicker mat that lay by the entrance. He smiled apologetically at the woman, seeming to take no notice of her beauty, and then he turned back to Deborah shrugging his jacket off as he did so and wiping his face with his mittened hand.

"Sorry I'm late. It's crazy out there." He nodded towards the window, but it was hard to see out through the steam. Deborah walked over and rubbed the glass with her sleeve. Thick drifts of snow had settled over everything. Huge chunks were falling from the sky. They hurtled straight down, not seeming to swirl and dance as they usually did. It was if they were magnetised towards the ground. The sky had turned black quickly and there was not a soul on the street.

"Wow!" was all Deborah could muster. "It's coming down fast." She immediately felt stupid. As if that wasn't obvious.

She turned back to Luke and gestured to the table where she had been sitting. They both sat down in silence as the woman brought over Deborah's tea in a huge, steaming white mug. She placed a little baked biscuit on the side which tasted of cinnamon and coconut when Deborah tried it, nodding her appreciation to the woman who beamed back at her. The woman then turned to Luke and tapped her notepad with her pencil expectantly. Her smile seemed to fade a little when she looked at him. Luke did not notice, as he was staring at Deborah's tea dubiously.

"Do you have anything alcoholic?" he asked, not looking up. Deborah could tell he struggled with this, not wanting to be judged. The woman simply nodded and then went through the door by the hatch.

"Sorry," Luke smiled sheepishly, "I just reckon I need something a bit stronger for this. What happened to your chin?"

Deborah touched it self-consciously. "Nothing," she muttered. There was something about him which immediately made her feel like a silly girl. All scabs and stains. Deborah kept her hand on her chin and looked away from him.

The woman then reappeared clutching a large, heavy-looking crystal bottle with an emerald green glass stopper. She placed it on the table in front of them and then set down two matching thick-rimmed crystal glasses and a large metal pot of freshly-boiled water.

"I make this myself," she explained, neither boasting nor being coy. "Its base is fermented honey with nutmeg and cloves." She carefully tipped a little into each glass and then topped them both up halfway with the hot water.

"Go ahead. Try it," she urged. Luke picked up his glass and raised it to Deborah, who sighed. She knew she shouldn't; she needed a clear head. But she didn't want to insult the woman so she followed in suit and raised her glass. The liquid was strong, hot and sweet and the spices tingled delicately on her tongue.

"Thank you." Deborah smiled at the woman who nodded amiably and then went back into the kitchen, leaving the bottle on the table for them to share.

Deborah leant back in her chair and almost wished that they didn't have to talk about any of the things they were going to. The warmth of the alcohol heated her belly and she suddenly felt sleepy and content. She looked at Luke, who was mirroring her pose, and found herself suddenly very attracted to him. This made her nervous and she sat up, embarrassed, and cleared her throat.

"I don't really know where to start. Um, I guess I should apologise for last time. I'm really sorry about that. I just got a bit freaked out."

Luke had his hands up and was shaking his head. "No, I'm sorry," her replied. "I shouldn't have piled everything on you like that and I shouldn't have taken you to the pub. I didn't handle it very well."

Deborah opened her mouth in protest to apologise again but realised that they could go on forever this way, so instead she simply nodded and smiled. "I dreamt about you," she said.

Luke's eyes widened and he took a large gulp from his glass, finishing his drink, and immediately reached to make another. "Oh?" he said.

"Yes, that's why I wanted to get hold of you, to tell you, to tell you I had one, too. And I went to Doctor Vanilla's. I thought I might see you come out before me, and then I went in and had my session, and when I came out you were there, and, I don't know, I just felt..." Deborah paused, aware she was rambling, then leant forwards and lowered her voice to a whisper. "Do you ever get the feeling there is something not quite right about him?"

"About who? About Doctor Vanilla, you mean?" He said it cautiously, afraid that he had misunderstood.

"Yes, about him," Deborah replied. "The way he talks,

the way he's obsessed with our dreams, he just, I don't know, he seems so desperate to know, like it's not for me, but for him, that I'm just in the way of whatever he really wants, that me... getting better... isn't really what it's about."

Luke nodded slowly, carefully tracing the rim of his glass with his forefinger before he replied. "I know what you mean. I get that, that kind of uncanny feeling around him. From the first day I met him I felt like I had met him before. He made me feel uneasy. I was going to stop going but then, well I kind of started feeling better when I wrote my dreams down. He made me think about them, about what they might mean. I don't know – it's hard to explain but, for a while, I felt like I was getting close to something, and then... well then you appeared in my dreams and since then, to be honest, Deborah, I've just felt really confused."

He looked at her carefully and Deborah felt nerves rear up again in the pit of her stomach and her cheeks grow hot. He was leaning forward, arms resting on the table so that his hands were almost touching hers. "He does have some strange methods, that's for sure. Did he ever do that shoe thing on you?"

Deborah suddenly realised where she had seen Luke's shoes before; on Doctor Vanilla's feet, the first day she went.

"He made me take them off one time," she replied, "but he didn't wear them." She laughed nervously. "At least I don't think he did."

Luke frowned and looked away from her. "He told me it was something psychological like, you know the expression,'to walk a day in another man's shoes'? He said it was something to do with that, to do with getting to understand me better."

Deborah put her head in her hands and made a faint groaning sound. It was all too much. None of it made any sense.

"So what was your dream about?" Luke asked.

Deborah pulled her journal from her rucksack and flicked it to the correct page. She then handed it to Luke and watched his face, feeling a strange mix of excitement and embarrassment. She watched as his eyes scanned the page, following him as he read, and began to recall the dream herself.

She remembered the school and the lights and how Luke had stepped in front of her protectively, just before the bell had rung, as if he had known that something was about to happen. She remembered those faces – the ones all turned to her, the faces that were all her own, cruel twisted faces that blocked their way out.

In the dream she and Luke had clutched each other's hands and faced them. They had run fiercely forward as the clones had pawed at them both and tried to separate them. But they didn't let go. They'd made it to the other side and, when they'd pushed open those doors, Deborah had seen her old home and a light in the shape of a girl. Luke and Deborah had both stared at the light, still gripping each other's hands. The girl was in the distance and had her back to them. She was staring up at the oak tree.

Deborah remembered that tree with a pang. How often she had sat under there! The girl in the dream had golden hair which flowed to the small of her back, and she had been completely naked. Deborah hadn't recognised her but when the girl began to turn, Deborah had been filled with a strange desire in the pit of her stomach. The last thing she remembered was an overwhelming sense of peace, a certainty that everything would be OK, and the next thing she knew she'd woken up.

Deborah waited until Luke had finished reading. He then closed the journal and pushed it to one side. Staring down at the table, he spoke quietly:

"I had no idea how weird it would be the other way around, someone else dreaming about you. It's a bit strange, you know?" He started to apologise again for not realising this when he had told her, for not being more sensitive, but Deborah shrugged him quiet, not letting him finish.

"Doctor Vanilla told me my dreams were full of misery and fear," she said, "but this one wasn't. He doesn't know what he's talking about. And then he gave me these pills to help with that, I guess, but I feel like I'm getting better, that the dream, with you, made me feel different, good, safe. But I didn't want to tell him that. I felt like I shouldn't, for some reason...did you tell him you were feeling better?"

Luke nodded. "I did."

"What did he do?"

"He gave me pills, same as you."

"What were they like?"

"Small, yellow, plastic looking things. Yours?"

"The same." Deborah sighed, frowning. "I don't get it, though. Why would he give us both the same pills, if you said you're feeling better and I didn't?"

Luke shrugged and clasped his hands together. He crossed his legs and Deborah felt one brush her own. He felt it, too, and quickly moved it back.

"Maybe it's irrelevant," he said. "Maybe whatever the pills do he wants the same thing to happen to both of us. Have you tried them yet?"

"No – you?"

"No." They both stayed silent for a while. Deborah poured herself another drink and swallowed it quickly.

There was a rustle behind the kitchen door and the faint sounds of the woman singing to herself filtered through the hatch. Her singing, like her voice, was deep but soft. Deborah strained to hear. It was a song about a boy and a longing to go home.

"Have you ever seen anyone else in his office?" Luke asked.

"I saw a young girl in the waiting room once. She looked in a bad way. Apart from that, no, never."

"Me neither. It's a bit weird, isn't it, that we would be the only ones? Have you seen that girl again?"

"No."

"And do you know anything about him? I mean, how can we be sure he is who he says he is?"

"Luke, that's ridiculous. I looked him up. He's supposed to be very good."

"According to who?"

Deborah screwed her eyes tight shut, racking her brain to think about what she actually saw. It was crazy to think that Doctor Vanilla was some sort of impostor. He had an office with his name on it! There was no way. Yet the possibility that Luke could be right could not be ignored. Deborah couldn't deny her instincts and they told her there was something sinister about whatever it was Doctor Vanilla was trying to do. She looked up at Luke:

"I feel like he wants something from me, something that's not just money, something that I don't think I want to give him... do you get that?"

"Completely." Luke nodded his head. He paused, catching himself, and sighed. "I don't know what we can do about it, though." A helpless look crossed over his face. "I guess maybe we should just stop going?"

Deborah sighed and shook her head, surprised at how easily he seemed to give up. "No way. If he's doing something weird, if he's messing with my mind in some sort of way, for whatever reason, then I am going to find out." She looked up at him resolutely. "I think I'm going to take that pill."

Luke looked startled at her sudden determination. "Are you sure that's a good idea?" he asked. "I mean, if we don't trust him should we be taking medicine he gives us?"

Deborah shrugged. "I think it's the only way we can know what he's up to. I don't think he's trying to poison me or whatever, but there is obviously something that the pill does that he wants to happen to me, to both of us really, and I won't know what that is until I try it. Look, I'll take it tonight, and I'll set an alarm, and then when I wake up I'll call you straight away, and if I don't call you then you'll know something is wrong, yeah?"

Luke looked unconvinced. "It's not the most foolproof plan in the world, is it, Deborah? Just take a pill that you know nothing about and then see what happens, and if something goes wrong the only person who'll know will be me, when it's already too late? Maybe I should take it instead."

Deborah shook her head. "What difference does that make?" She was defensive now, annoyed that he was suddenly trying to be all noble. "If you're so worried about it then it makes sense for me to do it. I don't care what it does..." She trailed off, realising what she sounded like. "I didn't mean that," she continued. "Of course I care. I'm not saying, you know, I'm not saying I don't care if anything bad happens to me. I just... it's just something I feel like I've got to do, OK?"

"OK," he said. He leant over and touched her arm. "But call me as soon as you wake up." There was genuine concern in his eyes, and Deborah felt herself blushing again.

"I promise," she said.

They left the café together and stood awkwardly outside. The snow had died down and now only soft flakes plodded wearily from the sky. Deborah glanced up; it seemed to her that the stars were a little brighter, a little more full of hope. Or perhaps they were just laughing at these two strange and sad little people who had convinced themselves of something utterly preposterous, because that was the only way they could relate to other human beings.

"Well," she said, unsure of how to leave him.

He smiled at her, then scuffed his trainer against the side of the kerb like a shy child. Suddenly he moved forward, pulling her close. She could smell his skin, an earthy honest scent. His arms were strong and wrapped tight around her, and she could feel his breath hot on her ear.

"Good luck, Deborah," he whispered. Then he quickly released her and strode off down the street without looking back.

She walked back through the park, feeling her hands shaking and she was nervous, but different – in a good way. *Don't read anything into it, don't read anything into it,* she repeated over and over in her head. Her boots squeaked and puffed through the snow as she weaved her way across, trying to find parts of it that had not been walked on by others and, when she did, feeling that strange satisfaction at being the first to indent them with her footprints. She couldn't think of anything but Luke. She tried to push him out of her mind, to focus on what might happen to her when she took the pill, but she could not. This made her angry. *It didn't mean anything. He just hugged you. Why do you even care? You are such an idiot!*

The park was empty, but Deborah could see lights from the houses dotted on its edge and, as she got closer, she could see into the window of one, and a family sitting around their kitchen table. Both parents were focused on the child, who was carefully bent over a drawing, scribbling furiously with a felt tip pen. The adults smiled at each other across the table and a sudden sense of guilt gripped at Deborah's throat.

How could you? Her mind taunted. H*ow could you think of anyone else? You have a family!* She halted by their driveway, unable to stop staring. The woman inside then looked up and her smile turned into a frown. She nudged her husband and nodded to Deborah, he quickly got up pulled the curtains tightly shut.

Deborah stayed still for a moment, clutching the middle of her coat and twisting it between her hands until her fingers hurt. Every time, every single time that she had a moment where she got to rise above the smog that had seemed to suffocate her life since they had gone, every time she saw a glimmer of a future that might be different, a chance of happiness, of a life with someone else, the guilt would come crashing down on her. It would dig its claws deep into her shoulders and she would feel this incredible shame for even daring to think it.

At home Deborah stood in her kitchen, then turned on the hot tap before reaching into a cupboard above for a mug which she filled with an inch of water, just as Doctor Vanilla had instructed. Carrying this to the bedroom, she then took her dream journal from her rucksack, placing it beside the bed and checking a pen was there ready for when she woke up. Deborah kicked off her boots and threw her coat down on the carpet. She did not bother to wash, to clean her teeth or to get undressed. As she peeled back the covers, her tongue twister book fell to the floor with a clatter that made her jump. She bent down to pick it up.

It had landed open on the page of her favourite one; it was the one she had never managed to do. That's why she liked it so much, because it kept the moments going with her grandmother. Without that one they would have run out. Carefully placing the book on the bedside table on top of the journal, she reached for the pills, popping one into the mug which she clasped tightly in her hands. It dissolved almost instantly. Deborah then quickly shoved the bottle into her pillow case.

"Cheers, Doctor Vanilla," she said, raising the cup to her lips. She swallowed it in one gulp, lay back on her pillows, and immediately she was asleep.

CHAPTER 15

GRACE
The beginning of understanding

Grace and Peter hurried along the pavement. It was quiet in the city as was usual for a weekday morning, but they both knew all too well that things could change quickly. It just took one crowd, one boisterous group for them to end up in a dangerous situation, and that was the last thing that they needed. They turned the corner onto a narrow, cobbled street with shops either side and large, leafy trees growing in even spaces along the centre.

"It's just at the end there." Peter nodded his head to the left, where a neon sign flickered sporadically on and off over a shop window. He quickened his pace, pulling Grace along beside him so she had to break out into a jog.

"Calm down, will you?" she called to him. "I know we've

got to be careful and all that, but we're here now and hardly anyone's about."

As if fate were trying to prove his point, a group of teenagers suddenly rounded the corner. One of them had taken another one's phone and now they were chucking it about between them as the owner flailed about in the middle of them trying to intercept it.

Peter quickly pushed Grace against the wall as they went past. He then raised his eyebrows in an 'I told you so' look before continuing on. Grace scowled, and was about to say something to vocalise her annoyance, but suddenly she felt very dizzy.

"Are you OK?" Peter had reached the shop and turned round. He walked back towards her with a concerned look on his face.

Grace held up her hand and he stopped. "I'm fine." Then, changing the subject, she asked, "Have you got the key?" Peter opened his coat again and fished a small gold key from one of the hooks on the inside of his coat.

"Of course." Peter unlocked the door. He pushed it open with his fingertips and gestured for her to go in before him.

There was a small white table immediately to the right as they entered with various tattoo magazines sprawled across its surface. The floor was red and black checked Lino, and long benches upholstered in black leather stretched along either side of the walls. Laminated posters of different tattoo designs were pinned to the walls, and straight ahead was a counter with a phone and a till on the left. On the back wall there were white shelves which held various pots of creams and bottles of lotion, and to the right at the back was a black curtain which rustled slightly as Peter pushed past her. Grace shuddered; it smelt like the hospital.

"Come on, come on," Peter muttered impatiently. He

hurried behind the counter and pulled the curtain back. A set of winding stairs led down.

"Why are you so worried?' Grace asked, slightly irritated as she followed him. "You said they close the shop today, that they do it this time every week. I don't see why you're fussing so much."

"I'm just being careful, OK?" Peter snapped back. He then stopped and turned round. "I just want to make sure you don't get hurt again. I mean, you got restored last time. We don't know why, and we don't know if you'll get so lucky if it happens again, all right?"

Grace pushed her hair back from her face. She had obviously underestimated how much it had affected him. "I'm sorry," she said softly and pulled him towards her, pressing herself carefully into him to show that she meant it. Suddenly the dizziness came back again and she sat down on the steps with a thump.

"Oh!" She bent forwards and put her head between her knees.

"Grace!" Peter knelt down beside her. "What's the matter? Are you OK?"

Grace looked back up at him and eased her head from side to side as everything began to settle. "Yeah, I just got dizzy for a second there." She looked him in the eye. "I'm OK, really." Peter looked dubious but said nothing further as he helped her up and they continued to the bottom of the stairs. At the end there were doors on either side of a short corridor ahead of them, every inch of which was covered in graffiti. Grace stared at the cartoon pictures with their big shoes and sprayed-on smiles. She felt a tug on her hand as Peter pulled her into one of the rooms.

The room was small with plain white walls and a lime green carpet. In the middle was another large black leather bench with a creased blue paper towel draped over it. Beside it stood a wooden chair which rocked unevenly when Grace walked past it. At the back of the room more shelves were lined along the wall, supporting tubes, creams and lotions and a huge roll of blue paper towel which was pressed into the corner. The whole place smelled strongly of antiseptic. Grace took a deep breath and tried to ignore it.

Peter walked over to the shelves and began rummaging around them before turning back to her with some cotton wool soaked in a pungent, clinical-smelling liquid. He patted the bench and she clambered on. He then sat himself down in the chair and began rubbing her arms.

"Are you sure you want to do this?"

Grace bit her lip and nodded. On the walls were pictures in frames of sturdy, kind-faced men with pony tails and long goatees. Their arms and legs were always uncovered and they grinned out from the pictures, showing off their tattoos. In between these were more laminated pieces of paper sporting the various designs you could get. Grace looked at the long, delicate flowers, the leafy vines, the pretty butterflies, the thick tribal designs and the delicate scatterings of stars. She then turned to the other wall and saw ones of crimson devils with their thick, stubby horns and evil grins, the screaming vampires with jaws that were dripping in blood, the twisted, disfigured faces of clowns, and pictures of huge, spiky spiders with claws and wings.

"Why would people want them?" she asked, shaking her head in horror and wonder.

Peter shrugged. "I guess it can be lots of things, you know. People like to be in control of their bodies. I guess this is one way to do it. Maybe getting ones like those is kind of like telling the world that you're not afraid, or that you don't care what people think. And then some people, like me and you, need them to be reminded of things. But I think some people do it as a way of cementing their memories like, if they achieve something, or they love someone, or they need to be encouraged and reminded of what inspires and pushes them, they might get something that makes them think of that."

Grace bit her lip. She felt her cheeks grow hot. She couldn't help but feel angry again. "I thought that's what we were for," she said. "Aren't we supposed to make them feel good and happy and inspired? That's the whole point of us, isn't it?"

Peter sighed. "We are, Grace, of course we are, but I guess maybe sometimes they need something more than us."

Grace brushed away a tear roughly, angry at herself for feeling so hopeless and sad. "I guess you're right," she said.

"Are you ready? Watch carefully 'cos you're going to have to do me after, OK?"

Grace nodded and watched as Peter reached for a huge, sleek metal pen, fascinated by the sight of it. Deborah had never been bothered by blood or needles, so Grace was not afraid. Peter leant forward. Taking her arm, he pulled it straight, and a low, whirring noise began to vibrate through the air.

Grace tried to keep still as she felt the heat and the sting of the ink spiking through her skin. There was something strangely wonderful about the pain and she smiled at Peter who had stopped to wipe the excess ink off her shoulder.

"Now this one," he explained, "this one is from the first dream I ever got pulled into. It was the day after I had arrived here so I had no idea what to expect." He smiled at her. "I wasn't lucky enough to bump into someone like me to show me the ropes. Anyway, so I got pulled in and I went through the tunnel and past the doors and the Creature was there and did his thing. I was completely bewildered by it all, of course." He paused. "It's funny now how it almost seems normal. Anyway, so the dream. It was strange and sad and terrifying in a way that's still really hard to explain. At first there was nothing, just total darkness. It was blacker than black, you know. It had an endlessness to it that made me think perhaps it was already too late for me. Then this silvery mist appeared. It came from everywhere and started revealing a picture, this incredible view, and there I was on top of this hill looking down. It was strange because it didn't feel like anywhere I had been before and yet it felt exactly like home."

He sighed and the whirring of the pen stopped for a moment.

"Go on," Grace whispered.

"So then I look down and I can tell that I am younger, that we are younger, you know? That this dream is about something that happened years back. I look into the distance and see these two boats floating in the sea, and I get this tug, you know? The tug that you know they are there. So I start to run. Just instinctively I ran down the hill, as fast as I could go. I could see those boats, and I could see that they were floating further and further away from the coast. I knew if I could just get to them in time that maybe I'd find him, or at least that everything would be OK. But the faster I ran the quicker the boats drifted from me. I remember looking down at my stupid, child-like legs and being sure that if I was older I could catch them. I got to the shore and dived in and swam but the smaller boat had already disappeared. I tried as hard as I could to catch up to the other one but then suddenly, just like that, I was pulled out."

Peter pulled back again and wiped her arm. "Done," he said. Grace peered at her shoulder to see two perfect boats, one slightly smaller than the other, floating side by side on a moonlit sea.

"OK, time to swap for a bit," he said, helping her down. "Now you have to do something about Deborah for me."

"I've only been in one dream," she said doubtfully.

"It doesn't matter. You need to think beyond that. Think about things that might appear for Deborah, think about moments that caused her the most fear or the most hate or the most love, her favourite colours or flowers or objects that are precious – anything like that is likely to come up, and if it does in a dream, it probably means that they're near. I know you think we might get pulled in together but, even so, it's so easy to lose one another. We need to be aware of every sign."

Grace nodded, thinking hard. "OK, well the most obvious thing is Jamie, her son. He conjures up more emotions in her, in us, than anyone else. All the love, all the sorrow, all the fear she's ever felt – it's all in him."

"Can you draw him?" Peter asked.

"I can," Grace replied. She then took the pen and bent over Peter's leg to begin.

The tattoos took several hours. They were much more resilient, the souls, so they could work faster than would have been possible on real human flesh. When they had both finished, they sat together comparing and explaining the stories for each one to make sure that the other understood. Grace had replicas of Peter's arm tattoos and they both had ones that would help them find Deborah on their calves and thighs.

"I kind of like them," Grace contemplated as she twisted her arm this way and that, admiring the work. It's weird how you can kind of tell stuff about them, about our bodies I mean, just by looking at them – how there's kind of a theme to them."

"How do you mean?" asked Peter, who was carefully studying a tiny symbol that Grace had tattooed on his ankle.

Grace gently tilted his head up to look at her arms. "Well, look at them. I mean, yours all seem to be linked to his past, don't you think? Your dreams are all so childlike; they seem to take you to places in the past. I know it's hard to tell but it seems to me like your body only dreams about things that have been and gone, like he's stuck there, stuck in the past trying to fix things that he can't."

She paused and looked at Peter to make sure she hadn't gone too far before pointing to the pictures on Peter's thigh, which were forming shiny black scabs on his skin. "And then there's Deborah's. I guess she's no better, really. She is consumed by the death of her son, her broken marriage. She still pleads for things to go back to the way they were, even though she knows it's impossible. But she still dreams forwards sometimes. When I was on the inside, sometimes she'd slip away, imagine herself happy, imagine herself getting married or growing old, of somehow escaping the life she was currently in." Grace gently grazed the picture of the apple tree she had drawn with her fingers. Its great sturdy roots were buried around the bones of Peter's foot and then it sprouted upwards, tall and strong on his calf bone, before blossoming out, bearing huge, dewy fruit, over his thigh.

"She still has hope," Peter said, understanding.

Grace looked up at him again as he pulled her gently towards him. She lay resting her head on his shoulders, trying to melt into him so she could share it with him, so that she could show him all the good things and all the bad things – everything. So that all the burdens they had ever had to carry could be relieved and mixed and shared with one another. All the pain and fear and beauty and love would rush together from both of them in a massive tide of emotion and pleasure, and they could be as one again.

But she could not do this, for as soon as she pressed herself into him again, and as he began to pull her urgently towards him, the dizziness swarmed through her head once more. She pushed him back hard, this time slipping from the bench and falling onto the floor.

"I don't know what's happening, Peter!" she cried. He stumbled down to get her and tried pulling her back up with his arms, but it just seemed to make it worse.

"Don't touch me!" she snarled at him, as a huge wave of nausea washed over her. "I'm sorry, Peter, but please don't touch me. I don't understand what's going on!" All of her skin felt hot and itchy, and she wanted to peel it off. Grace looked to the floor to see a faint patch of blood begin seeping through her t-shirt. The floor wrinkled and curved beneath her. Desperately she pawed at it, spitting onto the ground, trying to find her grip. She looked up at Peter, tears pouring down her face. "What's happening to me?!" she screamed again.

Peter's mouth had drooped open. His eyes were stern and full of worry but he had no words. This time he stepped away from her. Then he seemed to say something, but she could not hear him. For as his lips moved the familiar feeling came again. It took over the sickness and the dizziness and she felt her form go limp, her body elastic as she began to slip away. She felt it melt and drip and grow weaker; she was being pulled into the dreamworld once more. Grace stretched out her hand to Peter and gave one last anguished sob, and then she felt herself go.

CHAPTER 16

DEBORAH

The beginning of the understanding. Part II

Strings of light poked at Deborah's eyelids as she flickered into consciousness. She tried to open them, but they felt as heavy as rocks. She tried to sit up, but her head seemed cemented to the pillows. She tried to speak, but her tongue was cracked and dry. Faint noises blurred and echoed in the distance, slurring into her ears, but she could not make them out. She lay paralysed, her mind too fuzzy to panic, coffined inside her own skin.

After what felt like hours, she felt someone's fingers pressing into her arms. She moaned and tried to turn away, but they held her tight. Prising her eyes open into two tiny slits, she saw the blurry outline of a woman leaning over her. Deborah blinked, trying to focus, and moved her head in a gentle circular motion. She was in her room; she recognised the yellow floral pattern of her sheets. The window was open and the curtains were flapping furiously in the wind. A sharp pain suddenly pinched the skin across her face and a resounding smack echoed in her ears. This seemed to re-order her brain and she focused on what was in front of her. She could see her mother standing over her, screaming her name. The angle of her face meant that all the fat from her cheeks and neck were sagging down, and for a split second she looked as though her face was falling off. Deborah found this image incredibly funny and began to laugh. It started in a small, dry snigger, then slowly built its way up until she was shaking and crying and barely able to breathe.

She was dragged upright and propped back against some pillows as she continued to laugh uncontrollably, trying to wipe her eyes with a floppy hand. Her mother seemed older, with thick lines shovelled into her forehead and scraped around her lips. She also looked angry – her eyes were narrowed and her mouth, between shouts, was clamped down into a straight, quivering line. Her eyebrows jiggled about her forehead furiously as she tried to get her daughter's attention. Deborah took a deep breath, trying to regain control. She glanced at the clock by her bed. It flashed 2.02pm. She had been asleep for fourteen hours.

Deborah looked down at the floor by her bed. Several carrier bags were strewn across it. A chicken carcass could be seen sticking its stocky pink legs out from the end of one, and several potatoes and an onion had rolled out across the floor. Deborah suddenly remembered why her mother would be here.

"Oh God," she moaned softly, and pushed her head back against the pillows. This was her fault; she had invited her round. She had been so determined to take the pill last night, so excited and curious at what it might do, that she had blocked everything else out, and had completely forgotten.

Suddenly the waves of nausea turned to proper retching gulps. Deborah tried to stumble out of bed as the sickness flung itself up from her stomach. Her knees were weak, like puffs of cotton wool, and refused to support her as she staggered, weaved and then collapsed onto the floor. Her mother lifted her back up onto the bed and placed a basin under her chin. Deborah retched heavily. The sick was neon yellow in colour and tiny specks of black floated in a thin film on top of it like psychedelic frog spawn. Her mother held her hair until she was done.

"What did you take, Deborah? I'm calling an ambulance right now." The voice sounded muffled, as if she were speaking underwater. She carefully handed her daughter a glass of water from the bedside table and reached for her phone. Deborah grabbed at her hand, clamping her fingers down on her mother's wrist, and the phone spun across the floor.

"Please. Don't," she whispered. She took another gulp of the water, trying desperately to ease the pounding in her throat. "Please, Mum..."

Her mother looked at her. Deborah knew that look. It was exactly the same as when she had woken up in the hospital, that weak, withered look that was so unlike her mother. Usually such a strong, cold woman, she now looked as though all her strength had been sucked out of her with a vacuum cleaner.

"What did you take?" she repeated gently. "We need to get you to a hospital, dear."

Deborah leant forwards and put her hand over her

mother's. She tried to ignore the pounding in her head – this was going to have to be good. She carefully reached inside her pillow case for the pills.

"These," she said, handing them over. Her mother twisted the bottle, searching for information.

"Viatel?"

"My therapist gave them to me. They're herbal, to help me sleep. They certainly did that, but they must have disagreed with me somehow. Maybe I took too much or got the instructions wrong. But they're herbal, really – I don't need to go to hospital." She squeezed her mother's hand a little tighter. "Mum, I know what it looks like, but I swear, I swear that's the truth."

It felt strange not to lie. Even though she had left out the parts about how suspicious she was of Doctor Vanilla, the basic facts were, for once, the truth. She glanced at her dream journal, itching to write in it as snippets of the dream she'd had flashed into her head. But she had to convince her mother first, so she would have to wait. She studied her mother's face carefully for the reaction. She was staring at the pills dubiously.

"How can I believe you, Deborah?" She shrugged. "Your lies... you're always lying to me." She sounded broken and desperately sad as she nodded to the other bottles of unopened pills by Deborah's bed. "You told me you take all those, and clearly you haven't. Why would you take these ones when you won't take any of the others? The ones that were prescribed by the doctors when they first let you out of hospital?"

"Because I trust him, Mum," Deborah replied, the lies returning. "Doctor Vanilla, I trust him. I didn't trust the others..." She trailed off, realising how pathetic and insane it sounded. She doubted saying she didn't trust doctors was going to help her cause. Her mother, however, seemed to relent a little as she reached over to Deborah and tucked stray hairs from her ear.

"Why don't you get in the shower, all right?" she smiled. "I'm still not convinced but you seem a little better now so perhaps the need for an ambulance right this minute isn't absolutely necessary. So you go, clean yourself up, and then when you're ready we can have a good talk about it, all right?"

Deborah nodded weakly. It wasn't perfect, but at least this way she would have some time to think about what to say, then hopefully her mother would leave and she could write the dream down before she forgot. Her heart pounded faster as she allowed herself to think about it, before pushing it aside to concentrate on what she would say.

Deborah carefully crawled out of bed and unhooked a shabby beige towel from the back of her door.

"I won't be long," she said as she began to weave unsteadily towards the bathroom.

Her mother looked up at her with a smile that was stiff at the edges. "Take your time," she said, then immediately looked back to the floor.

In the bathroom Deborah quickly opened the window and pulled off her clothes before she knelt down in the bath and turned the shower to scalding hot and then vomited over and over again. Eventually there was nothing left inside, so she carefully cleaned the bath and then lay on her back, letting the water pour down over her face and chest. Gently she let it trickle over her stomach, now strangely used to the pain as it washed over the red mark. It would heal soon enough, she thought. She had better things to worry about now.

What on earth had happened? Doctor Vanilla must have known, or at least had some inkling as to the side effects, so why had he given her those pills? Surely it would be enough for any patient, even if they weren't already suspicious of his motives, to question his authority after what they did? Though perhaps they didn't have the same effect on everyone. That aside, however, Deborah already knew the reason he had given them to her, and the reason she would go back to him for another visit. Despite the sickness, and the pain they caused when she woke up, they had the most incredible effect on her dreams.

Deborah sat upright and closed her eyes as the water washed over her, easing her thumping head. Maybe she could call Doctor Vanilla, get him to explain to her mother that he had prescribed her the pills. Whatever he was up to, she felt sure that he didn't want to see her be taken away from him. He needed something from her, she just knew it, and besides, she would only be asking him to tell the truth...

Deborah's thoughts were interrupted as she heard a siren bellowing down the street. She quickly climbed out of the bath and, kneeling on the toilet, stuck her head out of her bathroom window as far as it would allow. Sure enough an ambulance was turning the corner into her road. No, it couldn't be... But it was. It carefully pulled up outside the entrance to her flat.

"Shit, shit, shit!" Deborah pulled the towel up from the floor and wrapped it around her, not bothering to turn the shower off, and burst from the bathroom. Her mother was standing in the hallway by the door. She turned around, looking startled as Deborah came up behind her, pushing her away angrily.

"How could you? HOW COULD YOU?" she screamed. Deborah gripped her mother's wrist tightly in her hand and dragged her into the bedroom.

Deborah flung open drawers and tugged on some jeans

and a T-shirt, her eyes frantically scanning the floor for her bag.

"You're not the only one who knows how to lie, dear." She said it firmly, though she took a step back away from her daughter and glanced at the door. "You need help, proper professional help. This therapist of yours clearly can't give it to you, and neither can I."

The doorbell rang. They both jumped and stood frozen, staring at each other.

"If you answer that..."

"You need help."

"Mum, I swear, if you answer that..."

Her mother kept her eyes on Deborah and took another step towards the door.

"No!" Deborah pushed hard, her mother fell backwards, hitting her head against the wall with a nauseating crack. Deborah covered her eyes and turned. She didn't dare look back; there wasn't time. She grabbed her bag, then ran into the hall, shoving her feet into some trainers by the door. A weak moan from the bedroom echoed behind her.

"I'm so sorry," she shouted. It came out wrong, like she didn't mean it at all. Deborah flung open the door and ran down. At the main entrance she could see two silhouettes of men through the frosted glass. She wiped her eyes and caught her breath, positioning a smile on her face as best she could before she carefully opened it.

"There you go," she said, cheerfully holding the door open for them. They looked confused, but nodded thanks and stepped past her, making their way immediately up the stairs. Deborah quickly walked down the street, waiting until she had turned the corner before breaking into a run.

After five minutes she stopped, feeling her heart burning in her chest. She hadn't run like that in years, and her lungs felt as though they were on fire. She wiped the drips of sweat from her forehead with the back of her wrist and tasted salt and bile in her mouth as she bent over, hands on knees, head bent down, trying to catch her breath. She was right at the bottom of Clapton Hill.

When she had recovered a little, Deborah began to walk across the bridge. The same sense of uneasiness filled her body as she did so. It was odd. Before she had met Luke there, she had never had a problem with crossing it, even though she hadn't been that way for a while. She certainly knew she didn't have a problem with heights or anything, so why now, every time she was in the area, would this sick sense of dread appear? She shrugged, realising this was the least of her worries, and then turned into a narrow side alley before crouching down with her head in between her knees. What had she done? She felt terrible thinking about her mother lying on her bedroom floor. She hadn't meant to hurt her at all.

Tears poured down Deborah's cheeks as she stuttered out wretched sobs onto the pavement. The situation had got totally out of hand. She reached into her bag, searching for her phone. Perhaps she could call, just to see if she was all right. But her phone wasn't there. In fact there was nothing in the bag apart from several used tissues and her house keys – not that she could go back there for now.

Christ! Luke! She hadn't called him and she'd told him where she lived. If he went round and those ambulance guys were still there – or worse, the police – what would he think of her? Deborah pushed herself up from her knees and wiped her face with her sleeve before walking back out of the alley. There was only one place she could go. Looking up she checked the street she was on and took a deep breath, racking her brains to try and remember which way they had come before. It was unbelievably cold. The snow from the night before had stayed and was sparkling like a duvet of diamonds under the winter sun.

A clatter from the back of the alley echoed behind her. Deborah turned back round with a start and felt a great wave of relief. There was John, round and red-faced in a huge fur coat and wellington boots, huffing and puffing as he dragged a large metal barrel behind him. He noticed her staring at him and stopped, confused, for a split second before he recognised her.

"Deborah?" He let go of the barrel he had been dragging and walked quickly towards her. "Are you all right love? Jesus, it's freezing out, what were you thinking?" He shrugged off his coat and draped it around her shoulders, gently guiding her back down the alleyway to a small arched wooden door in the wall. He ushered her through. Deborah muttered her thanks to him, suddenly exhausted and unable to properly speak.

John led her into a huge kitchen where boxes of rugged-looking vegetables lay on the counter. Large white freezers were lined up at the back of the room, and glinting hooks holding pots and pans hung from long hooks that attached to the ceiling. There was a row of hobs on the far right hand side and several gleaming, silver pots bubbled and hissed upon them. The whole room was wonderfully warm and smelt of sugar, onions and rosemary. John gently guided her through and sat her down on a small plastic chair in the corner. "Wait there," he said, disappearing, returning moments later with a glass of whisky. Deborah smiled and took a large sip before setting the glass on the floor.

"I need to get hold of Luke," she said.

John leant back on the counter. He looked at her cautiously. She could tell he was confused but, unlike his wife, he kept his questions at bay and simply nodded.

"I'll call him right now," he said.

Deborah strained to hear the conversation between them. She heard the words 'exhausted', 'terrible' and 'nervous breakdown' before she decided to give up. It seemed that John was doing most of the talking and from the silences, which were few and far between, that Luke was giving away very little.

When he returned, John announced that Luke was on his way and should arrive within the hour. He then took Deborah through to the bar and sat her at the same table she had been at before. He poured her another whisky and, without asking, he went to the kitchen and returned with a thick, steaming bowl of spicy stew. Deborah thanked him gratefully, feeling a little overwhelmed at the kindness of this man. Even Bingo, who had bounded over from the far corner of the bar, seemed to understand the situation and was now curled warmly around her feet.

About half an hour into Deborah's wait, the door was flung open as Linda returned. Her big orange face crinkled in surprise from underneath a dramatic white fur hat when she spotted Deborah wrapped in her husband's coat by the fire. John immediately intercepted her and pulled her into the kitchen. Deborah could hear muffled conversation which drifted over to her from behind closed doors. She sunk down in the chair and shut her eyes. The day had overwhelmed her and within minutes she drifted off.

The door tinkled again. She felt Bingo's head snap up and he made an inquisitive half-bark in the direction of the noise. The door creaked open and there stood Luke. Bingo immediately leapt up and padded over to him, whining in pleasure as Luke scratched behind his ears. He looked at Deborah and walked over.

"Are you OK? I called you, like, twenty times, and you never picked up. I was about to come over and then my phone rang and it was your number, but then when I answered it, it was this woman on the other end, demanding to know who I was and if I'd seen you – and when I said I didn't know, and why would I be calling you so much if I knew where you where, she got really angry and called me... something like a buffoon, and then hung up."

Luke's eyes were full of concern and Deborah couldn't help but smile. Her mother was definitely all right, that was something at least. She looked down. Luke had his hand on her arm. It felt warm and solid and she felt her stomach flip over as her insides seemed to pinch tight together under his touch.

"I'm so sorry I didn't call," she said. "That pill, it wipes you out. I slept for hours. I didn't wake up until my mother literally shook me out of it." She paused and smiled. "But the dream, the dream was amazing. I could almost control it."

Luke furrowed his brow. "What do you mean?"

"Well, I took the pill and I fell asleep immediately, I guess. But it didn't feel like I was asleep; it didn't feel like a dream. It's hard to explain. Everything was still dream-like, impossible things were happening, but it felt completely real..."

She trailed off and looked at him carefully, trying to work out whether he was accepting this or not. He looked confused but was nodding his head for her to go on. Suddenly the kitchen door creaked and John and Linda practically fell out of it. They had been listening.

"Do you think we can go somewhere more private?" she asked.

Luke shrugged then looked sheepish, his nervous

English gentleman persona reappearing. "Um, we can go back to mine if you like? It's a bit of a trek but my car's just outside."

Deborah nodded, almost too enthusiastically. She then pulled off John's coat and walked over to the bar to return it to him. "Thank you so much for everything," she said. Linda opened her mouth to protest, to demand an explanation. Even John seemed disappointed as he shook his head. "Keep it for now," he said, "and you're welcome." He smiled at her warmly, then nodded at Luke who nodded back and, with his hand resting gently on the small of Deborah's back, he guided her outside.

Luke gestured to a small battered-looking tin can of a car across the street. He opened the passenger door for her and Deborah settled herself into the seat which was covered in a peachy felt material that was worn at the corners. Luke climbed in next to her and they set off jerking down the road as he struggled with the gear stick.

"It'll take us about half an hour," he said. "I live down by the marina – do you know it?" Deborah nodded, surprised. It was one of the wealthiest parts of the city. She had been there rarely but once, a few summers ago, had gone there for an anniversary meal. She screwed her eyes shut and tried to remember the name of the restaurant but could not. She did remember the two of them sitting awkwardly opposite each other, talking in hushed whispers, unsure of what to order or which cutlery to use. When they had left they had both broken out into giddy hysterics and agreed that they were much more of a fish and chips and a can of beer type of couple.

Deborah opened her eyes, smiling, and realised Luke had been waiting for her to answer. "Sorry, yes I know it," she said. "It's pretty posh down that way, isn't it?"

Luke sighed. "I guess so," he replied, not offering any further explanation.

Luke drove slowly, weaving through the traffic. He had the heating turned up full blast. Deborah struggled out of the fur coat as the warmth pummelled into her face from the vents. She looked out of the glass as the marina came into view. "Mind if I open the window?" she asked. Luke shook his head.

Deborah wound it down and stuck her neck out, watching the boats with their crisp white masts bobbing serenely up and down on the water, making a clink and tinkle sound. The sun was still high in the sky, which was a crisp ice blue dotted with orange-tinted clouds. Deborah took a deep breath and smelt the freshness of wet soil and leaves. "It's beautiful here," she said as she turned to Luke and smiled.

"Yes," he replied. "It is."

Luke parked the car, carefully easing it into a space in the car park between a low slung red sports car and a large black 4x4. It looked hugely out of place, as did Luke with his shabby hair, stubble and scruffy clothes. He strode ahead of her, leading the way. They walked right down to the water and along the wooden pier which bobbed up and down under their feet. Deborah shuffled after him, confused.

"I thought we were going to your house," she called to his back.

He stopped and waited for her to catch up. "We are," he said, and pointed forward. "It's right over there."

In front of them, tied up in between two great white yachts, stood his boat. It was an old fishing boat, painted a deep navy blue with white stripes along the edges. 'The Locke' was painted down the side in neat red letters.

"My mother's maiden name," he explained, as he noticed

her looking. "I think it might have been the only time she was truly happy – when she had that name." Deborah nodded, watching him clamber on board before turning around to help her. The boat rocked unevenly as he grabbed her hands and pulled her on. Several thick ropes of different colours lay in coils along the bottom. There were wooden slabs along the sides and middle of the boat which acted as benches to squat on, a tiny door leading down below, and a raised area where the brass coloured steering wheel took pride of place in the centre of the boat.

"So you live here?" Deborah asked.

"Yep," said Luke. "I've been here for a few years now. It suits me, you know, and besides its all I can afford. Do you want to see below?"

He asked her so awkwardly that Deborah blushed, but she nodded and followed him down. The space below was surprisingly large; a booth with navy leather seats and a table was at the back, and there was a counter with a sink and a small hob with cupboards beneath it. A door on the left led to a tiny bathroom with a toilet, another sink and a shower overhead. Towards the front hung a floor length green curtain which Luke pulled back to reveal a double bed on a raised area with shelves either side where several dusty duck ornaments rested, as well as a gold-framed picture of a wide-eyed, raven-haired woman who was clutching a baby to her chest.

"Is that her?" Deborah asked. Luke nodded and stretched over the side of the bed to pick up the frame before handing it to her. The woman's eyes were unbelievably black. Her skin was olive and her face was gently creased around the eyes and mouth. "She's very beautiful," Deborah said, handing it back to him. Luke nodded again silently and turned around.

"Let's have a drink," he said, "and then you need to tell me all about the dream."

They settled into the seats and Luke poured generous portions of red wine into two large mugs, apologising for not having any proper glasses.

"So," he said, "what happened?"

Deborah curled her legs underneath and took a sip of her drink before she began.

"Well, as I said, after I took the pill I went straight to sleep. It was weird because I remember the going to sleep part very clearly. I felt myself being dragged down, through the bed, through the floor, into another world. Then suddenly I was just there, right there in the middle of something. It didn't seem to start; I was just there with everything going on around me." She pressed her head back against the side of the boat, trying to remember.

"I was in a fairground. Everything was black and white, and dull, hazy – just like you said. The air and the ground were damp, and everyone looked miserable. There were people everywhere – on the rides, playing the games, eating candyfloss, going through all the motions – but no one was having a good time, there was no one smiling or laughing. They seemed almost, well, they seemed almost lifeless, I guess."

Deborah paused and this time took a big gulp of wine, letting the warmth of it spread through her chest before she continued. "Well, that's when I realised that I was in charge, that I could control everything. I realised I was dreaming, that I was awake inside myself and, just like that, it was all colourful again. I could hear music. People were laughing and dancing and they all looked familiar but not quite themselves. The people – I knew all of them, people from work, my mother, this girl from the supermarket. They were all there, all lifeless at first, but then as soon as the colour came in, it all seemed real again, and the sky cleared and a big smiley-faced sun appeared in the sky. It seemed so great, on the surface. But I could feel something, like something wasn't right, you know, because I knew that all these people, they weren't really laughing, or having a good time. They weren't really happy because they weren't real... and there was something else there, something watching..." Deborah frowned as she trailed off.

"I'm sorry, Luke, I'm trying to remember it all. I didn't get a chance to write it down and I feel like, I feel like its fading, that I'm forgetting the important bits."

He leant over and took her hand. "It's OK," he said. "Just take your time, OK?"

Deborah nodded and glanced down to where his hand rested on hers before she went on.

"So then this woman came up to me, this huge woman. She was dressed in gypsy skirts, with bangles and jewels dripping from every part of her skin. She had bright red lips and when she spoke they didn't move at all. There was a big white wooden van behind her and she asked me if I wanted my fortune read. I said I did and she turned to the van so I followed her in, up the little white steps, and then she sat me on this pink and gold embroidered cushion inside and looked into this plastic bowl, and I remember thinking, 'I'm controlling this. I should get her to tell me the best fortune ever', but when the gypsy woman looked up her face was melting away. It was terrifying. I knew I had to get away so I ran out and it was pouring with rain and then..."

Deborah stopped and gasped as she remembered. "Then there was this shadow. It was peering out from behind a tent. I ran towards it and it ran away, and then I saw it, saw him, this little boy, and he looked just like..." She stopped again and swallowed hard. Her mouth was dry and she could feel a lump start to rise in her throat. She remembered now how, in her dream, that little boy had looked just like her son, just like Jamie, her perfect boy.

Deborah's forehead was crinkled in pain and she pinched her arm hard to stop herself from crying and went on:

"He looked just like my son. But it wasn't him, I could tell. That's when I stopped feeling like I was in control – because there was something so awful about this shadowy thing. I looked right in his eyes and there was nothing there. He was dragging a huge net behind him as he ran and he was screaming 'I will never grow up, I will NEVER grow up' over and over. And then we saw her..."

Deborah swallowed again. She was shaking. The memory was exhausting her. She looked up at Luke whose face tightened as he tried to smile reassuringly at her.

"It's OK, it's OK," he said reaching up to touch her cheek. "We can stop if you like."

Deborah shook her head. "I need to finish," she said and took a deep breath. "I saw the girl, the golden-haired one, again. She was facing me this time and I absolutely knew her. I did. And she was looking at the boy. I can't begin to describe the look on her face – like all the love and the joy in the whole world had been tangled up in her skin. And then she saw me, and started to run towards me, and as she did the boy began to run towards her. I tried to move, to reach her, but my feet were stuck in the mud. When she saw him, when she saw the boy coming closer, her face suddenly changed and she froze like a statue, she was like a goddess or an angel or something. But she looked so afraid. And then out of nowhere this guy appeared behind her – this scruffy long-haired guy – and he dragged her away. Then the little boy screamed and stamped his feet. The whole world started shaking when he did that. The sky tumbled in on me and I could hear voices screaming my name from the clouds. I was paralysed, rooted to the ground, I couldn't move. The next thing I knew I was back in my bed with my mum shaking me awake.

Deborah sat back, exhausted. It felt as though by telling it she had somehow relived the whole thing. She looked to Luke. His face had paled and he was chewing intensely on his lip.

"When you left me last night," he said quietly, "I was awake for hours. I couldn't sleep I was so worried about what might happen to you. But eventually, at God knows what hour of the morning, I thought sod it. If she's taking the pill I am going to take it, too, and, listen Deborah, I swear I am telling the truth. I dreamt I was at a carnival, too. I remember it so well. It was black and white but somehow sunny. Almost as soon as I arrived this kid grabbed me and dragged me off to the stocks. Then I was trapped and all these other kids were throwing sponges at me. I kind of got used to it and let it happen. It didn't seem to bother me for some reason. But then, Deborah, I saw that lady – that one you described with the gypsy skirts – I saw her pass me by. I remember it because the only thing in colour was coloured was her bright red lips, just like you said..." He stopped and looked up at her. They were now clutching each other's hands, both thinking the same thing but unable to say it.

"We were in the same dream," he finally whispered. Deborah nodded, scarcely able to believe it. "I swear Doctor Vanilla must have had something to do with it," he went on. "The pills – they must have had some weird psychological effect on us or something," Luke said, firmly shaking his head from side to side.

"But why would Doctor Vanilla want us to be in the same dream?"

Luke paused for a long time. "I don't know. All I know is that he wants something from us, and I don't know what it is, and whatever it is I don't think it's going to be good."

Deborah turned her head away; she felt as though it might explode or implode or both. It was ridiculous, impossible. Why would he want some part of her subconscious? It didn't make any sense. "Let's get some air," she said.

They climbed the steep stairs up to the deck and stood in silence for a moment, each trying to gather their thoughts. The sun had now dipped into the sea. The air was laced with a deep chill and the sky had turned a shade of rust, with faint blue scratches slashed across it that looked like rips in its very fabric.

"What do we do, Luke? It's too messed up. I don't understand what's happening to us."

He turned towards her. "I think we need to get into Doctor Vanilla's office," he said. "We need to look at those dream journals and find out whatever it is he writes about us in our sessions."

Deborah stepped closer to him, shivering. "I'm really scared," she said.

"Me too," said Luke.

They looked at each other for a moment and it felt like there was nothing left to say. Luke then roughly pulled her towards him and kissed her hard on the mouth. His lips tasted of salt and wine. She reached up and pulled at the back of his hair with small angry fists. Feeling half mad and half scared, she kissed him back as hard as she could, as if the pain might somehow take the fear away.

CHAPTER 17

GRACE

The sapphire ring

Grace clawed at the sides of the tunnel, trying to fight against the invisible force that dragged her through it. As soon as she had been pulled away, the sickness she had felt and all the pain had completely disappeared. Her head, however, was still swarming with terrifying thoughts and fears. What did it mean? Was Deborah dying? Souls that had been released from their bodies could feel things; they were vulnerable and could be hurt – she knew that. But this had felt different. It was a strange kind of sickness, a repulsion almost, and it had happened so suddenly. She had been fine one minute and then the next thing she knew she had been on the floor. Peter trying to help had only made it worse. In fact, the closer he came the more intense the feeling had become. What could possibly be happening? Nothing had changed, so why would this be happening to her now?

She knew logically that it must be something to do with Deborah. Perhaps her time was running out and her getting ill was somehow Deborah's subconscious telling her to hurry up. But Peter was fine and he'd been on the outside longer than her, so it couldn't be that, or maybe that was not how it worked.

Grace shook her head in the darkness and concentrated hard, trying to dig her heels into the sides. She needed more time, more time to think, to try and figure out what to do. She hoped that somehow Peter had been dragged in after her and tried twisting herself back round to see if, by some miracle, he was following her. She managed to angle her body, wedging her elbows and knees against the sides of the tunnel, and briefly ground to a halt. She turned around to check behind before she was swept off again, but there was no sign of anyone else. She was alone.

Grace grabbed in vain as the threads started to pull at her again. This time she tried to hold on. It was no good; they were slippery to the touch and no matter how hard she tried to cling on her hands simply glided off them as the force carried her onwards. She tried to cover her ears so she didn't hear the passing doors which still chanted mercilessly, their desperate voices screaming in agony as she went by, 'Mine, mine, MINE'. The Roman numerals above each one were the only clues but they became harder to see as she sped up and continued faster and faster, tumbling through the tunnel.

She only began to slow when her door glimmered in the distance. Grace squinted as she moved towards it. It looked a little more worn this time, the wood splintered across the middle, and the padlock had a smattering of rust on its surface. As she approached it she noticed the door right next to it. It looked strangely close to her own. Where the others had all been evenly spaced, these two were almost touching. Grace braced herself as she slowed further, readying herself to be pulled down. She looked at the Roman numerals above her door, and then the other. The numbers above were the same as her own!

She tried to claw her way backwards to check but it was useless trying to fight it. Coming to an abrupt halt outside her door, Grace watched helplessly as the blinding spotlight fell on her door and the lock dropped to the floor. The two hands glowed through the darkness just like before and she took a deep breath as they roughly pulled her down.

Landing with a thud face first onto the ground, Grace lay coughing into the sand before turning onto her back. It seemed later in the day then last time she had visited. The sun hung low in the air and heavy clouds were scattered amongst the sky. It was cooler, too. Last time the heat had been scorching but now there was a breeze and a slight chill in the air. It was as if the place was running out of fuel.

"Well, well." A shadow loomed over her and suddenly the Creature's face was pressed against her own. She pushed him away angrily and stumbled to her feet. He sat down looking bemused.

"There is really no need to be like that," he hissed, and grinned widely. Grace recoiled in horror. His teeth, which before had been flawlessly white, now looked sticky. They stuck out, protruding from The Creature's wide mouth, and a stench of something sour and rotting filled the air.

"Don't be so surprised, silly girl," the Creature continued. "What did you expect – for me to be the same?" He tilted his head back and roared with laughter. "Time waits for no one, you know – not even for time itself." He raised one of his paws and began scratching himself casually behind the ears. His huge claws sparkled strangely in the sun. As he stretched, Grace noticed his fur was a little duller and his ribs were sticking uncomfortably out from his chest.

"You took a while, though," he remarked. "You don't seem to be very good at this, do you?"

Grace felt her face grow hot. A fierce rage bubbled up from nowhere and she ran over to the Creature, ineffectually banging her fists on its huge chest. The Creature seemed bewildered by this but patiently let her tire until she collapsed at his feet, shaking huge, hot sobs of grief and frustration out onto the sand.

"I'm trying my best. How does anyone do any better than this? I don't understand what else I should be doing. I just want to find her," Grace stuttered through her gasps. "How could she do this to me? I miss her so much. Why haven't I found her yet?"

"Well, you're being distracted, aren't you?" he said.

"I don't know what you mean." Grace looked up at him defiantly and brushed the tears from her face. "All I have been doing is looking for her, and if I haven't been doing that then I've been thinking of what to do next time I get a chance."

The Creature snorted and moved away from her. He was limping slightly. Grace felt a wave of guilt wash over her. Of course there had been moments where being with Peter had caused her to momentarily forget, to find happiness without Deborah, but that didn't mean she wasn't trying to find her. She would never give up on Deborah. Without Deborah, there was no point in her at all. Grace felt herself grow angry again as a heat swelled in her belly. Perhaps the Creature was right. All this time she had spent with Peter, talking to him, listening to him as he told her about his body, perhaps it was all one big distraction. Grace swore to herself she would never be so stupid and would never allow herself to be distracted again.

"I'm so sorry, Deborah!" she whispered, her head bent towards the sand. The Creature pricked his ears towards her but said nothing. Grace shook her head resolutely. From now on she would concentrate hard and if she ever saw Deborah in a dream she would make sure that she got to her. It was all she wanted. She was sure it was all Peter wanted, too. To get back to his body surely was more important than anything, than her, than whatever kind of relationship the two of them now had. They needed to put all their energy into finding their bodies and when they did they could be together, all of them, as wholes, as one.

"I'm going to find her, and things will be OK. I just want for us to be together again, to share everything, like we used to."

"Impossible!" The Creature laughed. "Once you have been outside them and they have been without you, it will never be the same. Now really it is just a case of fighting for your own survival, don't you agree?"

Grace looked up at him, her mouth set in a hard line.

"No, I do not agree," she cried. "I don't believe you, and I will find her, and Peter will find his and we will go back inside and then we will be together just as we are supposed to be."

The Creature cocked his head. "Peter," he said. It was not a question; he just repeated the word as if it were foreign to him.

"Just show me the bloody shrubs and let me get on with it, OK?"

"Shrubs," the Creature echoed, tilting his head to the

other side. Grace glared up at him. She couldn't work out whether he was being intentionally frustrating.

"Yes, the shrubs. You know, you tell me to pick one and then I get to go into the dream, like what happened last time, although you made me waste too much time here so I was too late." She felt sure it had been his fault that the reason she had missed Deborah last time was because he had kept her for too long, with his prancing about and his showing off.

The air darkened a little and Grace looked up. In the distance silvery flickers of light were weaving in and out of the clouds like a school of fish darting through the sky. Fish. She furrowed her brow. There was something important about fish...

Glancing over to the Creature, Grace realised he had now stretched himself out on the ground. He had become weary and blinked his eyes slowly, looking at her as he spoke.

"Oh no, little lady," he purred. His eyes were clouded over and he seemed to be speaking more to himself. "I don't have any bearing on what you do. I am very tired now."

He rested his head on his paws and closed his eyes before rolling away from her onto his side.

Grace ran over to him. "NO!" she shouted into his ear, but the Creature had already fallen into a deep sleep. Grace leant against his side, feeling the sobs ache in the back of her throat once again. She looked around. There was nothing, just miles of desert and an ever-darkening sky. The clouds were weaving together now, almost blocking out the light, but through a gap a lone ray of sunshine poked its way through. It shone directly onto the Creature's paws and Grace saw them sparkle again as the light caught something in the fur around his paws before it faded away again. She tugged at it. The hair was matted and coarse.

Grace gasped. He had three rings on the front three claws of his paw. One was a thin gold band which was so shiny Grace could make out the reflection of her own face as she peered over it. The second one was a raised sapphire set on a silver band, and the third was a circle of rubies which glowed a deep crimson in colour.

The Creature languidly opened one of his eyes. "Pick one," he whispered, then let out a gentle sigh before his huge black tongue lolled out from the side of his mouth and he was once again fast asleep.

Grace studied the rings carefully. She tried to think what each one might mean. So there was a choice. She was in control of this. Or was she? She didn't even know if it was all some joke, whether her choice made any difference at all, or was it all predetermined somehow, anyway. Had she picked wrong last time? Is that why she had ended up behind in time? Or was it just the way it was always going to be? Grace sat back on the sand and rested her chin in her hands. She should make her decision quickly, she knew that. "Think of Deborah," she whispered to herself and shut her eyes. She leant back against the Creature's warm fur and let herself be pushed up and down in time with his breathing. She tried to think of Deborah's favourite things. One of the rings looked just like Deborah's wedding ring. But was that a symbol of good things or bad? Deborah had loved Jack more than anything but then their relationship had caused so much pain. If she chose it would she be choosing a door to the past and therefore be too late again? Grace moaned and pressed her fingertips into her temples. Why was it this hard? Was she just a terrible soul for not knowing? She shook her head and bent forwards, studying the rings harder. There was something about the sapphire one, something in the back of her mind that made her feel like she had seen it before. She couldn't put her finger on it, but time was running out and perhaps she didn't have to know why.

Glancing up, Grace saw night had closed in around her. The stars shivered vulnerably as if they were loose, as if at any minute they might drop from their places and come crashing down to earth. *At least I won't be going backwards,* she thought as she tugged at the sapphire ring and pulled it from The Creature's claw. It snapped off with a sickening crack as she did so. The Creature's howl followed her through to the next place as her surroundings immediately disappeared. She was sucked down through the earth, into darkness. Down and down she went, further and further, and then she fell through a ceiling and onto the floor.

She was in a corridor, and she recognised it immediately. It was Deborah's school. The lockers towered above her in neat rows and the strip lighting of the ceiling seemed impossibly far away. Grace shivered. The whole place was cold, completely isolated and creepily silent. She looked down and realised she was completely naked again. She felt a faint pull in her stomach.

Where are you?

A light went on overhead, then all the lights away from her, illuminating the giant corridor bit by bit, until they hit upon a figure standing alone and confused at the other end. *Deborah!* Grace tried to move towards her but she was so far away. She looked down at herself. Her movement was odd – she was bent and scuttling. *I'm not me!* She had taken on the form of something else. She didn't feel she was in her own skin anymore; she felt lighter, smaller, more graceful somehow. Peter had told her about this, about how sometimes you would take on the form of something else, even though you would look completely normal in your own eyes. Her stomach tugged again, making her cry out.

"Deborah, Deborah. Please!"

Her voice barely made a noise. Deborah was so far away, there was no way she could hear her. Nevertheless, Grace carried on relentlessly screaming and crawling towards her, every fibre of her body willing her forward.

From nowhere a shadow appeared beside her. It was a strange sort of energy, dark and flickering, in the vague shape of a man. It seemed to be sucking away at everything around it and Grace couldn't tell if it was good or bad, but it moved towards her and she felt herself being swooped away. She plummeted backwards and landed right back where she started.

"NO!" she screamed, turning around, searching desperately for something that might help her. There were two double doors behind her and one suddenly creaked open. Grace stopped and stared as a beautiful golden-haired boy poked his head around the corner and grinned at her slyly before disappearing again.

No. It could not be. Grace pressed her tongue to the roof of her mouth and swallowed hard. It was him! It was Jamie. She turned back to call out to Deborah, but she had disappeared. All that remained was the strange shadowy man slowly blurring everything and sucking it away as he moved down the corridor towards her. Deborah must have moved on.

Grace turned back towards the doors. Jamie! Surely Deborah would go towards Jamie? Grace ran as fast as she could and pushed the doors open. As they closed behind her she heard the faint echoing sounds of a school bell ringing.

Grace ran. She was herself again now. She ran into a beautiful green field and looked up at the sky. It was crystal clear with the sun blazing in a perfect tangerine sphere in the centre. Wild poppies pushed through the long sweet-smelling grass and she could hear the sounds of a shallow stream trickling gently somewhere on her left. Tall pine trees surrounded the field and at the bottom was a rusting red gate. Grace knew immediately where she was, at least what Deborah's dream was trying to recreate. It was back in Scotland, where they used to live.

Hearing children's laughter, Grace ran towards it and twisted her head left and right scanning for the boy as she continued through the field. Her heart was pounding, thud, thud, thud. She was overcome with a longing to hold him in her arms and stroke his hair. She would hug him and remind him of that wonderful time where she and him had both been inside Deborah together.

But it's not him. He's not real. He had not come back to life; he was just a presence in Deborah's mind. Her heart still pounded nonetheless, thud, thud, thud.

Grace glanced down at the tattoo of his delicate face on her calf and smiled. Even if she couldn't bring him back for Deborah it was good to know there was still a part of him alive in her dreams.

A fevered giggle echoed through the grass again. Grace came to the foot of an oak tree which was covered in soft green moss. It had a solid trunk and a line of ants were carefully marching out of a gap in the bark half way up. The branches spread out thick and sturdy at first, then multiplied infinitely twisting like a helter skelter up towards the sky. The boy was there. He was sitting on a low branch and had on a blue and white checked shirt and khaki shorts which were streaked with grass stains. On his feet were brown leather shoes and black socks which were pulled up to his calves, revealing two pink knees which were muddy and scraped and raw. He was holding what looked like an old fishing net, and he was beckoning her to come towards him with that same sly grin on his face.

Grace felt a pull between her shoulders, as though someone had attached an anchor to them and was dragging her backwards. She stepped back sharply, keeping her eyes on the boy who was now looking behind her, his little fist still clutched around the net. His eyes narrowed slightly, removing something from the innocence of his angelic face. Suddenly Grace knew. *She's here! Deborah's here!*

Not daring to believe it, slowly she turned round. She was too late. As she turned, Grace felt herself being propelled forward and she lurched past the tree. She turned just in time to see the little boy staring after her with a devastated look on his face. She saw him drop the net to the ground before he blurred into the distance. Facing forwards again with barely time to scream, an object rose up ahead of her and she slammed violently into the side of a huge white marquee.

Grace tried to scramble upwards, but the ground was soaked and she slipped about in the mud. Catching her breath, she rubbed her ribs, slightly winded by the fall. The entire scene had changed. Rain tipped from the sky in sheets. She looked down at her now bare feet, and saw she was wearing a thin grey dress that was streaked with mud. Grace pulled herself upright, using the ropes of the marquee to steady her. She looked at her hand and breathed a sigh of relief. On her middle finger was the sapphire ring. This was a comfort somehow. She was still in a dream; all was not lost.

Carefully she tiptoed round the corner and peered out. There were stalls everywhere. All were empty, and there was no sign of anyone else. At least fifty or so caravans stood to the left, all with their doors shut and lights off. There were bumper cars, a tea cup ride and a merry go round all next to one another in a neat row, and towering over this was a huge roller coaster whose carriages together made the shape of a giant bright green snake.

Grace heard a gentle humming behind her and turned round. There was a white caravan, parked away from the others, with a light glowing from its window. She gathered up the hem of her dress, trying to stop it from dragging through the puddles, and walked towards it. When she got to the front she climbed up the small wooden steps that led to the door, and then knocked.

There was a tinkle and a rustling sound as someone moved inside. The door was pushed open and a woman with fierce lime green eyes and flame red hair which flowed almost to her hips stood before her. She wore long flowing skirts and had large hoops dangling from her ears.

"Yes?" She was impatient.

Grace stared at her, completely at a loss of what to say.

The woman arched an eyebrow and sighed. "I'm trying to get ready here". She then looked Grace up and down. "Why aren't you getting ready? You know the brief, and I'm quite sure this..." She wiggled her finger up and down "...wasn't it."

"Um. I'm sorry. I couldn't find my costume." Grace decided that playing along was probably the easiest thing to do. The woman looked as if she wouldn't take any nonsense and Grace didn't want to have to explain to her that, as far as she could tell, she was a figment of somebody's imagination.

The woman sighed and ushered her inside. The space was impossibly huge. A vast gold decorative mirror which stood at the back was at least twice the height of the woman and was as wide as it was tall. On either side of this were two large chests of drawers which were half pulled open, and scarves in every colour imaginable poked out. On the tops of the chests were various pots of creams and pallets of paints with different-sized brushes resting on them. The woman left Grace by the door and rushed over to these, picking up a crumpled piece of paper which lay next to a large pot of black paste.

"What did you say your name was, dear?" she said, studying the piece of paper carefully.

Grace tried to think fast. She needed to pick someone Deborah would dream about, but who? She was quite sure this woman wouldn't understand if she explained who she was, and something told her playing along was the right thing to do. But Deborah had so few people in her life. Who would she possibly dream about? Her mother? Friends? People from her old job?

"Uh, Jo Jo," she said hopefully.

The woman's eyes scanned down as she muttered to herself. Then she looked up, smiling warmly.

"Ahh yes, here we are. Nice to meet you, Jo Jo. I'm Madame Mystic!" She said it with a grand fling of her arm and pirouetted around, ending the spectacle with a flamboyant curtsey. She then pulled Grace forward to the mirror. "Well, let's see. First what we need is to get you made up."

She handed Grace a sponge before taking one herself and dipping it in the black paste. She then wiped it quickly over her face, carefully avoiding her lips. Grace stared at her open-mouthed. She couldn't believe what she was seeing as the woman applied the paste all over herself, first her face, then arms and neck, slowly working her way down towards her feet. What was happening, well, it was impossible – she was colouring herself out!

"Come on, come on," she jostled Grace impatiently. "Really we don't have time for this." Grace took a deep breath. Looking in the mirror she carefully wiped the paste onto her own face, gasping in wonder as her own image also began to change. She, too, was changing to black and white, but as she applied the paste to her face all her features began to alter. Her cheekbones shifted higher, her eyes became slightly larger, and her lips plumped up into a sulky and seductive pout. The reflection in the mirror was no longer her, but exactly like Jo Jo from Deborah's work.

Grace studied herself in the mirror and smiled at her new reflection before she noticed Madame Mystic staring at her curiously. Vanity seemed an odd attribute for one to have in a dream, so Grace quickly stopped herself and turned away.

"What's next?" she asked.

Madame Mystic looked aggrieved again. "Really, child, haven't you seen the scripts? Haven't you learnt your lines? Really you cannot mess this up; this is my biggest part yet! Go back to your caravan at once and sort yourself out. We don't have long. She'll be here soon."

With that she began to usher Grace out of the van, who almost tripped down the steps as she found herself now wearing a pair of huge four-inch heels.

"Why are your lips like that?" Grace asked as she turned back round to face her.

"I'm to be noticed, of course!" The door was then abruptly slammed shut.

Grace turned around. The carnival grounds were still deserted, though faint flickers from behind caravan doors were now glowing dimly in the light and there was a tension in the air. The rain had ceased and the sun suddenly popped out from behind the clouds to applaud it. "Good show! Do that again later and you'll be a hit! Remember you're the final curtain," it called with a cartoon mouth. The rain took a sweeping bow, drenching both the land and Grace once again before it was chased from the sky. The sun then began to shine powerfully and the soil beneath her heaved and cracked as it slowly began to dry.

"What the hell is going on?" Grace muttered to herself. She twisted and turned, scanning the land for any sign of Deborah. Her hands were shaking and her head felt light. "Oh no!" she cried. The feeling was coming again. Deborah was obviously waking up. *No, I'm not ready. I haven't found her. Please!*

Grace braced herself, knowing there was no escaping it. She took one last look at her fading surroundings, trying to etch every detail she could into her mind, and then, just like that, the dream was over.

CHAPTER 18

DEBORAH

The truth about Luke

Deborah moaned and rolled over. She was stiff, her bones ached and her mouth felt dry. She could hear the sounds of water slapping carelessly against wood, the faint jingle of masts blowing in the wind and birds squawking restlessly overhead. She was freezing cold and tangled in a rough, grey blanket which scratched her bare skin and was not long enough to cover her legs. A similar groan escaped from under the blanket next to her and Deborah looked around. It was Luke. There he was, eyes closed with his hair perfectly ruffled around his face. His mouth was set in a hard line and the faintest hint of a frown crinkled on his forehead. One hand was strewn across his chest and the other was clasped tight around a bottle of rum. His skin was creased and shadowy and he looked angry as he slept.

Deborah looked up at the sky. It was a cloudless day and the sun streamed down upon them both. She squinted in the light and swallowed, easing her head from side to side and trying not to let the hangover take over. She needed to concentrate. She carefully eased herself upright, so as not to wake him, and tried to crawl away on her knees, spacing out her weight as evenly as she could and trying not to rock the boat. The blanket was still entwined around her foot however, and she pulled it off him as she moved away.

"Hey!" he cried angrily, sitting upright. He then checked himself as he saw her, on her hands and knees, her hair knotted over her startled face and her neck twisted around towards him. He raised his eyebrows and looked bemused at her position.

"Going somewhere?" he asked as he leant back on his elbows and grinned.

Deborah shook her head and wished that the base of the boat would suddenly give way and she could simply sink down to the bottom of the sea and wait there until the humiliation had passed. She was very aware that she must look more than a little ridiculous as she appeared to be trying to crawl away in nothing more than a T-shirt and not very flattering pants.

"Sorry. I just didn't want to wake you," she replied, pulling the blanket around her thighs and feeling her face go bright red.

Luke continued to look amused while tugging his hand through his hair.

"Jesus, it's cold up here," he said, getting up. "I've got some coffee downstairs. Want some?"

Deborah nodded. He seemed totally at ease, as if the events of last night had been perfectly natural. Deborah struggled to remember how it had all happened. She saw her jeans slung over the bow of the boat, dangling dangerously close to the water. She got up and walked unsteadily over to them, sitting back down to tug them on.

"Are you coming down then?" Luke called to her. He didn't wait for her to reply as he started making his way down but he looked over and winked at her just before his head disappeared below. He still seemed a little drunk. Deborah shrugged. "Just go with it," she muttered to herself, trying to ignore the fact that it felt as though her heart might beat right out of its chest. She then followed him down.

It wasn't until she had squeezed herself into the booth that Deborah noticed. He had a scar too. Deborah shook her head in wonder. "Luke?"

He turned to her, smiling. "Luke, where did you get the mark on your stomach?" He looked down and touched it self-consciously.

"To be honest I can't really remember. I just had it when I woke up after, well, you know..." He trailed off and looked at her uncertainly. "I noticed you had a bandage on your stomach too – I didn't want to say anything, didn't feel right in the heat of the moment, you know?" He smiled awkwardly. "How did you get yours?"

She looked at him, frowning. "Well, I woke up with mine too, but I just assumed it was part of, part of..." Deborah frowned deeper and shook her head. The cold of the night must have got to her, because now she felt she couldn't remember properly when it was that she had first noticed it. "It doesn't matter," she said.

Luke set about making the coffee and she watched him in silence. He remained barefoot, but had pulled on jeans and a bottle green, thick knitted jumper which suited the colour of his skin. Deborah found herself nervous at how

216

attractive she found him. For a moment she let herself forget about everything else and pretended that this was their life, that they were simply a normal couple who lived on a boat and drank coffee. She realised how much she wished that were true as Luke put a yellow mug in front of her and smiled. She leant forward to smell the aroma and feel the warmth of the steam on her face.

"There's more if you want it," he said.

She nodded her thanks and took a huge gulp, wincing as it scalded her tongue before setting the mug down.

"Are you hungry?" he asked.

His question made her realise just how much, and she nodded again, feeling strangely tongue-tied whenever he spoke. Luke turned and began rummaging in the cupboards for something to eat, pulling out a thickly sliced brown loaf, and then some butter from the fridge. He then put two eggs in a pan and began to boil them up. He gave both to Deborah before helping himself to some bread. He had cooked them perfectly and she tore off ragged crusts before dipping them in, watching in pleasure as the bright yolk dripped over the sides of the shell.

They ate in silence, and when they were finished Luke cleared the plates away and washed them, leaving them to dry on a little wooden rack by the sink. He then sat down next to her.

"I didn't dream," he said.

"Huh?" Deborah had been miles away, once again settled into a fantasy about how nice it would be if this were her real life.

"I didn't dream," he repeated, "or at least if I did I can't remember it." He looked frustrated and deep creases appeared in his forehead as he frowned. "I always remember them. I don't get it. Did you?"

"No," replied Deborah, surprised as she realised that she also hadn't. Luke leant his head back and closed his eyes. It all seemed to be getting to him today. Deborah shyly leant over and touched his hand, relieved when he didn't flinch or pull away.

"Let's not worry about it too much now, OK?" she said. There was so much that neither of them could work out. Not having dreamt was the least of their problems. "What we need to do is to figure out a plan, a way of getting into Doctor Vanilla's office without being caught," she said.

Luke leant back, resting his head against the leather of the seat, and leisurely poured himself another coffee from the pot. "I don't think that's going to be that much of a problem," he replied.

"What do you mean?"

Luke got up without answering and disappeared into the back of the boat. She heard a draw opening and a faint rustle and then a clinking sound as he reappeared with a key dangling in between his forefinger and thumb.

"Is that...?" Deborah trailed off. Surely it couldn't be what she thought it was but Luke was nodding eagerly, with a mischievous glint in his eye.

"Nicking stuff is about the only useful thing I learnt when I was in..." He suddenly checked himself and put his hand over his mouth. The mischievous grin had disappeared, replaced by a look of alarm. He tried to stammer something else out, some alternative to save himself from the slip up, but it was too late.

"When you were in where?"

Deborah looked at him carefully; she was once again reminded of how little she really knew about this man – none of the normal things anyway, the things that you would first ask when getting to know a person, like what they did for a job or when their birthday was or what their hobbies were. Those were the basics, the normal things to ask at the start. But with Luke – well, she didn't even know his last name. What she did know was that they were somehow connected through their dreams, and it seemed as though fate had brought them together in some way. But that didn't mean she had to trust him. She felt herself prickle and a knot of nerves formed in her stomach.

"When you were in where?" she repeated firmly.

Luke looked at her and when it became apparent she was not going to let it drop he pushed his head back and let out a resigned sigh.

"When I was in jail," he replied.

Deborah felt herself stiffen. It was shocking to hear, even though she had been half expecting the answer. She hunched up against the back of the seat, immediately fearing the worst. Had he killed someone? Had he even been released? Perhaps he was a psychotic mass murderer on the run!

"Please, Deborah," Luke implored as he saw her reaction. "You don't understand. Hear me out, OK? I know it's not good, and I should have told you all about this way before but, well, so much strange stuff has gone on between us, I just didn't feel like there was a good time. I mean we know nothing about each other, and then all this crazy dream stuff happened, but I promise I'll tell you everything, right now. I won't hold anything back, and then if you want, perhaps you can tell me about you, then we'll know everything there is to know, and if you feel like you can't take it then you can leave."

He dropped his hands to his sides and took a step towards her. "At least let's give each other a chance. I feel like we owe each other that if nothing else, right?" He gave her another imploring look. He cleared his throat, reaching up to tug at the neck of his jumper as if he were suddenly finding it difficult to breathe.

"God, this is all so hard," he muttered. He seemed to take her silence as a rejection. "Go then, if you want," he sighed.

Deborah looked him up and down. Despite all her instincts telling her to leave, she felt as though he at least deserved for her to stay and hear him out. Besides, it wasn't as if her track record was flawless of late, anyway. If he'd wanted to harm her he could have done it already, she reasoned, and besides, there was now too much at stake just to walk away.

"Tell me everything. Don't leave anything out," she said after another moment's pause. She patted the space next to her and let Luke slide in.

He talked first and Deborah listened without saying anything. She listened to him explain how he grew up, what had happened to his parents, and his mum becoming sick. She listened to how he had discovered his mother's affair, coming home from school one day and not understanding why this strange man was in his father's bed.

Then came the screaming matches between his parents, which eventually turned into long and desperate silences that culminated in his father leaving. Luke told her how afterwards the man his mother was having an affair with had moved in, and that it only took a few months before he had started to get drunk and violent.

He described how the man had got tired of his mother being sick all day, got bored with her and her 'weakness' as he called it, how Luke had listened to them fighting, and how the fights got worse and worse until one day the man had pushed his mother down the stairs. She had broken her back and never walked again.

The man left then and never came back. After a while of struggling to get by, some people came and took his mother away because she was too sick and frail and crippled and useless to care for him any more, and he was too young and helpless and scared and weak to care for her.

That's when he was taken to live with John and Linda. They saved him and loved him and treated him well. But it wasn't enough to stop his desire for revenge. When he was old enough Luke had searched for the man and when he found him he beat him. He beat him as hard as he could, and would have killed him if someone hadn't pulled him off.

When he got arrested he couldn't bring himself to tell John and Linda, so he hadn't contacted them until he got out. He'd got a year and served eight months; it could have been worse really. He'd kept being in jail a secret from everyone he knew. He thought it would be best for them and him, and that when he got out he could go back to his old life without anyone knowing what he'd done.

It was only when he got out and tried to go back to his old life that he found that his mum had passed away. He had missed the funeral. So, consumed with guilt and fear that the truth would come out, he kept away from everyone he loved, and with no one to love he had decided to end his own life. He didn't want to say how he had tried – he didn't want to remember. He'd woken up in the hospital so utterly scared and alone but something in him had made him want to try and get better. That's when he had found Doctor Vanilla. That's when he had met her.

When Luke had finished he leant back, closed his eyes and let out a deep sigh.

"I've never told anyone that. Well, not all at once anyway," he said, keeping his eyes shut. "I understand if you want to leave, and if you never want to speak to me again. I don't deserve anyone's friendship or sympathy and I'm sorry I didn't tell you all this before. But please know this: I will spend my whole life trying to make up for what I did, and I promise I will never, ever hurt you."

Deborah felt her head grow hot and heavy. She understood what it was like for a parent to leave. She understood what it was like to be trapped in a place with no way out. She understood what it was like to feel so angry and so vengeful that you ended up hurting or isolating yourself from everyone around you.

But still, he had beaten a man and tried to kill him. How could she be sure he wouldn't fly off the handle and do it again? She knew it was wrong. She knew she should leave him. She'd had enough of violent, angry people in her life, and it seemed after what she had done to her mother yesterday that perhaps she was becoming one, too.

Deborah looked at Luke who was staring back at her. In that moment she knew that if she didn't get up and walk away right then, no matter how hard they tried, the two of them together would never work, and that they would eventually destroy one another, bit by bit. They were both wrecks – messed up, sad little wrecks – and they couldn't help each other. She knew that she should stand up and get out and never look back.

But she did not do this. She was too far in now and she wasn't strong enough to go. So instead she told him her story – about the death of her son, her husband's violence and the sadness that consumed them both. Luke listened without saying a word.

When she had finished he leant over and held her face and whispered, "I'm so sorry," over and over again as if it had been all his fault. Deborah said nothing but allowed herself to fall into the embrace. After a while they were both silent and they stayed in each other's arms, gently rocking up and down in time with the water beneath them, until Deborah gently uncurled his fist and took the key which he had been holding all the while in his hand.

"So is this what I think it is?" she asked.

Luke nodded. "I got it the day I saw you in his office, the day you came out and told me not to tell Doctor Vanilla anything about you. There was something about the way you looked, like you were afraid almost. And I already had my suspicions, of course, so I decided to try and get his key. It wasn't difficult. He is always so engrossed in the journals, sometimes I think I could scream or set myself on fire and he wouldn't even bother to look up. It was just right there on his desk, and when he marched out with my journal I took it. He was too excited when he came back to notice anything."

Deborah frowned. "But surely he'll have noticed when he left at the end of the day."

"Not likely. When I left I went and made a copy at that key cutter's down the street, and then I came back. I pretended I had remembered something about my dream that I thought was important. He was so thrilled with it I'm sure he didn't suspect a thing, and I slipped the key back on his desk right where he'd left it. It was only gone for about half an hour at the most. There's no way he knew."

Deborah smiled at him and nodded. Her stomach was bubbling with nerves. This was it; they were finally going to find out what it was all about!

"So we'll go tonight?" she asked.

Luke nodded. "I'm game if you are."

She was.

CHAPTER 19

GRACE
The wicked boy

Grace threw up violently almost as soon as she opened her eyes. She groped along the floor, coughing and spluttering, until her hand found the leg of a chair. She clutched onto this, breathing heavily, and felt a strange coolness on her thigh. A bottle of water rested against it. She snatched at it, unscrewed the lid, and quickly gulped the water down, which almost immediately made her vomit again. This routine continued until the bottle was empty and, leaning back against the leg of the chair, her eyes rolled up towards the ceiling. She was back, back in the real world, back in the tattoo parlour where things were solid and actual, where sketchy demons snarled down at her from the walls.

"Oh, Grace." The sound of Peter's voice made her turn

towards the corner. She saw him in a watery outline as her eyes filled with tears.

"Roll the water back over to me and I'll fill it up," he said.

Grace did as she was told and pushed the bottle towards him. He picked it up from the ground, filled it, and then rolled it back to her. She drank it in small sips in silence, kneeling and bent with the floor scratching her knees. Finally her stomach began to settle.

Peter was crouching in the corner, looking at her with a wide-eyed, unblinking stare. His face was desperately sad, even though she could tell he was trying to smile. Grace wanted to touch him immediately, to make him feel better.

"Come over here," she called, and patted the space beside her. To her surprise he shook his head.

"I can't." His voice trembled as he swallowed hard. "God, I want to, I want to so much, but I can't."

Grace took another sip from the water bottle and stared at him. "What do you mean?"

She still felt weary from the journey and her head was throbbing. Squinting at him, she tried to work out his expression. Suddenly she had a thought and quickly reached up to touch her face to feel for cuts or scars. Grace looked around the room, twisting herself this way and that before spotting a small hand mirror which lay on the table in front of her. She stumbled over to it, her legs almost giving way with the effort, before clutching it to her chest, too terrified to look at herself. She must have gone back to being all scarred and deformed and ugly again. That's why he didn't want to come near her – because he was repulsed by her.

Grace felt a sickening lump form in her throat as slowly she brought the mirror up to her face and squinted at her reflection. No. She was fine. She looked no different – a little paler perhaps. Her eyes were still bright and her hair still flowed down in perfect golden waves around her shoulders.

Grace turned back towards him and stepped forward.

"NO!" he yelled, pushing himself back into the corner. He sounded savage and terrified. His eyes were bulging out of his head and his whole body was tense, all coiled up with fear.

"You have to stay away from me!" he yelled at her again.

Grace felt a hot lump appear in her throat. Why was he being like this? Peter reached out his hand to her and then withdrew it quickly.

"You stay where you are, OK?" he said this more gently, his voice quiet and firm.

Perhaps he's gone mad, she thought. P*erhaps that's what it does to you eventually, and you just give in and go insane.*

"It's me," he said, slumping to the ground when he was sure she would stay where she was. "I'm what is making you dizzy. I'm what is making you sick. And you do the same to me. We can't touch each other anymore."

Grace stayed still. "I don't understand," she said.

Peter gestured for her to sit down, so she did, cross-legged on the floor. He mimicked her position, and leant forwards as close as he dared while ensuring that no part of them would touch.

"I realised it as you were being pulled away," he said softly. "The reason you were getting all dizzy before, it was because of me. Something is happening with our bodies. They're doing something wrong and this is our way of knowing." He paused, battling to hold himself together before his face crumpled in anguish. "I don't think they are supposed to be together after all."

Grace struggled to understand what he was saying. She was desperate to reach out to him, to hold him or shake him or something. Really she wanted to show him how much she cared, how everything would be all right. But he looked so distressed, hunched and shaking in his corner, and she didn't know what to do.

After a while he stopped and looked up at her.

"I'm so sorry," he said, taking a deep breath, trying to get himself together. "This isn't helping either of us. How are you? How are you feeling?"

Grace shrugged and got up, watching crossly as he immediately tensed when she made signs of moving. "I'm OK. I feel a bit tired, but I'm fine. Look, Peter, you're going to have to explain this better for me, OK? What are you saying? That if we come near each other we'll get sick?" It seemed ridiculous. Their bodies had already been together. They had been interacting in a way for some time now. Why would they suddenly be repulsed by each other? It didn't make any sense.

Peter sat upright and leant his head back against the wall. "Essentially, yes," he said. "I figured it out as you went into the dream, that every time you'd gotten dizzy was when I had come near you, and when I backed off, you were fine again."

He sighed and began kneading his fingers into the floor. Then while you were away I thought about it, and I realised that it can only mean one thing. And that's that our bodies aren't meant to be together, so it's having a knock on effect with us – almost like they are trying to warn us, you know, that it can't work out? I guess it makes sense if you think about it. They both tried to kill themselves. They can't exactly be great for each other, can they?"

Grace shook her head incredulously, refusing to believe it. "But that's not what we decided, Peter. We said that we were intertwined, that our bodies somehow needed each other, and that's why we were brought together. We can't not touch each other! You're being ridiculous. We need to stay together, and our bodies need us to stay together. It's our only chance. It's why we feel the way we do about each other, which is why we... were together."

Grace moved further away from him, feeling tears prickle behind her eyes. She felt sick; she would never have been with him in that way if she hadn't been sure. She had been so certain that it was the right thing to do, that it would be all right because their bodies were also meant to be together. If they weren't, if that's not what was supposed to happen, then they had just made everything more confused. It made everything harder; it made everything worse.

She looked at Peter, who was staring back at her helplessly, and her heart drooped a little. Her stupid human heart. She hadn't asked for it, and now it was working against her, against her and Deborah both! She couldn't believe it. She wouldn't.

"Maybe I'm just sick?" Grace said. "I could just be sick, Peter. I mean, come on, just because I got dizzy a couple of times when you came near me, it could just be a coincidence. It's probably just an after effect of what happened to me in the shop or something – right?" She stepped towards him. "Right?" Grace repeated.

He looked up at her and shook his head. "Really, Grace, don't move, OK."

She took another step.

"Grace, I'm being serious now. Just stay where you are, OK?"

He looked afraid, but she wouldn't listen. She took a massive lunge towards him with her arms outstretched. She would touch him, and everything would be fine, she just knew it. She felt her hands clutch the back of his head and their bodies slid together as she pressed into him hard. Grace ignored the heat in her head, that fuzzy pain that started at the front of her temples as soon as she had got near him. It would pass; it was just a coincidence. She tried to keep breathing, steadying herself as her stomach heaved and tipped so all the acid rose to her throat. It was not unbearable. It was just the after-effects of coming out of the dream, that was all. It wasn't him. There was no way it could be him! Peter clawed at her back, struggling at first but then he, too, gave in to the embrace.

"It's fine, it's fine, it's fine," Grace repeated, trying to ignore the pain and the fact that the room was starting to close in around her. "It's fine, isn't it, Peter?"

She looked down at him and screamed.

He had turned a deathly shade of white and from the corners of each of his eyes two gooey trails of blood slid down the sides of his face, smearing across his cheeks where she'd pressed him to her chest. Grace scrambled away from him. The room around her was a whirlwind. She tried to clutch the chair but knocked it over as she crashed into the floor. Her head was pounding and she could barely see as she retched again and again and again.

"I'm so sorry. I'm so sorry," she gasped. "Peter, Peter! Please, are you OK? Say something!"

Grace glanced over at him. Peter looked awkward and lifeless as if his head had somehow been dislocated and then re-attached at a funny angle. His eyes were closed and his skin shone with beads of sweat. The blood was smudged across his face in crimson stripes. Grace looked down and saw that she was also covered in it. She wiped her hands on the sides of her dress. Bending her forehead to the floor she sobbed into the ground, and felt utterly helpless and utterly alone.

"I've killed him. I've killed him!" she wept, and banged her fists into the floor.

Peter moaned from the corner and Grace snapped her head round, immediately forgetting her own pain. She dragged herself to her knees and watched as he slowly opened his eyes.

"Peter. God, Peter. Thank God!"

Clambering to her feet as quickly as she could, Grace filled the water bottle at the sink before rolling it carefully towards him. It clumped uselessly into his arm as he stared up at the ceiling. His mouth opened and closed like a fish on land as he gulped in the air and struggled to speak.

"I..." His fingers closed around the bottle and he attempted to heave himself upright. He unscrewed the cap slowly and with a shaky hand he poured some into his mouth and then over his head. His eyes had stopped bleeding and the water washed the remains of the blood from his face. He looked at Grace who looked back at him anxiously.

"I told you so," he said, and drew his face into a wry smile.

Grace burst into tears again and began to apologise again and again. She only stopped when Peter yelled, "Enough!" at the top of his voice and began to laugh.

After they had rested a while, Grace went to get them some food while Peter cleaned up. She returned to find him sitting upright on the wooden chair with the tattoo pen clasped in his hand. She tossed him an apple and a hunk of bread, then eyed him suspiciously.

"What have you got that out again for?" she asked.

"For your dream, of course. You still haven't told me what it was about."

Grace propped herself up against the leather bench,

getting as close to Peter as she dared. She had completely forgotten about the dream. It wasn't surprising really, considering what they had been through, but when she thought back to what had happened she realised just how important it could be.

"Well," she said, swinging her legs over the side of the bench. "Where do I start?"

She started from the beginning, telling Peter of the Creature and how he had aged in front of her. She then explained about the dream with the field and the little boy, pointing to the tattoo of his face on her leg as she spoke. It was just like him. He had been there, she was sure of it, and he had been going to lead the way to Deborah! But then she had been flung forwards into the carnival place. Peter listened intently to this part, jotting down details and making little sketches in a little notepad he had pulled from his pocket.

"It was like they were in a play or something," Grace explained. "I can't really understand it, but it was like they were rehearsing for something, but there was no sign of Deborah anywhere. I didn't get that feeling – you know, the feeling like she might be there – like not even a little bit. It felt like I wasn't in the right place, or that I was in the right place but just at the wrong time."

She sighed and smiled at him. "Sorry, this probably doesn't make any sense. But you know, you know when before I told you about that dream where I was too late? It was almost like the opposite of that, like I'd come too soon, like I was in the future somehow. Do you think that's possible at all?"

Grace looked down at him and bit her lip. Regardless of all the mad things they had been through they still seemed nervous around each other when suggesting newer, even more insane-sounding theories, even though they both knew by now that anything was possible.

Peter nodded. "I don't see why not," he replied. "If you can be too late for a dream, I don't see why you can't be too early for one." He reached out to touch her and then retracted his hand quickly as he remembered. "Say it was true, say you'd been taken into a dream before it had happened, then assuming at some point you get pulled back into it, when Deborah is there, you can use what you saw to try and find her, right?"

Grace nodded. "Yeah. There was that woman with the lips. She said she was 'there to be noticed'. I'm guessing what she meant was she was there to be noticed by Deborah? She was acting all like she had a starring role to play. Maybe if I can get back to her, I can get back to Deborah!"

As soon as she said this Grace felt a familiar sensation sweep over her. She looked down at her hands and, sure enough, she was fading again. She looked at Peter desperately. There hadn't been enough time! Keeping her eyes locked on his until his image fuzzed and faded away, Grace blinked and suddenly she was back, right in the middle of the carnival.

It was entirely different this time. The whole place had come to life – if she could call it that. There were people everywhere, all with their black and white faces, moving, working, whispering to each other, but everything was quiet, like someone had forgotten to turn the sound on.

The people seemed almost unreal, like sketches on a 3D background. Grace weaved through the throng, desperately trying to find the gypsy lady with the bright red lips. She spotted a flash of crimson through a gap in the crowd and began running towards it. She tripped over tent ropes, urgently elbowing people out of the way, making sure not to lose sight of the woman who was walking briskly towards her trailer, her skirts gathered up in her hands.

Grace called out to her but she would not turn round. She yelled for people to get out of her way as she tried to catch up but the people ignored her. They all were going through the motions, playing their parts just as they had been instructed to do.

Suddenly, just like that, everything turned to colour, as if a rainbow had come crashing down through the sky. With it the gypsy woman's red lips faded into the crowd. Music started and the people began to laugh and play games, to queue up for the rides and the stalls. The crowd tightened, got denser around her. It was if they were all against her, and no one would let her get past.

The sun then disappeared with a pop and she saw the rain come in from either side, taking great sweeping bows across the land. The rain! He came in curtains like at the end of the show. She remembered how the sun had called to it before. That meant time was running out.

Grace twisted and turned, desperate to find Deborah, and suddenly she felt that familiar tug as she heard something like a child's laughter echoing through the sky. She moved forward, pushing and weaving and then stumbled into a clearing in the crowd.

There she was - Deborah! Looking confused, she was faltering clumsily over the ground, her hair slicked back from her face and her clothes speckled with mud. Deborah looked up and pushed her hair out of her face, and then her eyes locked onto Grace's.

She's looking at me.

Grace began to run forward, tripping and slipping over the ground, the tug getting stronger and more intense with each step she took. She was nearly there. She could nearly touch her!

The child's laughter which had been echoing behind her all the while suddenly changed. Lower, louder, it turned into a roar of fury. Grace turned round. Jamie! It was Jamie! Deborah's child! There he was again. He was running, with his huge net dragging on the ground behind him.

But he was different this time. The sly grin and the angelic face had hardened and his features were pulled together, set in a dark and spiteful glare. As he got closer, Grace could see the evil inside him pouring out of his mouth in thick black swarms. He began to scream, and the world around them started shaking. He was nothing like the sweet, gentle child that Grace had known. He was from a nightmare, and he was coming for her. Grace stood frozen in the mud. Every instinct told her to run from him, but she was so close to Deborah that she couldn't bring herself to move. The child drew nearer. Its blood-curdling scream raged through the skies as thunderous clouds rolled in from all sides. Its eyes were black as the harshest night and a dark, sinewy liquid poured from its mouth.

Grace felt someone beside her.

"Grace! Grace! Run!"

It was Peter. He was right beside her. Pure fear smacked across his face. He pushed her ahead of him.

"We've got to run. NOW!"

She nodded and felt the agony of turning away from Deborah course through her veins as they both sprinted through the mud, the rain pelting down on them with all its might. Grace twisted around to see the boy running after them, his face twisted, his black eyes bulging, his mouth wide open with that horrifying black liquid pouring out of it. She looked down at her feet. Her knees were weak and she felt herself sinking into the mud. She was going back! She was being pulled out! Grace looked for Peter, who was a few strides ahead of her, his T-shirt streaked with mud. Her knees gave way and suddenly she was gone.

All was quiet.

She opened her eyes. It had all happened so fast, and for a moment she couldn't believe it had been real. But then she heard a thud and a groan as Peter flashed back beside her. She quickly rolled away from him, making sure they didn't touch. She tried to sit up, but her head was throbbing, so she lay down on her back and stared at the ceiling, saying nothing until the pain had eased.

Once she was ready, Grace carefully sat back up, wincing as her skin tingled. It felt as though she was being pricked with a thousand needles. It certainly didn't get any easier each time it happened. But Peter! Peter had been there. He had saved her!

Grace shuddered at the memory of the little boy. What was that? He hadn't been trying to help her find Deborah after all. Instead he had been trying to catch her, to take her away!

Out of the corner of her eye she saw Peter roll onto his front and push himself up with his arms. His tattoos rippled and dented as he did so; momentarily they seemed to come to life.

"Wow," he muttered into the floorboards. He turned to Grace and ran his hands through his hair.

"We were in the same dream... at the same time," she whispered.

"I know."

Grace felt exhausted. It seemed it was just another thing to think about, another thing to try and work out. They had discussed the possibility that they might get pulled into the same dream at the same time but it was like nothing they could have imagined. They naïvely thought that if it happened they would have time, time to adjust, to work out a plan and to think about how they could help each other. But it was so much faster than that, and when Peter appeared all they'd had time to do was try and get the hell out of there, away from that... that... thing.

"I don't want to do this any more," Grace whispered. "I don't have the strength. I thought if I saw her then that would be it. We could just walk up to each other and she would realise how much she needed me and then I could go back inside. But it's so much harder than that. I can't even get to her, even when she's right in front of my face, and now it seems like something is trying to get to me first..."

Grace trailed off and began to cry softly. "I don't want to let it catch me." She turned to face Peter, who was watching her carefully. "I know it's the worst thing to think in the world, but sometimes, sometimes I just wish that I didn't have to find her, that I could just stay here with you."

Grace felt her face flush. Her stomach turned as the guilt of saying such a terrible, awful thing washed over her. It was impossible anyway, but to even think it was disgraceful. A soul's purpose was to serve the body – that was the only thing that would make them truly satisfied. Wishing for an independent life was just... it was just wrong.

"I'm sorry. I didn't mean that," she smiled wearily. "I'm just tired, that's all."

Peter was staring at her. "Grace." His voice was shaking, his eyes deadly serious. "It doesn't have to be this way, you know."

"What do you mean?"

"I mean there is another way. I've known for ages, I just didn't want to tell you before. I thought... you know, I thought you deserved to be with her, that that's what would make you happiest, but if you really feel that way, like you want to give up, then I know a way. We could have a different life; we could be together."

Peter looked up at her. His hands were shaking as he scrunched and un-scrunched the hem of his jeans.

"I met this guy, on the first day I got here. I couldn't believe I'd found another one, but I soon found out he wasn't like me. He wasn't searching for anything. He said he could help me. He could take me to a place where I didn't need a body any more. Of course at the time I thought he was crazy. I couldn't understand why anyone would ever want a life without their other, and I couldn't think of anything but getting back to mine. But now..." He trailed off and got up, walking over to where he had carefully folded his jacket over the chair, and pulled something from the pocket. "I told him where to go, of course, but before he left he said if I changed my mind I'd know where to find him, and he gave me this."

He placed a small piece of card on the floor and pushed it across so Grace could see. On it in neat black letters it simply read, '*Lost Soulz Bar*' and underneath was the name of a building and an address.

Grace picked up the card between her forefinger and thumb. She might never find her way back to Deborah. She might end up dead, or worse. Here was a chance to be with Peter, with someone that she loved, to have a life that was free from having to worry endlessly about the body, to juggle all its fears and woes. She stared at the floorboards.

"Take me there now," she said without looking up.

CHAPTER 20

DEBORAH

The Break-in

It was a bitterly cold night. Deborah wrapped the fur coat that John had lent her tight around her body and watched her breath as it puffed tiny clouds of white steam into the night sky. Luke, as usual, was marching ahead of her, a small rucksack dangling in between his shoulder blades. They had left just after dusk and decided to walk along the stretch of the river before turning north into the city. There was no one else around; just the faint glow of street lights from the lamps on the road above barely lit their way. The city was silent apart from the occasional low groans from cars driving past above them, and the faint rushing sound of the water moving slowly forward on its endless quest to mix with the sea.

They passed through a low archway with black bricks that dripped a slimy liquid, forming oily puddles on the floor. Deborah skidded into them as she struggled to keep up with Luke. She suddenly felt ridiculous in her oversized outfit, fumbling and stumbling behind him, but it was too late now; there was no going back.

At the end of the path Luke stopped and waited for her to catch up. Then they turned and walked up the narrow stone stairs until they reached the bridge over the main road. Doctor Vanilla's office was only a few streets in.

"So, you know the plan, right? You know what you've got to do?" His face was covered by his scarf so the words came out distant and muffled, but his eyes were deadly serious. Deborah did remember, of course she did. They had been over it a hundred times. For some reason, however, Luke obviously felt he needed her to say it one last time before they went in. Conceding, she smiled at him through the darkness.

"We go in together. When we get to Doctor Vanilla's office I go straight in, and you go and find out wherever it is he disappears to when he leaves us in his office alone. I immediately go to his desk drawers and see if there is anything useful in there – particularly the notebook he uses in his sessions. If I can't find anything I look on the shelves and if after ten minutes I still can't find anything I grab a few of the other journals and put them in here." She tapped the rucksack she was carrying with her finger. "Then I get the hell out of there and meet you on the corner of Duke Street. You might be a little behind me and I am not to panic. However, if you don't come back within fifteen minutes then I leave and come straight back to the boat, and then if you are not back within the hour I call the police."

She couldn't help but smirk a little as she finished. It suddenly all seemed so very ridiculous, as if they were robbing a bank or something. She really hoped it wouldn't come to her calling the police – what would she say?

"999 emergency."

"Uhh, yeh, I think my friend might be in danger."

"OK, please could you give me some more information and we will send someone out straight away."

"Well, we broke into our therapist's office because we think he is trying to control our dreams. My friend is an ex-criminal and we're both suicidal, but now I think our therapist might have done something to him..."

It was insane. They'd both be shipped off and locked up in a mental asylum or something.

"Deborah!" Luke was looking at her intently.

"Sorry, yeah, I got it OK. Just try... try and not be late, yeah?"

They had been walking as they talked and suddenly found themselves outside the entrance to the offices. The smiling family poster from the dentist's surgery was still there, peering out at them from behind the glass. This time, however, Deborah didn't envy their smiles and matching outfits; they looked phoney, and they were trapped that way forever. Deborah found herself feeling strangely sorry for them.

Luke unlocked the door to the main entrance of the building and carefully pushed it open. They both slowly walked inside. The building was so noiseless that every sound they made felt as if they were kicking bins or strangling cats or something.

Luke led the way as they climbed the stairs as quietly as they could. Deborah's throat felt as if it was closing in around her with each step she took. The absurdity of the situation had vanished. Where five minutes before she had found it almost laughable, now she suddenly felt very afraid.

When he reached the top of the stairs, Luke pulled the keys from his pocket again. They fumbled in his fingers and dropped to the floor with a horrible echoing clang. They both froze, immobilised and helpless as they watched the keys roll down the steps, landing at Deborah's feet with a hideous clatter.

Deborah clutched her hands to her mouth and Luke quickly turned towards her and pressed his finger to his lips. He then leant his head against the door and listened. Deborah's whole body felt stiff, like she'd been left outside too long on a cold night.

When Luke was satisfied, he turned and gestured for her to pick up the keys. Deborah bent down and slowly picked them up, wincing as they jangled, then she carefully climbed the stairs and slid the key into the lock.

They both stared at the door opposite them across from the waiting room, the one which led to Doctor Vanilla's office.

Deborah was taken back to the first time she visited. What a different sort of nervousness she had felt back then! It all looked exactly the same, of course. The dim light cast distorted shadows on the beige walls, and then there was the little table, the potpourri and the perfect ring of magazines. Nothing had changed – and yet, everything had.

They walked together towards the final door and stopped in front of it, then turned to face one other. Luke pulled Deborah towards her and kissed her roughly. She felt the prickle of his stubble dig into her face and when he pulled away her cheeks stung. He said nothing, but they both stood for a moment and looked at each other.

Luke carefully unlocked the door and ushered her in ahead of him. He pointed to the little door on the left, then pulled off his rucksack and drew out a small hacksaw, crouching down to begin work on the padlock.

Deborah watched him. She felt as though she might not see him again. Luke turned around and mouthed 'go', so she tiptoed away from him, weaving her way through the bookcases until she reached the main space of Doctor Vanilla's office.

It was swelteringly hot as usual, so she walked over to the window and drew back the heavy velvet curtains. A stale dusty smell wafted into the air as she moved them. She tried to lift up the window, and to her surprise this time it gave way and hoisted upwards. Deborah let the cool night air wash over her face, and then she turned back towards Doctor Vanilla's desk.

There upon it, positioned perfectly in the centre, was his notepad. Not quite able to believe her luck, Deborah hurriedly walked over and flipped it open. The paper was beautifully thin and crisp and made a delicate fluttering sound as she turned the pages one by one.

Wood
Water
Dances
Teeth
Shoes
Rum
Dogs

Deborah turned page after page, frowning as each one only perplexed her further. How on earth was this going to help them?

Each entry had a date at the top. She flicked to last week, when she had been in one of her sessions, but again it was just a list of seemingly meaningless words. They certainly weren't associated with anything she had done or said as far as she could remember, and they were nothing to do with the dreams she'd had.

Deborah put the notepad back on the desk and tried the drawers, which were locked. She glanced at her watch. She had already spent seven minutes in the office and so far had found nothing. There wasn't much time left before she had to get out. Maybe the journals would give her some sort of clue, but there were so many, and she couldn't exactly stuff them all into the tiny rucksack Luke had given her. How on earth was she supposed to know which ones to choose?

A shadow fluttered across the far side of the wall and Deborah whipped round. She pressed herself into a corner and squinted into the darkness. Her breath was shallow and rasping; it felt as if it was coming through a megaphone, so she put her hand over her mouth to try and muffle it.

There was nothing there. The painting of sunflowers hung on the far wall; it was a painting which haunted her whenever she saw it. Even in the darkness the flowers still seemed violently alive. They stretched out as if at any moment they would burst out from the picture and swallow her up.

She glanced to the bookcase to the left of the painting and noticed that one of the journals was sticking out a little, as if it had been only recently taken out and hurriedly put back in. Leaning over, she pulled it from the shelf. Luke's words echoed in the back of her mind. She knew she should put the journal in her rucksack and get out of there, but curiosity got the better of her. Deborah glanced at her watch again, she had a few minutes. She might as well read some of it to see if it was useful. Walking back over to the window she leant against the frame. The top of the page was dated in a scratchy black ink.

12th December 1623

I do it for you, Father, I do it for you.

The words were slanted forward and smudged in an excited scrawl, so Deborah struggled to make them out. She peered at the paper through the dim office light, slotting herself against the window and using the glow of the street outside to assist her. She steadied her breathing; her shallow, nervous breaths seemed so loud amongst the stillness of the office, and it felt as though her heart was beating right outside her chest.

The plant has become harder and harder to find. It is the damage of the fire that has made it almost impossible for me to hunt any more. I cannot sense where it grows like I used to; this is deeply troubling to me. I have tried to plant it and grow it myself. But no matter how much time and effort I invest, no matter how much care and attention I give to nursing and coaxing it to life, it rarely makes it past the first stages.

For many thousands of years, Father, the plant has sustained me. I have used it for the purposes you taught me and not ventured into experimenting with what it can do. You taught me of its power and also warned me against it, but why, Father, why? Look at what good it did you.

I have lived for so long now. I thought that would be enough, that using the plant to keep myself alive for as long as possible would somehow honour you and the life that was taken away from you. I have tried to come to terms with the pain.

A sickness grows within me, Father. It grows stronger each day and I fear it has finally taken me over. It has been within me for all this time. I am still not ready to leave. I am not ready to move on, knowing that there will be no one there for me waiting on the other side. What purpose do I have to follow the laws of our God, to follow the rules of the plant when it has done nothing to comfort me? You were all taken so unfairly and it made me realise how important it is to live. I am not yet done. I wish to live on and on and I do not wish to help these ungrateful people. No one believed in the powers of the plant when our family tried to help them all those years ago. Why should I now? They look at me with disgust. They cover their children's eyes when I walk past. They call me 'hideous' and scream and run from me, when it is they who inflicted these scars on my face – they! I will not use the last of the plant's power to help this wretched ungrateful race, but instead I will to learn how to catch them.

I am sorry, Father. I tried. I am so sorry, Father. I really tried.

A breeze rattled the blinds, darting shadows across the room, making the hairs on Deborah's arms stand to attention – stiff, alert, and sniffing for danger. She wanted to sit down, or to run, or to tear the pages from the book and burn them right there in the office. But she could not. She read on.

15th December 1623

It works! The plant has shown me that the world of dreams is concrete, finite. It is not a place conjured by the mind of the individual. When one enters it is as if they walk through a door, or alight from a train. We are all able to be in one another's dreams should we learn how to open that door, and the plant has shown me how. Now I know I can come and go as freely as I like. I have simply learnt to access others' doors, and enter. Tonight was my first time, Father! It was the most implausible, fantastic thing. I can barely explain the excitement. These worlds are unlike anything I have ever seen! The most beautiful things you could imagine, Father! I have seen them with my own eyes. The most dark and twisted thoughts you could conjure? I have experienced them tenfold over! These men, these creatures, they have such a capacity to create, to imagine, and they don't even appreciate how lucky they are, that they can escape to these impossible places where anything can happen! It is a gift, Father. This is what the plant should always be used for. I must go back as soon as I can!

2nd February 1624

These men are such a wicked and arrogant race! They believe their dreams are personal things and that they are only for them. It sickens me how foolish they are. The ones I wish to catch are the worst, the most weak, pathetic and helpless! They do not value life and that makes them careless and selfish. And not only do they not succeed when they try to die, but in doing so they lose their souls, their others!

Really, how hard can it be to end one's life? I know only too well of the ease in which death will take us, how it snatches us from those we love most.

How dare they think that they can take death into their own hands! How dare they think that it is not a gift to live! They are so depraved of mind that even in the world of dreams – their only chance to reunite with their souls – they do not understand what they must do.

They do not see the second chance that our God has given them and how lucky they are. They do not understand how easy it is to control their dreams, and so they wander through them time and time again learning nothing! This is why their souls have so much trouble finding their way back.

Now I have a way into the world of dreams of others and I cannot bear it. I cannot bear to see their sad, drooping, weary souls - ones that have fought so hard to come back to them but have been ignored time and time again. So I do what is right and noble, for I can offer them my own body as a home – my own body which is strong and good and full of life. In doing so I gain all the years that their own foolish bodies should have lived for, and their souls will suffer no more.

It is a fair process, Father, don't you see? These bodies chose to die. They attempted to take their own lives. By taking away their souls I am simply giving them what they wanted – for a body without a soul cannot last long. This way everybody gets what they desire. I choose to live on, and so I do, and those who chose to die will also be granted their wish.

I am not doing anything wrong, Father. I am honouring you. It is the right thing to do, Father, honouring you.

A floorboard creaked, startling Deborah, and she slammed the journal shut, instantly regretting it as the sound bellowed loudly around the room. She froze in fear as she noticed a dark figure silhouetted in the doorway ahead.

"My, my." The voice was hushed and dripping with spite. "Hello, Deborah. I thought I might find you here."

The hunched outline of a man blocked her escape and

Deborah recognised him instantly. Doctor Vanilla slowly moved into the light, his scar seeming to glow in the dark, highlighting his eyes so they blazed through the night. He wore a blood red satin shirt done up to the neck. He was huge, bloated, straining at the gut. His stomach now rolled grotesquely over the top of his trousers. In his hand he held a silver knife.

Deborah choked back a scream. Her head was buzzing, still trying to process the information she had just read. This man – he wanted to steal her soul!

Doctor Vanilla took another step towards her. "I don't want to hurt you, Miss Green," he said quictly, "but needs must."

He tapped the knife in a leisurely way against his hand. "You didn't need to make it this difficult for yourself, you know. You could have been like all the others, just attended the sessions like a good girl, and then quietly been taken away."

Deborah swallowed hard. "I don't understand. I checked you... I checked you out."

Doctor Vanilla scoffed and twisted his mouth into an ugly snarl. "Ha! How easy do you think it is to do that?" he spat. "Do you know how long I have been here for? Do you know how easy all this is for me, how much I know?" He tapped his temple hard with his finger and his eyes rolled back in his head as he continued.

"Besides, I only choose the ones that very few people will miss," he hissed cruelly, "and I'm always very, very sorry..."

He tilted his head to the side as he said this and batted his eyelashes, mocking innocence, as he put on a high pitched sing- song voice: "I'm so sorry, Mrs Green, there was nothing I could have done. She was so determined not to listen to me. It breaks my heart. She was so young..."

He laughed a laugh which bared his teeth as he moved towards her again. "So young," he repeated and ran his tongue over his lips.

Deborah pushed herself back against the window and glanced down to the freedom of the street below. What could she do? She could scream for Luke. Maybe he could get to her in time – if Doctor Vanilla hadn't gotten to him first that was.

Her stomach sunk as she realised that he must have passed the door Luke broke into on the way in. He must have seen the broken padlock on the floor. Oh, Luke! She kept her eyes focused on Doctor Vanilla's face. There was no way of negotiating with him. Perhaps she could somehow try to get past him, or... she looked down at the street again, trying to calculate the height. Could she make it?

The pavement below looked hard and unwelcoming but she didn't have a choice. She grabbed hold of the curtain with her fist.

"Not today, Doctor Vanilla," she said.

And then she jumped.

CHAPTER 21

100BC

The Apothecary's son

"Papa, Papa wait up!" There was a shuffle of tiny feet kicking up puffs of dust from the trail as he ran panting through his trunk which swung awkwardly back and forth, snapping off bits of branch from the low boughs of the trees which grew either side of the path. The day was foggy and thick with heat, so visibility was poor. Every time his father's rump disappeared into the dust, he would panic and begin to run.

Thud! He fell back on his forearms and laughed. His father turned around slowly. "That's the fourth time today, Ouranus! Why don't you just ride on my back like you used to?"

Ouranus shook his head vigorously from side to side. His

comical ears flapped in time with his shaking as he grinned, goofy-toothed, at his father. "I want to learn, Papa. I can't always ride with you. That's what you said to me, remember? That I needed to learn for myself. That this was a family business and you wanted to show me how to do it so I will run it myself someday. Don't you remember?"

Father nodded with mock austerity. "That's right, Son. I said it." He slapped his rump into the sand and pulled his son gently beside him. "It's a tough game, though. I told you that, too, didn't I? You know people don't always listen to us, don't you? That sometimes, because they see us as different from them, they become afraid. And fear can breed nasty things in a man. So I want you to make sure you want this. If you don't, then I don't mind. I just want you to know that I am not making you. You know that don't you my son?"

Ouranos tapped his claws impatiently on the ground. He curled his trunk around his father's ankles and yanked himself up again. He was no fool. He could see how much his father wanted him to continue the family business. He could see that his father wasn't as mobile as he used to be. His vision was poorer, which was no good for spotting, his trunk was withered and stiff so he couldn't smell as well, and nor could he reach the higher, harder to grab plants that towered above them. Besides, he had grown up listening to the tales his father would tell him about the surgeries he'd performed, the lives that he'd saved and the hope that he had given to all the families that had bothered to give him the time of day. That made it all worth it. His father was a thousand years old and he was the wisest and kindest of them all.

"I want to learn everything, Papa," Ouranus said softly. "Now come on – I think I can smell some over there!"

His father nodded and let his son gallop ahead. Sure enough, with a 'trump, trump, trump' a few minutes later, Ouranus made the call that he had struck gold.

The Viatel plant grew only in some of the toughest terrains in the world. They were hardy, needing little food or water to survive. They were of a solitary nature, growing alone and only producing one seed in the whole of their lifetime. They relied on the harsh desert winds to scatter this seed away in the hope it would land on fertile ground, and this was the only way the species could survive. Their roots were buried deep within the ground through layers of sand and silt and soil, and they stretched for miles around, making them truly impossible to knock over. They were deadly poisonous to all creatures. If frogs ate them they would turn to stone; if a mouse so much as even brushed his tail against a leaf it would shrink into nothing but a puff of fur. Even larger creatures such as the three-horned bullock could not handle the Viatel plant – one mouthful and their stomachs would swell up to ten times their size, and then they would explode.

There were, however, mysteriously enough, two species that could handle the plant, and for these creatures, if ingested in the right way, the power of these plants was truly unquantifiable.

Ouranos and his father stared up at the skies in silence. It was a remarkable find. Twelve, no, thirteen towering Viatel plants swayed above them, their giant prickly leaves swooping low in graceful arches tinged a perfect blue hue around the edges, making them seem as though they were dissolving into the sky.

"How can this be?" Father muttered. "It's impossible. How are they all together?" His eyes grew wide and he sighed a sigh of someone too old to comprehend new things.

Ouranos looked up at his father and felt overwhelmed with love. "It's a good thing though, Papa?" he said and began leaping about in excited, ungraceful circles. "Just think of what we can do with this much!"

Father seemed distracted. "Something is changing," he muttered, and furrowed his great grey monobrow.

Ouranus and his father lived five miles from the edge of the town of Kathacow in a small mud hut with a thatched roof. To get to the front door was a challenge, as wild ferns grew in thick tangled patches all around. Ouranus had learnt how to hack a path through with his trunk. Father had taught him this technique and as they approached the hut now, Ouranus relished how quickly and effectively he could do it. He swooped his trunk this way and that and his father followed in suit, each bent double with the weight of the Viatel that they had lashed to their backs with hunting rope.

As they approached the door, Ouranus pointed his trunk skywards and gave the long call to signal their arrival home. Seconds later the door burst open and his mother (or Dappha, as the Elephant people called her) heffalumped out of the entrance. Dappha was closely followed by a small bundle of skin and bones and lashings of strawberry blonde hair that was his sister, Pup. She was stark naked apart from a bonnet made out of rice sacks and reeds sitting lopsidedly on her head.

Dappha stopped abruptly when she saw what they were carrying and shook her head in disbelief. Ouranus untied the rope and let the bundle of Viatel fall with a thud to the ground. He then scooped Pup up into his arms, and smiled as she giggled in delight. Father looked at Dappha, whose mouth had slopped to the floor. Their eyes met for a moment and Father shrugged and began to laugh. It was not often that his wife was rendered speechless.

"Is it real?" she managed when she had caught her tongue.

Father nodded.

"But how can it be?"

Father shook his head. He had no explanation other than a miracle, but Elephant men had no time for miracles, only truth. He'd often wondered how strange it was when people got them confused – and how people, when faced with the truth, would not consider it to be so, instead shrouding it with suspicion and mystery and turning it into some dark potential evil that should not be trusted.

"My goodness!" Dappha exclaimed, clawing towards him. "My goodness gracious! Does this mean we can save them? Does this mean we can save them all?!"

Father nodded his head gravely. "If they will let us, we can," he muttered, but no one heard him. Dappha pulled Pup and Ouranus towards her and the three of them danced in a circle, throwing their heads back in laughter, tooting their trunks.

Father looked up to the skies; on the horizon blackish-blue clouds were creasing together and heading towards them.

"Better get it inside," he said quietly. "It looks like there's a storm coming."

CHAPTER 22

GRACE

The Lost Soulz Bar

Grace pulled up the hood of her coat as she hurried down the street after Peter. The afternoon sun was shining brightly, but she wanted to block it out. She folded her arms across her stomach keeping her eyes focused on Peter's laces which were trailing behind him. She tried to reason with the voice in her head, which was telling her she was about to make the worst decision of her life.

The laces suddenly stopped moving and she looked up to see Peter holding up his hand which had been their agreed signal to stop. He turned around and smiled. He had been in a particularly good mood since Grace had asked him to take her to the Lost Soulz bar and had practically skipped out of the bedsit where they had returned to get their things before setting off.

It seemed that this was what he had been hoping for. It made sense. He surely had much less time than she did and was getting no closer to finding his body. She did find it strange that he didn't seem a little more remorseful, though. What they were doing was surely one of the worst and most selfish acts of cruelty a soul could do – they were essentially sentencing their bodies to death. Regardless of the circumstances it went against everything they had been conditioned to believe, and yet Peter seemed to be barely thinking about it at all.

"We've still got a way to go," Peter called to her. "Are you OK? Do you want to take a break or anything?"

Grace nodded and stepped a little closer to him. They then sat about a metre apart on the grassy verge of the road and Peter pulled a bread roll from his pocket, tearing it in half and throwing a piece to her. They ate in silence.

They were on the outskirts of the city now, near to where Grace had first arrived. The road had narrowed and there was no pavement, so they had been walking along in single file to make sure they didn't touch one another as they went. The sun meant it wasn't particularly cold, warmer than many Grace had seen since she had been on the outside, but this had done little to cheer her up.

She stared down at her feet and watched as a shiny black beetle crawled over the tip of her boot and then carried on its way through the grass. Sighing, she took a large bite of the bread, her nose wrinkling in distaste. It was dry and stale. She pulled a bottle of water from her pocket and took a sip to try and wash it down before throwing the rest of the roll onto the ground. At least she wouldn't have to put up with this kind of food any more very soon. Peter had told her that once you gave up your other for good it no longer mattered if other humans touched you – that you would feel no pain. So once they had done it there would be no more sneaking around and sticking to outdoor markets to try and find food; they could have their pick of it.

Grace nodded her head silently, trying to reassure herself that she was making the right decision. She had to be selfish now. If Deborah hadn't got rid of her in the first place then she wouldn't be in this mess, so it was time to think of herself for a change. Deborah obviously hadn't given a damn about her when she'd tried to end it. Why should she give a damn about her now?

However, despite her best efforts to be strong and to not think of what she was doing to Deborah, Grace could do little to relieve the sickly, guilty feeling that throbbed in the pit of her stomach.

After a short break they continued on their way and soon the sun dipped low in the sky before eventually falling behind some tall hills in the distance. Night had set in, and with it came a bitterly cold wind which numbed Grace's face and fingers. She shoved her hands deep into her pockets and bit her lip as she felt the now too familiar feeling of tears beginning to swell in her eyes. She followed the outline of Peter's back; he would regularly call to her to make sure she was OK. Grace tried to focus on how great it would be when she could hold him again. He would look after her. He would fill the space that Deborah had so cruelly taken away.

"We're nearly here... Grace, STOP!"

Peter had been holding up his hand but, too caught up in fighting with herself, Grace had not noticed and nearly walked into him. She stopped herself just in time.

"Sorry," she mumbled.

"Look."

Peter pointed ahead of him. The road curved round, and breaking off to the left was a dusty track that led up to the top of a hill. An old stone farmhouse stood at the crest. Grace gasped as her eyes were drawn upwards. The moon shone so brightly overhead it looked like it was ready to pop out from the sky, which was packed tightly with thousands of glittering stars.

"It's beautiful," she whispered. Peter nodded his head. She could tell he wanted to tell her he loved her but she knew he would wait, wait until he could say it as he should do – with her in his arms.

When they reached the top of the path and stood and stared at the farmhouse, there were no lights in the windows and the door was padlocked shut. Peter walked over and pulled at them. They shook, but refused to give way. He stood in the middle of the courtyard looking uncomfortable and confused as he shifted his weight from one foot to the other.

"What do we do now?" Grace called to him. He shrugged in response.

Suddenly the door to the farmhouse was flung open dramatically, an imposing figure silhouetted in its frame in front of a great, blinding beam of light.

"Ahhhh, whaddyya know! Peter man, is that you?' The voice was a drawling boom as it bellowed out, echoing around the courtyard walls.

The man stepped out and the light flooded out, illuminating the entire area. Shielding her eyes, Grace looked the man up and down. At least six and a half feet tall, he made for an imposing figure and towered above the pair of them. He was dressed entirely in white. His suit fit him perfectly and on his head he wore a matching white top hat. Waist-length dreadlocks with colourful beads woven into the ends jangled as he spoke. He came forward with huge, lunging strides, kicking up dust as he went until he stopped in front of Peter and warmly shook him by the hand.

"How ya doing, man?" he roared. Peter looked dwarfed next to him as he nodded his reply. He then turned his eyes on Grace. "I can see you brought a lady with ya," he said, looking her up and down in approval before breaking out into a dazzling smile.

"Abeid," he said gently, giving his name and not waiting to hear hers. He nodded his head and bowed to both of them. "Greetins to both of y'all. Now we must make haste – get inside quick!"

He glanced at the sky and then turned around with some urgency and strode back inside. Grace looked at Peter, who shrugged at her and grinned before following him in. She took a deep breath and paused at the entrance, looking back at the landscape one last time before she walked in after them.

The inside was a brightly-illuminated corridor which seemed to stretch on as far as she could see. The walls were painted a dazzling white and the floor was dark varnished mahogany which made no noise as they walked along it. Framed pictures hung on either side of the walls with photographs of generations of men all in the same perfectly white suit and top hat as Abeid wore now. Below the pictures were neat silver plaques with dates engraved on them.

Grace tried to keep up with the men, who both strode quickly down the corridor. She wanted to stop and look at the faces of those who she assumed were the generations of leaders of whatever this place was, but Abeid seemed in no mood to be leisurely and she had to jog to keep up. They were yards ahead of her and talking earnestly. Peter spoke in a whisper and Abeid boomed back his answers, though Grace could barely understand what he was saying.

They approached a dark archway at the end, where a steep drop of stone stairs led them to a dimly-lit bar. Several murky figures were slouched around. One was hunched over a battered juke box from which an old country tune crackled out through the speakers; another pair were playing a game of pool, though they stopped to stare at the newcomers as they approached.

Abeid gestured for them to stay at the entrance and strode over to the bar. He whispered something to the bartender, a stocky-looking man with a thick grey moustache, then turned and nodded to Peter and Grace before retiring to a booth at the back of the bar where a young man sat biting his lip, looking nervous and ashamed.

Grace stared back at the shadowy faces looking at her. They must be other souls! She was desperate to go up to them and find out their stories. She stared at the booth, where Abeid was now talking earnestly to the young man, whose head was now in his hands. He must have been about the same age as them. He certainly didn't look too happy to be there, but Abeid, who was now gently clasping the young man's wrist, seemed determined to convince him otherwise.

The bartender was beckoning them over. He must have been in his mid-forties and wore a chequered waistcoat with a small yellow handkerchief that poked from his top pocket. His cheeks and nose were farmer's red and, as he smiled at them, they saw he was missing two of his front teeth.

He nodded over to the booth where Abeid was sitting and leant his head in close to Grace so he could whisper.

"Don't worry about him, love. He's just new, that's all. Like the both of you. It's normal to be nervous, and a decision none of us took lightly, believe me." He sighed and trailed off for a moment. "But trust me, love, sometimes the decisions that are the hardest to make turn out to be the best. Now can I get you something to drink while you wait for your guide?"

He sniffed and tugged out the yellow handkerchief before blowing his nose dramatically. He then nodded to a pair of stools that stood by the bar and Grace and Peter walked over to them. Peter peered over the edge of the bar, looking confused. All the drinks were alcoholic.

The bartender laughed as he saw the expression on Peter's face. "It's OK here," he explained. "You can drink and it won't matter. You haven't got anyone to look after any more, remember? Go on! Relax a little."

Peter glanced at Grace and shrugged before ordering two beers, which the bartender poured into metal tankards and set in them on card place mats in front of them. He then busied himself at the other end of the bar polishing glasses and setting them on the shelves above, whistling to himself quietly as he worked.

Grace turned to Peter and lowered her voice. "So that Abeid guy, is he the leader here?"

Peter nodded his head. "I guess so. I was asking him about it on the way in, but he wouldn't give much away. He said we had to wait for a guide, that they would show us around and explain everything to us. All he really told me was that he's the only one allowed outside the building. He's the only one who goes looking for lost souls."

"So, wait a second." Grace frowned at him. "Are you saying that's it – we can't go back out there, out to the real world again?"

Peter nodded. "I didn't expect that either, but Abeid says we will have everything we need here, all the comforts, all the food, everything we could wish for. It's going to be wonderful, Grace. Trust me, OK?"

Grace frowned at him again and took a sip of her drink,

enjoying the malty taste of the beer on her tongue before swallowing. She had a thousand more questions to ask, but she would have to leave them till later, because just then a young girl approached them from the shadows.

"Hi," she said softly. She couldn't have been more than fifteen. Her mousy brown hair hung forlornly around her face and cascaded down to her waist. Her other features were small and delicate – except her eyes, which were huge and a piercing azure blue.

"I am your guide," she said, doing an awkward half courtesy. "Are you ready for me to show you around?" She was nervous. The bartender came back over and nodded at her encouragingly. "Go on, love." He smiled at her before turning to Grace and Peter. "It's her first one, see," he explained. "But we've all got to do it, it's part of the job."

He gave her a wink and she responded by flashing him a shy grin before turning back to them expectantly.

"Yep, OK, we're ready," said Peter before gulping down his drink. Grace followed suit and then looked around, confused. There didn't seem to be any other doors leading off from the room apart from the stairs, which only led to the corridor they had just come from. She slid off her bar stool and stood up.

The young girl smiled at them. "I'm Lara," she said. She stamped on the edge of the floorboard that she'd been standing on. It flicked upwards and she caught it in her hand. "Follow me," she said, and jumped down underneath the floor.

As soon as they had jumped they were engulfed in darkness. They were falling so fast Grace felt weightless. She spun herself round and could just make out the outline of Peter, who was falling beneath her. A light appeared ahead and before she knew it she'd come to a gentle standstill. She was carefully tilted upright and her feet found the ground. Lara smiled at them and brushed down her skirt.

"Welcome," she said, turning with an open arm and gesturing at the landscape.

Grace gasped. Golden-coloured hills rolled out around them; shimmering waterfalls cascaded down the sides, forming huge swollen pools in the valleys where red brick houses with thatched roofs were dotted around. Tall, leafy chestnut trees stood proudly in every garden. Forests with thickly-knitted pine trees surrounded the area, seeming almost too dense to penetrate.

Lara beckoned them to follow her and led them over the brow of a hill where a railway track with a huge, puffing, shiny blue steam engine stood waiting for them.

"We'll go on a tour, shall we?" she said and smiled sweetly before climbing on board. Peter followed her immediately and then turned, offering Grace his hand. She looked at it dubiously.

"It's OK here," he said.

She reached out her hand and clasped her fingers around his, gasping softly as he pulled her on. They hugged tightly. She felt nothing but the warmth of his arms and the weight of his body as he pushed against her. She pressed her forehead deep into the dip of his collarbone and bit back tears of happiness as he stroked her hair.

"Everything's going to be OK now, Grace," he said gently, and she nodded.

Aboard the train Lara showed them to their seats, cream leathery cushions that stuck to the back of Grace's thighs as soon as she sat down. Lara sat opposite them and composed herself before pushing a large red button overhead. The train lurched laboriously into action, slowly at first, but soon it was chuffing through the hills at some speed as she began to point out what was around them.

"That," she said, pointing to an oppressive-looking grey stone building with tiny windows and a black slate roof, "is the library. There is all sorts of information there that has been written by our ancestors and other souls who once lived here. You may use it freely except on Sundays – nothing is open then. Each soul is allocated an individual cottage unless," she looked at them and blushed, "...you choose to live as one. The cottage is where you will live; you are expected to keep it clean and neat. Food is handed out to everyone equally at the town hall every Monday. The town hall is over there." She pointed to a tall wooden barn which stood in the centre of the valley. "Abeid is our leader and he and the elders decide our laws and rules, which we follow explicitly. We must be in our houses by the time the sun sets and we must not leave until sunrise. The forests mark the edge of our land. No one is permitted to go into them. On Sundays we gather for the cleansing. This takes place over there." She gestured to a tall white tower with no windows that stood just beside the edge of the forest. "That is Abeid's house."

"I'm sorry," Grace interjected. "The cleansing? What is that?"

Lara furrowed her brow and seemed agitated at the question. "It is to ensure we are totally free of our bodies," she said simply. She then leant across and hesitantly took Grace by the hand. "We live a simple life here," she said. "We cannot be complicated by regret or worry. If we choose to stay we choose to live a life of peace. It is a good life." She bit her lip and turned away. A flash of sorrow crossed her eyes. "It is the best life we can wish for."

Lara set her mouth in a hard line which told Grace she

had no more to say on the matter. She then reached up and pushed the red button once again. The train ground to an immediate halt.

"This is where you shall stay."

They clambered off the train and were faced with their new home. A small white picket fence cornered off the land that had been allocated to them. Little paving stones raised out of the grass led the way to the front door. On either side of these, bulbs were poking out in neat rows from the soil. "Bluebells," Lara said, nodding towards them. "They should flower soon." A cawing from above made them all look up to the chestnut tree which stood at the back of the garden. A large black bird was busy building a messy nest high up in one of the branches. It paused as they approached, looked down at them and squawked again. Lara tutted and carried on up the path. At the entrance she handed Grace a key who unlocked the door and pushed it open.

Inside they stepped into a large living room with dark wooden floors and pretty arched windows at the far end. There was a small oak table by the windows with a vase of yellow roses in its centre. On the left, a cosy fireplace was built into the rough brick walls and the newly-lit fire crackled and bathed the room in a warm glow. Some winding stairs by the door led up to a small loft-style bedroom. The bed stood in the centre of the room and a scent of lavender was in the air. More roses had been placed in a blue vase on a small table by the bed.

Back downstairs, Lara led them to the kitchen, which was by far the most impressive room in the house, with high ceilings, huge windows and red tiled floors. A large bottle-green Aga stood in the centre and filled the room with a comforting heat. A basket of fresh bread had been placed on the side of one of the wooden counters which stretched the length of the wall and several pots and pans hung on gleaming hooks which dangled down from the ceiling.

"You should find enough food in the cupboards and fridge to last you for now," Lara said gently. "Please feel free to look around, but remember you must be back inside before sunset. I will leave you now. I'll be back in the morning. You have until then to decide if you wish to stay."

She then nodded her head to them both and walked towards the door.

"Remember," she said, "you must decide tomorrow and, if you choose to stay, you will no longer be able to step beyond the forest."

Lara then walked quickly out of the door, closing it softly behind her without looking back.

CHAPTER 23

DEBORAH

No going back

Deborah clamped her lips together, stifling the screams that rose up from her throat with every step that she took. She clung onto the wall, her hands sliding down the slime as she desperately groped her way back through the tunnel. She could hear the water rushing along to her left and pressed herself against the side to make sure she didn't trip and stumble into it. It was almost pitch black and, bar the water, she could only hear the sound of her own whimpers, which echoed through the tunnel and into the skies as she limped along the riverbank.

The path was frosty underfoot and the night air wrapped itself around her, cruelly chilling her though to her core. Deborah had left John's coat in Doctor Vanilla's office, along with her rucksack, not having had time to grab them before she'd jumped. The only thing she'd managed to take with her was the journal, which she now clutched as best she could, wedging it uncomfortably under her arm.

She glanced down and tapped the light on her watch. The figures glowed through the darkness, telling her it was over half an hour past the time when she was supposed to have met Luke. God knows where he would have thought she'd got to – if he had even got out, that was.

Deborah wondered if he was looking for her now. Perhaps he'd gone back to Doctor Vanilla's office to find her. She shuddered at the thought. She'd been too afraid to go to where they were supposed to meet; it was too close to Doctor Vanilla's office and she was sure he would come looking for her. After she'd jumped she'd gone as fast as she could away from him, not thinking about where she was going.

It was only when she paused for a moment that Deborah had realised the severity of her injuries. One of her arms swung loosely from its socket and her foot and ankle were almost certainly broken. Deborah could feel the warmth of her blood as it oozed and swilled around her shoe. Her stomach flipped as she pictured what was underneath, all crushed bones and skin. She took a deep breath and tried not to pass out from the pain. She froze with every noise that she heard, convinced that Doctor Vanilla was coming after her. He might even know where Luke lived and be there waiting for her when she returned. But what else could she do? She could no longer return to her own house, and had nowhere else to go. Deborah struggled to keep her composure as those words resonated in her head: *I have nowhere else to go.*

Slumping back against the wall, she tried to steady her breathing. It all seemed so unfair. She'd tried, she'd really tried to get better for her mother, and for herself, but she had only ended up hurting her mother more and, as for her... Deborah glanced down at her foot. It wasn't just physical harm she was causing either – she was also falling in love with a man who was surely no good for her, a violent criminal who had also tried to kill himself and, to top it off, she had chosen a psychotic therapist who appeared to be out to steal her soul.

Deborah stifled an urge to laugh hysterically, feeling it brewing in her stomach, trying to force its way out. But if she did, she might be crossing that point of sanity where she was still able to stop, so instead took a deep breath and exhaled slowly.

As she reached the end of the tunnel, the faint glow of the marina shone in the distance. With her head bent down, she struggled on. Eventually she arrived back at Luke's boat, pausing as she looked it up and down, using the light of her watch to try to see whether there were any obvious signs of intrusion. It didn't look as if anyone had come back. There was no light glowing from the hatch. This meant that Luke had probably not returned. Shaking her head and blocking out the thoughts of what might have happened to him, Deborah tried to concentrate on getting herself on board and inside.

She lowered herself to the ground and bit her lip. Taking hold of the arm that had come out of its socket, she held it firmly and shut her eyes. Then, with a sickening click, she popped it back in. The pain was blinding, excruciating, but she didn't make a sound.

She slowly dragged herself onto the boat. As she tumbled inwards both her arm and foot banged the sides, and a wave of agony swept right over her. It rushed through her veins and seemed to tighten the whole of her skin. She couldn't help but cry out in pain.

"Who's there?" a voice sounded below and she heard footsteps and the rustle of paper.

"Deborah, is that you? Who is out there?" the voice demanded. It was Luke.

Deborah called out to him and heard him scramble up the stairs. Suddenly she felt hot tears pouring down her face.

"It's me and I'm hurt, Luke. I'm really hurt. Rolling onto her back she sobbed with relief and gasped for breath. The hatch was pushed open and Luke, armed with a torch, came rushing over to her.

"Oh my God! Deborah, what happened to you?"

"I thought you weren't here. I thought he'd got to you, too," Deborah whispered.

"No, no, Deborah. I'm OK," he replied. "I waited for you. I didn't know what to do. I was going to go back but then I saw him, leaning out of his window looking at the ground, and there was blood on the road, a load of blood. I thought he'd killed you."

He was half shouting as he tried to soothe her, his eyes desperate and bulging as he carefully moved her into an upright position. Reaching under one of the seats, he pulled out a large yellow box and rummaged around in it until he found a cloth, some antiseptic and some bandages.

"I'm going to fix you up and then we'll get you warm, OK?" He smiled at her, trying to sound reassuring.

Deborah nodded faintly as he began to gently wipe away the blood from her wounds. He removed her shoe and looked at her foot. Deborah watched his face carefully, she could tell it was bad from the way he swallowed and then briefly closed his eyes.

"I think I'd better get you to hospital," he said.

Deborah shook her head. "I can't go there. I know what my mum is like. She'll have alerted every hospital, every police station around. If I give them my name, she'll find me. She'll get them to take me away." She looked up at him firmly. "I can't go there, Luke. We'll just have to make do."

He paused and looked down at her quietly for a moment, before relenting. "OK, I'll do what I can."

He gently lifted her up and carried her downstairs, where he placed her on the booth and lifted her leg up high onto the table. Deborah twisted her head away as she saw a flash of bone and blood. Luke quickly bandaged it up before handing her several large pills and a mug of whisky.

"It's the best I can do, but these should help with the pain at least," he offered. Deborah nodded and swallowed them down. After a few minutes the pain began to ease and she felt herself relax a little. Luke went to the bedroom and returned with some pillows, which he arranged carefully under her head so she was propped upright.

"Do you want to sleep?" he asked. "I can carry you through to the bedroom if you like."

She shook her head. She could feel the painkillers begin to take effect, but with them the drowsiness would soon kick in and she needed to stay awake a little longer.

'I want to know what happened to you," she said.

Luke nodded and eased himself in beside her so she could lean on his shoulder. "Christ, I don't even know if you'll believe it," he said. "I managed to get through the lock. God knows what it was made of but it took forever to saw through. Anyway, when I opened it I stepped through into this room. It was just like a normal room – like a living room, really. But it didn't have any furniture – just this massive mantelpiece and a blazing fire. It was so hot in there I could barely breathe and when I stepped in I saw this thing. It was like a dog or something but it was different... I don't know, like some weird crossbreed I guess. Its legs were all huge and spotted and it had like a cat's head or something and the strangest mouth. It looked at me when I came in. I thought it might attack me and almost left right then, but it didn't pay me any attention. It was massive but I could tell it was really old; its fur was all wrinkled and patchy and stuff.

"Anyway, as I said it barely paid me any attention, so I decided just to be brave and get on with it. So I had a look around. It was only then that I noticed that the whole room was covered in hundreds of thousands of padlocks and keys."

"What?" said Deborah, sitting up further and momentarily forgetting her pain.

Luke nodded excitedly. "They were all over the walls, covering every inch of them, and beneath were names, of people. There were so many of them. Some of them were really old and rusty and stuff, and then others looked brand new. And then I saw ours. Our names were up there, Deborah, up there on his wall!" He paused, catching his breath, and took a big gulp of whisky from his mug.

Deborah twisted herself round to face him. There was only one thought on her mind. "Luke! You got our keys, didn't you? Please tell me you took our keys away from that bastard!"

Luke pulled the mug away from his face, looking crestfallen. "They weren't there."

"What?"

"I would have. Of course I would have, but they weren't there. In fact, as far as I could see, they were the only ones that were missing. Anyway, then I heard something. I heard something coming in, so I hid behind the door. I could see that weird creature turn its head round. It was getting ready to get up, to greet or eat whatever was coming through. I didn't stop to find out. As soon as the door opened and whoever it was stepped through, I slipped out and then I came to meet you."

Deborah pushed her head back against the pillow and moaned. "He's trying to kill us," she said weakly, closing her eyes. She felt Luke tense up against her and turned to see him open his mouth in protest at the absurdity of what she was saying. When he saw her face, however, he closed it again.

Deborah nodded to the journal which lay beside her. She hadn't released it from her grip since she'd returned. "I only read a bit of it," she said, "but it's all in here."

Gently, Deborah positioned the journal in front of her so that they could both read it together. She opened it to the front page and let Luke read in silence, feeling his heart quicken in his chest as he did so. He then nodded for her to turn over and they both read on. The next page was entitled '*Ingesting the Souls*' and had been underlined twice in a thick red ink.

The trickiest part of the process is that the souls, though sometimes easy to catch once you have perfected the Viatel recipe and made it into the world of dreams, can be challenging to store until they are ready to be ingested. It is of utmost importance that they blend in seamlessly with one's own soul so as not to cause any upset to the constitution. To do this incorrectly will send a man quite mad, for it would be as though you were tearing yourself apart from the inside. Because of this I take the utmost care and pride in ensuring that the souls I catch have been correctly stored and subjected to my own until they become accustomed to the way I live. Only then can I ingest them into my body.

To store a soul first you must ensure the container is hot. Souls do not do well in the cold; they become slow and sluggish. Heat is needed to keep them lithe and active so they burn off the excess imprint of their former bodies. Of course it is undeniable that this is not a pleasant habitat for them. However, since I subject my own soul to the very same conditions I have little sympathy for any such complaints. I am doing them a favour after all, for without me, where would they live? I took a risk too. By removing my own soul to blend with the others I must constantly ensure a fresh supply to keep me alive. My soul complains of course, begs me to take him back in. But I must be strong. A single soul is not enough! Sometimes I feel as though these souls aren't grateful for the second chance I give them. I explain to them that their bodies didn't want them, that they were rejected, not needed, selfishly left to die. But still they whine and beg and scream to be let go, to be taken back. They do not know any better, Father, so I forgive them for that, and soon they will understand that I only mean to end their suffering. If, in doing so, there is a little discomfort, a little loneliness and pain, then so be it. There is no going back now, Father. I will live forever to honour you.

It is the only way to do it, Father, because your life was so cruelly taken away from you, from me, by this wicked and selfish race. Now I will do my best to stay alive, to take the souls from those who so carelessly discard them and live on and on. You may think, Father, that this is a cruel fate for the souls of others who do not wish to be in a body other than their own, but they must learn to sacrifice themselves. They must learn that their bodies no longer wanted them, that they did not do their jobs well enough to keep them from trying to die, and so they, too, must suffer the loss and the pain just like I did. I do it for you, Father. I do it for you.

The time is takes for a soul to integrate fully with my own depends on the strength of character of the body from which it was taken. The younger ones tend to be the easiest to transition. Some older souls, however, can take many years. If this is the case, it often becomes hardly worth ingesting them at all. They have become rotten and therefore I simply dispose of these ones. It may be sad, Father, but if they choose to be so stubborn they are no good to anyone anyway, not even themselves.

However, the good ones, the ones who are willing to cooperate, when ready, are then prepared for ingestion. I cannot take in a whole soul at once. No matter how well acclimatised they are, the process is slow and must be done bit by bit.

Dissection is achieved using a pure silver knife and cutting the soul into appropriate sized pieces which are simply to be eaten. It is important, however, to ensure that the soul remains alive during this process and therefore one must leave the heart and eyes until last. Does it hurt them? Of course. But they suffer the pain to be loved again. It is all they want, to be loved again, I am sure of it.

The process is then complete and I then gain all the years the soul should have lived for in their own body. I live on, the souls live on, and those selfish human bodies get exactly what they deserve.

I know you may think the worst of me, Father, but it's too late now, and I do it for you, Father. I do it for you.

Deborah glanced up at Luke as he read, his eyes wide and disbelieving. When he got to the end of the page he looked up at her and shook his head. "This is insane," he muttered. Deborah nodded her head and gently turned the page.

To catch a soul I simply learn from their bodies the nature of their dreams. Once I have understood this enough I give them the Viatel plant, which ensures that they fall into a deep and dreamful sleep. It is during this time that I have my best chance of finding the souls. Of course, the world of dreams is a dangerous place, even for me. Things become tangled in the dream worlds and although the Viatel plants allow me to enter the dreams of others, it does not mean I have complete control. The bodies, weak and pathetic as they are, still influence the dream worlds. People and places, memories and things can all become intertwined. Sometimes they can feel that they are being violated, that something foreign has entered, and so their subconscious will do everything in its power to stop me. Still, I do not care for my own safety, Father. To catch the souls is my only aim.

Deborah slammed the journal shut, unable to read on. Her hands were shaking and her stomach churning. She swallowed hard as wells of sour saliva swelled up into her mouth.

"Jesus!" Luke muttered. He seemed unable to take it in and had refilled his mug several times while reading. He stared out of the window and sighed helplessly. "Do you believe it? I mean it can't be true, can it? It sounds mad, I mean. God, if it is true, is there a way we can even stop it?"

Deborah looked up at him, feeling suddenly angry. She didn't know if it was at him, or the bleak horror of the situation, but it bubbled up in a hot pool inside her and she banged her hand on the table, which made Luke jump in his seat.

"Of course it's true and of course we can stop it!" she yelled. "We started it, after all! If we hadn't been so stupid, so selfish, in the first place none of this would have happened." She eased herself out of the booth, ignoring Luke's cries of protest and the pain which shot through her arms and legs.

"Where are your pills?" she said to him, her eyes darting around the room looking for likely hiding places.

"What?" said Luke. "Deborah, calm down, will you?"

"WHERE ARE THE PILLS?" she screamed. She tore at her hair, feeling herself growing hotter and more frantic by the second. Feeling Luke's arms around her waist she collapsed into them, sobbing hysterically. "We need to go back into the dreams. We need to find our souls before he does."

Luke gently pulled her away and kissed her before brushing back the tears from her cheeks and nodding carefully.

"OK, we will. We'll take the pills. We'll take them together, and we'll find our souls and get them back." He paused and looked at Deborah. "Do you think that's why we sometimes dream of each other, that our bodies know what's happening, that somewhere in our subconscious we are working together, trying to help each other fight him off?"

Deborah smiled at him. "I hope so," she replied.

Luke pulled her tightly toward him again. "OK, we'll do it – but not tonight, OK? Not tonight, Deborah. I just want one more night of you and me and nothing else. We'll stay awake – we'll make sure we do – and we can just lie next to each other, OK? I just want one night of it. Then tomorrow we'll take the pills and we'll fix everything and it'll all be OK."

He looked at her face, studying it carefully for signs that she agreed. Eventually she nodded her head, pulling away from him to wipe her the tears away with her sleeve.

"Tomorrow then," she said firmly.

"Tomorrow," he agreed. He then picked her up and slowly, softly, carried her onto the bed.

CHAPTER 24

100BC

The village of the two pronged tongues

The wind howled through the night and the rain pummelled down, beating at the door of the straw hut. Ouranus and Pup huddled together by the fire, their trunks intertwined for warmth. Dappha ran around putting pots and pans underneath the gaps in the ceiling where big drops of rain had leaked through. Father was silent, his back to everyone, staring at the mammoth pile of Viatel they had stashed in the corner and covered with rice sacks to try to keep them dry.

"Cheer up, love." Dappha nestled up beside him. "It can't go on forever. Besides, the plants will be fine. We've sealed them in proper, and they can handle a little rain. For God's sake we all can – we've survived far worse storms than this."

Father smiled at his wife and nodded his head, draping his trunk over her shoulders affectionately. "I know it," he replied, unconvinced. "I am sure everything will be fine."

"That's right," Dappha confirmed, emptying a pan of water into the drain hole. "Tomorrow the sun will return, mark my words, then we can set the plants out to dry, and then, in a couple of days, we should be ready to go into the village"

Father nodded. "If the sun comes out then a couple of days should do it. Then, yes, I guess we can go in."

Ouranos pricked up his ears and lifted his head sleepily. "Can I come too, Father? Please let me. I want to help as well."

Dappha and Father exchanged a glance. "I'm sure it will be fine, love," Dappha whispered. "It's different to last time. So many of them are sick now. They'll have to listen to us. They'll just have to."

Father closed his eyes as he remembered last time – the shouts, the torment, the disgust as people slammed their doors in his face. Why hadn't they listened to him at the start? He could have stopped all of this when that first boy got infected. But they hadn't, and so, as he had predicted, it spread.

It was only in the shadows of night, as a last desperate hope, dragging their poor relatives wrapped in cloaks, rags in their mouths to stop them from screaming, that they had sought his help. He'd done what he could but often it was simply too late. He hadn't had enough Viatel to cure them. All he'd managed to do was prolong their lives, but who wants to live longer when your skin is falling off your very bones and your blood is boiling inside you? He'd just made it worse. And that hadn't helped matters. The people then blamed him, blinded with fury at the pain of their loved ones. They'd screamed curses in his face, called him and his family 'devil people', and cast them out to live in this shack away from the town.

Father looked towards the pile again. Dappha was right, though. There was so much this time. He could make a cure. He was sure of it. He could put an end to this. All they had ever wanted to do was to help, to preserve life just as their great God had told them to. That was the mission of all Elephant men, to wander the Earth and to protect its people, no matter what. It was the promise he had made and he would do everything in his power to make it so. He turned to his son.

"Yes, you can help me, Ouranos. You will be an excellent help, I am sure." Ouranos wriggled his legs and let out an excited squeal.

Dappha and Father exchanged a glance once more. She nodded at him, her eyes full of love and trust. "I'll make us some cocoa," she said and turned to the stove.

The sickness had started three months ago. The whispers had spread around the town like wildfire. The butcher's boy was poorly. At first it was nothing. Sympathies were exchanged. A few of those close to the butcher had sent gifts of decorative wheatlips bundled together with string. Then the boy got worse. His cries were heard throughout the night and the townspeople became afraid. It sounded as though a devil was in him, they whispered. *There is a devil come into our town,* they thought.

The Elephant family until that point had been generally left alone. The townsfolk did not care for them as such but they were widely regarded as gentle, unfortunate-looking folk who meant no harm. They kept themselves to themselves and caused no trouble. They had lived in that time on the edge of town in a nice but simple two-room mudhouse which let them carry on in comfort. On a weekly basis Dappha and Pup would come into the town centre and buy wheat and milk and sell baskets of fruit and freshly-baked bread to the locals who, although they found it hard to admit, all secretly agreed that the fruit was the most succulent and sweet they had ever tasted and the bread the softest and most delicious.

Father had earned a little money doing odd jobs here and there for the local townsfolk. They were more than happy to employ him to do the heavy labour jobs that they couldn't manage, for he worked hard, charged little and never addressed them more than he had to. He would often bring Ouranos along to help him, but mostly they left Ouranos to guard the home and to keep on with his studies of the Viatel plant which would be essential to his success if he wished to take over the true family business.

They led a quiet and simple life, giving no reason for trouble. Therefore the people of the town, while keeping their distance, remained happy to have the Elephant family live amongst them. Of course, the reason that Father had brought them to the town in the first place was because he had been guided there, so they all knew that this simple life of relative peace and harmony wouldn't last forever, that one dark day a sickness would come and it would be up to them to try to save the people from it. But until then all they could do was wait and try to gain the trust of the townsfolk so that when the time came they would let them help.

The sickness, however, came sooner than Father had predicted. When the butcher's boy first got sick Father had suggested that he could help and explained about the healing properties of the Viatel plant, but the butcher and his wife were conventional people and preferred to stick to the modern medicine of the time, so they had refused.

The local doctor was summoned and concluded that a nasty fever was the cause, so he set up a course of droplet medicine for the boy, estimating he would recover in a few days. When he did not, Father had returned to the butcher's door, quite insistent that he could help. By this time the butcher and his wife were half crazed and starved of sleep. They took Father's words to be aggressive, his strange face wrinkled with that ghastly trunk protruding out and his voice gruff and stern.

"Leave us alone, witchman," the butcher's wife had screamed and they pushed him away and closed the door.

Days later the butcher's boy was dead and the wife had taken to her bed with a fever just like his. Within a week she too was dead and two of the farmer's children were reported sick as well.

The town became nervous. People stopped going out. The markets dried up and everyone who so much as coughed was suspected of infection. Within a month the village was changed. Big red crosses covered the doors. No one ventured out and screams of the dying clotted the air both day and night.

All the while Father would make regular trips into the village clutching bottles of dried out Viatel, begging the villagers to let him try and help them. But the sickness got hold of people in many strange ways. Even those who weren't infected were crazed, unable to bear the constant screams of the dying, and so they too shooed him away.

It was Freddie Soot, the coalman's son, who was the first and only one that Father eventually got to treat. He remembered the night, the knock at his door and Mr Soot tumbling in, eyes red and wild with despair, clutching a cloaked-up, sputtering, boneless bundle that was barely a shadow of his son.

"Do what you can," he'd begged. "I already lost his mam, and his sister went yesterday. Please don't take him, too. Please make it stop. I can't lose him, too."

He'd gently laid his son on the floor who thrashed and howled violently with a sound barely resembling that of a human being. Pup and Ouranos dashed to their mother and curled themselves into her arms.

"Take them out," Father had said calmly. He'd looked at the boy. "How long has he been like this?"

Mr Soot had shrugged and shaken his head. He was barely able to string his words together. "A week. Two perhaps. I been the way of the Doctor and he gone and gave me some Drop medicine but it's useless. We all know it's useless but there is nothing else. You've got sumfink though, ain't you? A plant. Give him the plant leaves you said 'n' that'll cure him, make him normal again, that's what you said."

Father knelt beside the boy and looked into his eyes. There was no colouring left, only two huge, frantic black pupils screaming back at him. He was so far gone. Could it even work? He'd hurried to check his Viatel stocks. It had been a rough summer for spotting and they hadn't stored nearly enough. If the people had listened to him at the beginning he would have been able to save the butcher's boy and have enough left over to make a small vaccine for the rest of them, but now, if he wanted to try and save this boy, he would have to make a hit so strong that it would use up his entire supply in one shot.

However, he had taken a vow and his vow was to help all the people that asked him, so Father had set to work, shredding and mashing and bubbling and boiling until the medicine was ready. He knelt beside the boy once more and tilted his head back and poured the medicine in.

Almost immediately the boy went deathly still. Father

had held his trunk, not daring to breathe, and then slowly, slowly, a little colour came back to the boy's eyes.

Mr Soot had looked up at Father, not daring to believe. "He's getting better?" he asked, bewildered.

"I think so," Father had replied. Mr Soot then fell to his knees, sobbing with gratitude. He had hurriedly gathered the boy up and carried him back to his village to recover his own bed.

A day later the boy was sitting up, still sickly sore but with shrunken pupils, and his screaming had stopped. Mr Soot sung the praises of the Elephant family and when the townsfolk refused to believe, he had invited them around to look at his son, bringing Father along, too, to witness the progress.

Father sighed at the memory. It had been timing really, nothing more. Timing that had been against them all. Perhaps, if Mr Soot had brought his son just a few days earlier then the medicine might have been strong enough to give him a full recovery. Perhaps, if it hadn't been that very hour where half the village was crowded around his bed that the medicine had chosen to wear off... Perhaps... so many things... perhaps.

But it happened as it did, and what happened was that the boy had begun to deteriorate fast, right in front of their eyes. It started with a violent cough that startled them all enough to step back. Father remembered the cough and the sinking feeling that went with it. Seconds later, blood had trickled from the boy's ears, his eyes had clouded over and he had begun to fit and moan and thrash about. Mr Soot shouted wildly and used the weight of his body to press his son's arms to his sides, trying to pin him down. That's when the biting started, with Freddie Soot gnashing wildly at his Father's face.

The villagers screamed, the women folk pushing and trampling over each other to get out. Some of the men had gallantly tried to help. Some had turned to Father and yelled at him to do something. But the Viatel had all been used up and there was nothing Father could do but look helplessly on.

Four days. Four whole days the coalman's boy had lain in bed screaming a scream that no man should hear, his arms lashed to his sides, his huge black eyes twisting up towards the ceiling, his mouth foaming and the horrible sound of frantic, chomping teeth so desperate to bite. In the end they'd put a stick in his mouth to stop the gnashing and the splinters had trickled down his throat and he'd choked to death. It was a blessing really. God only knew how long he would have remained like that if he had not.

After that the villagers had turned against the Elephant family. The ones that remained healthy turned out in force on Father's doorstep, their faces thunderous with rage.

"Out, witchman!" they'd screamed, many believing that these strange creatures must have been the cause of the infection in the first place. "Out, filthy murderers!"

So Father had gathered his peaceful little family together and in the dead of night they'd left their home to live away from the villagers' wrath.

They did not give up, however. Father was quite insistent about that, despite Dappha's fears for her family.

"We're here to protect them. We can't let the sickness win," he'd replied to her frantic protests. Eventually she agreed, and so it began with Father and Ouranos out every day, stockpiling the Viatel when they found it in the hope that one day they would have enough to make a cure.

The wind howled through the night and Father turned to look at the great pile of Viatel once more. Dappha softly plodded up beside him and handed him a cup of sweet cocoa. She nodded to Ouranos and Pup, who were huddled in a perfect sphere in the corner, swaddled in rice sacks to keep out the cold. "We are lucky," she whispered and leant her chin softly on his shoulder.

Father nodded. She was right, of course. They had been blessed with a perfect family. Despite the troubles with the village they had never wanted for anything, happy to live a simple and solitary existence. As long as they kept their mission in mind and did what they could to save the people then they would be rewarded at the end.

Father sighed. Finding the Viatel had been a great blessing, a dream come true. Now, after all these months, they finally had a hope of helping the townsfolk. He knew it would be difficult but as Dappha had pointed out there were so many of them now sick that surely they had to listen. He just wished he could shake off the uneasy feeling, deep in the shadows of his brain, that something truly terrible, even more terrible than being outcast, even more terrible than the sickness itself, was lurking, waiting for them, right around the corner.

CHAPTER 25

GRACE

The cleansing

Grace and Peter sat on top of a hill and looked down at the scene below. The sun was lowering down onto the hills, flexing its golden rays far over the valley and casting everything in its deep orange glow. It seemed to be a different season in this strange place, for the temperature was warm and spring flowers were popping up their heads through the grass in every shade of pink, yellow and purple that was imaginable, creating a rippling kaleidoscope of colour as they swayed back and forth in the breeze.

Grace rested her head on Peter's arm and he stroked her hair, which shone like a golden crown in the sunshine. They had spent hours exploring the grounds and the buildings of this place. They had first gone to the library, which was a breathtakingly beautiful building on the inside. Its grey brick walls led up to a wide vaulted ceiling supported by ornate marble columns. The windows were stained glass and dappled the room in a rainbow of lights as the sun shone through. The shelves which ran along all sides had wooden ladders which stretched as high as the ceiling to ensure even the topmost shelves could be reached. Large tangerine silk cushions were scattered in heaps on the floor, making comfortable resting places for those who wished to sit and read. The air smelt of paper and dust.

Grace had wandered up and down the shelves, pulling out various books which told of the history of the place. She settled on one of the cushions to read. She took a deep breath, and the faint scent of lavender from the bushes which grew outside reached her nostrils through an open window. She read that the valley had apparently been discovered over two hundred years ago, where one desperate soul who had been drinking himself to death in the bar had got up to leave. Because he was so full of liquor, he had tripped and stumbled gracelessly onto the floor, flinging up the floorboard exactly as Lara had done for them just hours before. He had then discovered, seemingly by chance, a timeless place where souls could rest and live on without their bodies. He went back out to find others, to spread the word, but he sadly never made it back in time to live out his days in the beautiful place he had discovered. Too far gone to make it back to the outside world, he had been found by another soul, face down in the river. They had dragged him out and in his pocket had found a soggy note with instructions and a map of how to get there. It seemed he had known his own fate.

The man who found the map was Abeid's great great great grandfather. Over the years his ancestors had built the place into a community and souls were actively sought out to be rescued and brought here by whoever was appointed leader. The community rules were simple: everyone would be treated equally, everyone must be cleansed and, once committing to stay, no one would again be permitted to leave.

After Grace had had her fill of the books, they had gone to the town hall. It had looked like a functional barn from the outside, but inside it had been fit for a king. Statues of gold dragons dripped wine from their mouths and huge crystal chandeliers hung high from a ceiling where thousands of flowers had been carved out of the wood. There was a raised platform at the end of the hall and a huge grandfather clock stood in the middle. It had been carved from a rich piece of walnut and swirled and curved as if it could move. When Grace came closer, she realised the pattern was made up of hundreds of creatures just like the Creature she had met when she had been first pulled into the dreams. Their strange human eyes seeming to watch her as she ran her hands over the carvings.

She had called Peter over to see. The creatures were all in differing stages of youth and death. Peter shuddered when he looked at them and had pulled her away from the platform, instead turning her attention to the centre of the room where a huge table stretched out, ready and set for festivity. Thin china plates decorated with gold leaf lay between gleaming silver knives and forks. The glasses were crystal. Huge copper jugs had been placed, evenly spaced, along its length and the entire surface had been scattered with orchid petals which filled the room with their sweet, heady scent. He gushed about how beautiful it all was and speculated what the table could have been prepared for. Perhaps there would be a celebration? Grace had nodded, for he was right; it was spectacular. Neither she nor Peter had ever seen anything like it.

"So," Peter said, breaking the silence and pulling Grace away from her thoughts. "What do you think?"

He was obviously nervous. She could tell from the moment he had stepped foot in this place that there was no question in his mind that he wanted to stay. Yet she also knew that he wouldn't leave her if she chose to go. She looked up at him. Was it enough to be in love? Was that a reason to abandon Deborah? A few weeks before the idea of agreeing for Deborah to be cleansed from her life would have been the most disgusting and vile suggestion anyone could have made, but now, here she was, actually considering it.

She gently took Peter's hand and led him out of the hall. They climbed up to the top of the hill which was the highest peak of the land and gazed down towards the village. Grace turned to him.

"Peter..." she began.

She was interrupted, before she could continue, by Lara, who had shyly appeared behind them. She was wearing a black net dress which brushed the blades of grass as she walked. She nodded to the sun which was now only barely peeking over the hills. "We must be inside now," she said softly. Peter nodded at her before scrambling to his feet and then helping Grace up. They walked hand in hand down the hill back to their cottage. All the while Grace was reminded of how wonderful it was to be able to touch him again. They were safe here. They were at peace. There would be no more pain, no more struggling. They could be happy here, together.

Peter and Grace walked up the garden path and, just before going inside, Grace turned round and watched from her little cottage doorway as the last of the sun disappeared behind the hill. She turned to Peter, who was already inside, leaning against the table, watching her nervously. Grace pushed the door behind her and walked towards him until they were only inches apart. She brushed his lips with her fingers and looked deep into his hopeful green eyes.

"Let's stay," Grace sighed and forced her mouth into a smile. She wanted to stay. At least she thought she did. It made sense for them, but somehow she couldn't quite bring herself to feel happy about it.

Peter seemed not to notice the uncertainty in her voice or the unhappiness in her eyes and was immediately overjoyed. His eyes sparkled and he lifted her up and twirled her round above him.

"Yes! Yes! Oh, Grace, we're going to be brilliant here. It's going to be so good. I know it!" His laughter was infectious and eventually Grace forgot what was troubling her as they tumbled together to the floor and became as one again.

They were woken by a sharp knock at the door. Peter moaned as Grace moved, trying to disentangle herself from him and the pile of cushions that they had strewn around them. They had not made it upstairs and she felt a stiffness in her bones; the hardness of a night on the floor had taken its toll.

She squatted on her knees and squinted, holding her hand up to her face as the pallid morning sunlight streamed in through the windows. The knock sounded again. Grace scrambled up and pulled her dress over her head, reaching the door just as a third knock started. She pulled it open. There stood Lara, who looked desperately nervous. Her eyes were wide and her mouth set in a stern, thin line. She wore a blueberry-coloured puffed-out skirt and a ruffled white shirt that was done up to the collar. A small pink flower was entwined in the end of her hair, which she had braided into a loose plait. She held a small cloth in her hand which she was rolling through her fingers.

Grace smiled at her. "Hello Lara," she said.

"I guess you know why I'm here," Lara replied, fingering the cloth anxiously. "Have you decided to stay or not?" She peered behind Grace as Peter came up to the door. Grace felt him wrap his arms around her waist and his breath was hot on her neck.

"Yes," he mumbled into it. "We're going to stay, aren't we, Grace?" There was a pause where Grace said nothing. She felt Peter's arms stiffen around her and him draw his head back. "Grace?" She turned and looked from him to Lara whose face now looked as though all the blood had drained from her cheeks.

Grace couldn't help herself. She needed to ask. She needed to know.

"What would happen if we weren't, just out of interest, of course?" She could feel Peter's grip loosen and turned to see him wipe his brow with the back of his hand as beads of sweat formed on his forehead. She felt guilty for playing with him like this but she felt there was something strange about the way business was conducted in this place, and needed to know that if she was going to stay it was her choice, not because she would be forced to.

Lara remained impassive, though her face was still startlingly white. "Well, nothing, of course," she replied in a deadpan voice. "You would simply have to leave."

Grace studied Lara's expression. She couldn't help but feel as though she was hiding something from them. She seemed so young, yet she had none of that carefree or youthful nature about her that a teenager should have. Still she said nothing and there was no time. So Grace shrugged, remaining unconvinced as she conceded.

"Yes," she said. "We're going to stay."

Both Peter and Lara seemed to breathe huge sighs of relief and Grace could see that Lara immediately relaxed her hands. Her shoulders dropped and the colour came flooding back to her face.

"Great," she said, smiling brightly. "I shall let Abeid know at once." She then turned to go before stopping half way down the path to call back, "Oh, it's Sunday today so there is a cleansing at noon. We gather in the town hall and walk over to the tower from there." Lara then turned and walked away. Grace frowned as she watched her, for she could have sworn that, just for a moment as the sun beamed down on Lara's back, she had seen a flash of silver spark underneath the cloth she'd been holding.

Noon came round sooner than they expected and Peter and Grace found themselves running hand in hand over the grass to make it to the town hall in time. They were the last ones to arrive and were greeted to a rippling murmur as they rounded the corner to the thirty or so other residents who all turned round to stare at them.

Abeid was sitting on a huge white throne which had been placed on the raised platform right beside the clock at the end of the hall. He was wearing the same blazing white suit as before. His top hat, however, had been removed and replaced with a small, intricately-beaded cap. He nodded serenely to them as they approached. All then turned around to face him as he stood.

"Howdy and good day to ya all!" he roared. "It is that great time again for the people of this fine place to be cleansed. Come with me. Follow me, and I will show ya'll the way to true freedom!"

There was scattered applause as Abeid then leapt down from his chair and led the way across to his tower. The souls began to follow him, marching across the grass. Grace clutched at Peter's hand as they followed. A dark feeling began to press down on her.

"Peter, I don't know about this," she whispered.

He squeezed her hand. "I know it's scary but we'll be fine. Once we've had it once we'll realise that it's nothing, I'm sure. I'll be with you the whole time, OK?"

She nodded. They entered the tower through a small arched door at the back. As soon as they were all inside this was immediately shut so no natural light could come in. Several souls busied themselves by lighting candles and placing them in rings on the ground. Grace looked up – there was nothing above them apart from a huge, flat neon light that was fitted into the ceiling which hurt her eyes if she looked directly at it. Apart from this, as far as she could tell, the tower was simply a big white tube of cement. There were no doors leading to rooms, no way of getting to the top of the tower and no way of getting out bar the way they had entered.

The souls had arranged themselves in neat rows so Grace and Peter followed suit, standing next to one another in the second row back. She glanced sideways and recognised the young man from the bar the previous night. His expression had changed; it was now one of a strange and empty calm like the faces of many of the others. Grace couldn't help but stare at him. There was something about him that she recognised but she didn't know why, yet it was something that made her feel desperately, desperately sad.

Suddenly all fell silent as Abeid stood in front of them and was helped into a long white robe which skimmed the floor and was embroidered with swirls and slashes of brown and gold. He lit a solitary candle and placed this at his feet. He then scanned the room up and down until his eyes settled on Grace.

"All right, sister." He beckoned her forward. "Come over here to me. Don't be afraid."

Grace planted her feet firmly on the ground. All her instincts told her not to go forward. She didn't want to be cleansed, especially not by this man she barely knew and did not trust. Suddenly and overwhelmingly, she knew she had made a mistake. Despite the life she might be choosing, she had to find her way back. She felt a wretched tug deep in her heart. It was Deborah! Deborah was calling for her, she knew it!

But before she could do anything, Grace felt a sharp shove in her back and stumbled forward. She turned to see Lara glaring viciously at her. Peter looked aghast and seemed to be about to protest but Lara turned and glared at him, too, so he did not speak. Instead he settled his face into a smile and nodded at Grace encouragingly.

As Grace turned around she saw that Abeid had appeared by her side. "Don't be afraid, sister," he whispered in her ear, making all the hairs on the back of her neck stand up. He then grabbed her by the arm and led her into the centre of the room. Quick as a flash, he produced a small silver knife from a pocket concealed within his robes. It filled her with horror.

"No, NO! I don't want this!"

Abeid gripped her firmly as he traced the knife up and down her chest. Grace could feel Deborah tugging at her and was overcome with horror and disgust. How could she? How could she give up on Deborah? Deborah needed her! She wanted her back. She could feel it! She was pulling as a sign, and the pain of the separation was more intense than ever. Grace squirmed in agony as every time Abeid's knife skimmed over her chest and stomach it got stronger and stronger. She tried desperately to break free as he ran the knife right over the spot where she could feel Deborah's pull the most. It seemed, however, that the knife could feel it too. Her stomach seemed to drag up like a magnet towards the tip of the blade, and Abeid's hand shook as he kept it from plunging in. His lips curved upwards. "Aha! Hold still, sister. I need to get this demon out!"

Abeid raised his arm, clutching the knife high above his head. Grace shut her eyes and screamed. But instead of the cold metal being plunged into her skin, she felt herself being pulled away and Abeid's grip loosen. Peter had appeared behind him and had hold of his wrist. He twisted Abeid's arm hard behind his back and did not let go until the knife clattered to the floor. Peter shoved him backwards into the crowd of startled souls before grabbing Grace's arm.

"Let's go!" he shouted. They bolted for the door, hearing a roar of anger from Abeid behind them. Peter pulled the door open and out they ran as fast as they could over the field and towards the pine trees that marked the edge of the land.

Grace's heart was pounding. She clutched at her stomach as the pain throbbed still. She glanced behind her. Peter was right on her heels and, behind him, the souls, streaming over the land! They were coming after them! They weren't going to let them peacefully leave as Lara had said.

"Get to the woods!" Grace cried out, as Peter grabbed her arm, pulling her faster. The souls were catching up with them, headed by Lara, whose face was set in a thunderous scowl. But they were so close, and suddenly they were at the foot of the trees, and ran into the forest.

The trees were packed so tightly together that they snagged and slashed at Grace's skin. She could hear the angry screams of the souls grow distant, and she ran until she could feel warm trickles of blood dripping over her arms.

Grace looked up and could barely see the sky through the dense branches that towered over her. She panted like a dog as she tried to keep up with Peter. Her mouth was dry and her heart was burning in her chest. What had Abeid been trying to do, had he been trying to somehow cut the connection she had with Deborah? It wasn't humane! No one told them that 'cleansing' meant ripping your heart right out of your chest!

"Peter, Peter, wait!" she called ahead of her as she struggled to catch her breath and leant against the rough bark of the tree. He stopped and waited until she came to his side.

"How do we even know we're going the right way?" she cried. "We could be lost in here forever. How do we know they won't come after us?"

Peter shook his head. "There's no way. Didn't you see the way Lara looked when she talked about the edge? She looked afraid. They've had their hearts ripped out. They can't come back into the real world now. They would die straight away."

"And Abeid?" Grace asked. "What about him?"

"I guess he kept his heart," Peter shrugged. "That's the only way he'd be able to go back out there. It must be pretty torturous for him, though."

"Well, maybe he deserves it with what he does to us," Grace said angrily. Her hands were shaking. It had been so close. She shut her eyes, not daring to think about what could have happened if Peter hadn't got to her in time.

"Thank you," she said and took his hand. Grace smiled at him and leant forward to show him how much she meant it, but suddenly the smile was wiped from her face. The dizziness was returning. Grace felt it swarm in from either side as the pain began, like a huge hand crushing her skull.

"Oh no, Peter. No!" she cried as her stomach began to lurch and bile swilled in her mouth.

Peter quickly dropped her hand and immediately the pain went away. Grace looked up at him as she rubbed her head. He was staring at her with his big green eyes, which had suddenly filled with tears.

"I guess that's it then," he said, looking away and wiping his eyes angrily with his sleeve.

Grace looked at the ground. She hadn't expected it to happen straight away. She had thought that they would have more time, more time to say goodbye, to hold each other for the last time. "I'm so sorry, Peter," she said, not looking at him, "but I can't live without Deborah. I just can't."

"But I guess you can without me," he replied.

They reached the edge of the forest by nightfall. Peter was right; no one came after them. Grace couldn't help but wonder if she had somehow made a mistake. Perhaps they had simply put the rules in place because that's the way it had to be. Grace dug her nails into her palm as she remembered how strangely cold Lara had been, and the way Abeid had refused to let her go, despite her cries. No way – they were definitely doing the right thing, besides she couldn't let Deborah go, she knew that now.

Peter had not spoken a word to her since they had discovered they were no longer able to touch. Grace had wanted to call out to him, to tell him that she did love him, that she did want to be with him so much, to try to explain that if it was only her then she would do anything for him. But what good would it do? She was Deborah's, and Deborah was calling her back, and there was no way she could ignore that call.

Peter turned around as they reached a road and they

both looked down towards the bright lights of the city once again. It seemed so small, so harmless, from where they stood – a little noiseless, twinkling metropolis in the distance. If only this were true. Now they were both alone, fighting for themselves against the city, against the dreams, and against time itself. It seemed so impossible that they would survive. Grace turned to Peter, trying to find the words to apologise again.

She frowned. Peter had his head bent towards his chest and was looking at his hands which were shimmering under the moonlight. She could see outlines of trees through his body. He was fading.

He looked up at her and the same furrow of confusion lined his brow. "You're being pulled in!" she called to him. Her voice came out shadowy, as if it were an echo of itself.

"So are you," he called back.

Suddenly she felt it. She quickly stepped closer to him while she still had control and they stared into each other's eyes, watching as, bit by bit, they both became transparent, like liquid outlines, as the dream-world took them over. Neither of them looked away until the very last moment and then, at exactly the same time, they disappeared altogether.

CHAPTER 26

DEBORAH

The brutal morning

It had been a long night. Both too fearful to go to sleep, they had fought to stay awake. For Deborah it was hardest; the painkillers had made her drowsy so she had refused to take any more, and once the first ones had worn off the pain in her foot had been excruciating. Luke had suggested that they wait until morning before going to sleep, and he was right. Despite all of the pain she was still grateful for one more night with him. They had talked a little, first about what they should do if they got into the same dream and then what they would do if they survived it. All the while Deborah had leant her head on Luke's chest and listened to the sound of him breathing and his heart beating. It was a strong heart, she could tell. No matter how much it had been battered and bruised it was still beating loud and hard, and the rhythmic noise comforted her as the hours of the night passed by.

Eventually the sun yawned and stretched its rays across the sea, prickling the birds into life, and they listened in silence to the caw of seagulls circling overhead. The alarm which they had pointlessly set then bleeped and Luke gently kissed Deborah on the forehead and slid quietly away from her. She heard him walk up the steps to the hatch and close it behind him.

Deborah suddenly felt incredibly lonely and tired, even though she knew he was coming back. The loneliness sat like a hole in her stomach. While he was gone she pulled the journal onto her lap and began to read:

25th December 1923

It is a surprisingly good time of year to catch them. Christmas. Such a time of joy for so many. Such pressure to be happy. It really can be hard to hold it together. Today I caught the soul of a young woman, only 14 years old, due to be married to the local farmer in the New Year. He was a forty-five year old man but had more money than the girls family could ever hope for, so they had welcomed the idea. Stupid girl. She should have been grateful for the chance at a better life, no matter what. We were grateful people, weren't we, Father? We appreciated every day we were given, no matter what came our way.

The Creature is getting to me again. He is a wicked sort! Taunting me with threats that I'll never make it, that time runs out eventually for all men. He does not know to whom he speaks. I have locked him in chains in my attic. He is, of course, useful to have around. I need to keep an eye on him to make sure he does not get too weary. The thing is, you see, that no matter how young I ingest their souls, I can't be sure of how long they were going to live for; this girl may have died young anyway. So I keep the Creature and if he starts to look weary I make sure I make haste to find another soul so I don't find myself in any trouble. He sometimes struggles and howls through the night, but it seems no one else but me can hear him. No matter, Father, I am used to the screams. They do not bother me now.

Deborah pushed her hair back from her face. The Creature! That must have been what Luke saw in his office. She didn't understand it, though. Why did he need to keep it alive? From what she had read it seemed as though this Creature was linked to him somehow, that if the Creature got tired then so would he. It was absurd, of course, but then so was everything that had happened to her in the last few weeks.

When Luke returned, Deborah filled him in. He reacted in much the same way – disbelief at first, then weary acceptance that probably it was somehow true. Doctor Vanilla had not meant for them to read the journal. Why would he lie?

Luke set about making breakfast as Deborah leant her head back on her pillows and listened to the sounds of him rummaging in the kitchen. She heard the click and bubble as the kettle boiled and soon the dark, rich scent of coffee filled the air. Moments later Luke arrived with a tray which he carefully balanced on a space on the bed between them. Two steaming mugs of coffee, thick slices of malty toasted bread, which sat upright in a toast rack, and two little pots of butter and jam. Deborah struggled upright and peered into her coffee cup as Luke arranged the pillows around her.

They ate in silence and despite the simplicity of the meal, Deborah relished every mouthful. When they had finished Luke cleared the tray away and sat on the edge of the bed.

"You should take more pills now," he said. "It won't matter if they make you drowsy if we're going to sleep soon anyway."

Deborah nodded and reached for the bottle, but didn't open it; instead she simply tipped it one way then the other, listening to the rattle of the tablets inside.

"I'm so sick of pills," she sighed. Luke turned around to face her and reached for her hand.

"I know," he said. "Me too."

"Do you have anything cold, though, for my foot? Something in the freezer, like ice-cream or something?"

Luke shuddered. "No way. I hate the stuff, always have. I could soak a cloth in cold water, though?"

Deborah nodded. Luke did as she asked, then sat beside her again and gently pressed the cloth to her foot.

They each held the other's gaze. It was as if, since they had shared their pasts, they knew each other better than they knew themselves. Deborah couldn't even explain to herself how she now felt about this man. It was a need. She needed him. She would no longer be whole without him.

Deborah leant her head back on the pillows and thought about her soul. She had never bothered to contemplate the idea of having a soul before, she wasn't a religious person nor particularly spiritual. She had, in fact, never really considered anything other than her own existence, as it was, day by day. It was only after she had found herself without her boy that Deborah had even really thought about death, and had assumed it would bring her peace, a wonderful nothing that would end the pain and sweep her away into darkness. But now, now it seemed she had a soul, a soul she had been carrying around within her for all these years. She felt suddenly empty now knowing that she was without it. It was not only the knowledge that she needed it back to live, there was also the guilt, a deep shame that she had been so unaware, so self-involved that she had tried to take her own life and caused it to leave her.

"What are you thinking about?" Luke asked, reaching over to gently tuck a strand of hair behind her ear.

Deborah struggled upright, brushing him away.

"Oh you know. Just about how our souls are out there, and if we don't find them..."

She bit her lip. There suddenly seemed so much to live for.

"I know," Luke replied. "It's all pretty overwhelming, isn't it? I mean, I've been thinking about it all night and going over that journal of Doctor Vanilla's again and again, and I still can't believe that it's real. It's almost like this is a dream and when we go to slecp it's just a continuation of that. I feel like I barely have a grip on reality at all."

Deborah nodded. "I know what you mean, but it is real, isn't it? I mean we are both here, both experiencing this, right?"

Luke smiled at her. "I guess so, unless you're a figment of my imagination, that is!" With that Deborah leant over and pinched him hard on the arm, laughing a little as he winced.

"Well unless that was a figment of your imagination, too," she grinned. "Ow! No, don't do it back to me. I'm in enough pain as it is!"

Deborah laughed again and then sighed. "I almost don't want to do it. It seems so impossible. I mean, we've got no idea what to expect. And what if the pill doesn't work the same on you as it did for me? I mean, for all we know yours could be different. They could just look the same but they might do something else." She frowned. "Maybe you should stay here and I'll just take it again and you can watch over me while I sleep... and then you can wake me up if it looks like something is going wrong?"

Luke shook his head. "I don't think there's time for that," he sighed. I mean, Doctor Vanilla knows that we know. I don't know how long we get to survive without our souls but it can't be that long, can it?" He paused, then set his face in a determined stare. "The pills will be the same. I know it. They have to be. None of it makes sense otherwise. It's obvious he didn't prescribe them to us because of anything we were saying. His aim is the same for both of us; he wants us in the dreams so our souls will be drawn to us, and then he'll make his move."

"What if we can't stop him?" Deborah asked despairingly. "I mean, we've never done this before. He's done this God knows how many times, judging by all those journals in his office..." She trailed off and continued to tip the bottle of pills back and forth in her hand. "What if we can't beat him?"

Luke sighed and shifted his weight on the bed. He looked at her earnestly. "If we don't, then we die," he said. "And that's why we can't let him win."

Deborah nodded, though she still could not believe it. There were so many things which could go wrong. The world they were soon to enter could hold things that could defy everything they had ever thought impossible. In this world, they would not only have to find their souls, which they had only just learned existed, but do so before some monstrous evil stole them away. Deborah didn't even know what a soul was supposed to look like.

She tried not to betray her feelings to Luke, who seemed so full of unusual confidence it hardly seemed right to try to put doubts in his mind. Deborah wondered how he could be so sure. Perhaps he wasn't. Perhaps he was only trying to keep her from knowing his doubts too.

"So," she said finally, "when are we going to do it?"

"Soon," he replied, "but let's go on deck for a while." Without waiting for her consent he gently placed her arms around his neck and lifted her from the bed. He carried her with astonishing ease up the narrow steps that led to the hatch, and when they reached the top of them he placed her leaning against the bow of the boat. It was still early. The sky was striped with slabs of pink and violet cloud. Behind them the sun glowed fiercely. It was redder then Deborah had ever seen it before, both beautiful and ominous at the same time.

"Red sky in the morning," Luke breathed, almost reading her thoughts.

Deborah smiled. "I think we've had enough bad luck, don't you? Besides, I imagine the skies might be very different once we go to sleep. It'll be of little consequence what they are like here any more."

"Until we wake up," Luke said.

"Until we wake up," she repeated.

Luke crouched down beside her and placed a rough chequered rug around her shoulders which smelt of salt and scratched her bare skin. He then stretched out his legs beside her and squeezed her hand as she tilted her head so it rested on his chest, just underneath his chin. She could feel the bristles of his stubble catch on her hair as he spoke. He spoke about how, when it was all over, they could take this little boat and sail it up the coast; how they could visit all the seaside towns and play on the slot machines at the piers, and eat fish and chips on the pebbles. He talked of a life that was so nearly theirs, ignoring the huge black mountain they had to climb before they could achieve it.

"It's just one sleep," he said finally. "It's just one dream."

Deborah stretched her neck up to kiss him. It was an uncomfortable kiss with her head tilted back and his lowered at a funny angle to meet hers, but each refused to end it, as though it might be their last, and Deborah felt a surge of love and despair start as a lump in her throat as she choked back tears which were both happy and horribly sad all at once.

Finally she pulled away. "It's time," she said softly. Luke nodded and got up. He picked her up carefully in his arms and they both looked at the sky one last time. It was a perfect and brutal morning that seemed just right for what they were about to do. He carried her below, laying her gently on the bed before settling beside her. Deborah pressed the backs of her knees into the mattress, feeling the comfort of soft cotton sheets beneath her. Luke prepared the pills and she watched as he leant over the mugs, making sure each of them had dissolved before handing one to her. She reached for his hand and held it tightly.

Together they drank.

CHAPTER 27

100BC

The sickness overcomes

Dappha was right of, course. Her trunk was a fine tool for predicting the weather and just as she had prophesied, the storm calmed and abated throughout the night. The skies had cleared and the morning greeted them with bright rays of sunshine streaming through the gaps in the roof of the hut.

Dappha was the first of the family to wake and set about making a breakfast of scrambled Toot's eggs and wheatgrass tea. As the others slowly shrugged into life she stepped outside, smiling up at the cloudless blue skies that greeted her.

"Everyone wake up!" she hooted happily. "Breakfast is ready and the sun is shining!" The others stretched and yawned and then ambled out to the small lake at the back of the hut to wash. The family then sat down in a ring and ate their breakfast together. The Toot's eggs were delicious – fresh and perfectly cooked, as always. When she had licked the last of her plate, Pup parped eggily and giggled. Dappha tutted and tried to be stern but soon the whole family had collapsed into laughter. Ouranos then joined in and Father, whose spirits seemed to have been lifted in the night, gave his wife a cheeky wink before doing the longest and loudest egg parp of them all. "Oh, for goodness sake!" smiled Dappha, clearing the bowls and shooing them away. "Get on with you, all of you. There is work to be done!"

The rest of the morning was spent organising the Viatel into manageable piles so they could boil up batches of it for the first part of the process. Father and Ouranos dragged the thick-stemmed plants from the back of the hut, wrapping their trunks tightly around the ends, careful not to drop them or damage their leaves. Dappha and Pup then carefully peeled the leaves from the stems and placed them gently into huge steel cooking pots filled up to the brim with water. They then lit the fire and all gathered round waiting for the brew to boil. It was very important to keep watch at all times, for as soon as the water first started to bubble the steam had to be caught and sealed in jars for later use.

Once all the water had evaporated the leaves were left out in the sun and, when they were completely dry, Ouranos carefully crumbled them up and added them to the jars where the steam had been collected, cooled and now left a clear, deep blue liquid in the bottom. Once the first batch was ready the family started the process again. Never before had they this much Viatel to cook up all at once. The work was hard and cumbersome and the family worked in silence. Even Pup could sense the awe and magic as jar after jar was sealed up and placed in wooden boxes at the back of the hut, ready to take to the village.

It was just as the sun was beginning to set that the last batch of Viatel was completed. Father held the jar in his hands, tilting it this way and that, watching as the leaves swirled and tipped like tiny islands in a perfect blue sea. He then quietly shuffled to the back of the hut and placed it in the box. Two hundred and one jars had been filled. It was more than he had ever seen in all the centuries through which he had lived. A great surge of thankfulness filled his bones and he gently knelt on the floor and lifted his trunk to the skies.

"Please let it be enough," he whispered to the great God. "Please let it be enough."

Ouranos stood quietly at the entrance to the tent watching his Father, so strong and so wonderful as he prayed with all his might that he would be able to rescue the people of the village. He was once again overcome with love, yet something about the way his father was kneeling, the positioning of his trunk, the way his knees were trembling, made Ouranos realise how fragile he was. Even the greatest of all the Elephant men would not live forever and a sense that Father was perhaps drawing near the time where he would end suddenly overwhelmed him. Ouranos looked down and saw two soft, damp patches of mud below his feet as great, sad tears, weeping for a time not yet come, ran down his trunk and dropped to the floor.

After a simple supper of gant fruit and stonereeds, Ouranos and Father carefully lashed the boxes onto their backs. The sun was gone now and the moon hung round and full in the sky. Dappha carefully lit a couple of oil lamps and handed the first to Ouranos, gently kissing him on his forehead after she had done so. She then passed a lamp to

Father and they stood facing one another. Father raised his trunk and Dappha did the same. They gently touched one another for a moment before Father pointed his trunk skywards and gave out the great hunting call, a long, low trump that echoed through the hills. Then, without another word, he and Ouranos set out towards the village.

The path to the village was a simple mud track and they walked in single file, Father first and Ouranos behind. At the entrance to the town Father stopped and pricked his ears for a moment and frowned. Ouranos did the same. However, much as he strained to hear, there was nothing apart from the echoes of crickets chirping in the summer nights heat. "What is it, Father?" Ouranos asked quietly, moving beside him. "What can you hear?"

Father turned to his son. "I hear nothing," he said gravely, "and that is just the problem. The last time I was here there were cries and moans and, though it was terrible to listen to, it concerns me far more that I hear none of that now." Ouranos understood and nodded, and they continued silently into the village.

The town houses looked old and worn. Some had great planks of oak nailed across the windows. Almost all had dripping red crosses painted across the doorway. There were no lights, no noises, and the strange acrid smell of smoke drifted across the pathways.

Father gently unleashed the jars from his back and motioned for Ouranos to stay where he was before slowly making his way to one of the houses and carefully prodding at the door with his trunk. It swung open with an eerie creak and Father stepped into the entrance, leaving Ouranos alone in the street, where he found himself strangely shivering despite the stifling heat.

A few minutes later Father emerged, shaking his head.

"There is no one there," he said, furrowing his brow. "It looks as though someone was there very recently; there is food on the table, and the beds are made. Clothes still hang from the rails, there are many, many bandages on the floor and a bucket of crimson water sits by the bed. A course of unfinished droplet medicine was by the bed. There is no doubt that someone very sick was here, but now they are gone."

He sighed and his frown deepened. "I would think that perhaps they had packed up and left, perhaps tried to escape the sickness, or having seen that the doctor's medicine failed to work, perhaps they tried to go to other villages to seek help there."

Father looked stricken at the thought. "God forbid they went elsewhere. The sickness is wild and will spread like no other. If they have gone to another village it will surely get them too..."

He trailed off and shook his head. He wasn't looking at Ouranos but instead staring straight ahead and continued to talk as though lost in his own thoughts. "The strangest thing was that they appear to have left in a hurry and there were several broken plates on the floor. It is almost as if they left without any warning, or perhaps, perhaps, they had not intended to leave at all. Perhaps they did not have any choice."

Father sighed. "Stay here for a moment, son," he said gravely and then continued up the street, checking every house along the way. Each time he emerged he shook his head again. There was no one left; they had all disappeared.

As he watched his Father enter the last house on the row, Ouranos suddenly heard something. It was faint, far in the distance, but he was sure he was not imagining it.

"Father!" he cried. "Father, I think I hear something!"

Father came towards him and they listened carefully. There it was again, the faintest crackling sound coming from the old town hall on top of the hill at the peak of the village. Ouranos squinted into the night and sure enough he could make out a dim orange glow in the distance. "Father, look!" he cried and pointed his trunk towards it.

Father nodded and his heart lifted. Perhaps all was not lost. The surviving villagers had gathered together and simply moved to higher ground in an attempt to escape the sickness. "Follow me closely," he instructed his son, and began to walk in the direction of the hill.

It took around twenty minutes before they reached the base of the hill and, sure enough, as they got closer the noises became louder. A low groaning chant seemed to echo about the hills and they could see great black twists of smoke drifting into the air. In silence they began to climb. Ouranos was tense and he could see that Father was, too. There was something hesitant in his gait which suggested that his senses were telling him not to go up there – and an Elephant man's senses were usually right.

Ouranos would never forget the moment they reached the summit, the second when his eyes first settled on the huge pile of burning bodies whose limbs were all tangled together, mouths open, eyes burnt right out of their sockets. And the group of men with their billowing black cloaks, their stony faces, their seeming detachment from what was happening, as they used pitchforks to shovel the bodies onto the flames, one by one.

"Stay behind me," Father whispered, and waited until Ouranos had moved before giving out a loud trump to announce their arrival. The men turned, startled, and looked flustered at first. Then, on realising who approached them, they grew menacing. They pointed their pitchforks towards Father and gathered in a circle around him.

"What do you want, devil-man?" one of them called gruffly and spat on the ground in front of Father's feet. "How dare you come here! How dare you show your face!"

Father raised his head defiantly. "I demand to know what is going on here. I have come to help you."

The men, crazed with loss, began to laugh – a slow, mean chuckle at first, which ascended into a frightening hysterical howl, one that only madmen can make.

While Father was trying to placate them, Ouranos noticed something out of the corner of his eye: a muffled moan, a shadow shuddering in the distance near the hall. It was just by the side of the cluster of carts the men had used to pull the bodies up the hill. He looked up at Father, who was busy with the men, and slowly turned toward where he had seen the movement. The moaning grew louder as he approached.

Ouranos squatted by the side of the truck and peered around the corner. "No!" he cried. "It cannot be!" He covered his eyes with his trunk, unable to believe what he saw. For there, on the ground, at least thirty people, all bound and gagged, all terribly sick, were writhing in the mud. Some saw him and began desperately trying to wriggle their way towards him, eyes bulging in a desperate plea for help. Ouranos turned away.

"Father!" he screamed. "Father, come quick! They are alive. They are burning them alive!"

Ouranos felt Father by his side in a flash. He could hear him groan and felt the earth shake as he collapsed heavily onto his knees. "Oh no, no, no," he kept muttering over and over. "Oh no, no, no. How has it come to this?"

Ouranos felt the glare of cloaked men behind him and suddenly a heavy hand landed on his shoulder, clutching at the rolls of fat that hung under his neck. "Father!" Ouranos screamed. "Father, help me!"

Immediately Father leapt to his defence, tussling with the men as they prodded at him, swiping viciously with their pitch forks.

"Don't you see, devil-man?" one of them cried. "Don't you see that it is you that has done this to us, you that has spread this disease, the disease that has cursed us all from the very day you and your crippled, deformed family stepped foot in our village? How dare you come here, devil-man! How dare you show your face!"

Father wailed and begged them to stop. Ouranos was caught in the middle, frantically darting this way and that to try to avoid the stinging prongs of the pitchforks. He could feel the jars of Viatel loosening as the ropes began to give way. Why were they doing this? They had come to help! He could hear Father pleading with the men.

"You must listen to me!" he cried. "We can help you. We have the cure!" At this, one of the men signalled for the others to stop. He lowered his hood, revealing a pale pocked skin and bloodshot eyes. He came in closer and leant over Father, who was kneeling, head down and breathing heavily, on the ground.

"The cure?" he sneered. "The cure? Don't you think it's a bit late for that? There is no cure for us now. Can't you see what we have been driven to? This pitiful handful of men, burning our brothers, our wives, our children! We do it because there is no cure, because this is the only way to stop it killing us all!"

Father raised his head. His eyes were streaming with tears. "You don't understand," he begged. "I have the antidote. Last time I came there was not enough, but we, my son and I, we have found more, so much that I can reverse all the sickness in those folk you have tied up over there. I can reverse it and wipe it out forever. You have got to believe me!"

The man snorted. "Believe you? Believe you? Why on earth should we believe you, devil-man? Last time you came we saw what your so-called medicine did. It poisoned that poor boy, made him worse, gave him the most excruciating death of them all. Don't think we don't know what you are up to out there, you and your freakish family all alone, isolated from the village. We know how you feel outcast, and rightly so! But don't you come here and try to take your bitter revenge out on the last remaining few of us who still have life. You would see us all die the most painful deaths imaginable. Don't think we don't know it. What we are doing may be terrible, but at least we are putting them out of their misery. You with all your talk of cures! You simply want to harm us and we won't fall for your devilish trickery. Out, devil-man! GET OUT."

He raised his pitchfork high above his head and drove it into Father's side. Father rolled over in agony, and as he did so the jars that had been lashed to his back came undone and went crashing, one by one, to the ground. Ouranos squealed and flung himself towards his father, trying to protect him, to stop them from doing it again. He realised too late that his ropes were loosened, too, and he turned in horror as the final jars crashed, sending glass and liquids flying everywhere. Ouranos turned frantically, expecting to see a pitchfork ready to plunge into him. But it seemed that the men had had enough. The leader pulled his hood back onto his head and spat once again on the ground near to where Father lay. He then nodded to the others silently and they began their low chant once more, moving quietly to the pile of live bodies who lay squirming, silently screaming, desperately protesting their fate.

Father groaned as Ouranos nestled in beside him. "Father, oh Father!" he cried. "Father, are you OK? Are you hurt badly, Father?"

Father shook his head. "I'm fine," he muttered, though this was not the truth, and he made an attempt to stand. His skin was dented with holes where the pitchforks had been relentlessly driven into his flesh. Blood flowed freely down the top of his legs and his knees quivered and buckled under his own weight. "The Viatel," he muttered, "is there any left?" Ouranos looked around and shook his head. Every single jar had been smashed. He gently picked up the remains of one with his trunk; a few drops of the cool blue liquid remained in the bottom. "Here, Father," Ouranos said gently, and carefully poured the drops into his Father's wounds. There was not enough for all of them, but he could see almost immediately the biggest ones starting to seal up.

"Come now, Father," Ouranos said and lifted his Father's trunk with his own, carefully draping it round his shoulders for support. Father said nothing, his eyes wide with disbelief. He was trembling all over, clearly in shock from the events that had just happened and the devastation all around them. "It's OK, Father. I have got you," Ouranos said, feeling almost at once the sudden shift from Father to Son, the wisdom, the energy being passed through his Father to him. He was the man of the family now and it was his duty to get his Father back home safely. Gently he eased him upright and slowly, heads bent and trunks low, the two Elephant men made their way slowly back to the hut.

CHAPTER 28

GRACE

The end of time

Grace had her eyes screwed shut, not daring to open them in case it wasn't true. The wind from the tunnel tugged and whipped around her and she could feel the same slippery strings begin to pull at her arms and legs.

"Peter?" she cried, twisting round, not daring to believe he could be with her. Her words echoed loudly down the tunnel and disappeared into the distance. Grace opened her eyes. She was alone.

"Peter!" she cried again through a half-choked sob. They had been pulled in together, she was sure, and he'd come into the same dream as her before, so where was he? He should be here with her, and yet, as she looked around once again, he was nowhere to be seen.

Suddenly Grace heard a noise in the distance, so faint it was barely perceptible but it was definitely there. Straining her ears to hear it again and using all her strength, she wedged her arms and legs against the sides of the tunnel and turned against the wind, which seemed to get stronger with each second that passed. With an almighty effort, Grace twisted herself around and there she saw him, far in the distance, hair whipped over his face, twisting and tumbling down the tunnel.

"Grace." She heard him again, louder now and she could make out his dark outline in the distance. "Grace, wait up!"

The winds were pulling her forwards; they were so strong she felt as though they were stretching her limbs out into threads of spaghetti. "I can't, Peter, hurry!" she called.

Suddenly he was upon her. He had been travelling at such a speed that he cannoned into her. Grace yelled out, expecting to feel the pain and sickness that his touch brought once again. But it did not come. Instead they twisted, spiralling onwards, their limbs, their hair, all bound together. As they passed the doors Grace buried her head in Peter's chest, unable to bear hearing their desperate screams again.

Eventually they came to a halt. Grace opened her eyes and she was in front of her door, which was lit. A huge crack had appeared across the front of it and the padlock was covered with rust. This time, however, she noticed that the door next to hers was also lit. She looked at the number above it and let out a gasp of surprise. She had been right before, after all. The numbers were the same.

As the hands came up to pull her through, so did hands from the other door. Both pairs clawed at the couple, each desperately fighting for them to be theirs. One pair clutched at Grace's wrists while the other had managed to grip

Peter's ankles. They were being pulled apart.

"Don't let go, OK? Whatever you do, don't let go!" Peter yelled. Grace could feel his fingers digging deep into her arms. She could feel herself stretching and sinking closer to her door.

"I can't hold on!" she screamed. It was too hard. The pull was too great. With a final cry, Grace felt herself being sucked down and then a bump as she landed on the hard ground below. Lying on the ground and breathing in the dusty earth, she coughed and spat, trying to lift her head. It was as though all the breath had been kicked out of her body. Night had come and the air was cold. Grace thought about staying there forever. She could just lie here until it was all over. Peter was gone again and it was too much to bear. She couldn't do this alone. She couldn't do this without him. Grace pressed her head into her knees, let out a miserable sob and thought about giving up.

Suddenly, she heard a screech through the darkness and her head snapped up. Two glowing pairs of eyes were dancing wildly about ahead of her through the darkness. Grace could recognise the pale blue glaze of them anywhere; it was the Creature. She had expected to see him, of course, but now, though seemingly impossible, it looked as though there were two of them.

Tilting her head, and staring harder into the black sky, her eyes adjusted and she knew they had not been deceiving her. There were indeed two Creatures, and they appeared to be engaged in a vicious and bloody fight.

She was about to crawl towards them when she heard a faint groan to her right. Slowly she turned about, not daring to believe. It couldn't be! And yet it was. There was Peter, lying dusty and exhausted, on the ground.

"You made it!" she exclaimed, crawling over to him.

"Oh, Peter, you made it!" She helped him up and hugged him tightly and felt him breathe in her hair. It was so good to touch him even if they could now only do it in dreams.

When he had got his breath back, Grace pointed to the scene in front of them. Both Creatures looked as if they were no longer made for fighting. Their yellow crooked claws snapped and spun into the air as they swiped fiercely at each other's chests. Through their snarls only a few crooked teeth remained, and their coats were grey, patchy and covered in scabs. It looked as if neither would last the night, yet they both fought as if their lives depended on it.

"It's us, isn't it?" Grace whispered to Peter, her eyes fixed on the fight.

Peter nodded. "Because we're both here at the same time, it makes sense, I guess. We can't have two checkpoints; we can't exist in two lots of time."

"Should we try to stop them?"

Peter shook his head. "I don't think we could if we tried," he replied. "We just have to wait until one of them wins."

So they waited and watched as the two once majestic and powerful Creatures fought it out. Eventually, with one final blow which ripped out his opponent's eye, the slightly less weary-looking Creature won the battle. The other dropped to the ground with such a final thump that Grace had to bite her lip to stop from crying out to it.

The victor stood over his opponent, head hung low, breathing heavily. Its ribs were pumping in and out through its skin. A less victorious image could not be imagined. Finally, without lifting his head, he spoke.

"It's your fault, you know. We all end, and I know our time was soon to be up anyway, but there was no need for it to be like this."

Grace stepped forward; she was now certain that the remaining Creature was hers, the one she had met before.

"I'm sorry," she said. "Really, I am sorry. Please, we need your help, and we really can't stay here long."

The Creature snapped his head round. Blood dripped from his jaws.

"Oh, I'm sorry. You're in a rush, are you? Well don't let me stop you. Please be on your way." He then turned his back to her and thumped his tail warningly on the ground.

Peter, now at Grace's side, then spoke. "No," he said firmly. "We need you to show us the choices, like always. Now stop playing your games. This isn't a game, you know. Can't you see that?" He stepped forward and marched up to the Creature's side, pointing down at the other one whose life was spilling out in a sticky red pool around their feet.

"That was my time there, and now it's gone. So we only have you left. You're all we have left, so help us. Please! Just give us the choices!" His shout echoed through the air.

Grace felt tears begin to stream down her face. Why was the Creature wasting their time like this? If he didn't give them the choices now then it would be too late, and this was their last chance. If Peter didn't find his body now, his time would be up when he came out of the dream. As for her, well she still had some time, but very little.

The remaining Creature looked as though it did not have much life left in it. She stared at it solemnly as it seemed to struggle to pull the air into its lungs.

"Please," she whispered. She stepped right up to the Creature's side. It looked down at her and its eyes softened a little. She reached up and tugged gently at its fur. "Please," she said again.

The Creature breathed a rasping sigh that seemed to go on forever. He turned to face them both and locked his eyes onto Grace's, winding his bloody, toothless mouth into one final terrifying grin.

"There are no choices now," he hissed, and collapsed dead on the ground.

Grace leapt back with a gasp and then stood silently for a moment, watching as the dust settled around the Creature's lifeless body. She could feel Peter watching her as she collapsed to the ground and banged her fists into the earth.

"This is all Deborah's fault. I hate her. I hate her!" The dust caught in the back of her throat as she coughed and sputtered the words out in between huge, desperate sobs. "She's so selfish! I hate her!" she screamed again. Grace felt Peter pull her upright and press her into his chest. He held her as tight as he dared, squeezing all the anger and the fear out until he felt her calm down.

Pushing her away from him, still holding onto the sides of her arms with his hands, Peter spoke. "You don't mean that, Grace," he sighed, pushing the hair carefully away from her eyes. "I almost wish you did, because then maybe somehow we could get back to the Lost Soulz bar. Maybe it wouldn't actually be so bad there, after all. We could try again. At least we'd be together there, you know? But I know you, and I know you can't do that. You can't be without her, can you?"

Grace stared at him defiantly and tried to shake her head. Why did she feel like this? It was so hard, such an inexplicable feeling. She knew he was right. She was so angry for what Deborah had put her through yet she would always forgive her. She would always choose her over anyone else. Why did she have to feel like this? She had to try to find her again. She just had to.

The alternative life that she and Peter could have at the

Lost Soulz bar wouldn't be enough. Images of Abeid, his arm raised above her clutching the knife, flashed before her eyes. Grace bit her lip and shook her head, trying to muster a smile. It was no good. There was no going back now. Besides, their time was up; the Creatures were dead. This was their very last chance to find them. She bit her lip. "So what do we do now?" she said.

Peter let go of her arms and glanced around him. They could barely see more than a few metres ahead and the breeze had turned into a wind which was so cold it went right through them, chilling their bones to the core.

"This can't be it," he muttered. His eyes were darting back and forth, desperately scanning for something they might have missed. Grace wandered over to the Creature. The wind made his remaining hairs dance about so it looked as though he was still faintly alive. She knelt down beside him and rested her head on his shoulder. A drip of wet dropped onto her nose. She wiped it away, but then another came, then another and another.

Grace looked up to the sky. It was raining. Peter hurriedly sat down beside her as they huddled closely together, trying to use the Creature's body for shelter and warmth. The sky, without warning, seemed to split and tip and the rain came down in torrents. The ground quickly became swampy, so Peter crawled onto the Creature's back before helping Grace up. The rain came down so hard that soon the earth was flooded and they held on tight as they felt the Creature suddenly begin to rise and float along the surface of the water. Grace screamed as she slipped down its leg and nearly fell off altogether.

"Hold on!" Peter called. He leant down and pulled her back to safety. 'Hold onto me, as tight as you can, OK?'

Grace nodded and clung onto Peter's coat. The wind was

tossing and twisting them this way and that. The earth now turned into a huge river with strong currents and they went faster and faster in every direction. Peter was clutching onto the remains of the fur, trying now to keep them both balanced as the Creature bobbed furiously up and down. It was almost impossible to make out if they were travelling forwards or backwards or neither or both, and the water was ice cold as it lapped and splashed at their feet.

"Whatever happens, make sure you don't let go of me!" Peter called to her again. "Even if you are going to fall off, we'll fall off together, OK? We have to stay together whatever happens."

"OK!" Grace screamed back to him. The howl of the wind whipped at her ears; she could barely hear his shouts even though he was right next to her. Each raindrop that hit her skin felt like an icy needle ripping through her flesh and right into her blood.

Suddenly the Creature's body began to turn. It swooped in wide circles at first but then they got tighter and tighter, faster and faster. They were caught in a giant whirlpool. Grace could feel them being taken down, being sucked into the bed of the ocean. She screamed and gripped Peter as hard as she could. She could feel it coming and who knew what would be waiting for them under there? Grace shut her eyes and felt them being dragged in. She took a huge breath, praying that it would not be her last, and then the water hit them like a wall of solid ice.

CHAPTER 29

DEBORAH AND GRACE

The beginning of the end

They were underwater, and Deborah was afraid. She knew it was cold, so cold that she should have been half frozen to death. But her flesh didn't seem to react here; it didn't seem to matter. She was terrified to open her mouth, scared that the water would instantly suffocate and choke with its wet, black fists. But she knew she had to breathe, and so eventually did, and found that there was no reason to be afraid, that this was a place she could breathe without air.

Looking around, her eyes strained through the murk of the water. Deborah tried to remember why she was here, why she had come. The water closed in on her like a fog.

Suddenly Luke was beside her, holding her hand. Deborah clutched it tightly, not daring to speak. He nodded his head forwards, and together they began to swim. Craggy rocks towered above them; Deborah couldn't help but feel as though they were being watched.

***

They were sucked down through the epicentre of the whirlpool, Grace still clutching Peter's arm as tightly as she could. Then they landed. It was softer than she had expected, and her bare feet felt the grainy grit of sand beneath them. They had settled on the bed of the river. Grace still clutched Peter's arms. She could feel the water all around them, so close it was as though they were part of it.

Slowly she opened her eyes and was surprised that she could see perfectly well. She glanced down at her knuckles, which were ghostly white. Pulling her hand away, she stepped back from Peter and watched as tiny trickles of blood spurted out into the water from where her nails had dug into his arms. She looked at him apologetically. He looked at her and smiled. He looked ethereal down here, Grace thought, with his red hair swaying upright from his head, and the pale moonlight which seemed to cut through the water and illuminate his face in a pallid, dewy glow.

Violet plants sprouted from the seabed and tangoed back and forth with the currents. Grace took Peter's hand again. She noticed a flash as the sapphire ring she still wore sparkled under an invisible light. Together they moved forward.

***

Deborah didn't know which way to go, and she didn't know what she was looking for. The weight of the water began to press down on her like a heavy hand on her heart. She weaved slowly in between the jagged charcoal rocks, desperate for a sign, but it was endless and none were to come. She was searching for something, this she knew, but what? What? Distant memories swirled like the pockets of shingle that were lifted up by the currents from the sea bed. There was danger around them, she knew that, yet felt removed from it, like she didn't need to care.

Something cold and flat was pressed up against her hip and she could feel it shift as she swam. Deborah looked down and noticed a glint of silver poking out from underneath the rim of her jeans. She pulled it out, and was surprised to find a shiny silver knife glimmering through the darkness of the water, looking strangely menacing in her hand. She frowned. Had she brought it, and if so, why? Her thoughts were cloudy, tangled like the weeds that grew all around her.

Luke tugged at her ankles and pointed to a school of fish which had appeared from a crevice on his right. They split and came in around them either side, herding them forwards, their bulbous white eyes stretched open, unblinking, curious and ever alert. Deborah could feel her heart beating through her skin and it felt as though she was the pulse of the ocean.

***

Grace felt a tug deep in her stomach and stopped immediately, dragging her feet along the bottom of the seabed, feeling the sting as tiny shards of rock dug in between her toes. She knew the feeling; it had happened before, that pull, the one which then spread into an overwhelming sense of desire and sorrow, that strange paradox of both love and of hurt.

Grace turned to Peter, who nodded and tapped his stomach; he had felt it, too. That meant they were together. That meant they were close.

***

A spark of blue flashed through the water like a bolt of lightning between two great twisting lumps of coral. Deborah felt Luke tighten his grip on her ankle. He had seen it too. She felt her heart swell when she saw it, as if its capacity to feel had somehow doubled in size. Deborah knew immediately that she should swim towards the light. She needed to get to its source as fast as she could, and so together they went, pushing back the rainbows of weeds which tugged and pulled at their arms and legs as they passed. Through an arch of rock and into a clearing they went and, suddenly, there they were.

The golden-haired girl and the shaggy-haired boy were there, swimming towards them. It was only then that Deborah knew what she was doing, and why she had come. It all came flooding back to her, and she felt all the pain and the sorrow and the anger a thousand times more intensely than ever before. It felt as though she was reliving every part of her life that led up to the point where she had tried to kill herself in one intense shot of feeling.

She doubled over in pain. It felt like a knife in her heart, but when she looked up at the golden-haired girl whose arms were stretched out towards her, she finally understood. She knew she was being given a second chance, that she was being forgiven, that she was being saved. Deborah began to swim towards her.

The fish suddenly darted away.

***

There they were; she could see them! Grace could not believe it. Deborah was right there, right in front of her. As soon as she saw her she had instantly forgiven what Deborah had done to her, the pain she had felt by being without her, the loneliness and sorrow. All she felt was an overwhelming love, and all she wanted now was to be back inside. Grace began to swim as fast as she could towards Deborah, propelling her arms in huge circles and kicking her legs. But she was stuck. Something was holding her back. Her legs couldn't move properly. When she kicked them, it felt as though she was swimming through treacle. Grace glanced up. Peter was ahead of her. He was almost at Luke's side. But Deborah, Deborah's face was frozen, her jaw slack and her eyes so wide it looked as if they might pop right out of her head.

Deborah pointed and Peter, who had noticed her expression, twisted himself round to look. Then they all had this look, all three of them. It was the same look as that time when Grace had been pushed onto the outside, when she had seen Deborah and Jack's faces watching Jamie being knocked down; that desperate terror of knowing nothing could stop it, that nothing could be done.

Grace used her arms to turn herself around, even though her legs would not move. It was only then that she understood why they all looked so afraid. A huge, black swamping thing was enveloping her. She screamed. She knew. It was the thing that had been trying to catch her, that was coming to steal her away.

Struggling and desperately kicking her legs, Grace tried to escape, but it was no use; she could feel herself being dragged inside it. There was nothing she could do.

Hysterical now, she glanced up again. There was a flash of skin and a flicker of silver through the darkness. The black thing was up to her shoulders now. She could feel it hot and sticky on every part of her ready to swallow her up. It whispered dark secrets to her as she felt it lick at her ears. It told her she would be burnt and cut and put inside another. Grace tried to scream again, but no sound came out. Then the spark of silver flashed through the water again.

The water filled her ears with a thunderous, blood-curdling screech. Grace felt two hands pull her away as the black thing thrashed and screamed huge piercing screams, echoing into the ocean. Grace saw Deborah with her arms raised above her head, plunging a knife into the blackness over and over again. She felt herself being released and, as she turned back, Grace saw the shape, with one final cry, separate and mix with the sea.

It was gone, and just like that the water drained away, as if someone had pulled the plug on the ocean. Grace felt herself being sucked upwards, propelled out of the water into the sky. She shut her eyes and cried out for Deborah.

When she opened them again she found herself standing in a bright, white room. She coughed and spluttered on the floor. Her hair dripped down over her face and the water splashed her feet. She gulped in the air and stared at her shaking hands, the sapphire ring still firmly on her finger.

"Grace."

She turned, and there they were. Deborah, Peter and Luke were all standing before her. Deborah took a step forwards, and Grace saw that her eyes were filled with tears.

"I'm so sorry," she said. "I'm so sorry I made you leave."

Grace shook her head. "You saved me," she smiled. "You saved both of us."

Deborah did not reply, but the two stayed smiling at each other until Peter cleared his throat. Grace turned around to see that he and Luke were staring at each other uncertainly. Something wasn't right; they should be so happy to see one another again. Peter turned to her.

"Grace," he whispered. His voice was so quiet it was barely audible. "Grace, something's wrong."

"What is it, Peter?" she asked. His skin turned a greenish colour and he looked as though he was going to be sick.

"It's not him, Grace. It's not mine."

"Peter, you're scaring me. What do you mean?"

Peter turned back to Luke, who was staring at him intensely. "You are not my body." He said the words slowly and deliberately so that there was no way anyone could misunderstand them.

Luke shook his head. "Come on. That's ridiculous." He turned to Peter and shook his head defiantly. "Of course I am. Why would you be here otherwise?"

"No. I'm sorry, all right, whoever you are. But you aren't for me." He looked towards Grace, then to Deborah and stepped towards her. "I can't explain it very well. It's only now that I see you together that it's beginning to make sense to me, but somehow I think I am here not because of him, but because of you."

Grace walked over to Peter and gently took his hand. "I know how overwhelming this is," she whispered gently. "But Luke must be yours, it doesn't make sense any other way. We should be happy, Peter. We found them. We can save them."

"NO!" Peter shouted and pushed her away. "Why don't you get it? There is something else going on. I can't understand it, but there is no way that he's mine. Please, Grace, you have to believe me."

Grace shook her head and stepped towards him again. She tried to take his hands but he shrugged her off.

"No, Peter, please don't do this, OK? I'm sure it will be fine. Just go with him and you'll see, OK?" She turned to Luke. "He'll see, won't he, that we can all be together, on the outside, in real life, right?"

Luke nodded his head. "She's right. I'm different now, I promise."

"NO!" Peter yelled again. He tugged his hands through his hair and then turned his back to all of them. Grace could see his shoulders were shaking as he took a deep breath. "You're all stupid if you think it's going to work. I get that you need us to live – I get that – but I can't go back with him. I'm sorry, but it would never work." He turned to Grace. His voice cracked as he took her hands. "Don't you see? That's the reason, the reason we started getting sick around each other. It all makes sense now. It won't work, Grace. Please, don't go back with her. We make each other happy, don't we?"

Peter reached out and stroked her hair before angrily brushing back the tears which were now falling freely down the sides of his face.

"Please, Grace, I'm begging you. I love you and we still have a chance to go back to the Lost Soulz bar. We still have time. If you go back inside her then we'll never be together again. I know it."

"I can't go back there, Peter. We know what they would do to us – I can't live like that. Besides, I am not leaving her, not now. Please, Peter, just go with him. It will be OK, you'll see."

Grace felt her heart rip in two at that moment – the moment Peter got to his knees and pressed his head against her thighs. It didn't make any sense, though. He had to be

Luke's soul – he just had to be. The dreams, the sickness – what else could it possibly mean? She shook her head, looking firmly down at Peter, and tried to tell herself everything would be fine. She had made her choice. What he was asking her was pointless; she couldn't say yes to him. Even if she believed him it didn't matter. She loved him, they both knew that, but her need to be with Deborah was stronger than love.

"I'm so sorry," she whispered, turning around and leaving him, sobbing, on his hands and knees beside Luke who stood uncomfortably by his side.

Grace walked over to Deborah, refusing to look back. "It's time," she said. Deborah nodded, then ran to Luke and embraced him fiercely. "I'll see you on the outside," she whispered, then returned to Grace who led her to the far corner of the room. Taking Deborah's hands, Grace then pressed herself into Deborah's body. They smiled at each other.

"Just before we do it," Deborah said, "I have a question. Why the name Grace?"

Grace smiled sadly and fought back the tears. "It's to do with him," she smiled nodding at Luke, and stepping closer to Deborah. "He loved some old movie star called Grace, right?"

Before Deborah had time to answer she pressed herself in as hard as she could, trying to forget how she had done the same with Peter only a few days before. As she did, she felt her flesh grow red hot and begin to shimmer and melt into the air.

Poor Grace. It was only right before the end, in the very last few seconds, that she realised the truth: that Peter was right – he was not Luke's soul. As her flesh melted into Deborah's she suddenly remembered how she knew Peter, why he had found her, and how she had loved him all along. And she remembered that young man in the Lost Soulz bar who had made her feel so strangely and peculiarly sad, though at the time she hadn't been able to figure out why. That had been Luke's soul! His soul who, she now realised, had clearly given up on him for good. But Peter, well he belonged to someone else entirely.

Suddenly Grace realised the reason she and Peter had begun to get sick around each other. It was because Peter's body was getting sick, and the sicker it became the more it had been subconsciously trying to pull them apart so that neither of them would get hurt.

But that wasn't the worst thing, for it was only in the very last few seconds as she melted back into Deborah's body, whom she loved and cared for more than anything else, the body for whom she had sacrificed everything, that Grace suddenly realised it had all been lies. It was only then that she saw all the lies that had been let loose into Deborah's head, the ones that had been there slowly growing like tumours inside her: lies that had festered and twisted and gripped around her, lies that had been so strong that even Grace had somehow believed them, too. As she realised this, Grace opened her mouth to speak and desperately tried to pull away.

It was too late, though. The heat took over until, finally, she was gone.

CHAPTER 30

100BC

The fire at sunrise

Dappha screamed when she saw them. She'd had a vision in the night of dark creatures with sharp claws. She already knew it hadn't gone well, but she had no idea it would be this bad. Father was obviously badly hurt, and she could hear him breathing heavily as they approached. Ouranos laid him on the ground in front of the hut and tried to comfort his mother.

"This isn't the time for tears, not now," he said, as calmly as he could. "Father needs our help. I poured some Viatel on the worst of his wounds, but the others need seeing to. Fetch some hot water and some bandages, and keep Pup inside."

His mother stared at her son for a moment. It seemed he

had returned from the village a decade older. She did not have time to contemplate this wise, strong and courageous creature that seemed to have replaced the playful and naive child that left her earlier that evening. However, she was grateful to have him – that's all that she knew. She rushed inside the hut and glanced at Pup who was sleeping prettily in a tight ball, her ears fluttering as she anticipated happy dreams. Quickly and quietly, Dappha gathered all the medical supplies they had, as well as a pail of water and some firewood which was stocked at the entrance.

Together, they carefully washed Father's wounds, sprinkled them with leaves from the ancient frothic tree and then helped him inside. Dappha knelt beside him and lovingly stroked his head. '

"What happened?" she asked.

Ouranos shook his head. He was exhausted and defeated and couldn't bring himself to share with his mother the horrors they had seen.

"They didn't want the Viatel," he offered by way of an explanation. "They didn't want us to help them and they smashed all our jars." He shrugged his shoulders at a loss of what to say next.

"And your Father?" Dappha asked. "How did he come to be like this?"

Ouranos sighed. "They attacked us; they don't want us here. They think we are the cause of the disease, that we have brought some sort of curse on all of them, that because of what happened last time we are out for some sort of terrible revenge. We tried to explain to them, mother, truly we did, but they just wouldn't, they just wouldn't..." He trailed off, suddenly feeling the weight of the world on his shoulders.

Father let out a moan and both he and Dappha

immediately rushed to his side. "Father?" Ouranos gently brushed his cheek. "Father, can you hear me?"

Father opened his eyes. "Ouranos," he whispered and tried to smile. "Ouranos, my boy, my brave boy. Where is the Viatel, my brave boy? Did you save it?"

Ouranos turned away and his eyes filled up with tears. "No, Father. I didn't save it. It's gone, remember? I told you, it's all gone. I saved you instead, Father. I saved you instead." His Father said nothing more; he simply rolled away from Ouranos and closed his eyes. "Why doesn't he remember?" Ouranos cried, feeling hot tears roll down his trunk once again. Then he shook his head, pulling himself together.

"We have to get out of this place, mother, you understand? As soon as Father is stronger we are leaving, OK?"

Dappha nodded quietly. "Whatever you say, my son," she replied. "You are the head of the family now." She gently nudged him with her trunk. "Fetch some blankets, will you? We should all try to get some sleep.

Ouranos did as he was told, and once they had made Father as comfortable as possible, they both lay down either side of him, nestled in scratchy blankets. The warmth of the night bore down on them. Ouranos, who usually couldn't sleep in the heat, found himself surprisingly drowsy and soon enough he succumbed to the weight of his eyelids and fell into dark and fitful dreams.

Men with red hot eyes stood in a ring around him. He tried to move, tried to call out for help, but it was no use. He was lashed down and his trunk stuffed with cloth so he could no longer make a sound.

The hooded men leered over him. "It's your fault, devil-boy," he whispered. "You thought you could be the head of the family, did you? How foolish you are! You are just a boy, a fool. But now it is you we blame."

From behind them, Ouranos suddenly noticed a thousand pairs of eyes staring at him unblinkingly through the darkness. The hooded men parted to reveal an endless stream of bodies, burnt and bloody, with their limbs outstretched, all pointing down to where he lay.

"You did this to us, devil-boy," they chanted. "You must pay for what you have done."

The crowd moved closer around him and suddenly Ouranos recognised the eyes of Father, Dappha and Pup. They were all staring at him, eyes full of hatred just like the others, their trunks shrivelled, skin blackened by smoke. "You did this to us, devil-boy," they chanted along with the rest. "You must pay for what you have done."

Ouranos woke and sat up with a gasp. He glanced around, his eyes adjusting to the darkness. There was Dappha curled protectively around Pup, who was twitching and purring lightly, still happily oblivious to the goings on of the night. Father was breathing with trouble, wrapped tightly in blankets, agitatedly murmuring to himself through waves of sleep. Ouranos leant back and breathed a sigh of relief.

It was just a dream, he thought to himself, and let his eyelids drop down once more.

He could not tell, upon awakening again, whether he had been asleep for hours or minutes. All he instinctively knew was that something was horribly wrong. He couldn't work it out at first. As he looked frantically around the room, everyone was still there, everyone still sleeping, and as far as he could see nothing had been moved or changed. He got up slowly, stretching out his limbs, ears and trunk both pricked up, trying to figure out what why he felt so anxious.

It was only when he got to the door that he realised. He'd wanted to go outside, to march the perimeter of the hut, just to put his mind at rest and make sure that nothing untoward was going on. When he nudged the door it wouldn't budge. At first he thought it must have got stiff. With the weather having been so changeable of late this was easily possible. So he tried again, but still he could not move it. He pressed his ear against the door, and sure enough he could hear hushed voices whispering outside. Their tone was tense and urgent, but he couldn't quite make out what they were saying.

Ouranos looked back at his family. He was the head of the household now. Usually he would have woken Father the minute he had suspected danger, but Father was in no fit state to help anyone. He didn't want to worry his mother, and Pup was too young and would surely get hysterical if she was woken. What could he do?

Whenever Ouranos thought back to this day, which he did as little as possible, he would never remember whether he heard it or smelt it first. It seemed as though both his senses realised what was happening almost simultaneously. The crackling of flames and the woody smell of burning hay both hit him at once. It wasn't until a few seconds later that the smoke began billowing under the door of the hut and the first lick of flame poked through the walls.

Ouranos banged on the door fiercely and cried out. "Hello? I can hear you out there. What are you doing? My family is in here! We're trapped! Help us!" He pressed his ear against the door once more. He could feel it beginning to get hot and the smoke stung his eyes. There was a silence where he heard nothing but the crackle and sputter of the fire beginning to take hold, then, as clear as day, came a voice on the other side of the door, low and loud through the cracks, which made the hair on his trunk stand up straight as if trying to separate from his skin. It was a voice he recognised from earlier that night as the leader of the hooded men from the hill.

"We know you're in there, devil-boy," it said. "We know."

Just as quickly as it came, it went. Ouranos banged on the door once again, heaving and clawing at it with all his might. Flames were now appearing through the walls and the temperature of the hut was soaring. Ouranos turned and saw Father stir in the middle of the room. He ran over to him.

"Oh, Father! Father!" Ouranos cried. "What do I do, Father? They've set the hut on fire and I can't get out."

Father opened one eye and focused on his son. "I'm sorry, Ouranos," he whispered. "I should have taken us far away from here long ago. This is my fault and I only hope the great God will have mercy upon me. You must find a way out, Ouranos. Save your mother and your sister. Forget about me."

Ouranos felt huge tears fall from his cheeks. If only he could cry enough to put out the flames. "Oh, Father," he sobbed, trying to find the words that would mean what he was trying to say. "You have been the best Father I could have wished for. I feel honoured, Father, and I will save you all. I promise."

He ran across to Dappha and Pup, who had miraculously managed to sleep through the disturbances so far. "Wake up!" he cried, shaking his mother vigorously. Dappha woke with a start, causing Pup to do the same. Pup took one look around the hut and immediately opened her mouth and let out a big bawling scream.

Dappha swept Pup up in her trunk. "Ouranos!" she screamed. "Ouranos, what's happening?"

"It's the villagers," Ouranos gasped breathlessly. "They're trying to burn down the hut. They are trying to burn us alive! I am so sorry, mother. They've barricaded the door. I should have made us leave tonight. I'm sorry, mother. How could they do this to us?"

Dappha coughed, unable to answer her son. The smoke was now billowing freely into the hut and flames covered the walls. Pup's stifled sobs were barely audible above the noise of the fire.

"Stay low," Ouranos instructed. "I will be back as soon as I can." He ran back over to the door, which was now engulfed in flames. Surely it must have been weakened? He pushed it again, wincing as his trunk was scalded in the fire. Turning back, he could see Dappha and Pup cowering together in the corner. Flames licked at the edge of Father's blankets.

Ouranos took another look at the door, feeling strange and foreign feelings of anger and hatred begin to boil up inside him. How could this have happened? The Elephant men were put on this earth to protect the human race - the selfish, wicked, cruel human race! They had no respect for one another. They had no idea of the value of things like honesty and friendship and love. Father had tried to help them. He had dedicated his whole life to hunting for Viatel and journeying across lands to find those in need, to rescue and to cure them, to prolong their lives. How had they repaid him? By casting him out, by prodding him with pitchforks and cruelly taunting him, by injuring him so badly that he could no longer help his own family, by setting fire to their home, by murdering them all!

Ouranos could feel himself engulfed in rage, and suddenly through the smoke and the fire and heat it became crystal clear to him. The Elephant men were fools. No matter what their so-called Great God said, they had been helping the humans for hundreds of years, and yet what did they get in return? Nothing but cruelty and distrust. They could never settle down, never have any true home of their own. They spent all their time trying to save these people, these terrible people who didn't even want to save themselves.

Despite the smoke and the horror of the moment, Ouranos made a promise to himself then and there that if he got through this he would never try to help the humans again.

With all the rage still boiling up inside him, Ouranos backed himself into the furthest corner of the hut. He coiled himself up like a spring, fixated on the door and, with all his power, he galloped full pelt towards it, slamming the whole weight of his body against it. He could feel his skin screaming as the fire ripped through his veins, then suddenly it gave way and he rolled, on fire, out into the darkness of the night. Fresh air hit his lungs as he tumbled onto the ground. He could feel heat on his face and a searing pain running up and down his trunk as he beat it on the earth, desperately trying to put out the flames. Then he lay for a moment, gasping, looking up at the stars. He twisted his head to the side and looked at the hut, now completely engulfed in flames. The others! He had to go back for them!

There was now a gap where the door had been. Although still raging with fire, it was big enough for him to get back through. Ignoring the pain that now seemed to throb throughout his whole being, Ouranos struggled to his feet and dashed back into the hut. He firstly prised Pup from Dappha's arms and ran out, placing her hurriedly back on the ground a safe distance away from the hut. It seemed as though Dappha had managed to comfort her well enough, as she was back fast asleep. Ouranos then ran back towards his mother, who was still curled and barely conscious. "Mother, come on!" he cried, pulling at her trunk. He levered himself beneath her and, though still only about half her size, managed to throw her onto his back and hobble out. He lay her next to Pup, where she wheezed heavily.

"You can't go back, Ouranos," she whispered. "It's too dangerous. Please."

Ouranos looked back. The roof of the hut was sunken, a concave flaming mess, ready to collapse in on itself like a dying star. "I have to get Father," Ouranos shouted and, ignoring his mother's cries, ran back in a third time.

Inside, he could barely see because of the smoke. He shielded his eyes with his trunk and frantically searched for Father. There, under a huge pile of flames, he found him. "Father, come on. Please get up. Come on!" Ouranos screamed, pulling uselessly at Father's trunk.

Father's eyes were closed and he made no movement. "Father, please. Oh, Father!" Ouranos cried. He knew there was nothing he could do. His father was already dead.

At that moment there was a huge groan that seemed to come from within the walls of the hut itself. Ouranos looked up to see a section of the roof collapsing down towards him in a great fiery whoosh. He pulled himself out of the way just in time; the sparks and the smoke burnt his eyes and skin. "I'm so sorry, Father," he choked before pulling himself upwards. He could just make out the gap, a poke of night sky urging him out. He shut his streaming eyes, took one huge breath, and ran towards it with all his might.

CHAPTER 31

DEBORAH

If only it were all but a dream

Deborah opened her eyes and winced as the sunlight streamed in. She reached up to touch her head and let out a soft moan before trying to sit up. For a moment she couldn't work out where she was; then she glanced to the window and recognised the thick green curtains flapping in the wind. The air was brutally cold, heavy and damp, as though a storm had come.

She clutched the edge of the desk and pulled herself to her feet, careful not to put any weight on her ankle. She had expected to feel the searing pain as soon as she woke up, but there was none. Gingerly she bent down and unwound the bandage. Her foot had completely healed.

She heard another groan stretching out from behind one

of the bookcases and ran over to it. "Luke!" She cupped her hands underneath his armpits and helped him up as he stared at her, groggy-eyed and unable to speak.

"We're in Doctor Vanilla's office, I don't understand, how can we be here?" Deborah whispered.

His eyes widened and he was soon on his feet. They looked around. The office was a mess; it looked as though it had been ransacked. Several vases had been smashed, and the bits of them were now sticking like jagged teeth up from the carpet. The Chaise Longue had been overturned and ripped open, with its stuffing scattered all over the room. Almost every journal had been pulled from the shelves. It looked as though it was snowing when the wind blew in again and all the leaves of paper which were strewn about suddenly lifted and danced about the room.

Deborah knelt down to try to gather some of them up and screamed.

"Oh my God, Luke, look!" She pointed to the desk.

Luke frowned and tilted his head; from where he stood he could see nothing. Deborah, however, from her crouching position could see underneath, and there Doctor Vanilla was, curled into a tight ball. Perfectly round he lay, like a pale naked egg balancing serenely on top of a dark pool of blood which was gradually deepening as it soaked through the carpet.

Deborah clapped her hand over her mouth and turned away. She thought she might be sick.

"It's him, isn't it?" she said through her hands. She heard Luke softly walk behind the desk to crouch down.

"Jesus," he muttered. "Jesus."

Deborah swallowed the bile in her mouth and forced herself to look as Luke carefully dragged Doctor Vanilla's lifeless body out from behind his desk. The blood was pouring out of him in great glossy streams, and Deborah could see several large gashes deep in his back.

"Oh God!" she whispered, suddenly feeling faint. She stumbled back before steadying herself on one of the bookcases. "It was me. I've killed him. I must have."

Luke snapped his head round and glared at her. "Don't say that!" he shouted. "Don't say that, OK, Deborah? Don't be so bloody ridiculous, OK?"

His eyes seemed blacker than before and his face was twisted with panic.

"Ridiculous?" Deborah backed away from him. "You are telling me not to be ridiculous? I'm sorry, but what the hell have you been doing for the past few days, because as far as I'm aware it's all been ridiculous, but that doesn't mean it's not real!" She clasped her hands together to stop them from shaking. She wanted to run over to him and hit and scratch and kick him. How could he say that? After all that they'd been through, how could he?

They stood glaring at each other for a moment then, before she knew it, he was upon her, squeezing her tightly and whispering in her ear.

"I'm so sorry," he said. "God, I'm sorry. I just panicked. I mean, he's dead, Deborah... dead." Luke's hands were covered in blood from where he'd touched him and they left smears of crimson on Deborah's hips.

"What do we do?" she mumbled into his chest.

Luke pulled her back and looked her in the eyes. When she looked back at him she could see they had glazed over. There was no compassion, just an emptiness that sent shivers up her spine. Something twigged inside her and, in that moment, everything changed between them. Peter had been right. How could they have thought they would be OK?

Deborah stepped back. "What do we do?" she repeated.

"We burn it," he replied.

They piled the papers on top of one another to make a starting point for the fire. Luke shut the window to keep out the wind and pulled the desk near to the centre. Deborah scrabbled around in the drawers looking for matches. Finally, Luke pulled Doctor Vanilla by the ankles near to the pile, leaving a rainbow-shaped smear of blood on the floor.

Deborah threw the matches to Luke and positioned herself by the door. She rubbed at her chest as she felt something inside telling her not to go through with it.

Luke struck a match.

"Wait!" Deborah called. She ran to the far wall and tugged down the painting of sunflowers, throwing it onto the top of the pile. She had expected something to happen, something momentous, like all the flowers bursting from the canvas and shooting off into the sky. But nothing did, and suddenly the painting seemed very ordinary and real.

"Go ahead," she nodded.

Luke struck a second match and tossed it on. The paper blackened in an instant as the flames took shape. They poked their heads up and over until one found the hem of the curtain and swelled. Up and up it climbed until thick twists of smoke began to billow about the room.

Deborah watched from the doorway, her eyes never moving from the painting. She watched as the flowers began to sweat and droop under the heat and then one daring flame popped its head through the centre and it began to disappear as if it was being dragged down into hell itself.

"Deborah, come on!" Luke was tugging at her hand. She could feel the heat on her face and the smoke start to find its way down to the bottom of her lungs. He pulled her backwards and then they were gone.

Once safely outside, they stood around the corner and listened as passers-by gasped and pointed. Eventually they heard the sound of fire engines roaring in the distance. Deborah looked around them. Rubbish and leaves were teasing each other, scuttling in circles, and crumbled stones and twigs had been scattered all over the road.

"Looks like there was a big storm or something," she whispered.

Deborah looked at Luke, who was looking back at her with a funny expression on his face, as if he was trying to force a smile. He pushed the hair from her eyes with both hands, leaving a smudge of soot across both cheeks. His lips were curved upwards but quivering as if any moment they might crack and break and reveal something she did not wish to see.

"What's the matter?" she asked.

"It's Peter," he said. "He couldn't do it. He said I wasn't his body and he couldn't come back with me."

"What?" She looked at him. His lips were trembling. "But that means, that means..."

"I know." He smiled softly at her.

Deborah shook her head defiantly. "No, Luke. No. There must be a way. We can't let it happen, OK? We won't."

Luke smiled at her again. "OK, you're right. Of course you're right. Nothing is set in stone. We can change this. I don't need him. I don't need a stupid soul or whatever. As long as I have you, things will be fine." He nodded his head and smiled at her unconvincingly.

"Listen," he whispered, drawing her closer. "Why don't you head home and get some things. I will head back to the boat and then let's just go somewhere, anywhere, OK?"

"Sail off into the sunset, you mean?"

"Exactly."

"Sounds perfect."

They held each other's gaze for a moment before Luke leant down and gave her a gentle kiss.

"See you on the other side, Deborah," he said and then turned and walked away.

Deborah felt frozen to the spot. She glanced down at her chest, hoping for a sign of life or a sign of something, a reason to show that it hadn't all been in vain. She watched until Luke's back disappeared into the crowds and rubbed her arms, strangely overwhelmed by a feeling that she would never see him again. She rubbed them until they hurt, as if, once she stopped, there would nothing to think about apart from the huge, throbbing lonely hole that had burst inside her as soon as he had walked away.

Leaning back against the wall, she closed her eyes. Apart from the smell of soot in her hair and the screams of the sirens which were now so close, it felt as if she could have almost imagined all of it, as if it had all been a dream. But she hadn't, and now she was alone, alone but still alive. She began to walk towards her flat.

When she arrived at the end of her street she realised how much damage the storm had done. Rubbish was strewn across the road and roof tiles lay smashed across the pavement. Then she spotted the apple tree. It was lying knocked over on the grass, brown petals and rotten fruit spilling out onto the road. Its huge roots lay turned up to the sky. A crow had landed on one of them. It turned to her, staying silent, its head cocked to one side. Deborah felt a desperate wave of emotion. She stepped towards it suddenly, waving her hands.

"Go away, just go away will you?" she flapped her hands towards the crow who remained sitting undisturbed on top of the roots of the tree. Deborah could feel hot tears brewing in her eyes as she turned away from it.

She didn't stop until she got to her front door, pausing outside to learn her head against the cool paint. So much had happened. It seemed ludicrous to be back, back in her little flat. How was she supposed to go inside?

Suddenly the door opened and she stumbled forward, crying out as she was immediately enveloped in two plump, wrinkly arms. She could hear her name being repeated over and over again.

"Deborah! Oh my God, Deborah! I thought you were dead. I thought we'd lost you." Her mother pressed her tightly into her chest until Deborah coughed and pushed herself away to take a breath. She saw a large red scab on her mother's forehead and her skin looked bruised around the temples. Huge, thumping sobs suddenly burst from Deborah's mouth and she was all tears and snot like a child as her mother gently led her up the stairs.

Men were waiting there, in her living room. They looked like doctors; she had seen them before. They stood quietly in the corner of the room and raised their eyebrows as Deborah entered, as if to say 'here we go again'. There was a woman there, too. She was sitting on her sofa in a long floral skirt and a cream blouse buttoned up to the collar. She smiled as Deborah entered, and got up.

"Deborah." The woman said her name softly. It was annoying, and Deborah quickly wiped her face with her sleeve, but the sobs would not stop coming.

"Why can't I stop bloody crying?" she said. She must have said it louder than intended, as the woman looked startled and one of the men stepped forward.

The woman held up her hand, which put a stop to the man, and then she sat back down on the sofa, patting the space next to her. Deborah turned around. Her mother was blocking the door. She nodded for Deborah to go and sit down.

"Deborah," the woman said again. Softly again. Annoying again. "I'm Doctor Knox." She smoothed her skirt down and shifted in her seat before continuing. Deborah noticed her dream journal sitting on the coffee table in front of her. *How did that get there?* She touched the sides of her head. Her temples felt hot and were beginning to throb.

Doctor Knox continued.

"Now your mother and I have been having a little chat and we think it's best, just for a little while, that you come and stay with us." She glanced up at the two men when she said this and smiled primly. "We don't want you to make a fuss, and your mother has already packed a bag for you so, unless you can think of anything you might need right now, then it's probably best for everyone if we all head off as quickly and painlessly as possible, OK?"

Deborah turned towards her mother, who was taking solace in the door frame, clutching it tightly with one hand, the other clasped to her mouth.

"Where did you get my dream journal?" Deborah asked, again too loud. It didn't feel like it was too loud, but everyone around her seemed surprised.

"Deborah, please." Her mother stepped forward.

Deborah reached out for the journal, stretching across the woman, who backed away. She misjudged the distance, instead pushing it away from her so that it toppled off, clattering noisily to the floor. The men took another step forward, but Doctor Knox shook her head at them.

Deborah got up and slowly walked around the edge of the coffee table. She could feel them all looking at her as if she was an animal that had escaped from its cage. The journal landed open on the ground. Deborah stared at the pages. Her forehead crinkled. The date read four days earlier, but underneath it was not what she had dreamt about. It in fact wasn't anything she had ever dreamt about.

Peter Piper pecked a pickled pepper. Stop. Pretty Polly picked a peppered pickle. Stop. How many precious pickles did Peter Polly Pop? STOP.

Deborah twisted herself around. The room was getting blurry. She could hear her mother, wailing loudly now from her corner. One of the suited men appeared to be comforting her while the other stared, arms by his sides, leaning slightly forward, waiting to pounce.

"I didn't write that," Deborah whispered. No one said anything.

"I did not write that," she said again as though they had not heard her, and pointed to the floor. It all made sense now. He'd set her up! He'd taken her journal away and written other stuff in it to make her seem crazy!

"Deborah, please," her mother whispered again.

"No, mum, no. You don't understand. I can't take it any more. How the hell do you expect me to cope with this? My son is dead, my husband beat me near to death, and now I am being set up by a bloody therapist that's not even a therapist, that's some sort of creature. God I sound insane, I know, but let me explain. Listen to me!"

Doctor Knox frowned and patted the sofa next to her so Deborah sat down and took some deep breaths to try to stay calm. Her mother came over and sat on her other side.

"Is this what you were talking about?" Doctor Knox asked, not talking to Deborah.

Her mother nodded. "Yes, it's happening again. Oh,

Deborah!" She tried to smile at her daughter, though her eyes were full of fear.

"I'll explain it to her, shall I?" she asked nervously. They both seemed to be talking over her.

Doctor Knox nodded.

"Explain what, mum? For God's sake, what is going on?"

"Jack didn't beat you, love."

"What?"

"Jack didn't beat you. It's just... well, it's just something you say. We don't really know why."

Doctor Knox raised her hand and spoke. "Well, we think it's your way of coping, Deborah. It's hard to process what really happened, you see. It's called FMS, False Memory Syndrome."

"Do you remember, love?" Her mother leant in closer and tried to take hold of Deborah's hand. "We've explained this to you before."

Deborah shook her head. Her ears were buzzing. Nothing anyone was saying was making any sense.

"Should we show her the pictures?"

Doctor Knox nodded again and put her hand on Deborah's shoulder. "Just remember, you have seen these before, Deborah. I know it's a lot to take."

She took a slim brown envelope from her purse and handed it to Deborah. Inside were several photographs, some of her, some of Jack, both in hospital, both bruised and beaten.

"I don't understand." Deborah felt tears well up in her eyes and heard them land with a satisfying drip on the floor.

"You did it together, love."

Her mother took her hand and gently pressed it between her own. "You and Jack. After Jamie, it was so hard for you both. I don't know why you felt like we couldn't help you any more, but you both decided that life without him was too hard, so you did it together. Neither of you were very good at it, mind. Throwing yourselves off that Clapton bridge. You both survived. Jack's still at the hospital, in a coma. He's been there for six months now. Don't you remember Deborah, don't you remember my love?"

Deborah shook her head as her mother continued. What were they talking about? Nothing made any sense.

"It was your idea to do it, you see, love. I think the guilt, plus everything else, well it's not surprising really." Her mother trailed off. "You need help love, OK?"

Deborah was suddenly bent double and clawing at her stomach. She shook her head over and over again as hard as she could. "No," she said, looking up and around each person in the room one by one. She stood up and walked over to the mantelpiece where the letter from Jack sat.

"Look at this." She thrust it into her mother's hands. "It's a letter, from him. How can he be in a coma if he is writing me letters?"

Her mother bit her lip and looked at Doctor Knox first, before sighing and turning to her daughter.

"It was from me."

"What?"

"I'm so sorry. I just wanted you to feel better. I thought if you got some closure it might help, you know?"

Deborah shook her head again. A faint ringing sound had lodged in her ears.

"You're wrong, Mum. I remember what happened perfectly. I did it in the bath, after months of torment from Jack. There is no way we did it together. There is no way."

Deborah banged her hand defiantly on the sofa. And suddenly she began to remember. She remembered how she and Jack had desperately clawed at each other as a coffin so tiny and wrong was lowered into the ground; the months and years that went by when nothing got any better. Deborah shook her head more vigorously this time. No, it wasn't true. It wasn't true. Jack had left her. She had done it in the bath. The porcelain, the blood, the scar.

She suddenly jumped up and walked over to the mirror. "Ha! If I didn't do it in the bath, then what is this?" She pointed to the scar on her neck triumphantly.

Her mother let out a moan. "Oh, my love," she whispered, her eyes full of sadness and longing for her daughter to be all right. She came up behind her daughter and placed a hand on her shoulder, Deborah turned.

"There's nothing there, love."

Deborah turned back wildly towards the mirror. Another memory jumped forward – the night where she had confessed to Jack how she sometimes wanted to end it all. He had been shocked at first but then they talked about it. For hours they talked, holding hands with teary faces. They went on and on and on, and finally the only thing that seemed to make any sense was for them to do it together.

No. It wasn't possible. She shook her head. Here came another – the night where they had walked hand in hand. They had sat by Clapton Bridge for a while, talked about nothing and everything while taking it in turns to swig from a bottle of vodka. When the time was right they had wrapped themselves around each other, kissed one last time and then jumped. It was all supposed to have been over then. It was supposed to have worked.

Deborah gasped. "Grace!" Grace – that was what her soul had called herself. She had tried to explain it in the split second before she went back inside. She had nodded over at Peter and Luke. '*Some old movie star called Grace*' she'd said.

Grace Kelly had been Jack's favourite film star. They'd spent hours snuggled up in the evenings watching films like *Mogambo* and *The Country Girl*. Jack had always joked that Grace Kelly was the one girl he would leave her for, but obviously she didn't have to worry about that.

Peter had been right, after all. It hadn't been Luke he was searching for, but Jack! How could he ever have expected to find him though, if he really was in a coma – a strange permanent state somewhere between dreams and death? That's why Peter had found Deborah's soul and named her Grace, because Jack somehow had been trying to save her, even though he couldn't save himself!

Deborah crouched to the floor and put her head in her hands. She couldn't put her finger on the reason why, but the need to laugh gurgled up from inside her. She tried to press her hands over her mouth, but it felt as though her face might split she was smiling so hard. It was all so absurd! She found herself creased up and shaking, overcome with mirth.

"It's not real," she giggled and looked at her mother whose tears now streamed freely down her face. "Oh my God, Mum. How can this be real?"

The laughter rendered her helpless and she slipped from the sofa to the floor. Tears streamed down her face as she lay there, helpless to the hilarity of it all, and she barely noticed as two pairs of strong male hands took her underneath her shoulders and carried her towards the door.

"He's dead." She whispered it, giggling into one man's ear. She tilted her head back. "HE'S DEAD!" she bellowed and roared with laughter. That was the last thing she said before the prick and sting of the needle went into her arm. The darkness swooped over her like a waiting vulture. The last thing she remembered was tilting her head back and roaring and shaking and sweating with laughter at how fantastically, wonderfully and outrageously funny it all was.

CHAPTER 32

100 BC

The end of the Elephant people

Ouranos woke to the feeling of light rain spattering on his skin. He opened his eyes and shifted his head from side to side groggily in the mud. It took a few moments to register the pain, a few more to remember the events of the night before.

"Father!" he sat up and screamed. It felt as though he had been skinned. His trunk hung loosely, dislocated from his face, and his whole body ached and wept with blood and mud and sores.

He struggled to his feet, fighting the pain, and looked back at the smouldering remains of the hut. The entire roof had collapsed in. There was nothing left but a smoky pile of rubble – and somewhere underneath, his poor father's broken body.

"Mother! Pup!" Ouranos cried. Where had he left them last night? He turned this way and that, desperately trying to find them. Suddenly he spotted Dappha's legs sticking out from behind a huge smoking fern. As quickly as he could, Ouranos limped over to her. There she was lying quietly with Pup curled up in her arms.

"Mother!" Ouranos cried, and tried to nudge her awake. "Mother! Wake up, Pup. Pup, please, come on, wake up." He shook them both harder, trying not to think about how cold they both felt. It was no use though. Neither of them stirred.

"No!" Ouranos cried, sinking to his knees. "No! No! No! You can't be gone. Please, no. You can't be!" Ouranos pulled his mother and sister close to his chest and sobbed. His whole family was gone, his beautiful, wonderful, magical family: little Pup, so gentle and innocent, Dappha who was so caring and strong, and Father. Oh Father – the wisest, kindest, most extraordinary creature he had ever known! How could they be gone? Ouranos felt as though he couldn't breathe; the sadness was suffocating him, swallowing him up. He lay down beside his mother and sister and cried and cried, holding their trunks gently in his own.

Ouranos lay like this for many days, and every day it rained a little more until the mud became a sea and the three bodies were lifted, and they drifted away. Ouranos was powerless to stop it. He didn't want to stop it. He just held onto his mother and his sister as tightly as he could. He couldn't let go, for he knew if he let go they would be gone forever.

One day, as they were sailing along through this great flood, Ouranos, now barely alive himself, still holding onto the lifeless bodies of his family, hit upon a rock. He dunked deep under the water, and as he was pulled down so he pulled the others down with him, coughing and spluttering and choking as he went. The current gripped his heels, pulling him in one direction while the bodies he held onto so fiercely were pulled in another. He tried to hold on to them, but he had not eaten in many days and he was too weak.

Ouranos remembered the moment he felt them slip from his grasp, the way that he opened his eyes and felt a strange sense of peace as they both twisted and floated gently away from him through the shadows of the murky water. He almost immediately felt a sudden and desperate urge to live, and used all his remaining strength to push his way upwards, pulling himself out and onto a rock.

Ouranos lay there for three more days and nights, waiting until the rain stopped and the water finally turned back to land.

For those first few days alone, he was delirious. He barely knew who or what he was. It was only after happening upon a nest of toot's eggs, which he devoured hungrily, that he began to finally come to his senses. Slowly he began to rebuild his life. In the first few weeks he built a small shelter and began foraging for nuts and berries, which luckily were plentiful in the spot where he had landed. These he ate by the gallon. Some he ate raw, some he roasted and made into huge steaming stews. He slept a lot. Slowly but surely he regained his strength, until one day he awoke and felt fully restored.

Ouranos thought long and hard during those weeks, trying to come to terms with life alone and the loss of his family. He remembered the promise he had made to himself in the burning hut that night, and vowed he would never deny it. Try as he might he would never forgive the humans for what they had done and, as the weeks turned into months, the months into years and the years into centuries, Ouranos lived on, using the Viatel plant to sustain him. He walked through many villages and encountered many sick humans, but could not bring himself to help them. Instead of finding forgiveness and letting go of the past, he grew bitter and filled with hatred.

It was a cold and sleepless night, with the winds raging at the walls of his hut, when Ouranos suddenly realised what he must do. It was revenge he wanted, revenge for Father and Dappha and Pup. It was his only reason to live. The humans did not value life, so he would teach them how important it was. They would pay for the lives they had taken away from him, the lives they seemed so readily able to take away from each other. If they did not see how precious it was, then he would take their lives and use them himself. Father had taught him a lot about the powers of the Viatel plant over the years. He had stressed its healing properties, of course, but also had suggested that it could be used for all sorts of magic.

It was during his experiments with the plant that Ouranos first encountered one – a strange, ghostlike figure, a lost soul. He had noticed him straight away, this dark-skinned, wide-eyed fellow all hunched up at the bar. The soul did not flinch at Ouranos' disfigured face when he looked at it. He did not gape in horror at the great wriggling scar which was where his trunk should have been. Instead, the soul could not believe that Ouranos could see him.

'You are not like the others then,' he'd whispered after they'd introduced themselves. He nodded to the bodies which sat slumped around him, too caught up in their own booze-soaked problems to give them a second glance. 'They don't even know I am here.'

Ouranos simply thought it was the drink talking, though as the evening went on he realised the soul was speaking the truth.

They talked for hours in the dimly-lit tavern. It was innocent at first. Ouranos found it funny how drunk the soul seemed to get so quickly. It amused him to see the soul staggering about, lost in his own world of despair. However as the night went on the soul's tongue loosened, and he told Ouranos the story of how he, too, dedicated his life to looking after the humans – not the whole race, mind you, but a particular one. One which he loved so fiercely there were no words to describe it. The soul told how the human had rejected him, tossed him outside without a second thought, selfishly, cruelly deciding to end his own life without a care about who else got hurt.

Ouranos listened to this story carefully. At first he did not believe the soul's mumblings, about who he was and how he was pulled into the dreams of his body, how this was the only way he could get back to him, could save him.

"Impossible, man. You're drunk," he'd laughed and handed him another beer.

The soul had turned to him, his sunken eyes brimmed up with anger and sadness. He'd slammed down the tankard and raised his fist to Ouranos, then grabbed him by the throat.

"Do not speak of what you do not know," he whispered. His arm was shaking and his breath was thick and heavy with the sour scent of alcohol. Ouranos pushed him away and the soul fell drunkenly in a shaking, sobbing heap on the floor.

Ouranos looked round. The bar had gone quiet. It was in that moment that something miraculous happened. The soul suddenly faded away. Ouranos watched with awe as he shimmered and moaned then disappeared altogether, just like that. He had turned, called out, gestured to the others at the miracle he had just seen, but they had all scoffed

'You're drunk, you blind fool' one of them jeered and they had returned to their dark corners to drink away the rest of the night and contend with their sorrows alone.

Ouranos wasted no time. He'd flung some coins on the bar, and hurried back to his hut where he stayed up all the hours of the night. He boiled and chanted and cracked up the Viatel, racking his brains for every last thing his father had told him about the plant.

Dawn broke with the sharp tweeting of birds and a grey mist that made it look as though someone had scribbled over the sun. Still Ouranos worked and worked until his fingers were bleeding and the skin on his hands was cracked and raw. Tirelessly he continued until he had the perfect recipe – a flawless capsule which, if swallowed, would allow him into the world of dreams.

It was only then that Ouranos finally understood how he could avenge his family. He would go into these dream worlds and capture the lost souls. He would use the humans to find out the details, the outlines of what kind of dreams they would have, then he would get there first. He would take their wretched souls and with it take all their years, the years they could have lived if they had truly valued their own lives.

Ouranos knew the true value of life and if they did not, he would take theirs away, just as his family's lives had been taken from them.

It was at that moment that Ouranos vowed to keep a document of his travels, of his strange journeys into the dreams of others, of this unexpected life he now had. So late that night, after he had returned from the first dream, his heart pounding and his face flushed with excitement and greed and the true knowledge that it could be done, he pulled a brand new leather-bound journal from a candlelit shelf on the side of his hut. He dipped his quill in ink and began to write his first entry. Neatly putting the date at the top, he began:

I do it for you Father, I do it for you...

EPILOGUE

The creak and whirr of the lunch trolley can be heard in the distance. Deborah hears the jangle of keys and the thump of heavy, swollen feet, which pause outside her door. It creaks open and she twists away from the light, away from the matron in starchy white whose fat sigh squeezes all the air from the room.

She hears the rustle as pillows are plumped and sheets are straightened, and then a clunk as the tray is placed by her bed, the tap, tap, tap of the foot, until she turns, smiles and reaches for the baby blue beaker which contains her pills. Swallowing without water, she opens her mouth for inspection. A satisfied nod and then she is left alone.

She stares from her window, refusing to blink at the sun.

Spring has arrived and puffs of blossom have spurted from the ends of the trees. The grass is greener. The birds which occasionally come to rest on her window sill look stout and healthy, pushing out their chests as they sing.

Here she will stay on her small wicker chair until night arrives with a thump and snuffs out the lights. It is only then that she pulls the tray towards her and eats her food with a little plastic knife and a little plastic fork until there is nothing left.

And she lets it take her over – she accepts the misery with grace, her lips pinched together, eyes pegged shut, for no one believes what she knows is true, because no one can see it. So instead she sits by her window and makes her lists and waits for the pills to trap her in sleep. When she feels it lurking, she crawls into bed, and stares at the flower in the painting, that lone sunflower which glowers through the midnight storms like a beacon. She longs for the man to release it, to set it free so its petals can swirl like a flock of tangerine birds through the sky.

She stares until her eyelids grow heavy, still pricked with the hope of release. It is only then she allows herself to think of them, of Jack and of Jamie, of her two boys. She wills the lost soul to find its way back and clings to the impossible, to the thread of hope that she may see them once more.

Then, finally, with a sad smile that slowly creeps across her lips, she is asleep.